PRAISE FOR

THE WAY I USED TO BE

★"This is a poignant book that realistically looks at the lasting effects of trauma on love, relationships, and life. . . . Teens will be reminded of Laurie Halse Anderson's *Speak*. VERDICT An important addition for every collection."

—*School Library Journal*, starred review

"*The Way I Used to Be* explores the aftermath of sexual assault with a precision and searing honesty that is often terrifying, sometimes eerily beautiful, and always completely true. It is The Hero's Journey through a distorted circus mirror—one girl's quest to turn desperation into courage, to become a survivor instead of a victim. Amber Smith gets it exactly right."

—AMY REED, author of *Beautiful* and *Clean*

"Edy's exploration of the meaning of sexuality and intimacy will be thought provoking for teen readers of various experience levels, and this title is likely to find space alongside [Laurie Halse] Anderson's *Speak*."

—*Bulletin of the Center for Children's Books*

"*The Way I Used To Be* is an intensely gripping and raw look at secrets, silence, speaking out, and survival in the aftermath of a sexual assault. A must-have for every collection that serves teens."

—*School Library Journal*/*Teen Librarian Toolbox*

"Readers will root for her as she gathers the courage, at last, to speak up."

—*B&N Teen Blog*

"This is far from a feel-good read, but I can't implore how *necessary* it is to read a book like this one. . . . As unforgettable and stirring as Laurie Halse Anderson's *Speak*, Smith's provocative debut is best described as a survival story with hope and anger serving as prominent themes so fully explored they simmer off the page."

—TheYoungFolks.com

THE WAY I USED TO BE

AMBER SMITH

Margaret K. McElderry Books

New York London Toronto Sydney New Delhi

MARGARET K. McELDERRY BOOKS
An imprint of Simon & Schuster Children's Publishing Division
1230 Avenue of the Americas, New York, New York 10020
This book is a work of fiction. Any references to historical events, real people, or real places are used fictitiously. Other names, characters, places, and events are products of the author's imagination, and any resemblance to actual events or places or persons, living or dead, is entirely coincidental.

Also available in a Margaret K. McElderry Books hardcover edition
Book design by Debra Sfetsios-Conover
The text for this book was set in Minion Pro.
Manufactured in the United States of America
This Margaret K. McElderry Books paperback edition March 2017
20 19 18
The Library of Congress has cataloged the hardcover edition as follows:
Smith, Amber.
The way I used to be / Amber Smith. — First edition.
pages cm.
Summary: "After fourteen-year-old Eden is raped by her brother's best friend, she knows she'll never be the way she used to be." — Provided by publisher.
ISBN 978-1-4814-4935-9 (hc)
ISBN 978-1-4814-4936-6 (pbk)
ISBN 978-1-4814-4937-3 (eBook)
[1. Rape—Fiction. 2. Emotional problems—Fiction.] I. Title.
PZ7.1.S595 Way 2016
[Fic]—dc23 2015003952

To You.

To every *you* who has ever known the feeling

of needing new ways to be.

PART ONE

Freshman Year

I DON'T KNOW A LOT of things. I don't know why I didn't hear the door click shut. Why I didn't lock the damn door to begin with. Or why it didn't register that something was wrong—so mercilessly wrong—when I felt the mattress shift under his weight. Why I didn't scream when I opened my eyes and saw him crawling between my sheets. Or why I didn't try to fight him when I still stood a chance.

I don't know how long I lay there afterward, telling myself: Squeeze your eyelids shut, try, just try to forget. Try to ignore all the things that didn't feel right, all the things that felt like they would never feel right again. Ignore the taste in your mouth, the sticky dampness of the sheets, the fire radiating through your thighs, the nauseating pain—this bulletlike thing that ripped through you and got lodged in your gut somehow. No, can't cry. Because there's nothing to cry about. Because it was just a dream, a bad dream—a nightmare. Not real. Not real. Not real. That's what I keep thinking: *NotRealNotRealNotReal.* Repeat, repeat, repeat. Like a mantra. Like a prayer.

I don't know that these images flashing through my mind—a movie of someone else, somewhere else—will never really go away, will never ever stop playing, will never stop haunting me. I close my eyes again, but it's all I can see, all I can feel, all I can hear: his skin, his arms, his legs, his hands too strong, his breath on me, muscles stretching, bones cracking, body breaking, me getting weaker, fading. These things—it's all there is.

I don't know how many hours pass before I awake to the usual Sunday morning clamor—pots and pans clanging against the stove. Food smells seeping under my door—bacon, pancakes, Mom's coffee. TV sounds—cold fronts and storm systems moving through the area by midday—Dad's weather channel. Dishwasher-running sounds. Yippy yappy dog across the street yips and yaps at probably nothing, as always. And then there's the almost imperceptible rhythm of a basketball bouncing against the dewy blacktop and the squeaky-sneaker shuffling of feet in the driveway. Our stupid, sleepy suburbia, like every other stupid, sleepy suburbia, awakens groggy, indifferent to its own inconsequence, collectively wishing for one more Saturday and dreading chores and church and to-do lists and Monday morning. Life just goes, just happens, continuing as always. Normal. And I can't shake the knowledge that life will just keep on happening, regardless if I wake up or not. Obscenely normal.

I don't know, as I force my eyes open, that the lies are already in motion. I try to swallow. But my throat's raw. Feels like strep, I tell myself. I must be sick, that's all. Must have a fever. I'm delirious. Not thinking clearly. I touch my lips. They sting. And my tongue tastes blood. But no, it couldn't have been. *Not real.* So as I stare at the ceiling, I'm thinking: I must have serious issues if I'm dreaming stuff like that. Horrible stuff like that. About Kevin. Kevin. Because Kevin is my brother's best friend, practically my brother. My parents love him like everyone does, even me, and Kevin would never—could never. Not possible. But then I try to move my legs to stand. They're so sore—no, broken feeling. And my jaw aches like a mouthful of cavities.

I close my eyes again. Take a deep breath. Reach down and touch my body. No underwear. I sit up too fast and my bones wail like I'm an old person. I'm scared to look. But there they are: my days-of-the-week underwear in a ball on the floor. They were my Tuesdays, even though it was Saturday, because, well, who would ever know anyway? That's what I was thinking when I put them on yesterday. And now I know, for sure, it happened. It actually happened. And this pain in the center of my body, the depths of my insides, restarts its torture as if on cue. I throw the covers off. Kneecap-shaped bruises line my arms, my hips, my thighs. And the blood—on the sheets, the comforter, my legs.

But this was supposed to be an ordinary Sunday.

I was supposed to get up, get dressed, and sit down to breakfast with my family. Then after breakfast, I would promptly go to my bedroom and finish any homework I hadn't finished Friday night, sure to pay special attention to geometry. I would practice that new song we learned in band, call my best friend, Mara, maybe go to her house later, and do dozens of other stupid, meaningless tasks.

But that's not what's going to happen today, I know, as I sit in my bed, staring at my stained skin in disbelief, my hand shaking as I press it against my mouth.

Two knocks on my bedroom door. I jump.

"Edy, you up?" My mother's voice shouts. I open my mouth, but it feels like someone poured hydrochloric acid down my throat and I might never be able to speak again. Knock, knock, knock: "Eden, breakfast!" I quickly pull my nightgown down as far as it will go, but there's blood smeared on that, too.

"Mom?" I finally call back, my voice scratchy and horrible.

She cracks the door open. As she peers in her eyes immediately go to the blood. "Oh God," she gasps, as she slips inside and quickly shuts the door behind her.

"Mom, I—" But how am I supposed say the words, the worst words, the ones I know have to be spoken?

"Oh, Edy." She sighs, turning her head at me with a sad smile. "It's okay."

"Wh—" I start to say. How can it be okay, in what world is this okay?

"This happens sometimes when you're not expecting it." She flits around my room, tidying up, barely looking at me while she explains about periods and calendars and counting the days. "It happens to everyone. That's why I told you, you need to keep track. That way you won't have to deal with these . . . surprises. You can be . . . prepared."

This is what she thinks this is.

Now, I've seen enough TV movies to know you're supposed to tell. You're just supposed to fucking tell. "But—"

"Why don't you hop in the shower, sweetie?" she interrupts. "I'll take care of this . . . uh . . . ," she begins, gesturing with her arm in a wide circle over my bed, searching for the word, "this mess."

This mess. Oh God, it's now or never. Now or never. It's now. "Mom—" I try again.

"Don't be embarrassed," she says with a laugh. "It's fine, really, I promise." She stands over me, looking taller than she ever has before, handing me my robe, oblivious of my Tuesday underwear crumpled at her feet.

"Mom, Kevin—" I start, but his name in my mouth makes me want to throw up.

"Don't worry, Edy. He's out back with your brother. They're playing basketball. And your father's glued to the TV, as usual. Nobody'll see you. Go ahead. Put this on."

Looking up at her, I feel so small. And Kevin's voice moves like a tornado through my mind, whispering—his breath on my face—*No one will ever believe you. You know that. No one. Not ever.*

Then my mom shakes the robe at me, offering me a lie I didn't even need to think up. She starts getting that look in her eye—that impatient, it's-the-holidays-and-I-don't-have-time-for-this look. Clearly, it was time for me to get going so she could deal with this mess. And clearly, nobody was going to hear me. Nobody was going to see me—he knew that. He had been around long enough to know how things work here.

I try to stand without looking like everything is broken. I kick the Tuesdays under the bed so she won't find them and wonder. I take my robe. Take the lie. And as I look back at my mother, watching her collect the soiled sheets in her arms—the evidence—I know somehow if it's not now, it has to be never. Because he was right, no one would ever believe me. Of course they wouldn't. Not ever.

*

In the bathroom, I carefully peel off my nightgown, holding it at arm's length as I ball it up and stuff it in the garbage can under the sink. I adjust my glasses and examine myself more closely. There are a few faint marks on my throat in the shape of his fingers. But they're minor, really, in comparison to the ones on my body. No bruises on my face. Only the two-inch scar above my left eye from my bike accident two summers ago. My hair is slightly more disastrous than usual, but essentially I look the same—I can pass.

By the time I get out of the shower—still dirty, after scrubbing my body raw, thinking I could maybe wash the bruises off—there he is. Sitting at my kitchen table in my dining room with my brother, my father, my mother, sipping my orange juice from my glass—his mouth on a glass I would have to use someday. On a fork that would soon be undifferentiated from all the other forks. His fingerprints not only all over every inch of me, but all over everything: this house, my life, the world—infected with him.

Caelin raises his head and narrows his eyes at me as I cautiously approach the dining room. He can see it. I knew he would see it right away. If anyone was going to notice—if I could count on anyone—it would be my big brother. "Okay, you're being really weird and intense right now," he announces. He could tell because he always knew me even better than I knew myself.

So I stand there and wait for him to do something about this. For him to set his fork down, stand up and pull me aside, take me out to the backyard by the arm, and demand to know what's wrong with me, demand to know what happened. Then I'd tell him what Kevin did to me and he'd give me one of his big brother-isms, like,

Don't worry, Edy, I'll take care of it. The way he did whenever anyone was picking on me. And then he'd run back inside the house and stab Kevin to death with his own butter knife.

But that's not what happens.

What happens is he just sits there. Watching me. Then slowly his mouth contorts into one of his smirks—our inside-joke grin—waiting for me to reciprocate, to give him a sign, or just start laughing like maybe I'm trying to secretly make fun of our parents. He's waiting to get it. But he doesn't get it. So he just shrugs, looks back down at his plate, and lops off a big slice of pancake. The bullet lodges itself a little deeper in my stomach as I stand there, frozen in the hallway.

"Seriously, what are you staring at?" he mumbles with his mouth full of pancake, in that familiar brotherly, you're-the-stupidest-person-on-the-face-of-the-earth tone he had perfected over the years.

Meanwhile, Kevin barely even glances up. No threatening looks. No gestures of warning, nothing. As if nothing had even happened. The same cool disregard he always used with me. Like I'm still just Caelin's dorky little sister with bad hair and freckles, freshman band-geek nobody, tagging along behind them, clarinet case in tow. But I'm not her anymore. I don't even want to be her anymore. That girl who was so naive and stupid—the kind of girl who could let something like this happen to her.

"Come on, Minnie," Dad says to me, using my pet name. Minnie as in Mouse, because I was so quiet. He gestured at the food on the table. "Sit down. Everything's getting cold."

As I stand in front of them—their Mousegirl—crooked

glasses sliding down the bridge of my nose, stripped before eight scrutinizing eyes waiting for me to play my part, I finally realize what it's all been about. The previous fourteen years had merely been dress rehearsal, preparation for knowing how to properly shut up now. And Kevin had told me, with his lips almost touching mine he whispered the words: *You're gonna keep your mouth shut.* Last night it was an order, a command, but today it's just the truth.

I push my glasses up. And with a sickness in my stomach—something like stage fright—I move slowly, cautiously. Try to act like every part of my body, inside and out, isn't throbbing and pulsing. I sit down in the seat next to Kevin like I had at countless family meals. Because we considered him part of our family, Mom was always saying it, over and over. He was always welcome. Always.

IT'S TOTALLY SILENT IN the house after breakfast. Caelin left with Kevin to go play basketball with some of their old teammates from high school. Dad needed some kind of special wrench from the hardware store to install the new showerhead he got Mom for Christmas. And Mom was in her room, busy addressing New Year's cards.

I sit in the living room, staring out the window.

A row of multicolored Christmas lights lining the garage flicker spastically in the gray morning light. The clouds pile one on top of the other endlessly, the sky closing in on us. Next door, a mostly deflated giant Santa rocks back and forth in the center of our neighbors' white lawn with a slow, sick, zombielike shuffle. It feels like that scene in *The Wizard of Oz* when everything changes from black and white to color. Except it's more like the other way around. Like I always thought things were in color, but they were really black and white. I can see that now.

"You feeling all right, Edy?" Mom suddenly appears in the room carrying a stack of envelopes in her hands.

I shrug in response, but I don't think she even notices.

I watch a car roll through the stop sign at the corner, the driver barely glancing up to see if anyone's there. I think about how they say when most people get into car accidents, it's less than one mile from their home. Maybe that's because everything's so familiar, you stop paying attention. You don't notice the one thing that's different or wrong or off or dangerous. And I think about how maybe that's what just happened to me.

"You know what I think?" she asks in that tone she's been using on me ever since Caelin left for school over the summer. "I think you're mad at your brother because he hasn't spent enough time with you while he's been home." She doesn't wait for me to tell her she's wrong before she keeps talking. To tell her that it's really her who's mad that he hasn't been home enough. "I know you want it to be just the two of you. Like it used to be. But he's getting older—you're both getting older—he's in college now, Edy."

"I know that—" I start to say, but she interrupts.

"It's okay that he wants to see his friends while he's home, you know."

The truth is, none of us knows how to act around one another without Caelin here. It's like we've become strangers all of a sudden. Caelin was the glue. He gave us purpose—a reason, a way to be together. Because what are we supposed to do with each other if we're not cheering him on at his basketball games anymore? What are our kitchen table conversations supposed to sound like without him regaling us with his daily activities? I'm certainly no substitute; everyone knows that. What the hell do I have going on that could ever compare to the nonstop larger-than-life excitement that is Caelin McCrorey? At first I thought we were adjusting. But this is just how we are. Dad's lost without another guy around. Mom doesn't know what to do with herself without Caelin taking up all her time and attention. And me, I just need my best friend back. It's simple, yet so complicated.

"It wouldn't hurt you to branch out a bit either," she continues, shuffling the stack of envelopes in her hands. "Make a couple of new friends. It's officially the new year." She smiles. I don't. "Edy, you know I think Mara's great—she's been a great friend to you—but a person is allowed more than one friend in life is all I'm saying."

I stand and walk past her into the kitchen. I pour myself a glass of water, just so I have something, anything, to focus on other than my mom, the pointlessness of this conversation, and the endless train wreck of thoughts crashing through my mind.

She stands next to me at the kitchen counter. I can feel her staring at the side of my face. It makes me want to crawl out of my skin. She reaches out to tuck my bangs behind my ear, like she always does. But I back away. Not on purpose. Or maybe it is. I'm not sure. I know I've hurt her feelings. I open my mouth to tell her I'm sorry, but what comes out instead is: "It's too hot here. I'm going outside."

"Oh-kay," she says slowly, confused.

My feet quickly move away from her. I grab my coat off the hook near the back door, slide my boots on, and walk out to the backyard. I brush the snow off one of the wooden swing-set seats. I feel the bruises on my body swell against the cold wood and metal chains. I just want to sit still for a second, breathe, and try to figure out how things could have ever gotten to this point. Figure out what I'm supposed to do now.

I close my eyes tight, weave my fingers together—and though I know I don't do it nearly as much as I probably should—I pray, pray harder than I've ever prayed in my life. To somehow undo this. To just wake up, and have it be this morning again, except this time nothing would have happened last night.

I remember sitting down at the table with him. We played Monopoly. It was nothing, though. Nothing seemed wrong. He was actually being nice to me. Acting like . . . he liked me. Acting like I was more than just Caelin's little sister. Like I was a real person. A girl, not just a kid. I went to bed happy. I went to bed thinking of him. But the next thing I remember is waking up to him climbing on top of me, putting his hand over my mouth, whispering *shutup-shutupshutup.* And everything happening so fast. If it could all be a dream, just a dream that I could wake up from, then I would still be safe in my bed. That would make so much more sense. And nothing will be wrong. Nothing will be different. I'll just be in my bed and nothing bad will ever have to happen there.

"Wake up," I think I whisper out loud. God, just wake up. Wake up, Edy!

"Eden!" a voice calls.

My eyes snap open. My heart sinks into the pit of my stomach as I look around. Because I'm not in my bed. I'm in the backyard sitting on the swing, my bare fingers numb, curled tightly around the metal chains.

"What are you doing, splitting atoms over there?" my brother shouts from the back door. "I've been standing here calling your name a hundred times."

He walks toward me, his steps are wide and swift and sure,

the fresh snow crushing easily under his feet. I sit up straighter, put my hands in my lap, and try not to give away anything that would let him know how wrong my body feels to me right now.

"So, Edy," Caelin begins, sitting down on the swing next to mine. "I hear you're mad at me."

I try to smile, try to do my best impression of myself. "Let me guess who told you that."

"She said it's because I'm not spending enough time with you?" His half grin tells me he half believes her.

"No, that's not it."

"Okay, well, you're acting way weird." He elbows me in the arm and adds with a smile, "Even for you."

Maybe this is my chance. Would Kevin really kill me if I told—could he really kill me? He could. He made sure I knew he could if he wanted to. But he's not here right now. Caelin is here. To protect me, to be on my side.

"Caelin, please don't leave tomorrow," I blurt out, feeling a sudden urgency take hold of me. "Don't go back to school. Just don't leave me, okay? Please," I beg him, tears almost ready to spill over.

"What?" he asks, almost a laugh in his voice. "Where is this coming from? I have to go back, Edy—I don't have a choice. You know that."

"Yes, you do, you have a choice. You could go to school here—you had that scholarship to go here, remember?"

"But I didn't take it." He pauses, looking at me, uncertain. "Look, I don't know what you want me to say here. Are you serious?"

"I just don't want you to go."

"All right, just for fun let's say I stay. Okay? But think about it, what am I supposed to do about school? I'm right in the middle of the year. All my stuff is there. My girlfriend is there. My life is there now, Edy. I can't just drop everything and move back home so we can hang out, or whatever."

"That's not what I mean. Don't talk to me like I'm a kid," I tell him quietly.

"Hate to break it to you, but you are a kid, Edy." He smiles, clapping my shoulder. "Besides, what's Kevin supposed to do? We're roommates. We share a car. We share bills—everything. We're kind of depending on each other right now, Edy. Grown-up stuff. You know?"

"I depend on you too—I need you."

"Since when?" he says with a laugh.

"It's not funny. You're *my* brother, not Kevin's," I almost shout, my voice trembling.

"All right, all right." He rolls his eyes. "Apparently you gave up having a sense of humor for your New Year's resolution," he says, standing up like the conversation is over just because he's said what he wanted to say. "Come on, let's go inside." He holds out his hand to me. I feel my feet plant themselves firmly in the snow. My legs begin to follow him instinctually, as they always have. My hand rises toward his. But then just as my fingers are about to touch his palm, something snaps inside of me. Physically snaps. If my body were a machine, it's like the gears inside of me just grind to a halt, my muscles short-circuit and forbid my body to move.

"No." I say firmly, my voice someone else's.

He just stands there looking down at me. Confused because I've never said no to him before in my entire life. He shifts from one foot to the other and turns his head ever so slightly, like a dog. He exhales a puff of air through his smiling lips and opens his mouth. But I can't let him say whatever smart-ass remark his mind is churning out.

"You don't get it!" I would have yelled the words if my teeth weren't clenched.

"Get what?" he asks, his voice an octave too high, looking around us like there's someone else here who's supposed to be filling him in.

"You're my brother." I feel the words collapsing in my throat like an avalanche. "Not Kevin's!"

"What's your problem? I know that!"

I stand up, can't let him try to get away before he knows the truth. Before I tell him what happened. "If you know that, then why is he always here? Why do you keep bringing him with you? He has his own family!" My voice falters, and I can't stop the tears from falling.

"You've never had a problem with him being around before. In fact, it's almost like the opposite." The sentence hangs in the air like an echo. I look up at him. Even blurry through my tears I can tell he's mad.

"What do you mean"—I shudder—"the opposite?"

"I mean, maybe it's time to drop the whole little schoolgirl-crush thing. It was cute for a while, Edy—funny, even—but it's played itself out, don't you think? It's obviously making you, I don't know, mean, or something. You're not acting like yourself." And then he adds, more to himself, "You know, I guess I should've seen this coming. It's so funny because me and Kevin were just talking about this."

"What?" I breathe, barely able to give the word any volume. I can't believe it. I cannot believe he's really done it. He's managed to turn my brother—my true best friend, my ally—against me.

"Forget it," he snaps, throwing his hands up as he walks away from me. And I can only watch him get smaller, watch him fade from color to black and white, like everything else. I stand there for a while, trying to figure out how to follow, how to move—how to exist in a world where Caelin is no longer on my side.

That night I close my bedroom door gently. I turn the lock ninety degrees to the right and pull on the knob as hard as I can, just to make sure. Then I turn around and look at my bed, the sheets and comforter clean and perfectly made up. I don't know how I can possibly go even one more minute without telling someone what happened. I take my phone out of my pocket and start to call Mara. But I stop.

I turn on the ceiling light and my desk lamp, and then pull out my sleeping bag from the top shelf of my closet. I roll it out onto the floor, and try to think of anything but the reason why I cannot bring myself to sleep in my bed. I lie down, half falling, half collapsing, onto my bedroom floor. I pull my pillow over my head and I cry so hard I don't know how I'll ever stop. I cry for what feels like days. I cry until there are no more tears, like I have used them all up, like maybe I have broken my damn tear ducts. Then I just make the sounds: the gasping and sniffling. I feel like I might just fall asleep and not wake up—in fact, I almost hope I do.

IF THERE'S A HELL, it must look a lot like a high school cafeteria. It's the first day back from winter break. And I'm trying so hard to just go back to my life. The way it used to be. The way I used to be.

I exit the lunch line and scan the cafeteria for Mara. Finally I spot her, waving her arm over her head from across the crowded, rumbling cafeteria. She was able to secure us a spot in the drafty corner near the windows. Every step I take is intercepted by someone walking in front of me, someone shouting, trying to be heard over the noise but only adding to the disorder of everything.

"Hey!" Mara calls to me as I approach. "Stephen got here early and saved us this table." She's smiling hugely, which she's been doing all day, ever since she got her braces off last week.

"Cool," I manage. I knew scoring this table was like hitting the jackpot. We would be inconspicuous, not as much of a target as usual. But I can only give Stephen a small smile.

Stephen Reinheiser, aka Fat Kid, is a nice, quiet boy we know from yearbook who occasionally sits with us at lunch. Not really a friend. An acquaintance. He is a different breed of nerd than me and Mara. We are club-joining, band-type nerds. But he just doesn't fit in, really, anywhere. It doesn't matter though, because there is a silent understanding among us. We have known him since middle school. We know his mother died when we were in seventh grade. We know his experience has been just as tragic as ours, if not more. So we look out for each other. Meaning, if one of us can snag a decent lunch table, it belongs to us all and we don't have to talk about why this is important.

"Edy?" Stephen begins in his usual hesitant manner. "Um, I was wondering if you wanted to work together on the history project for Simmons's class?"

"What project?"

"The one he talked about this morning. You know, he handed out that list of topic ideas," he reminds me. But I have no recollection of this at all. It must show because Stephen opens his binder, smiling as he pulls out a sheet of paper and slides it across the table. "I was thinking 'Columbus: Hero or Villain?'"

I look at the paper for what I'm sure is the first time. "Oh. Okay. Yeah. That sounds good. Columbus."

Mara takes out her compact mirror and examines her new teeth for the millionth time, obsessively running her tongue over their smooth surfaces. "God, is this what everyone's teeth feel like?" she asks absently.

But before either of us can answer, a whole fleet of corn kernel pellets shoot down over our table. Mara screams, "Ew, God!" As she shakes her hair the little yellow balls tumble to the floor one by one. I follow the path of the ammo, leading to this table full of sophomore guys, each one in his pathetic JV jacket, keeled over in their chairs laughing hysterically at Mara as she frantically combs her long hair with her fingers. I hear her voice, almost like an echo in my brain, "Did I get it all?" I look at her, but it seems like it's all happening at a distance, in slow motion. Stephen sets his bologna sandwich down on top of its plastic baggie and clears his throat like he's about to do something. But then he just looks down instead, like he's concentrating so hard on the damn sandwich, there's no room to think about anything else.

"Fire in the hole!" I hear someone shout.

My head snaps up just in time to see one of them—the one with the stupid grin and pimply face—line up his sight, the cheap, malleable metal spoon poised to launch a spoonful of pale green peas right at me. His index finger pulls back on the tip of the spoon slightly.

And some kind of hot, white light flashes in front of my eyes, harnessing itself to my heart, making it beat uncontrollably. I'm up from my seat before I even understand how my body moved so quickly without my brain. Zitface narrows his eyes at me, his smile widening as his tablemates cheer him on. His finger releases like a trigger. The spoonful of peas hit me square in the chest and then drop to the floor with these tiny, dull, flat thuds that I swear I can hear over all the other noise.

Suddenly the planet stops orbiting, pauses, and goes silent for just a moment while all the eyes in the world focus on me standing there with mushy pea splat on the front of my shirt. Then time rushes forward again, the moment over. And cacophony erupts in the cafeteria. The Earth resumes its rotation around the sun. The sounds of the entire cafeteria's oooohhhhs and shouting and laughter flood my body. My brain overheats. And I run, I just go.

I'm aware of Mara watching me storm out of the cafeteria, her palms facing up toward the mind-numbing fluorescent lights, mouthing, *What are you doing?* Aware of Stephen looking back and forth between me, Mara, and his bologna sandwich, his mouth hanging open. But I can't stop. Can't turn around. Can't go back there. Ever. Without a hall pass, without permission, without a coherent thought in my head except *Get the hell out*, I get the hell out.

In the hall I walk fast. I can barely breathe, something strangling me from the inside out. On autopilot, my feet race down the hall and up the stairs, looking for a place—any place—to just be. I shove through the double doors of the library and it's like I've just walked outside. Things are somehow lighter here, and everything moves at a more normal pace, slowing my heart down along with them as I stand in the entryway. There are only a few kids scattered throughout the entire library. No one even looks up at me.

The door behind the circulation desk opens and Miss Sullivan walks through cradling a stack of books in her arms. She smiles at me so warmly. "Hello. What can I do for you?" she asks, setting the books down on the counter.

Hide me, I want to tell her. Just hide me from the world. And never make me go back out through those doors again. But I don't. I don't say anything. I can't.

"Come on in," she gestures me forward. "Here's the sign-in sheet," she tells me, centering a clipboard in front of me.

I take the pen tied to a string tied to the top of the clipboard. It feels like a chopstick between my fingers, my hand shaking as I press the pen against the paper. You're supposed to fill in the date, your name, the time, and where you're coming from. We have to do this every time we come or go anywhere.

Miss Sullivan looks at the scribble that's supposed to be my name. "And what's your name again?" she asks gently.

"Eden," I answer, my voice low.

"Eden, okay. And where are you coming from?" I've left that box blank.

I open my mouth but nothing comes out at first. She looks up at me with another smile.

"Lunch. I don't have a pass to be here," I admit, feeling like some kind of fugitive. I can feel my eyes well up with tears as I look across the desk at her.

"That's okay, Eden," she says softly.

I dab at my eyes with my sleeve.

"You know, I think I have something for that." She nods toward the green stains on the front of my shirt. "Why don't you come in my office?"

She pushes open the half door at the side of the counter and leads me inside. "Have a seat," she tells me as she closes the door behind us.

She rifles through one of her desk drawers, pulling out handfuls of pens and pencils and highlighters. Her office is bright and warm. There's a whole table in the corner just filled with different plants. She has all these posters pinned to the wall about books and librarians, and one of those big READ posters with the president smiling and holding a book in his hands. One of them says: A ROOM WITHOUT BOOKS IS LIKE A BODY WITHOUT A SOUL—CICERO.

"Ah-hah. Here it is!" She hands me one of those stain removal pens. "I always keep one of these nearby—I'm pretty klutzy, so I'm always spilling things on myself." She smiles as she watches me pressing the spongy marker tip into the stains on my shirt.

"Please don't make me go back there," I plead, too desperate and exhausted to even attempt to make it seem like I'm not desperate and exhausted. "Do you think maybe I could volunteer during lunch from now on? Or something?"

"I wish I could tell you yes, Eden." She pauses with a frown. "But unfortunately we already have the maximum number of volunteers for this period. However, I think you would be a great fit here, I really do. Is there another time you would be interested in, maybe during a study hall?"

"Are you really sure there isn't any room because I really, really can't be in lunch anymore." I feel my eyes getting hot and watery again.

"May I ask why?"

"It's . . . personal, I guess." But the truth is that it's humiliating. It's too humiliating to be in lunch anymore, to have to hide and still get food thrown at you anyway, and not be able to do anything about it, and your friends are too afraid to stand up for you, or themselves. Especially when you just got attacked in your own house—in your own bed—and you can't even stand up for yourself there, either, the one place you're supposed to be safe. For all these reasons, it's personal. And questions like "why" can't truly be answered, not when this woman is looking at me so sweetly, expecting a response that leaves her with something she can do about any of it. But since there's not, I clear my throat and repeat, "Just personal."

"I understand." She looks down at her fingernails and smiles sadly. I wonder if she really does understand or if that's only something she says.

Just as I'm about to stand up and leave, something in her face changes. She looks at me like she's considering letting me do it anyway, like she's going to take pity on me.

"Well," she begins. "I do have this idea I've been toying with, something you might be interested in?"

I inch closer, literally pushing myself to the edge of my seat.

"I've been thinking about trying to put together a student group, a book club that would meet during lunch. It would be open to anyone who's interested in doing a little extracurricular reading. It would be like an informal discussion group, more or less. Does that sound like something you'd want to do?"

"Yes! Definitely, yes, yes. I love books!" Then, more calmly, I add, "I mean, I love to read, so I just think a book club, um, would be great." I have to force my mouth to stop talking.

"Okay, well, that's excellent. Now, according to school policy, any club must have at least six members to be official. So, first things first—do you know anyone else who you think might be interested?"

"Yeah, I think so, two people maybe—one for sure."

"That's a start—a good start. If you really want to do this, I'll need you to do a little bit of the legwork, okay? Because basically my only role is to be a faculty adviser, a facilitator—the group itself is essentially student run, student organized—it's your group, not mine. Does that make sense?"

"Yeah, yeah. So what would I need to do then, to make it happen?"

“You can start by making flyers, putting them up around school. Start by seeing if we can get enough people interested.”

“I can do that. I can do that right now!”

She laughs a little. “You don’t have to do it right now—although I do appreciate the enthusiasm. In fact, you don’t have to do it at all. You can take some time to think about it if you want.”

“I’m sure. I want to, really.”

“Okay. All right then. I’ll take care of the paperwork this afternoon, how does that sound?”

“Great!” I shout, my voice all high and trembling as I fight the urge to jump over the desk and throw my arms around her neck. “That sounds really great!”

I make the flyer right then and there and have the walls plastered by the end of the day.

SATURDAY MORNING, PROMPTLY AT TEN, the doorbell rings. I call from my bedroom, "I'll get it," but Mom beats me. I get to the living room just as she's swinging the door open.

"Good morning, you must be Stephen! Come on in, please, out of the rain."

"Thanks, Mrs. McCrorey," Stephen says, walking through our front door cautiously, dripping puddles of water all over the floor, which I know is making Mom secretly hyperventilate.

I stand there and watch as Stephen Reinheiser hands my mom his raincoat and umbrella. Watch as this person who knows me in one very distinct way crosses this unspoken boundary and begins to know me in this way that's entirely different.

"You can just leave your sneakers on the mat there," Mom tells him, wanting to ensure he does indeed take his wet shoes off before daring to step onto the carpet. This is a no-shoes house he's entering. Watching him stand in my living room in his socks, looking uncomfortable, I realize that he has boundaries too.

"Hey, Stephen," I finally say, making sure I smile. He smiles back, looking relieved to see me. "So, um, come in. I thought we could work at the table."

"Sure," he mumbles, following behind me as I lead him to the dining room.

We sit down and Stephen pulls a notebook out of his backpack. I readjust the stack of Columbus books I've checked out from the library.

"So what are we working on, Minnie?" Dad says too loudly, suddenly appearing in the doorway between the kitchen and dining room, holding a steaming cup of coffee. Stephen jumps before turning around in his seat to look up at my dad.

"Dad, this is Stephen. Stephen, my dad. We're doing a history project on Columbus."

I try to silently plead with him to just keep this brief. Both my dad and my mom were making such a huge deal of me having a boy over. I told them before he got here that it's not like that. I don't even think of Stephen in that way. I don't think I'll ever think of anyone in that way.

Stephen adds, "Hero or Villain."

"Ah. Hmm. Okay," Dad says, grinning at me before walking back into the living room.

"Who's Minnie?" Stephen whispers.

"Don't ask," I tell him, rolling my eyes.

"So, you stopped coming to lunch this week?" he says, like a question. "Sorry."

"What for?"

"What happened Monday. In the cafeteria. I wish I would have said something. I should've said something. I hate those guys—they're morons."

I shrug. "Did Mara ask you about the book club thing?"

He nods.

"Will you do it? We need people to come. At least six people. Miss Sullivan's really nice. She's been letting me stay in the library all week." I try to make this seem cooler than it probably is. "I think she gets it, you know?"

"She gets what?"

"You know, just, the way things are. How there are all these stupid cliques, and rules you're supposed to follow that don't make any sense. Just all of it, you know?" I stop myself, because sometimes I forget we aren't really supposed to talk about this. We're supposed to accept it. Supposed to feel like it's all of us who have the problem. And we're supposed to deal with it like it's our problem even though it's not.

Still, he just stares at me in this strange way.

"I mean, you get it, right?" I ask him. How could he not get it, I think to myself. I mean, look at him. Total geek. Overweight. No friends.

"Yeah," he says slowly. "Yeah, I get it. No one's ever really said it like that, I guess." He looks at me in this way he's never looked at me before, like I've told him some big secret he never knew about himself.

"Well, consider it, anyway—the book club." I pause and take a breath. "So, Columbus?"

"Right," he says absently.

"So, what do you think?" I try to steer our conversation to

our project and away from all this dangerous honesty. "Hero or villain?"

"I don't know," Stephen says, still preoccupied. "I was reading online that there were all kinds of people that got here before Columbus. I mean, Native Americans, obviously, were already always here. But also the Vikings. And then there were people from Africa and even China who got here first."

"Yeah, I read that too."

"It's more like Columbus was the last to discover America, not the first," Stephen says with a laugh.

"Yeah," I agree. "And I've been reading all these books from the library." I open up one and slide it across the table to him. "Did you know he kidnapped all these people and he would cut off their ears or nose or something and send them back to their village as an example?" I point to one of the illustrations. "They basically just took anything they wanted."

Stephen reads along in the book. "Exactly: food, gold . . . slavery . . . rape. . . ." I flinch at the word, but Stephen keeps reading. "Crap, it says that they would make them bring back a certain amount of gold—which would have been impossible for anyone—so when they failed, they would cut their hands off so they would bleed to death! And when they ran away, they sent dogs to hunt them down and then they would burn them alive! Sick," Stephen says, finally looking up at me.

"So, I think we have our position—villain, right?"

"Yeah, villain," he agrees. "Why did we ever start celebrating Columbus Day?" He grins. "We should discontinue the holiday."

"It's true. Just because someone has always been seen as this incredible person—this hero—it doesn't mean that's the truth. Or that's who they really are," I say.

Stephen nods his head. "Yeah, totally."

"Maybe they're actually a horrible person. And it's just that no one wants to see him for who he truly is. Everyone would rather just believe the lies and not see all the damage he's done. And it's not fair that people can just get away with doing these awful things and never have to pay the consequences. They just go along with everyone believing—" I stop because I can barely catch my breath. As I look over at the confused expression on Stephen's face, I realize I'm probably not just talking about Columbus.

"Yeah," Stephen repeats, "I—I know, I totally agree."

"Okay. Okay, good."

"Hey, you know what we should do?" Stephen asks, his eyes brightening. "We should do, like, Most Wanted posters for Columbus and all those guys. And, like, list their crimes and stuff on the posters." He smiles. "What do you think?"

I smile back. "I like that."

LUNCH-BREAK BOOK CLUB. I named it. The next week we have our first meeting. We bring our brown bags to the table in the back of the library by the out-of-date reference materials nobody ever uses. It is me, Mara, Stephen, plus these two freshmen girls. The one girl looks to be about ten years old and transferred from a Catholic school at the beginning of the year. She dresses like she's still there, always wearing these starchy button-down shirts under scratchy sweaters, and embarrassingly long skirts. The other girl chews on her hair. She looks so out of it, I'm not sure if she even knows why we're here.

"We're one short," I announce, hoping this doesn't spoil everything.

Miss Sullivan looks at me like she knows just as well as I do that this is basically bottom of the barrel here. Then she looks up at the clock. The minute hand clicks on the one. "There's still time," she says, reading my mind. "Besides, it's all right if we don't have all six people the first day."

Just then this guy I've never seen walks toward the table—this severe-looking guy—skinny, with pale skin and deep black hair with blue streaks that match his bright blue eyes. He wears these funky, thick-rimmed glasses, and two silver rings encircle his lower lip.

"Wow," Mara whispers to me, grinning ear to ear.

"What?" I whisper back.

"Just . . . wow," she repeats, not taking her eyes off him.

"Cameron!" Miss Sullivan greets him. "I'm so glad you decided to come."

"Oh," he says, pulling out the chair beside Stephen. "I mean, yeah. Hi."

"All right," Miss Sullivan begins, clearly encouraged by our new addition. "Why don't we get started? I thought maybe we could just go around the table and introduce ourselves, tell everyone a little bit about your interests and why you're here. I'll start. Obviously, I'm Miss Sullivan." She laughs. "I'm your librarian. But when I'm not here, I'm actually a real person, believe it or not. I spend a lot of time volunteering for the animal shelter and I foster rescue dogs while they're waiting to be adopted. As far as this book club is concerned, as I mentioned to Eden, this is your club, so I want each of you to shape it. I think this will be a great way to do some reading for fun, outside the usual classroom setting, where we can have discussions and debates, talk about issues we don't normally get to address in your forty-minute classes."

She waves her hand in my direction, as if to say *you're up*. I sink into my skin a little deeper. "I'm Eden—Edy, I mean. Or Eden. Um, I guess, I just like reading." I shrug. "And I thought this book club sounded like a good idea," I mumble. Miss Sullivan nods her head encouragingly. I hate myself. I look to Mara, silently begging her to just please interrupt me, just start talking—say anything.

"My name is Mara," she says sweetly, flashing her new smile at all of us. "I'm a freshman. I'm interested in music—I'm in band. I like animals," she adds, so naturally. Why couldn't I have thought to say something like that? I'm in band too. I like animals—I love animals. "What else? I really think this will be a great way to spend our lunches—it's a lot nicer, and quieter, than the cafeteria." She adds a little giggle onto the end of her sentence, and everyone smiles back at her. Especially this new guy. Mara kicks my foot under the table, like, *Are you seeing this?*

"That's great, Mara—we could always use more volunteers at the animal shelter, you know," Miss Sullivan says with a smile. And I really wonder how people get to be normal like this. How they just seem to know what to say and do, automatically.

"I'm Cameron," the new guy says, skipping over the two other girls. "I'm new here this year. I'm interested in art. And music," he adds, smiling at Mara. "I like reading too." He breaks his gaze away from Mara to make eye contact with me. "And dogs," he smiles, looking at Miss Sullivan.

Miss Sullivan smiles back at him like she means it.

"I'm Stephen," Stephen mumbles. "When Edy told me about this, I thought it sounded like a good alternative to having lunch in the cafeteria. Oh, and I like art too," he adds, looking at Cameron. "Photography, I mean. I'm on yearbook."

"Awesome, man," Cameron says, flashing Stephen one of those smiles. This New Guy stepping all over my territory—first with

Mara, then Miss Sullivan, now Stephen. And he's going to try to smile at me like he's some kind of nice guy.

He catches me staring at him, trying to figure out what kind of game he's playing. I don't know what expression I must be wearing, but his smile fades a little, and his eyes look at me hard too, like he might be trying to figure out why I'm trying to figure him out. Somewhere, my brain tells me I should be listening as the two other girls introduce themselves, but I can't.

"Thank you for the introductions—this is great. So, I think the thing to do at this meeting is establish some logistics," Miss Sullivan says through the fog of my brain. Cameron redirects his attention to her, and I follow. "What sounds reasonable to you? Two books a month? One? Three? I don't know. We can vote on which books we would like to read together—we'll do the reading on our own time, and then these lunch sessions will be for discussion. Thoughts?"

"Two a month sounds good," Cameron offers, just before I was going to say the same thing.

"Yeah, two sounds right," Mara agrees, with this strange twinkle in her eye.

"Why not three?" Catholic Schoolgirl asks.

"I don't know if I have time for three extra books, with regular schoolwork and everything," Stephen says uncertainly, looking around the table for support.

"I agree." I say it firmly, just so I have something to say. Stephen smiles at me. He had, after all, supported me on Columbus.

"All right. I think we have a majority then. Two books per month it is!" Miss Sullivan concludes.

*

"Edy, this book thing was the best idea you've ever had!" Mara squeals the second we cross the threshold of the outside world, as we prepare to walk home after school. "That guy today was, like, so cool."

"You mean the guy with blue hair and all the piercings?" I ask in disbelief.

"It's not blue. It's black with little steaks of blue. It's awesome—he's awesome."

Okay, I mouth silently.

"Things are about to get good, Edy, I can feel it," she says, clasping her hands together.

"What are you talking about?"

"This is just the beginning—me and Cameron. We can only get closer from here on out, right?" She trails off, looking into the distance. And I know I've lost her; she's gone into her obsessive fantasizing state: "Yeah," she continues, finally looking at me again, her eyes wide. "We'll get to know him now that we're all doing this book thing. We'll become friends first. They always say that's better, anyway. It will be—"

I have to tune her out, though, because she could go on like this for hours, planning out how things will be.

"You noticed the way he was looking at me, right, like, *looking* at me?" I hear her say.

Sometimes I wonder if she gets it, like Miss Sullivan and Stephen—how they just get it. Most of the time I think so, but then sometimes it seems like we're on different planets. Like now.

"Maybe I should dye my hair blue?" she concludes, after a

monologue that's lasted almost the entire walk home from school.

"What? No, Mara."

"I was just making sure you're listening." She smirks.

"Sorry, I'm listening," I lie. We stand at the stop sign at the corner of my street. This is where we part. I go straight. She goes left. Except I can't force my feet to move in that direction. It's like I'm in quicksand. She stands there looking at me like maybe she really does get it. Like she knows something is wrong.

"Wanna come over?" she asks. "My mom won't be home until later."

I nod my head yes and we start walking toward her street.

"Okay, so I won't dye my hair blue"—she grins—"but I am getting contacts. I already guilted my dad into it. We're going to the eye doctor next weekend."

"Sweet," I tell her as I push my own glasses back up over the bridge of my nose.

We have no choice but to walk past his house to get to Mara's. Kevin's house. It hardly matters that he's not there. I can feel my legs weakening the closer we get. I suddenly hate this neighborhood, loathe it, despise the way we're all so close that we can't get untangled from each other's lives.

I already see Amanda in the front yard as we approach their house. His sister. She always seemed so much younger than me—I always thought of her as this little kid, but as I'm looking at her right now she doesn't seem so little. She's only one year behind us in school. We used to play together a lot when we were little, before Mara moved here in the sixth grade and took her place as my best friend. Their youngest sister is with her, along with another little kid—probably a neighbor—bundled up in layers, playing in the snow. It looks like they're trying to assemble a snowman, but it's really just a big blob of cold white. Amanda stands next to it, winding a scarf around and around the place where the top blob and the middle blob meet, while the two little kids scream and throw snowballs at each other.

The kids are oblivious to us, but Amanda sees us coming. She ties the scarf in a final knot and then places her mittened hands in her coat pockets; she stands there watching us. She doesn't say anything, which is strange. Even though we weren't technically friends, not like we used to be, we still talked, still got along at the occasional family get-together.

When I don't say anything either, Mara fills in the blanks: "Hey, Mandy!"

Mandy. It's what we all called her after they first moved here. It didn't stick. I remember that's how they introduced her the first time we met. It was at my eighth birthday party, back when our two families started celebrating everything as one, because Kevin and Caelin were inseparable from the very beginning. Kevin was always included, and his family by extension. But I guess that was a million years ago.

"Hi, Amanda," I offer, trying to smile.

She crosses her arms and stands up a little straighter. "Hey," she finally replies, monotone.

"So, did you have a nice Christmas?" I try, anyway, to act like things are normal, but all I can think of is Kevin.

She shrugs slightly, staring at me. The seconds drag by.

The thing about the Armstrongs—the thing I never really gave much thought until now—is that when they came here, they weren't just moving here. They were leaving something else. Something bad had happened wherever they were before. I'd overheard Mrs. Armstrong telling Mom about it. She was crying. And then later I was eavesdropping while Mom told Dad about it. I didn't get most of it, other than it involved Kevin, and Mr. Armstrong's brother, Kevin's uncle.

"Actually"—I turn to Mara—"I think I am gonna go home instead. I'm not feeling great, honestly."

"Really, what's wrong?" Mara asks, her voice genuinely concerned.

"Nothing, I just—" But I don't finish, because I'm literally backing away from them. I turn to look only once, and they both stand there watching me.

Mara raises her arm to wave, and yells, "I'll call you!"

I start running after I round the corner, my head pounding harder and faster with each footfall, my whole body in this cold sweat. By the time I make it home I'm so nauseous I'm actually crying. I run into the bathroom and am instantly on the floor kneeling in front of the toilet, gasping for air.

I lie down on the couch after, not even bothering to take my coat off.

I close my eyes.

The next thing I know, my mom is leaning over me, touching my forehead with the back of her hand. "She sick?" I hear Dad ask as he tosses his keys down on the kitchen table.

"Edy?" Mom puts her freezing hands on my cheeks—it feels so good. "What's the matter? Are you sick?"

"I guess so," I mumble.

"Well, let's get your coat off, here." She puts her arm around my back to help me up. And I wish more than anything that she would just hug me right now. But she pulls my arms out of my coat instead.

"I threw up," I tell her.

"Did you eat something weird today?" she asks.

"No." In fact, I didn't eat anything today. I was too busy trying to figure out that Cameron guy during lunch break to actually eat the peanut butter and jelly sandwich that I packed for myself.

"Oh, honey, I'm sorry." She stands and looks down at me like she really is. "Why don't you go get in your pajamas, and I'll make you some soup, okay?"

"Okay," I answer.

I go into my room to get changed, careful not to stare too hard at the fading gray bruises that still line my thighs. Careful not to dwell too long on the bruises on my hip bones and ribs. They'll be gone soon, anyway. I pull on my pajama bottoms and button the matching flannel shirt all the way up to my neck to hide the remnants of bruises still on my collarbone.

"Chicken noodle?" Mom calls out from the kitchen as I take my seat at the table.

Before I can answer, she sets a cup of steaming tea down in front of me.

I don't actually feel like soup at all, chicken noodle or any other kind. But she has this big smile on her face, like the kind she would always get running around after Caelin. I think she must like having someone to take care of, something concrete to do for me.

"Yeah, chicken noodle," I agree, in spite of my churning stomach.

"Okay. You drink that," she tells me, pointing at the tea.

I nod.

Dad sits down at the table across from me. Making his hands a tent, he says, "Yep. Some kinda bug going around, I guess."

If only I were sick all the time, things might feel a little more normal around here.

THE NEXT WEEK WE sit with our brown-bagged lunches at the table I reserved in the back of the library. Mara takes the seat directly next to Cameron, instead of me. His arm accidentally brushes against hers, and I watch as she turns slightly toward him. I can tell from here he's not actually into her. And that makes me feel too good.

"So, Lunch-Break Book Club is a democracy," Miss Sullivan begins as she wheels a book cart over to the table. "I pulled a number of books that we have at least six copies of in the library. I think the way to start is for each of us to pick a book that we'd like to read and then we can put it to a vote. Sound good?"

We all nod and begin combing through the rows of books. We finally make our way back to our seats with our books.

Cameron looks across the table at my selection. "Anne Frank? Excellent choice."

"I know, I picked it."

I look at his: *Brave New World.*

"My favorite," he explains.

"I've never read that," Mara tells him.

"Oh, it's really good. It's about this guy . . . ," he begins, moving in closer to her. Everyone starts listening to him, but all I want to do is pick the book up and hit him over the head with it. Why does he keep trying to take over my book club?

"Well, then, we might as well start there," Miss Sullivan says. "All those in favor of *Brave New World,* show of hands?"

I refuse to raise my hand. But all the others shoot up. They wait for me to join, looking at me like maybe I just didn't get how cool it was when Cameron was talking about it.

"Veto." I have to restrain myself from shouting it at him.

"Why?" Cameron asks, a hint of a laugh in his voice.

I feel my face flush. I open my mouth, not knowing what I'm going to say next. "Because." I pause. "Because everyone knows we're all going to have to read that in English when we're seniors."

"Oh yeah, that's true," Stephen agrees quietly, withdrawing his arm. I want to high-five him, but I just smile. He smiles back shyly, before he looks down at his famous bologna sandwich, dog-earing a corner of his napkin.

"So what? Wasn't Anne Frank summer reading?" Mara asks. I can hardly believe it—she's taking his side.

"Yeah, what's the difference?" Cameron asks, the two of them against me.

"It was summer reading," I start, trying to come up with any reason other than I hate you and I can't let you win. "But the difference is we never got to actually discuss it in class or anything. And we should've."

"But we haven't read *Brave New World* yet," Hair Chewer adds. "This way, we'll be prepared when we do have to read it senior year."

"That's true," Catholic Schoolgirl agrees.

"Well, I think that's idiotic." The words just roll off my tongue like the most natural thing in the world. I shut my mouth quickly, but it's too late.

Mara lets her mouth drop open like she can't believe I just said that. And then her face gets all scrunched up in that way that makes her look exactly like her mother. I honestly can't believe I just said that either.

"All right, guys, it's not that serious," Miss Sullivan intercedes. "Majority rules. So, we'll start with Mr. Huxley's *Brave New World*." Then she squeezes my shoulder gently and whispers, "I promise you'll enjoy it, Eden."

Everyone looks at me like I'm the biggest jerk in the world.

Mara takes a deep breath as we leave the library.

I look at her face, studying me.

"I know, I know—I don't know what happened, Mara," I admit. "Was that really bad?" I whisper.

"Kind of." She winces. "Are you okay?"

I nod.

"Are you sure you're not still sick from last week? 'Cause you're acting really weird."

"I guess not."

It's unnervingly quiet between us as we make our way to our lockers.

"Hey, can we do something this weekend?" I finally ask her. "Just us?" I clarify, thinking I really need to just tell her what happened with Kevin. Need to tell someone. And soon. Before I explode.

"I can't. I'm with my dad this weekend. Remember, we're going to get my contacts?"

So, it will have to wait.

AFTER SCHOOL THE NEXT day the halls are flooded with people trying to get the hell out. I was on my way to band practice, Mara walking alongside me, talking enough for the both of us—filling in the spaces I was leaving empty. I feel like I've gone off somewhere else, like I've just sort of slipped into this other realm. A world that's a lot like the real world, except slightly slower. This alternate reality where I'm not quite in my body, not quite in my mind, either—it's this place where all I do is think about one thing and one thing only.

"Black," Mara declares with finality. "No, red. I don't know. What do you think?" she asks, holding a strand of brunette hair up in front of her face. "I think black. Definitely," she answers. "I know my mom will flip out," she says, as if I had brought it up. "Well, I don't care. I just need a change."

"Another change?" I ask, but she doesn't hear me over the lockers clanging and the voices shouting, or maybe it's just that I'm not talking loud enough.

"Oh—did I tell you my dad wants me to meet his new girlfriend this weekend?" She says it as if she just remembered, as if she hadn't told me twenty times already. "Can you believe that?" She says "girlfriend" like it's this impossibility, like a unicorn or a dragon or something.

I know she's been having a hard time with it all—her parents getting divorced, her dad moving out, her mom getting crazier, and now this alleged girlfriend. I know I need to at least make an attempt to be the best friend I was only a month ago. I shake my head in what I hope looks like disbelief.

"Edy," she says. "You can come over after school today, if you want."

I manage a smile. But that's about all I can manage.

"You can help me pick a color. We could do your hair too!" she shouts.

I shrug. I try to stay close to the wall as we walk. Lately it feels like my skin, just like my mind, has been turned inside out. Like I'm raw and exposed, and it almost hurts to even be brushed up against. I hug my clarinet case to my chest to make myself smaller, to be my armor.

That's when I see him, this guy running down the hall, toward us. Number 12, it says on his stupid, pretentious varsity jacket. I have a distinct sinking feeling in my stomach as I watch him gaining speed, weaving between bodies like he's on the basketball court and not in the hallway. I hear someone shout his name and something about being late and how the coach will make him do laps. He turns his head and looks behind him, laughing as he starts to yell something back. I see that he's not looking ahead, that he's about to collide into me. I open my mouth, but nothing comes out.

I could see it happening before it happened.

And then it does. Crassshhh: him into me, my shoulder into the wall, clarinet case into my stomach so hard my body keels over involuntarily. It jolts me back into reality. Time rushes ahead, my brain and body overloaded in only an instant. Hunched forward, my abdomen aching like I'd just been stabbed, I stare at my dirty no-name Kmart sneakers. Number 12 grabs my forearm. It feels like his fingers are burning holes through my shirt. I hear his voice, muffled, in the background of my mind, saying "Oh shit—shit, I'm sorry—are you okay?"

But I can't listen all the way because I seem to have only one thought. Just this: *Fucking die fucking asshole fucking kill you fucking die, die, die.*

I don't quite know what to do with this thought. Surely it can't be mine. But how can I explain those words? They're on my tongue, about to spill right out into the open air. And I've never said such words out loud, to or about another human being, yet there they are. In fact, I can't think of any other words in the entire English language; my complete vocabulary is suddenly composed of nothing more than an endless string of obscenities punctuated with expletives.

As he stands there in front of me and I stand in front of him clutching my stomach, he looks at my outfit and my glasses and my stupid hair, but not at me. "Sorry," he repeats, and when I still don't respond, he adds, "I didn't see you." He enunciates his words precisely, as if he truly believes I might be deaf.

He repeats them, those four words: "I. Didn't. See. You." Each word like a match striking against that thin, sandpapery strip on the back of a matchbook, failing one, two, three, four times.

Let him say just one more word.

"Ohh-kaay?" he says slowly.

Lit. On fire. My God, I burn.

It's something new, this feeling. Not anger, not sadness, not embarrassment. It burns up everything inside of me, every thought, every memory, every feeling I ever had, and fills itself in the space left vacant.

Rage. In this moment, I am nothing but pure rage.

I watch him pick my clarinet case up off the floor. He holds it out to me. My hands shake as I take it from him. Carefully, I hug it against my torso again, this time for a very different reason. Because everything in my brain and body is telling me to beat him with it, to hit him repeatedly with the hard black plastic case.

I hear Mara saying, "I think she's hurt. You should watch where you're going!" And then to me, "Are you all right, Edy?"

Only, I can't answer her, either, because the gory scene of this basketball player's death is reeling through my mind, and it is truly terrifying. Because I'm not supposed to be capable of thoughts like that, I'm not built that way. But I feel it tingling in my bones and skin and blood—something barbaric, something animal.

I force my feet to start walking. If I don't move, I'm afraid I might do something crazy, something really bad, and if I open my mouth, I'll say those horrible words. After a second I hear his feet running again, away from me. He should be running; in fact, they should all be running. I'm dangerous, criminally dangerous.

Mara catches up with me and speaks the one word that says it all: "Asshole." Then she looks over her shoulder and adds, "Although,

I wouldn't mind if he crashed into me a little. Just sayin'."

I look at her and feel the corners of my mouth pull upward, and it almost hurts, but in a different way than my stomach. It hurts like it's the first time I've smiled in my whole life. She laughs, and then touches my shoulder gently. "Are you really okay?" I nod, even though I'm not sure if I am—if I ever will be.

"IT'S TIME," MARA DECLARES as we sit in the middle of her bedroom floor. I just finished cutting a big wad of pink bubble gum out of her hair that someone had stuck in at some point during the day. It had hardened beyond the point of peanut butter and careful untangling.

The debate has been going on for months now.

"So, red," I confirm, as we stare at the box of hair color standing upright in the space between us. I didn't say anything when she stopped showing up to band practice, or when she started sneaking cigarettes from her mom's purse, but I have to say something now, before it's too late. "Mara, you realize that's really, really red?" I ask, looking at the girl on the box.

"Cranberry," she corrects, picking the box up gently with both hands, studying the picture. "Do you think you could cut it short like this girl's?" she asks me. "I'm so sick of having long hair—it's like I'm inviting them to throw things in it."

It's true; she's had the same long brown hair falling to the middle of her back ever since I can remember. "Are you sure it has to be right now?" I double-check. "'Cause if you wait just three more weeks, it'll be summer, and then if it doesn't turn out, you'll have time to—"

"No," she interrupts. "That's all the more reason it has to be tonight—I can't go through this for another year. I can't go through this for three more weeks. I can't go through this shit for another day!" she almost shouts.

"But what if—"

"Edy, stop. You're supposed to be helping me."

"I am, I just—do you really think coloring your hair is going to change anything?"

"Yes—it's going to change *me*." She rips open the lid on the box and starts pulling out the contents one by one.

"Why right now, though—did something else happen besides the gum?" It was the question I had been waiting for her to ask me for months.

"Like anything else needs to happen? It's been years of this—every single day—stupid names, gum in the hair, 'loser' signs stuck on my back. Can only be expected to take so much," she says, her voice getting chopped up by the tears she tries to hold in.

"I know." And I do know. I get it. She gets it. It has to happen, and I understand why.

"Well, let's do it then," she says, holding the scissors out to me.

I take the scissors from her like a good friend.

"You realize I have no idea what I'm doing, right?" I ask her as strands of hair begin to fall to the floor.

"It's okay, I trust you," she says, closing her eyes.

"No, don't," I say with a laugh.

She smiles.

"Can I ask you something and you'll promise not to get mad?" I begin cautiously.

She opens her eyes and looks at me.

"This isn't about Cameron, is it? Because he should like you the way you are. I mean, if you're doing this so he'll be interested, or so he'll think you're cooler, that's not—"

But she stops me. "Edy, no." She's calm, not mad at all. She talks quietly, explaining, "Yes, I like him, but I'm not trying to be like him. I'm just trying to be like me. Like the real me. If that makes any sense at all," she says, laughing.

I don't even need to think about it—I know exactly how she feels. "It makes sense, Mara."

"Good." And then she closes her eyes again, like me cutting and coloring her hair is the most relaxing thing in the world. It's quiet for a while.

"Can I ask you something else?" I finally say, breaking the silence.

"Yeah."

"You're not coming back to band, are you?"

"No."

"Thought so."

She turns around to look at me. "Sorry, Edy. It's just not me anymore; I'm interested in other things now."

"It's okay, I was just missing my stand partner is all." I try to make light of it, but it really does make me sad. "You know they're gonna stick me with that smelly girl who's always messing up, right?" I tell her as I start mixing the hair color.

She laughs. "I'm sorry. Just hold your breath!"

"I kind of need to breathe in order to play!"

"True," she admits, still smiling.

I start brushing the mixture into her hair in sections, trying to be as neat as possible. "So, what other interests?"

"I don't know. I think I'll start taking art classes next year. And I know what you're gonna say, but it's not about Cameron. But becoming friends with him, it's just made me realize I want to try new things."

I've never known Mara to be interested in art. "Well, that's cool." I kind of mean it too. Because I can't think of anything in the world that I'm interested in anymore.

"Do I look tough?" she asks once we've finished, giving herself dirty looks in the mirror.

I study her reflection too. "You look . . . like a completely different person," I tell her, consumed equally with admiration and jealousy. She walks past me over to the window and cracks it open. Then she pulls out a cigarette and a lighter from the rhinestone-studded jewelry box in her desk drawer, watching herself closely in the mirror as she brings it up to her demetallized mouth. "I look mean, don't I?" she asks. "I look like a bitch," she says slowly, her smile perfectly straight.

"So you want to look like a bitch now?" I laugh.

"I don't know, maybe. Why not?" She shrugs. "I'm reinventing myself. Everyone else gets to change." I know that what she really means by "everyone" is her parents—they get to change their minds, change their lives, and hers.

"I guess." I can't exactly protest too much, because honestly, the idea of reinventing myself sounds pretty appealing. I'm not sure who I'd want to be, though.

"I really don't care what anyone thinks about me, as long as they don't think I'm just going to sit back and take it anymore!" She exhales a cloud of smoke with the words. "I'm just sick of getting pushed around, treated like shit. I mean, aren't you?"

She shifts her gaze from the mirror to me. I can't lie. Can't admit the truth, either. So I say nothing. Instead, I walk over to her and take a cigarette out of the pack. I place it between my lips. Mara doesn't say a word. She just smiles cautiously and brings the lighter up to light it for me. I breathe in. And then choke on the horrible chemicals. We laugh as I cough and gasp.

"That's so gross!" I tell her, choking on my words. But then I bring it to my lips again anyway.

"Don't breathe in so deep this time," she says with a laugh.

I don't. And I don't choke this time. I watch Mara watching me, and I think maybe I can change too. Maybe I can become someone I can actually stand. I take my glasses off, take another drag, and look at Mara. "Seriously, what do you think? Should I get contacts?"

"Absolutely!" She keeps the cigarette dangling from her mouth as she reaches over and swoops my hair back from my face. "You could do this," she tells me, her words muffled through the smoke.

"I could?" I ask her, not sure exactly what she means by "this." Just my hair. The contacts. Or everything.

"You could be so hot—so beautiful, I mean—if you would quit hiding."

"Do you really think so?"

"Yes, Edy. I know so."

I smile again, letting the chemicals go to my head, and imagine what I could be, all the things I could do.

THE SUMMER TOOK FOREVER to get here and now it's here and it's just flying. Mostly, I've spent the days thinking a lot about what Mara said to me. About how I was hiding. How I could be beautiful if I would just stop. Mostly, I've spent the whole summer trying to figure how you go about not hiding when that's all you've ever done your entire life. Caelin wasn't around. He was taking some kind of special summer sessions. It was actually better that way anyway. Because it meant Kevin would stay away too.

"Mom?" I use my I-want-something-and-I'm-such-a-good-girl-so-please-hear-me-out voice. "I was wondering . . ."

"Mm-hmm?" she murmurs, barely caffeinated, not lifting her eyes from the sales ads.

"What do you want and how much does it cost?" Dad interferes, trying to hijack the conversation.

"What, what do you need?" she asks, finally looking across the kitchen table at me.

I slowly remove my glasses.

“Don’t you think I look better without my glasses, Mom?”

“You look pretty no matter what.” She’d already gone back to the paper. Obviously that approach was not going to work.

“Okay, so school’s starting in what, like, three weeks or something, and I was thinking—I mean, well—Mara got contacts and she thinks—I mean, I think—I think that—”

“All right, Minnie, come on, just spit it out.” Dad makes this rolling, speed-it-up gesture with his un-coffee-cupped hand.

“Okay. So, um, I was wondering if I could get contacts too?”

Mom and Dad share a look, like, *Oh God, why can’t she just leave us alone?*

“They’re really not that much more expensive,” I try.

“I don’t know, Edy,” Mom says, nose scrunched, not wanting to disappoint me, because after all, I really am a very good girl. Except for the small detail about me smoking every single day with Mara, and blowing all the back-to-school money they gave me to buy too many clothes at the mall and makeup and hair products, but not school supplies, like they wanted. Other than that, I really am good.

“But, please. Please, please, please. I look like such a dork. I look like a loser. I look like I’m in band!”

“You are in band,” Dad says, grinning, missing the point, of course.

“But I don’t want to look like I’m in band.”

“Oh, well, now I see.” Dad rolls his eyes. Mom smirks. He shakes his head in that condescending way he always does whenever he thinks someone is an idiot.

“Mom?”

Her stock response to any and everything: “We’ll see.”

"So no?" I clarify.

"No, I said we'll see," she repeats sternly.

"Yeah, but that means no, right? This is so unfair! Caelin can get all kinds of new stuff and I ask for one thing, one thing, and you say no!"

"Caelin got new stuff when he left for college," Dad says, as if Caelin went off to go cure leprosy. "He needed all those things. You don't need contacts. You want them, you don't need them."

"I do need them!" I can feel the tears beginning to simmer behind my eyes. "And just so you know," I continue, my voice falling in on itself, "I'm not wearing my glasses anymore even if you don't get me contacts!" I throw my glasses onto the table and then I stomp off to my room.

"Oh, for Christ's sake, she has to start first thing in the morning?" I hear Mom say just before I slam my bedroom door shut.

And I hear fragments of Dad's response: "Jesus . . . melodramatic . . . girl . . . spoiled rotten."

Spoiled? I'm spoiled? I never ask for a thing! I never even ask for attention. That's it. The last goddamn straw. I fling my door open and march back out there, bracing myself with both hands against the kitchen table. I open my mouth, not caring what comes out, for once not having a plan.

"I hate you both!" I growl through my teeth. "Sorry, but I'm not Caelin! Sorry I'm not Kevin! Sorry you're stuck here all alone with me. But I'm stuck here with you too!" The words just tumble out one after the other, louder and louder.

They are stunned. They're shocked. I had never so much as looked at them the wrong way.

Mom slams the paper down onto the table, speechless.

"Don't you dare talk to your mother and me that way ever again!" Dad stands up, pointing his finger in my face. "Do you understand? Go to your room!"

"No!" The word claws its way up my throat. My vocal cords ache immediately, never having achieved this volume before.

"Now!" he demands, taking a step.

I stomp away, my feet like bricks. I slam my bedroom door again as hard as I can, then press my ear against it. My chest heaves with frantic breaths as I listen.

"All right, Conner," I hear Mom say, her voice low, trying to whisper. "We have got to do something—this is crazy. What are we supposed to do?"

"It's hormones, Vanessa. She's a teenager. They're all the same. We were like this too when we were her age," he says, trying to calm her down.

"I never would have said 'I hate you' to my parents," she argues.

"Yes, you would have. And I'm sure you did. And so did I. And so did Caelin, if you remember. They never mean it."

Except maybe I do mean it. A little, at least. Because I let them push me around just like I let everyone push me around. I let them make me into a person who doesn't know when to speak the hell up, a person who gives up control over her life, over her body, over everything. I do what they tell me to do, what everyone tells me to do. Why didn't they ever teach me to stand up for myself?

Even though they don't know what happened, what he did to me, they helped to create the situation. In a way, they allowed it. They let it happen by allowing him to be here and making me believe that everyone else in the entire world knows what's good for me better than I do. If I hate them, I hate them for that. And I hate Caelin, too. Except I hate him because his loyalties are with Kevin, not me. I know that. Everyone does. Especially Kevin.

And what about Mara? Why couldn't she be the kind of friend who would just get it out of me? Why do I feel like after all this time I still can't tell her, that even she wouldn't believe me, or that if she did, that she would somehow blame me? Why do I feel so completely alone when I'm with her sometimes? Why do I feel like, sometimes, I have no one in the entire world who knows me in even the slightest, most insignificant way?

Why do I feel like—God, it makes me sick to admit—that sometimes I feel like the only person in the world who knows me—really, really knows me—is Kevin? That's sick. Demented sick. Like, I-should-be-locked-up sick. But he's the only one who knows the truth. Not only the truth about what happened, but the truth about me, about who I really am, what I'm really made of. And that gives him tyranny over everything in this world.

Most of that hate, though, I save for me. No matter what anyone else did or didn't do, it was ultimately me who gave them permission. I'm the one who's lying. The coward too afraid to just stop pretending.

This is bigger than contacts. It's not over the clarinet, Environmental Club, FBLA, French Club, Lunch-Break Book Club, Science Club, yearbook, or any of the other things I had checked off the list in my head, things in which I was no longer going to participate. It's over my life, my identity, my sanity—these are the things at stake.

When I come out of my bedroom later that night, I force myself not to apologize to them. Because I desperately want to, want their approval—crave it. But I have to start standing up for myself. And it has to start with them, because it was with them that it began.

The next week I have my contacts. It is my first small victory in the battle over control of my life. No more Mousegirl. No more charades. No more baby games.

PART TWO

Sophomore Year

IT'S SURPRISINGLY EASY TO completely transform yourself. I had my contacts. I had new clothes that my mom did not help me pick out at Kmart. I had finally figured out my hair, after fourteen years of frizz and headbands. Finally let my bangs grow out, instead of that perpetual in-between state they had been in for years. I pierced my ears at the mall during one of our back-to-school shopping trips, little rhinestone studs that sparkle just enough to be noticeable. Mara got her second holes done before it was my turn, just so I wouldn't be afraid.

I don't put on much makeup. Just enough. Lip gloss, mascara. I don't look slutty or anything, just nice. Just normal. In my normal, fashionable jeans that fit me right. A simple T-shirt and cardigan that doesn't hide the curves I finally seem to have grown into over the summer. I just look like someone who's not a kid anymore and can make her own decisions, like someone about to start her sophomore year—someone who's not hiding anymore.

I slip my new sandals onto my bare feet before I head out the door.

“Oh my Lord!” Mom shouts, pulling on my arm before I can leave. “I can’t believe how beautiful you look,” she squeals, holding me at arm’s length.

“You can’t?”

“No, I can. I just mean there’s something different. You look so . . . so confident.” She smiles as her eyes take me in. “Have a great first day, okay?”

Mara got a ride with Cameron, whom she started hanging out with again toward the end of the summer. So I wait for her on the front steps of the school. People look at me as they pass. It’s strange. I’ve never been seen like this. As a regular person. I test out a smile on this one girl I’ve never seen before. As an experiment. Not only does she smile back, but she even says “hey.”

I spot another lone girl walking up the steps. Just as I’m about to try it on a new test subject, I stop short as she looks up at me, her dark, dark eyes burning against her warm, tanned skin, her black hair shining in the morning sunlight.

“Amanda, hi,” I finally say, taken back by her presence—by the hot sinking feeling her presence leaves in my stomach—by all the memories of the past, of growing up together, of her and Kevin, and Kevin, and Kevin, and Kevin.

Stop, I command my brain.

It can’t quite stop, but it slows down just enough for me to try to smile anyway. Because all of that is in the past, I remind myself. It’s not something I need to think about ever again. And Amanda has nothing to do with it anyway.

“I guess I forgot you’d be going here this year.” Smile.

She moves in close to me, so close I want to back up. And then quietly, but firmly, she hisses, "You don't have to talk to me."

"No, I want to—"

"Ever," she interrupts.

"I don't—I don't get it."

She shakes her head ever so slightly, like I'm missing something completely obvious, and then smiles coolly before shoving past me. I turn around and watch in disbelief as she walks away. I hardly have time to worry about it, though, because the second I turn back there's Mara, shouting, "Hey, girl!" with Cameron following along behind her. Mara kisses me on the cheek, and whispers in my ear, "You look A-MAZE-ING. Seriously."

"Hey, Edy," Cameron says, looking off somewhere past me.

"Hey," I mumble back.

Mara frowns a little, but she's used to it by now. Cameron and I are never going to be friends.

"All right, you ready?" she asks me, her face glowing with excitement, her short cranberry hair framing her features perfectly.

I take a deep breath. And exhale. I nod.

"Let's do this," she says, locking her arm with mine.

After homeroom, it's trig, which makes me want to scream already. Then after trig, it's bio. Stephen Reinheiser is in my class. I can feel him looking at me, staring with his glasses and his fresh haircut and his brand-new clothes—his trying too hard—craning his neck eagerly, begging for me to look up at him when it's time to pick a lab partner. I quickly turn to the girl next to me and smile, as if to say: I'm friendly, I'm normal, smart—I'd be a great lab partner. She smiles back. And we exchange nods—done. The last thing in the world I need this year is another Columbus project with Stephen Reinheiser. The last thing I need in my new life is a Stephen Reinheiser. When the bell rings, I'm ready to bolt. Because I know he's dying to say hello and ask me about my summer.

In the hall I hurry to my new study hall. I've never had one before because I'd always had band. There were always lessons, practice, rehearsals. Never just free time. As I walk I keep smiling at random people. And most of them smile back. I even thought I noticed a few guys smiling at me first. No, I definitely don't need a Stephen Reinheiser holding me back this year.

Just as I'm floating along, I hear someone call my name. I stop and turn around. It's Mr. Krause, my band teacher. Suddenly gravity drags me back down just a little.

"Edy, I'm glad I ran into you. I was really surprised not to see your name on my roster this year. What happened?" he asks, almost looking hurt that I'd dropped out.

"Oh, right. I just—" I search for the words. "I've been in band for so long. I just kind of wanted to branch out this year, I guess. Try some new things," I tell him. He still looks at me like he doesn't quite comprehend. So I test out my smile on him. And suddenly his face softens.

He nods his head. "Well, I guess I can understand that." But just then the second bell rings. I open my mouth to tell him that I'm late, but he stops me. "Don't worry, I'll sign you a late pass." And as he scribbles his signature on the slip of paper, he tells me "We'll miss you. You're welcome back anytime, you know."

"Thank you, Mr. Krause." I smile again.

He smiles back.

This is the way the world works, apparently. I can't believe

I'm only figuring this out now. I wonder, as I walk to my new study hall, if other people know about this. It's simple really. All you have to do is act like you're normal and okay, and people start treating you that way.

I arrive at my new study hall late. There's a buzz of light chatter. Which is good. It's never easy for me to study if it's too quiet. I make my way to the front of the room to hand in my late pass.

Then I scan the room for an empty spot as I pace the aisles of desks. I see that guy—Number 12. He sits in the back of the room, at the tail end of a cluster of jock types, wearing his Number 12 jacket. There are no empty seats anywhere. I start to panic as I notice more and more eyes beginning to look up at me, afraid they might see that underneath my new outfit and hair and makeup and body, maybe I'm really not that normal or okay. I start up the next aisle when I hear a voice behind me: "There's one back here."

I turn around. It's Number 12. He clears a stack of books off the top of the desk next to his, and looks up at me. And I actually have to look behind me to make sure he's really talking to me. This is the same guy who so completely didn't see me that day last year, he could've seriously injured me. He points at me and mouths the word *you*, with a small lopsided grin.

I walk toward him slowly, half wondering if this is some kind of sick joke to lure me into unfamiliar territory only to do something humiliating, like throw spitballs in my hair. I move into the seat cautiously, trying not to make any noise as I pull out my notebook and pen and planner. I open the planner to today's date, and make a note: Smile.

"Eh-hem." Number 12 clears his throat kind of loud next to me.

I just trace my pen over the word, over and over, branching out into designs that outline the letters until they're barely visible. I consider taking out my trig homework, but that would just upset me, and I'm actually feeling okay—normal, almost.

"Eh-hem-hem." Number 12 again.

I pivot away from him.

"Eh-hem." He does it again. "Eh-hem!" I look up, wondering if he's choking or something. And he's turned toward me—facing me—smiling.

"Oh," I say, not really knowing what else there is to say. "What?" I whisper. Maybe he said something to me and I just spaced.

"What?" he repeats.

"Oh. Did you say something?"

"No."

"Oh, okay." I start to go back to my doodling.

"I mean, I didn't *say* anything," he whispers.

I look at him. He leans toward me. So I lean toward him slightly and try to listen as hard as I can. That's when I notice his eyes. They're this intense brown, so deep it makes me want to just fall all the way into them. "What?" I ask again.

He laughs too loud. His jock people turn around and stare at me for a few seconds before returning to each other. "I said, I didn't say anything. I was just trying to get your attention."

"Oh." I pause. "Why?"

"I don't know." He shrugs. "To say hi."

"Oh. Hi?" I say it like a question, only because I'm really confused about what's going on here.

"Hi," he laughs the word.

I look down at my planner. The word "Smile" stares at me through the scribbles. So I look at him again, and give him the smile that had been working for me so far this year. He inches his whole desk closer to me, making a screeching noise against the floor, again drawing the attention of his friends.

"So," he whispers. "Are you new?"

"New?" I repeat.

"New this year, I mean?" he asks.

"No."

"Seriously?"

I nod.

"Oh. Wow, okay." He narrows his eyes at me and turns his head slightly, like he doesn't quite believe me.

That's when I realize he has absolutely no idea who I am. No idea I was that girl he nearly ran over in the hall last year. No idea how he grabbed my arm and asked me if I was okay. No idea that I ever existed. And somehow, I really like the way that feels. I smile again.

He smiles back. "What's your name?"

"E—den." I almost say Edy but stop myself just in time. "Eden," I repeat, clearer. Because I can be anyone to this guy. I can truly be this new person. Because he knows nothing different.

"Eden?" he verifies. And it suddenly sounds like the best name in the world.

"Yeah." I smile. I start sifting through the collection of random facts—these small things that I know about him. Like his name and the fact that he's a senior and a basketball star and has had previous cheerleader girlfriends. The term scholar-athlete comes to mind. I know who he is, of course; it would be impossible to not know something like that. Like when his name comes up in the morning announcements for leading the boys' varsity team to victory over blah, blah, blah, or for scoring x number of points in whatever quarter in last night's game against whomever, I obviously have an image in my head of who it is they're talking about. But it's different, somehow, actually sitting next to him.

His eyes meet mine. I'm staring. I look down and think: Chocolate. That's what his eyes remind me of. I look up again. The color of dark chocolate. And I realize that those small random facts don't really add up to anything when you're up close like this. When someone like him is looking at you the way he's looking at me.

"Josh," he tells me. And then does something just . . . insane. He reaches across the aisle, extending his hand toward me for a handshake. It seems a little silly, but I raise my hand to meet his. His skin is warm, just like his voice and his eyes and his laugh. It seems like we're holding each other's hands for way too long, but he just smiles like there's nothing weird about this at all.

But then the bell screams. I drop his hand, shocked back into a world not composed solely of this guy's chocolate eyes. I gather my things quickly so I can get out of there, because I don't know what just happened—what's happening. I don't know if it's scary or exhilarating. I don't dare look back at him. I rush for the door.

THE NEXT DAY IT'S like my entire world revolves around preparing for study hall, even though I know it's the least important part of the day. I should be worrying about my trig quiz next week, and the fact that I have no clue how to even properly work my calculator yet. I can't tell if I'm obsessing over seeing Josh again because I'm dreading it or because I can't wait. Or both, somehow.

When I get there, he's already sitting with his friends. I stand in the doorway, not knowing what to do. I can't go over and just sit there. But then if I sit somewhere else, I don't want it to seem like I don't want to sit with him again. He's laughing with the guy in front of him, who's turned around in his chair, gesturing wildly.

But then the second bells rings. People are still filing in, and they push past me as I stand in the way. My heart starts racing as I try to make the decision. If he would just look over here and give me a sign that I'm invited to sit back there again. But he's not paying attention. He doesn't see me. He probably doesn't even remember yesterday.

"Okay, find your seats, everyone!" the teacher yells. So I sink into the seat closest to the door. I keep my eyes glued on the back of the kid's neck in front of me while the teacher takes roll call. I am the biggest coward in the universe.

"Eden McCrorey?"

I raise my arm, but he overlooks me.

"Eden McCrorey?" he repeats, louder.

"Here," I call back. And I can't help myself; I look behind me to the back corner of the room where he's sitting. He's looking at me. I turn back around quickly. When the teacher finishes taking attendance, I hurry to the front of the room to have him sign my pass for the library. When I turn around to head for the door, Josh waves at me and points his thumb toward the empty desk next to his. As I get closer he motions for me to come over there. I really just want to run, though. But I remember about acting normal and smiling, so I walk over to him. His friends turn to look at me; it's like they're evaluating me—inspecting me for flaws. Quietly, Josh says, "Hey, Eden, I saved your spot."

"Oh. Well, thanks. I'm going to the library though."

He looks disappointed. "Tomorrow then," he says with a shrug, brushing it off.

"Sure."

And then he looks up at me with his smile, and I can feel his eyes watching me as I leave. I'm barely breathing. My heart feels light and fast—too fast.

I walk through the doors of the library, quietly making my way to her office. I see her sitting at her desk going through some papers. I knock softly.

"Eden, come on in!" She smiles, her voice warm.

I sit down in one of her chairs. "Hi, Miss Sullivan."

"So, to what do I owe this pleasure?"

"I just wanted to say hi." I just needed a place to hide. Again.

"That's so sweet. Thank you, Eden." There's this pause—this silence that lasts too long. Thankfully, she fills it. "You know, I was just thinking back to last year. I remember you had initially wanted to volunteer?"

"Oh yeah, I did." I'd nearly forgotten.

"Well, there're still some spots open . . . if you're interested, that is."

"Really? Yeah, I am. I mean, yes. Definitely!"

"Okay. When are you free?" she asks, pulling up the schedule on her computer.

"Now, I guess. I have study hall, and then directly after I have lunch, so I could even volunteer third and fourth periods. I mean, if you need me. If you need help, I mean."

"Well, I do need help, but I want you," she says pointedly, tracing her finger along the boxes of her calendar. "Okay! We're in luck; it looks like that's going to work out perfectly!"

"Great. When do I start?"

"No time like the present," she says, opening her arms in this welcoming gesture. Miss Sullivan takes me through the checkout process and teaches me about the database and how to locate the books on the shelves. She watches while I check out my first customer.

"You're a natural!" she tells me. I smile back at her, not with my new smile but my real one. I'm glad to be around her again—she makes me feel like maybe I really am normal. Like things really will be okay.

“SO, SOMETHING REALLY WEIRD happened yesterday,” I tell Mara as we begin our walk home from school.

“Oooh, what?” she asks eagerly.

“So, do you know that guy Josh Miller? He’s a senior on the basketball team?”

“Of course.”

“Yeah. Of course. Well, he was talking to me. Like *talking* to me. It almost seemed like . . . I don’t know. No, forget it. It’s stupid.” I laugh.

“No, what? You have to tell me now—I’m hooked!”

“Okay. But first, believe me, I know full well exactly how stupid this is going to sound,” I warn her.

“Oh. My. God—just tell me!” she demands, laughing.

“Well, you know how I dropped band? So, I got put in this study hall instead. And he’s in there—Josh—and he gave up the seat next to him so I could sit there. And then he was trying to talk to me, almost like he was actually . . . interested.” I wait for her to start laughing, but she just continues to look at me. "Interested in me, I mean," I clarify.

"Okay, first of all, why would you think I would think that's stupid? And second of all . . . WOOO-HOOOO!" she screams, jumping up and down right in the middle of the street. "YEEEEESSSS!"

"Oh my gosh, stop! You're crazy!" I yell. But we're both laughing uncontrollably.

"So what happened next?" she asks, her laugh fading as she tries to catch her breath.

"What do you mean? Nothing. Was something supposed to happen next?"

"I mean, how did you leave things? What exactly did he say to you?"

"He said he was going to save me a seat tomorrow."

"Perfect!" she shouts. "So then tomorrow you—"

"Wait." I interrupt her. "I'm not actually going to be there tomorrow, though."

"Why not?"

"Well, I kind of volunteered in the library for that period," I admit.

She stares into my eyes, unblinking, her smile fading rapidly. "I'm sorry, did you suffer a blow to the head?"

"You think I should've stayed in the study hall?"

"Duh-uh!" she yells. "Of course, Edy. Have you learned nothing this summer?"

I think about it for several minutes as we walk. Mara keeps letting out these small exasperated breaths, and looking at me and shaking her head, periodically sighing. "Oh, Edy."

“You’re right,” I tell her once we reach the corner where we need to part. “You’re totally right. I don’t know why I did that. I just got scared, I guess.”

“Scared of what? It’s Joshua Miller—this is a great thing, Edy.”

I just shrug. Because I can’t tell her exactly what I mean. And I know she wouldn’t be able to understand even if I could.

I HAVE BEEN WORKING in the library for a full week. I like being around Miss Sullivan again. And I have nearly forgotten all about Josh Miller and the seat he was saving for me. Forgotten everything except for those eyes, that is.

I'm nice and safe in this little corner of the world. It's like a break from life. I realize quickly I actually love shelving the books, putting things back in the proper order. Everything has a place—a right way to be. Here, I don't have to worry about who I am or if I'm being it right. No one bothers me, not even myself.

"You're a very hard person to find, you know that?" someone says, suddenly very close to me.

I turn around. I almost can't believe it. It's him. Josh. And his eyes, looking at me. He leans against the bookshelf and smiles. I didn't realize how tall he was when we were sitting together, and that day in the hall I guess I was too crazed to realize much at all. To realize how irresistible he is when he stands in front of me like this. We're so close to each other, tucked away in this quiet aisle; it's like there's no one else in the entire world. Still, I take a small step toward him because it's like he's some kind of magnet, and I can't not move closer.

"You were trying to find me?" I ask.

"Well, I've been saving that seat for you, and people were starting to look at me funny." He grins, that small lopsided smile again. "I kinda started thinking you were never coming back." He looks around the library and then at the stack of books in my arms. "I guess I was right?"

"I didn't think you were serious about that." I feel my grasp on the books tighten as my heart begins to speed up.

"Why don't people ever think I'm being serious?" he asks with a laugh.

Maybe because you look like that, I want to say. Maybe because you always have that ridiculously charming smile on your face. Maybe people don't want to take you seriously because then you're real. Then you're not just Number 12. Or maybe that's just me. "I don't know," I tell him instead.

"Well, I was."

And we just stand there staring at each other.

Finally he says, turning his head at me suspiciously, "Do you not like me or something?"

"No," I tell him right away. "I mean, not no. I mean I do. I mean, I don't not like you."

"Okay. I think," he says, laughing. "Well, now that that's all cleared up. I was thinking maybe we should do something sometime?"

"Like what?" I ask.

"Like what?" he repeats. He grins that grin of his again. "Oh, I don't know, I thought we'd knock over a couple of ATMs, do a little vandalism, steal some identities, and then head for the border. Carrying illegal substances, of course." He laughs. "Or we could get really crazy and go see a movie. Possibly even eat at a restaurant."

I can't help but smile.

"Is that a yes?" he asks.

"I don't know," I tell him. "Maybe."

He looks at me more seriously now. "What, do you have a boyfriend or something?"

"No."

We just stand there, saying nothing.

"All right," he finally says with an exhale. "I guess, let me know then."

As I watch him walk away, God, I wish I would've just said yes. I step out from the aisle to see if I can still catch him. But just as he walks out the door, I see Amanda standing there at one of the shelves, absently touching the spines of books. She's looking back and forth between me and Josh. This time I glare at her. Pretending she doesn't see me, she pulls a book and starts randomly thumbing the pages.

SITTING IN THE GRASS next to the tennis courts, I pick those fuzzy white dandelions, absently blowing the little seeds off into the wind. Almost October, this is probably one of the last truly nice days of the year. There's a chill, but the sun feels so warm, it makes the actual coldness of the air inconsequential. I want to breathe it in. Hold it there in my lungs forever.

Mara's staying after with Cameron to work on something for their art class. I guess I could go home, but I really don't want to be there, either. So I wait for her instead, whether she wants me to or not.

"I hope you're making wishes when you do that," I hear someone call out behind me. I turn around, shielding my eyes from the sun. It's the silhouette of a boy, and a blazing pink and orange sky behind him. A tall boy in a T-shirt, gym shorts, and a knee brace, toting a duffel bag and a water bottle. He's wearing this old, beat-up black cap that makes it hard to see his face, but as he steps closer, his features gradually come into focus. "Otherwise you're just making more weeds," he finishes.

I clear my throat, try to sound casual. “You’re always sneaking up on me, aren’t you?”

“Not *always*—just twice.” He smiles.

It had been almost two weeks since I’d seen him at the library. I’m shocked he’s even talking to me. I figured I’d pretty much blown it.

“So, what are you wishing for?” he asks, taking off his hat as he drops down on the ground next to me, uninvited. His face is flushed, hair damp. And his eyes are slightly glazed, like he’s really tired. I remember my brother always having that look when he came home from practice.

I think about my answer for a second while I watch him settle in next to me.

“I don’t wish,” I decide. Not for things that can be taken care of by delicate white pixies surfing aimlessly on haphazard currents of air, anyway. He looks disappointed—I’m not playing right. I’m supposed to make up some cute thing I want more than anything in the world. And then he’s supposed to spin me a web of bullshit about all the ways he could make that thing happen. Of course, he couldn’t. And I wouldn’t. So, we’re left to our own devices.

“Everyone wishes,” he insists.

“Not me.” I would look so much tougher if I had a cigarette hanging out of my mouth. I’m not to be messed with, that’s the impression I want to give him. I’m not naive or stupid. In fact, I’m not even nice.

Now he looks more than disappointed. He looks like he wants to wish on a weed that he hadn’t just sat down next to me. He doesn’t say anything as he looks out at the nothing, at all the people who are not here, and thus will not rescue him.

"Well, okay—" I start. Out of the corner of my eye I can see that he's stopped sweeping the deck for a life jacket and faces me now. "Even if I did wish for something—and I'm not saying that that's what I was doing—I still wouldn't tell you what it is." I steal a glance. He's grinning. He's cute, and he knows it too. The sun filters through his irises, pulling out all these kaleidoscopic caramel and mahogany colors that had been hiding behind chocolate. I have to force myself to stop looking. He inches closer. I feel my heart accelerate.

"Because then it won't come true, right?" he asks.

I nod. "Exactly."

"Yeah, but do they ever really come true anyway, even when you don't tell?" Interesting tactic—playing to my cynicism. He's good.

"You have a point," I admit. I can see his mind working as he looks at me, deciding which move, which play to make in order to win, to beat me.

"You know, I did a project once on the life cycle of dandelions," he tells me, nodding toward the now empty stem in my hand. "Second grade or something like that."

I don't think this is in the script. I rack my brain. No, I don't have anything to say to that. He reaches somewhere behind us and picks something out of the ground; I hear the flimsy stem snap. I just silently tap my shoe against the yellow weed at my foot.

"Well, you know how they're yellow at first? And then after the petals fall off you get that white, fluffy stuff so the seeds can float away?" he asks, examining the one he just plucked from the ground.

I nod.

"See, this one . . . is sort of in between." He holds it close to my face so I can get a better look. "The yellow petals are gone, and the white's starting to come through, but they're not really light enough to start flying away yet." He blows at it, but nothing happens.

We are so close, I can feel his breath on my skin, feel the warmth radiating from his body. He looks directly into my eyes as he waits for some kind of response on my part. But his breath and warmth and eyes undermine my ability to think or speak or understand anything other than his breath and warmth and eyes. I finally force myself to just look away.

"Well," he continues, after I don't respond. "They're pretty hard to find—I had to track down a dandelion at every stage of growth for that project. And you'd be surprised how rare these ones are."

I dare myself to look him in the eye again, but I can't hold it for long, so I refocus on the dandelion.

"I guess that's not very interesting, is it?" He rests his elbows on his knees and lets the weed dangle between his fingers.

I smile. I did actually think it was a little interesting, but I'm not about to tell him that.

"Nice out," he says, looking up at the sky.

"Yeah," I agree.

"Yeah." He sighs.

I feel bad for him; he is probably really good at making small talk with girls. This isn't his fault.

"So, what are you still doing here?" he asks, the silence rapidly becoming unbearable.

"Just waiting for my friend. You?"

"I'm waiting for my ride—I just got out of practice."

"Did you, like, get hurt or something?" I gesture to the bandage around his knee.

"No, it just acts up sometimes. It's fine, though." He smiles slowly as he stares at me.

"Oh." I nod, looking away, careful not to appear too concerned about him—or anything for that matter.

"So," he says, nervously twirling the dandelion between his thumb and index finger. "You have me in suspense, you know that, right?"

"Oh," I say again. "Sorry."

"So, should I just take that as a no?" he asks, still smiling. "It's okay. I just don't wanna keep feeling like such an idiot." He laughs.

And I want to laugh at the fact that he's the one feeling like an idiot here. I wish I could somehow make him understand that I want to say no as much as I want to say yes. "No, that's not it. I just—" But I can't finish because I don't even fully understand it myself.

"Well, what is it?"

"I don't know," I mumble.

The shape of his mouth looks a little confused, uncertain if it should smile or frown. "Are you doing this on purpose? I really can't tell."

"Doing what?"

"Screwing with me—not giving me a straight answer."

"No, I'm really not. I swear."

His eyebrows pull together, a vertical line forming in the center of his forehead. He looks at me appraisingly. "Forget it," he finally says. "I just can't seem to get you right, I guess." With this sad, awkward smile and a wave of his hand. "Forget it, really."

"Yes," I hear myself say. Because maybe this is my chance—a second chance—to be initiated into all this boy-girl stuff.

"Wait, yes?" He looks at me closely, his eyes lighting up. "So you're actually *saying* yes?"

I take a deep breath and repeat it: "Yes."

"Finally!" he yells, raising his arms to the sky, laughing. "Tomorrow night, are you free?"

"Yeah, I guess."

Just as he's about to say something else, a car pulls in at the far end of the lot—a navy blue hearse-looking vehicle, most definitely a parent's car.

"Shit, that's my ride. Here." He takes my hand.

"Wait." I pull away. "What are you doing?"

"Hold on," he says with a laugh. "It's okay, it won't kill you. Just relax," he says in this soothing, dreamy way that probably makes other girls melt. He unclenches my fingers and puts something there in my palm.

I look down. It's the dandelion, the in-between one.

He stands and shoulders his bag. "So, let's just meet here after school tomorrow?"

I nod.

"Cool." He smiles. "Okay."

He gets into the hearse car with a woman who I assume must be his mother in the driver's seat. She waves her hand in my direction. I turn around to look behind me. But she's waving at me, I realize, as he sits in the passenger seat looking embarrassed. I raise my arm and wave back. "Does she need a ride?" I hear her ask through the unrolled window. He says either "No" or "Go." I can't tell which.

After the car drives off, I pull out my planner and open it to this week. Then I carefully set the soft white weed in the binding and close it gently between the pages.

I hear shuffling on the tennis courts. I glance behind me and do a double take. It's Amanda. Standing there with her fingers wrapped through the chain-link fence, staring at me.

"Hey!" I call over to her. But she turns and starts walking. "Hey!" I stand up and run over to the gate that leads inside the court. "What are you doing just standing there?" I yell, catching up with her quickly. "Spying on me?"

"No. And I can stand wherever I want." She crosses her arms and looks me up and down, her face changing slowly, her upper lip curling into this snarl of disgust.

"Why don't you just mind your own business, Mandy!" I start to shove past her, but I swing back around, my heart tugging on my courage. "Wait, what is your problem exactly?"

"I don't *have* a problem," she answers.

"Seems like it to me." I cross my arms as well, trying to calm down, trying to look as formidable as she somehow does. She steps in close to me, like that day on the front steps. And if I didn't know her better, I would think she was actually about to hit me.

"My name is not Mandy," she growls.

She stalks off the tennis courts without another word.

I BARELY SLEEP AT all that night. So I wake up early and get ready. Before Mom and Dad even. Nobody's at school yet by the time I get there. The burnt stench of cheap coffee wafts out from the teacher's lounge, but there's not a person in sight. I go into the girls' bathroom on the first floor and open the window to sneak a cigarette while no one's around.

I try to get my head together in here. I'm so terrified about seeing him later today, I can hardly think straight. I consider going home sick. That would be a good excuse. If only I didn't actually *want* to see him later.

I hear someone coming. I toss my cigarette and slam the window shut. This time of the morning, it has to be a teacher. I race into one of the stalls and lock it behind me. Stepping up onto the toilet seat, I hold my breath and wait.

The door screeches open and two voices whisper frantically to each other.

"Hurry up, hurry up. Lock it, lock it now."

"Okay, I got it. Here, here."

"Hurry! Hurry," they whisper breathlessly.

Their sheer excitement makes me need to know more. I cautiously position myself to look through the crack between the door and the wall of the stall, careful not to make a sound. That's when I see her: Amanda. I can't seem to get away from her lately.

"Okay, here," she says to this other girl—another freshman I've seen around, always with this snarky look on her face—handing her a marker.

"All right, and what are we writing again?" Snarky Girl asks, staring at the wall.

"You know—slut, whore, skank, bitch, whatever. All true, so just take your pick," Amanda tells her.

Armed with two wide-tipped permanent markers, they approach the bathroom wall. Amanda goes first. She presses the spongy tip of the marker against the grimy, pale pink tiles and it squeaks as I watch her carefully write the words:

EDEN MCCROREY IS A WHORE

I can barely believe it. I can barely breathe.

Then Snarky steps up and draws a little arrow between the words "A" and "WHORE," and writes in this sickeningly self-assured scrawl:

Totally Slutty Disgusting

"How's that?" she asks Amanda with a smile.

"Perfect!"

"And why is she a totally slutty disgusting whore, again?" She laughs.

"Trust me, she just is," Amanda says as they stand back and admire their work. "Besides, she practically screwed some guy out by the tennis courts after school yesterday!" she lies.

I cover my mouth with my hand. I would have killed her, would have pushed her out the window. I would have screamed at the top of my lungs at her. Except I'm paralyzed.

"Oh, gross!" Snarky shouts.

"Yeah, completely," Amanda agrees. "Okay, come on, we don't have much time."

Then they leave. I let them leave. But I still can't move. I'm frozen, crouched on top of the toilet, my mouth hanging open, my hand still covering it.

I don't know how much time goes by before I snap out of it. I push open the stall door and walk up to the wall in absolute disbelief. I touch the black, inky, hateful words with my fingers. I hear a voice in the hall. And a locker slams shut. People are getting here. I quickly pull a whole armful of paper towels out of the dispenser and soak them in soap and water. Then I go to the wall and scrub, scrub, scrub against those words, using the strength of my whole body, until I can't even catch my breath, until I'm crying. I look at the wall. The words still stare back at me. Unchanged. I let the sopping wad of paper towels fall to the floor. I clench my fists, digging my fingernails into my palms, wanting to punch the wall, wanting to punch anything.

Just then these three pretty, popular senior girls push through the door, midconversation. They assemble in front of the mirror.

I turn my back to them as I wipe my eyes dry. Then I walk to the sink to wash the wet paper towel crumbs off my hands.

"Oh, ouch!" one of them shouts. My head snaps up to look at her. She points to the wall with her mascara wand, and says, "Someone's been a bad girl."

They all laugh. My heart feels like a bird trapped in a cage in my chest. Its wings flapping violently against the bars of bone. I want to smash this girl's pretty face into the mirror so hard. Then another one of them asks, "Who the hell is Eden McCrorey, anyway?"

"A whore, apparently," the third girl answers, laughing.

"No," the first girl corrects, "a totally slutty disgusting whore, you mean."

And they cackle like little witches, following one after the other back out into the hallway. I just stand there and let them get away with talking about me like that.

I race out into the hall, my head in a fog, determined to find those girls and tell them they can't treat me like that. To tell them it's all lies. To go find Amanda and pound her into the ground. But I stop after only a few steps. The halls are beginning to fill with people and noise. And those girls have dispersed already.

I go to my locker instead. I try to act like nothing's different. Try to just get through the day as if I don't know, as if there's nothing *to* know. I manage to avoid every single person who knows me. But Mara finds me in the library during lunch.

"Hey," she whispers, coming up behind me as I'm shelving books. "Can I talk to you for a sec?"

It was inevitable. I let her pull me by the arm deeper into the aisle.

“So, Edy,” she begins, “I have to tell you something. It’s bad. But before I do, remember, it will be okay. I just—I think you should know.”

“I know,” I tell her.

“You do?” she asks, her face in a grimace.

I nod—try to smile, shrug like I don’t even care.

“It’s insane! I don’t know who would start rumors like that. About you of all people!”

“I don’t know,” I lie.

“Well, Cameron and I went through *all* the bathrooms and tried to scribble them out. We’ve been doing that *all* morning, so it’s okay. I hoped you wouldn’t have to see it, though,” she admits.

“Cameron went into the girls’ bathroom?”

“No, the boys’ bathrooms.”

I hadn’t even considered they would have gone into the boys’ bathrooms too. “Thank you for doing that, Mara. I mean it. I think everyone’s seen it already, though,” I tell her. “Can’t undo that.” I laugh bitterly.

“Well, fuck everyone!” she says too loudly, and a bunch of heads turn toward us. “I’m really sorry, Edy,” she whispers. “I don’t understand this at all.” She’s so sad it’s almost like it’s happening to her and not me. “Want to come over tonight? We can eat all kinds of junk food and just veg out?” she tries.

“I can’t. I actually have plans.”

“You do? With who?” she asks, shocked.

I look around to make sure no one can hear, and lower my voice so that I’m barely speaking. “Josh. Joshua Miller.”

"Oh my God! Are you serious?" she whispers, her smile stretching wide. "How did this happen?"

"I don't know, it just . . . happened. He asked me out."

"Edy?" Mara's smile suddenly contracts. "You don't think it was him, do you? Because if it was, then you definitely don't want to go out with him, right?"

"It wasn't him."

"Yeah, but how can you be sure?" she asks, rightfully suspicious.

"I'm positive," I assure her, but she doesn't look convinced.

"Edy, I'm worried now. You're gonna be really careful, right?" she asks, her voice trembling faintly. "Because he's kind of from this whole different world. He's older. I mean, what if he's expecting something, you know?"

"So what if he is?" I answer immediately. "I don't know, maybe that wouldn't be such a bad thing."

"Really?" she asks in disbelief. "But—but aren't you afraid?"

"No," I lie. I am afraid. But in this other way, I'm also more afraid of *being* afraid. Afraid of not doing it too. Afraid that maybe I would be too afraid to ever do it. That Kevin would continue to control me in these ways I had never even dreamed of. And suddenly the thought of having someone else there in place of him is something I required-wanted-needed, in the most severe of ways. And I don't really care who, anyone else at all will do. This guy, Josh, he's good enough. He did, after all, pick me a weed.

"Maybe the rumors aren't such a lie after all," I muse.

"Shut up, Edy," Mara says, her face completely straight. "Don't you ever say that again. That's not true and you know it!"

"Sorry," I tell her. She stares at me for a second too long, like she wants to keep arguing the point, but she doesn't. "I'm sorry," I repeat.

"Edy, you have to be sure," she says firmly. "If you're going to do it—like really, really sure. It's not like you get to take it back if you—"

But I have to stop her. "Don't worry, okay? Who knows if anything will even happen?" I lie, trying to make her feel better.

"Oh God," she moans, both horrified and delighted at even the possibility. "Joshua Miller—that's big. Like. Huge."

I grin in spite of my fear, at the thought of things being different—the thought of me being different. "Yeah, I guess it is."

I STAND ON THE sidewalk near the tennis courts after school. It feels like I've been waiting for hours, but it's only been seven minutes. I'll give him three more, and then I walk. I adjusted my hair and makeup in the bathroom before I left. I brushed my teeth. I even wore my new silky floral dress that I got before school started. I run my hands through my hair one more time. Just as I'm considering making a break for it, I see him walking toward me.

"Hey! You're really here?" he says, greeting me with that smile.

"I said I would be." I smile back.

"I know, exactly. That's why I wasn't sure," he says with a laugh. "Come on." He reaches for my hand. My heart stops. He doesn't seem to notice, as he leads us through the parking lot, that everyone is staring at us. He stops at the blue station wagon that picked him up yesterday and lets me in first. When he gets in the driver's side, he starts the car and looks at me sweetly. "You look really nice, Eden."

I mumble "Thanks," and look out the window so he doesn't catch me blushing. But that's when I see these guys—guys I'm sure he's friends with—staring and pointing and laughing.

"So, where you wanna go?" he asks me, clearly not seeing what I'm seeing. Not living in the world I'm living in.

"Anywhere but here."

"Okay," he says with a laugh. "Are you hungry?"

I shrug. I don't feel like eating after the day I've had.

"Okay, movie?"

"Is there anywhere to go where there won't be other people around?" I try to laugh, even though I'm entirely serious.

"Mostly everywhere has people around these days." He grins, still expecting an answer. "My parents were doing something tonight so I borrowed my mom's car just so I could take you somewhere. So come on . . . just name a place, any place, and we'll go."

"What are your parents doing?" I ask, an idea forming in my mind.

He looks at me like I might be crazy. "I promise they aren't doing anything we'd want to do, if you're looking for ideas."

"No, I just mean, what if we went to your house? No one's there, right?"

He looks confused for a moment, but then a wave of clarity passes over his face. "Um, sure. I guess we could. Isn't there somewhere else you'd rather go, though?" he asks, putting the car in drive.

"Not unless you know of some uninhabited island we could go to and be back by ten for my curfew."

He just smiles as he pulls away.

Next thing I know, we're in the middle of his bedroom standing opposite each other. "So," he says, shuffling through a stack of CDs on his dresser. "Do you want to listen to anything?" He still listens to CDs—that's unusual. But my mind is racing too fast to follow that thought any further.

"Sure."

"What do you like?" he asks.

"Anything."

He selects one of the CDs. It starts quiet and slow. He stares at me. He puts his hands in his pockets. He takes them back out. I shift my weight. "You like this?" he asks. I think he's talking about the music, but I also wonder if he means *this* as in being here with him.

The answer is the same either way, so I tell him the truth: "Not sure yet."

He sits down on his bed and gestures for me to follow. I feel everything inside of me start to race and pulse as I move to the bed. I could never have imagined a year earlier I would be in the bedroom of the guy I so violently had the urge to bludgeon to death that day in the hall. I find myself evaluating every detail of the situation: him, me, the distance between us, the way his comforter feels soft against my legs, and everything smells like clean laundry, the sports posters on his walls, the hardwood floors, the curtains parted just slightly. I try hard to keep breathing as the fear tightens its knot around my heart. His lips are also slightly parted. I wait for him to speak, but he doesn't. My jaw is clamped so tight my teeth throb.

I study his face closer than I have before. His nose, I thought at first, seemed large, except it's not actually—*aquiline*, my brain whispers, flashing back to seventh grade, when I had to look up the word after reading it in *Sherlock Holmes*—but now I can't imagine a nose that belongs more perfectly to a face. And his eyes again, the colors seem different every time. I look down at my hands in my lap, my fingers twisting around one another, and I wonder if his mind is racing like mine, if his brain is working in overdrive just to understand my face. Somehow, I think not.

"So," he begins. "You're Caelin McCrorey's sister? Or something, right?"

"Yeah, so?"

"I don't know." He shrugs. "Just conversation. We played together. He was a cool guy. I mean, I didn't actually know that he's your brother. I asked around about you. That's all anyone really could tell me—you're a mystery." He grins, raising his eyebrows.

I don't know what I'm supposed to say to that, though. I'm not such a mystery? Not so hard to unravel? And what about me being a slut all of a sudden, hadn't he heard that one?

He smiles out of the corner of his mouth and asks me, "What—you don't wanna talk?"

"Not about my brother."

He makes a sound like *phffsh* and I can't tell if it's a laugh or just an exhale, but then he adds quietly, "Yeah, me neither." He has this gravelly, running-words-together way of speaking, like he's not thinking much about how he sounds. Not like Kevin. Kevin always enunciates his words so that they come out smooth and hard and precise and borderline loud. His voice is different. But everything about him is different. This is going to be okay. I'm going to be okay. He smiles again, and reaches out to touch my cheek, so lightly. I think my heart stops. Nodding his head toward the space between us, he says, "Why are you way over there?"

I slide toward him slowly. He leans in. I close my eyes. It's too intense, too frightening to watch. I feel his lips press against mine. He's kissing me. I try to let him, try not to think of the last time a boy's mouth was on my mouth. I try to kiss back like this isn't my first kiss. Because I have never been kissed, not really.

I force myself to kiss him back, kiss him back with everything I have in me. Because I can. I can. I can do this. Before I even know how he does it, he's somehow managed to lower me down onto the bed and I'm on my back. He drapes his leg over mine, nimbly shifting his weight; his body slides in right next to mine. But just when I start to feel like this might really be okay, like this might actually have the potential to feel something other than terrifying, I feel his fingers trail down my neck. My stomach clenches because I can't forget the fact of the matter, that the last time a boy had his hands on my neck he was choking me.

Normal, be normal, I tell myself. *This is different.*

But his hand on my thigh—I go rigid. Can't get the thing out of my mind because he could—so what if he has chocolate eyes or an aquiline nose or a magnetic smile—technically, he could do it, could do anything he wanted, and I wouldn't be strong enough to stop him and no one would even know because we're here all alone and how the hell did I get here again? What was I thinking? His hand moves farther up my thigh; my dress slides up even more. I want to push him off me, I want to run. My heart is just pounding, banging, slamming behind my ribs. He pulls his mouth away and looks at my face. I try not to look scared. But I freeze.

"What's wrong?" he asks quietly. "You want me to stop?"

I can't say yes, but I can't say no, either. I close my eyes, trying to find the words. But the instant I do, I'm back there. With Kevin. Kevin holding my arms down against the bed. And his hands, his fingers like dull knives slowly carving their way down to the bone. The more I tried to get away, the more he had me. I couldn't believe how strong he was. How weak I was.

I open my eyes. I'm barely breathing. Too much time has passed. It's something worse than silence, this quiet. I know I need to say something, but I don't know what. So I just look up at the ceiling and breathe the words, "I have to go," too quietly for him to even hear.

"What?"

"I don't know," I whisper. Because I *don't* know—I don't know anything right now.

"No—I—I know," he breathes. But as I raise my head to look at his face, he doesn't look like he knows or understands—he looks as confused as I am. His fingers move through my hair as he leans in to kiss me again.

"I really, um—" I start to say, pushing my hands against his chest. "I have to go." But my hands do nothing. They can't move him. They can't even budge him an inch. "I have to go!" I shout this time. His eyes widen as he shifts his weight off me. I sit up fast and move to the edge of the bed.

He catches my arm and pulls me back. "Wait—"

"What—" My voice is too sharp, but I can't help it. My instincts tell me that I should start screaming, start hitting him. That I should saw-cut-gnaw the arm he's holding off my own body if it means getting away. But then again, my instincts are kind of fucked up now, so I adjust my tone and try again, more calmly. "What?"

"Nothing, just—what's going on, why do you have to go?" I look down at his hand, still holding on to my arm, and he lets go. "I thought we were going to—"

"Thought we were going to *what?*" I interrupt, feeling my eyes widen.

"Nothing—not that!" he says quickly. "I thought we were going to go out—go do something. I just thought we had time. I'm just confused. One second you're into it, the next you're leaving? I mean, did I do something?" he asks, talking fast.

I watch him closely. I don't even know how to answer him. *Did* he do something? Or is this just normal? Is this just what people do? My thoughts are spinning. I don't know what I feel, or think, or want.

"You're the one who wanted to come here," he says, but not in an unkind way, like he's truly reminding me of that fact.

"I changed my mind, okay?"

"Okay," he says, like it really is okay.

We both sit there next to each other at the end of his bed. I straighten out my dress. He adjusts his shirt. And then it's that horrible silence again. I look out his bedroom window. The sun is beginning to set. "I think I should go."

"Right here's good," I tell him as we approach the corner of my street. He stops the car and looks around, confused.

"Where's your house?"

"Just over there. This is fine."

He pulls in close to the curb and turns the headlights off. "So, are we cool?" he asks.

"Yeah. I think so."

He nods. "Okay. Well, even though I don't really consider this an actual date, since we didn't technically go anywhere . . . can I still kiss you good night?" he asks with that smile.

I look around quickly to make sure there's no one around. When I turn my head back, he's already there, leaning in. He kisses me, just once, softly.

"Tomorrow night," he begins, "you know, we have that big away game. But after, there's gonna be this party. Do you wanna go?"

"I don't think so." I can imagine all his friends pointing and whispering, those pretty girls from the bathroom laughing. Josh, a witness. Or worse, a participant.

"Why not?" he asks, offended. This is, after all, a highly coveted invitation; I am being given a chance to rub elbows with kings and queens of proms and homecomings past and future. And I, just a lowly mortal peasant, have the gall to turn him down.

"Because I don't"—how to say it, though—"I don't want to be your girlfriend."

He rolls his eyes, shakes his head, stifles a laugh.

Apparently, not that way.

He looks straight ahead for a few seconds, then turns to me in the passenger seat. "Ohh-kaay," he says slowly, the way he did that day in the hall a year earlier, when I was still just invisible Mousegirl. "I didn't ask you to be my girlfriend; I just asked if you wanted to go to this party."

"Well, I don't." There's this authority in my voice I never knew I possessed.

"Fine." He tries to act nonchalant. I keep my eyes on the

dashboard. The clock changes from 6:51 to 6:52. "So, this is it then?" he asks.

I shrug. "Maybe. Maybe not." So cool. So calm. So collected. How am I doing it?

"I'm sorry, I don't—I don't get you. What exactly are we doing, then?" he asks, an edge of irritation in his voice.

"I don't know. Couldn't we just get together sometimes—just, you know, keep it casual?" I ask him, the words flowing from my mouth like they actually belong to me.

He looks skeptical as he takes a few moments to consider. "I think that's probably the strangest thing a girl has ever said to me. You really don't want to go to this thing with me tomorrow night?" he asks again, unable to understand. "It wouldn't have to mean anything."

"Look, I'm not going to argue about it. If you don't want to see me again, that's fine, okay? But if you do, then this is the way it's going to be. The way it is, I mean."

He inhales through his nose, exhales slowly through his mouth. I sigh loudly. Feign impatience, fingers tickling the handle, ready to open the door and bolt. "I don't know," he finally says, hesitantly.

I leave without another word. I know he's watching me as I walk toward my house. I make sure I don't turn around until I hear the engine fade into the silence surrounding me. I look—nothing but two red taillights glowing in the distance.

BY MONDAY I START to notice something about the way people are looking at me. Like the world has suddenly divided into two distinct camps. The first is the one I'm used to, the one where no one knows I'm alive. But then there's this other faction emerging, one that throws looks of every type my way: disgust, pity, intrigue. I'm not sure if it's because of the graffiti or if it's due to the public departure with Josh on Friday. Or both.

But not here in the library.

Here, I'm safe. With all the subjects and letters and numbers to keep things in order: philosophy, social sciences, languages, technology, literature, A-B-C-D, point one, point two, point one-two, point three. It all makes so much sense, there's no room for mistakes or misunderstandings.

"Hey," he says, suddenly standing with me in the narrow aisle.

I jump, nearly dropping the book I'm holding. "You scared me!" I whisper.

"Again," he says with a grin. "Sorry." He stands really still, like he's afraid to come any closer. "Still mad at me?" he asks.

"You're the one who was mad, not me." Though, that's not completely the truth either.

"I was never mad. Just confused."

I want to tell him I was confused too. I want to tell him how happy I am to see him, how thankful I am he's not looking at me the way everyone else has been looking at me today. But I can't admit that. I have to be sure and strong and solid because there's something about him—I don't know what, exactly—that makes me want, so badly, to be vulnerable.

"Look, can we just start over?" he asks.

If anyone is going to be allowed to start over, it would be me, and I would start over at that night in my bedroom. But since that's not possible, I tell him, "No, not really."

He looks down at his hands like he actually feels bad, or upset, or disappointed, or something. "Right," he whispers, turning to leave.

"But we can just—" I touch his arm. He turns back. "Continue. Can't we?" I finish.

He takes a step toward me, this new light in his eyes. "Yeah, I think we can."

I nod. And I smile to myself. Because I just fixed this—me.

"Does this mean we're on a phone number basis?" he asks.

"I guess so," I say with a laugh.

He laughs too, as he takes his phone out. I recite my number to him, never wanting this moment—him standing close to me like this, smiling—to end.

Since we are now on a phone number basis, I decide it's time to lay down some ground rules when he calls me to invite me over later that night.

"Before I come over again, I just want to make sure you really understand that this isn't going to be like a boyfriend-girlfriend thing."

"Yeah, you made that pretty clear before."

"I mean, we're not going to go out on dates or anything like that. I don't want to be introduced to your friends. I don't want to go parading down the halls holding hands or having you wait for me by my locker. I'm definitely not going to be the girl cheering you on from the sidelines at your basketball games."

"Wow, you sure know how to make a guy feel real special, don't you?" he says, a trace of a laugh behind his voice.

"It's not about you," I tell him, and I can't believe how utterly selfish I sound—how utterly selfish I *am*.

"Ooh-kaay. Anything else?"

"And I never, ever, ever want to meet your parents."

"Well, that's one thing we can agree on."

"Oh." Wow, that stings. I guess that's a taste of how I must be making him feel.

"It's not about you," he mimics, pointedly.

"Okay."

There's a pause.

"Eden, how are old are you?"

"Why?"

"I don't know, just wondering. It's hard to tell. You seem—" He stops himself from finishing.

"I seem what?"

"You seem . . . I don't know. This all feels either really mature or completely the opposite."

"Do you really think calling me immature is going to help you in any way?" I laugh. "I'm almost amused. Or completely offended—it's hard to tell."

"No, no, no, that's not what I'm saying!" He backpedals. "I'm actually saying you seem mature."

"Or the complete opposite," I remind him.

"I didn't mean that," he laughs. "Really, what are you, though? Like sixteen?"

"Sure," I lie. Fourteen. But my birthday is coming soon, and then I'll be fifteen. Which is *like sixteen*. "Okay, you answer me now. Yes or no, what do you think?" I ask him.

After considering my list of commandments for several seconds, he breathes in and exhales, "I think you're really weird." He pauses. "But I still want you to come over again."

I feel my mouth curve into a smile.

SO THAT NIGHT HE smuggles me past his parents and up the stairs to his bedroom. And the next night. And practically every night for the past week. And each day things seem to go just a little further, his hands wandering over my body with just a little more freedom, like he's testing the limits.

But this is it—the night. I decided before I even got to his house. He told me earlier his parents are out of town at his cousin's wedding. Perfect. Because I can't stand the anticipation of it anymore. It needs to just happen already. So I can stop being scared every second we're together. Worrying about what it will be like, what he'll do, how he'll act, if he'll hurt me. And me—what I'll do, how I'll feel.

Except tonight, with my mind all made up, I'm more than scared. I'm so terrified I'm almost unable to breathe. I think I feel a rash working up my fingers to my hand to my wrist to my forearm to my whole body to my brain, and, oh God, I have this bullet stuck inside of me and I might throw up.

We stand next to his bed. He moves in to kiss me.

Be normal. Be normal, Edy, I tell myself. *Be normal,* I repeat in my head. Now. I take a breath and pull away from his kiss. I start unbuttoning my shirt—one, two, three, four, five, six buttons. My hands are shaking. They barely work. God, why did I pick a button shirt, anyway? I look up. He's staring at my new bra. It's lacy and purple and matches my underwear. I let the shirt fall off my shoulders. I try, inconspicuously, to glance at my arm. It looks fine, no rash. I'm fine. I'm fine and this is fine—I exhale—everything is fine, fine, fine. I coax the heels of my sneakers off with my toes and nudge them to the side. I unbutton my jeans, unzip them, slide them down over my hips, my butt, my thighs.

I look down at my feet. Socks. You can't have sex in socks—that's idiotic. I try not to tip over while I pull them off and stuff them in my shoes. The floor feels like ice on my feet. He's still fully dressed, just staring, making me feel ugly and stupid.

I start thinking maybe he's disappointed with what he sees; I know, of course, I'm not the prettiest, not the sexiest. I feel my arms twist together in front of my chest. I suddenly want to run. Run far and hard and fast, away from him, myself, my life, my past, my future, everything.

He snaps out of it right away. His shirt brushes against my skin as he pulls it up over his head and lets it fall on top of my pile of clothes. His socks pull off with his sneakers. The space between us rapidly closing in—his hands, on my waist so suddenly, make me flinch, no jump, no *lurch* away from him like some kind of wild, deranged rabid animal. I stumble over my shoes and my legs crash into the bed frame. He pulls back, looking confused.

I'm so stupid. My face burns. I want to die-hide-disappear.

"Sorry," we both say at the same time.

"Are you okay?" He extends an arm as if to help me stabilize, but doesn't dare touch me again.

"I'm fine," I snap.

He takes a step back, puts his hands in his pockets, and tries very hard not to stare at my bra. "Listen, you don't have to—I mean, we don't . . . have . . . to . . . if—"

He stops talking because I'm unbuttoning his pants. He stops thinking because now I'm unzipping them. He stops breathing because I pull his hands out of his pockets and put them on my waist again. And then my heart and lungs and brain stop too because my underwear are suddenly around my ankles and so are his and I feel his body against mine and then we're in the bed and our legs are tangled and things are happening so fast and his hands are all over me and my hands are shaking and I don't know where to put them and I hope he doesn't notice.

He stops kissing me. I open my eyes. He's looking down at my naked body. I, too, look down at my body. But all I can see is just one huge, gaping wound that somehow seems to still hurt everywhere sometimes. I hope he doesn't notice that, either.

He touches my skin lightly like it's something that should be touched lightly, and he speaks slow when he says, "Eden, you're really—"

"Shhh, please, please." I stop him before he can finish. "Don't say anything." Because whatever he thinks I am, I'm not. And whatever he thinks my body is, it isn't. My body is a torture chamber. It's a fucking crime scene. Hideous things have happened here, it's nothing to talk about, nothing to comment on, not out loud. Not ever. I won't hear it. I can't.

He looks at me like I'm crazy and mean and rude. "I was just gonna say that you're—"

And since maybe I am crazy and mean and rude, I interrupt him again, "I know, but just don't. Please don't say it, whatever it is, just—"

"Fine, okay. I won't." He looks like maybe he thinks this has just officially stopped being worth it.

I concentrate hard on doing this nicely. And I try not to look at his body because his body terrifies me. But I take my arms and wrap them around his back, my fingertips tremble against his skin, tracing outlines of bone and muscle. I pull him down so that his chest and stomach touch mine. He kisses me carefully, like I might be this fragile thing that needs to be handled with caution. But it feels too nice, too sweet, too meant for someone else, someone more like who I used to be, or rather, who I would have been.

He reaches for something from the nightstand next to his bed. I only realize what it is when he tears the wrapper open. The sound rips through my brain. It shakes something loose inside of me. And it's from this shaken place deep within that I want him to know. To know everything. I want to stop time and tell him every moment of my life right up until this one. Because he has no idea who I really am. I want him to know how innocent I still feel right now, somehow. To know exactly what I'm entrusting him with. But it's all too much to be held in this small, urgent space.

I can't keep my thoughts still long enough to even understand them.

My heart races dangerously fast. My skin burns. My chest

tightens, my lungs seem to go rigid. I'm not breathing quite right, I know that much. My fingers and toes tingle. Things begin to go out of focus, then back in, and out again. Like looking through a kaleidoscope, it makes me dizzy—the room, the way it's spinning—the way the world ceases to make any sense at all. I hear this buzzing in the background, like static. Static pulsing through brain waves, electric currents floating around in this strange place, making the air feel nervous, activated somehow.

"You okay?" he asks softly. I nod. Of course I'm okay, of course. "Okay," he breathes in my mouth, as he moves in to kiss me again, stroking my face and hair so gently. This, I'm sure, is the way he always kissed his perfectly respectable, perfectly normal, well-adjusted ex-girlfriends—those soft, breakable creatures that never harbored secret bullets in their guts.

He shifts his weight off of me. In all my planning and preparing and imagining, the realness of this moment had escaped me. Just a year earlier, I was still wearing those damn days-of-the-week underwear and now I am lying on my back, naked in a bed, watching a guy I barely know put on a condom. This is real. This is actually my life. And it's happening. It's happening right now. No turning back. Not that I want to. There's nothing to turn back to—nothing good, anyway. I want to get as far away from the past as possible, be as different from that girl as I can.

"Okay, you're sure?"

I nod.

I've only been this terrified once. I can feel my heart pumping. I can feel the blood, at first, rushing through my veins, but then I get the distinct feeling that it's stopped rushing, stopped pulsing, stopped coursing, and is just seeping out, uncontained, flooding my whole body and I'll surely be dead soon.

I focus my eyes on this tiny crack in the ceiling. It starts in the corner by the door and branches out like a lightning bolt, frozen in that one nanosecond of its existence, ending directly above the center of his bed. I try to calm myself down, try to not be afraid. I focus on him, on the way he breathes. And then I count all the ways he is not like him, the ways this is not like that, the ways I am not like her. And then someone switches off the circuit breaker in my mind and everything just stops. Like wires are cut somewhere. I am disconnected, offline. And then things fade to this still, calm, quiet nothingness.

I'm vaguely aware when it's over. Vaguely aware of him touching my face, vaguely aware of words coming out of his mouth. I am alive. I did it. I'm okay.

"You were so quiet, baby," he whispers softly.

It's like I've suddenly opened my eyes, except they were already open. And there's that lightning bolt I'm supposed to stare at, so I do.

"I didn't know if you . . . you know?" He runs his fingers up and down my arm; I pull the sheet a little tighter to my body. I can't tell if it feels good or not.

I can sense him staring at me, waiting for me to say something, looking hopeful. "Yeah," I whisper, trying to sound sure of myself. I know it's the right thing to say. He tries to put his arm around me, I think, but I don't budge. I don't move. I don't know what's supposed to happen next.

He seems to study my face longer than feels comfortable, and then finally says, "I don't know . . . you seem weird or upset or something."

"I'm not upset," I contest immediately. Although, as I listen to the edge of panic in my voice, I do sound upset, so I add, softer, "Really, I'm not."

"Why are you acting like this, then?"

"Like what? What am I doing?"

"Nothing," he says quickly.

"Then why are you getting mad at me?" I feel my heart pumping faster again.

"No, I mean you're doing nothing."

"What do you want me to do?" I sit up fast, suddenly aware that he could take something from me that I hadn't given. And apparently I hadn't given something he wanted. I grope around the bed frantically for any article of my clothing. "I don't know what else you want from me, but—" I'm not going to wait around to find out.

Now he sits up too. "Wait, what are you doing? Are you leaving?"

I find my bra. "Yes. Can you turn around?"

"What?" He laughs.

"Can you not watch me get dressed?" My hands are shaking. I can't get the clasp.

"Are you serious?" he asks, a dumbfounded grin on his mouth.

"Yes. Can you please not watch me?"

"Not watch . . . what are you talking about? Just wait. Wait a minute, okay?" he says, placing his hand over mine, uncurling my fingers. "Just stop. For just a second. What's happening?" he asks, his eyes locked on mine.

I can't say what kind of expression I must be wearing—indifference, smug hatred, maybe.

"It's time for me to leave," I say, my voice sounding really flat and unaffected. "Is that all right with you?" I can taste the meanness in my mouth as the words pass across my lips. And I'm not even sure why.

"You're mad?" he asks in disbelief. "You're mad at me?"

Am I mad? Maybe, but that's not all. I'm sad. And still scared. And confused, because I don't understand why I'm still scared, why I'm still sad, why I'm angry. This was supposed to fix things. This was supposed to help.

"Wow. Well, this is just perfect, isn't it?" he mutters to himself, smirking, but clearly pissed. "What, are you using this against me or something?"

"What are you talking about? I'm not using anything against you!"

He crosses his arms over his stomach, looking oddly vulnerable; I pull my knees into my chest and wrap my arms around them. "Look, I don't—I'm not—I don't know what this is." He's stumbling over his words. "I mean, is this like some sick game to you or something? Like some test, or something? Or is this just what you do with guys? Because that's really fucked up." He's short of breath, his voice shaking like he's actually upset.

"Sick game? No." Test? Okay, maybe. "I thought I was doing you a favor, okay?" I tell him, even though that's a total lie.

"Doing me a favor how? By making me feel like I'm forcing you to do something you don't want to do?" Then he adds, quieter, "It's more like the other way around, if you really wanna know."

It takes me a second to untangle the insult. "Wait, so I'm forcing you? Oh my God, I don't believe this!" It feels like my mind is being turned inside out, this situation getting completely backward.

"That's not what I'm saying, okay. I just—I mean—you act like—"

"I have somewhere to be," I lie, interrupting him. I stand up and pull the sheet around me, getting dressed as fast as I can. "I'm not going to sit around for this!"

I pull my shirt on over my head as I step into my shoes. I look down at him, sitting so still and quiet, just watching me. Then he says, not yelling, but almost whispering, "What the hell is wrong with you?"

"Nothing's wrong with me!" I hear the volume of my voice mounting; I feel all my muscles going tense and heavy. "I just don't like wondering what you're really thinking, what you really want from me!"

"How the f—" he starts, but then stops. "How do you think I feel?"

"Forget it!" I try to stay calm even though I'm so furious I'm shaking. I head for the door, but turn around to look at him, feeling some kind of pressure building up in my throat—pulsing words wanting to be screamed: "Just fucking forget it!"

This is this first time I've ever said the f-word at another person, out loud like this. As I look down at him, staring up at me like I'm insane, I feel my eyeballs boiling in their sockets. And then his image before me begins to blur and wrinkle like a mirage—I have to leave because the tears, I know, are on their way. And I don't cry in front of boys. Not anymore. Starting now.

I storm out of his room. He calls my name once, halfheartedly, like out of obligation, not because he actually wants me to come back. I slam the door behind me as hard as I can. I wipe at my eyes. I walk home.

The next day at school I see him walking down the hall in the midst of his herd. So, of course, I pretend to be absorbed in finding something in the very depths of my locker, pretend not to even notice. They're the kind of people who always have to be drawing attention to themselves—talking just a little too loudly, taking up just that extra bit of space, laughing like goddamn hyenas in that way that always makes me wonder if they're really laughing at me. I hate those kinds of people and yet I can't quite force myself not to look as they pass.

There's no chance of salvaging the wreckage of last night. I watch him say something to this Jock Guy he walks next to, and then Jock Guy looks at me. Looks at me as if he's calculating some unknown criteria in his mind. I let my eyes meet Josh's for just a fraction of a second. But I feel like I might die or throw up, so I promptly return to examining the contents of my locker, trying to remember how to breathe.

"Hey," he says, suddenly leaning against the locker next to mine, incredibly close. People were certainly staring now.

"Hi," I reply, but I feel so stupid, stupid, stupid—the way I screamed at him, the way I left. The way he sat on his bed looking at me.

We just stand in front of each other with nothing to say, both of us trying to pretend we don't notice the eyes of every passerby on us. I shut my locker, forgetting the one thing I actually needed for my next class. I fidget with the dial of my combination, spinning it around and around, unable to stop.

"So . . . ," he finally begins, but doesn't follow up with anything.

And more silence.

"Oh, just kiss and make up already!" Jock Guy shouts from across the hall. Josh waves his arm at him, in a get-the-hell-out-of-here kind of way.

"Sorry," he mumbles. "Look, I know you're still mad, but—"

"What did you say to him?" I interrupt.

"What?" He turns around to look at his friend walking away. "Nothing."

"Well, not nothing; obviously you told him something. I saw the way he looked at me just now."

"Eden, I didn't say anything. Look, I'm just trying to apologize here."

"Don't. Don't apologize, it's fine, it's just—it's whatever." The truth is that I don't want to have to apologize.

"Well, I am sorry." He pauses, waiting for me to tell him it's okay, waiting for me to apologize right back. After it becomes clear I'm not going to, he adds, "I'm not sure what for, but anyway . . . here." He holds out a folded-up piece of paper for me to take.

"What is it?" I ask.

He rolls his eyes; he's getting really good at that. "It's not anthrax. Jesus, Eden. Just take it."

I take it.

He walks away without another word, without so much as a glance back at me.

Eden,

I feel bad about last night. I still don't really know what happened, but I'm sorry. My parents are still out of town, so if you want to come over later, you can. I want you to, but I'll understand if you don't. You could even stay over. We wouldn't have to do anything, I promise. We could just hang. It doesn't matter to me. . . . I just want to see you. We have a game tonight, but I'll be home by eight. I hope I'll see you later.

J

AT HOME THAT NIGHT I hold the piece of paper carefully between my fingers. I'd read the note enough times to recite it. Still, I unfold it one more time: *I hope I'll see you later I hope I'll see you later I hope I'll see you later.*

But I had decided. No. This thing with him could not go any further. It was supposed to be simple, it was supposed to be easy and uncomplicated, but in one night it's suddenly become a dense, unnavigable labyrinth. And I'm lost in it. I just need out. By any means. I was a fool to think I was ready for this.

As I fold the note back up into its neat square, Mom yells my name from the living room as if it were a matter of life and death, as if it were her last word. I race to unlock my door, letting the note fall from my hands. As I swing open the door I almost run right into her, standing in front of me with her arms crossed tight, hands clenched, and knuckles taut.

"What's wrong?" I ask, my brain processing her rigid stance, the hardness in her face.

“Can you not feel that wind, Eden?” she asks between clenched teeth. But before I can respond or even try to understand what she’s even talking about, she keeps going. “I’ve been begging you for weeks—weeks—to put in the storm windows. Is that so much to ask? Is it? Is that too much for you to handle?” The volume of her voice rises steadily with each word.

“Oh my God, who cares?” I sigh.

Her eyes widen as we stand face-to-face. She looks behind her at Dad sitting on the couch in the living room, as if trying to rally some support. But he just points the remote at the TV and the volume bars dance across the bottom of the screen, 36-37-38-39, louder, louder, louder. Rolling her eyes at him, she returns her gaze to me. She inhales through her nose and exhales sharply. “Excuse me?” she finally manages, the words tight and hard. “I *care.* Your father cares. We’re supposed to be a family—that means pitching in! Do you understand?”

“And the windows are somehow an emergency all of a sudden?” I snap back at her.

“I don’t know who you think you’re talking to, Eden. And I don’t know what has gotten into you lately, but it stops right now!” She takes a step closer, her body blocking my exit.

We stare each other down, volleying this invisible ball of fiery emotion back and forth between us. But there are no words to explain to her what’s gotten into me. I don’t even know what it is. There’s nothing that I can say or do that will be right, anyway. I spin around to face my room. For just a moment I consider whether or not I can make a break for my bedroom window—that’s how bad I want to get away. But she grabs on to my arm before I can decide.

"Don't turn your back on me when I'm talking to you," she growls, pulling me back into the ring. "Did it ever occur to you that I might need a little help around here once in a while?"

"Look, I'll put the damn windows in—I just haven't gotten to it yet!" I wrestle out of her grasp easily and take a step backward. "I've been busy, okay?"

"And tell me, why exactly have you been so busy lately, Eden? Where is it you've been spending all your time? Not here, that's for sure."

She stands there waiting for an answer.

I roll my eyes, look away. I feel my mouth smiling, somehow, in spite of the tears menacing just under the surface. I shake my head.

She steps inside my room now, fully in my space. "You listen to me. I've had it, Eden—your father, too," she says in that clipped tone of hers that she always uses on Dad to make sure it's clear she thinks he's totally useless.

"What's the big fucking deal here?" I dare her, taking a step forward. And before I can even understand what's happening, there's a loud, hollow crack that echoes inside my head. And the side of my face is on fire.

She says something, but her voice is dulled by the ringing in my ears.

And because I feel like I could hit her back, I turn away. I grab anything I can and stuff it into my backpack. I pick the note up off my bedroom floor and shove it in my pocket. "Out of my way," I mutter, shoving past her.

"Edy?" she whimpers, her voice straining as if she has no air left in her body whatsoever. "Don't go. Please."

"I'm sleeping at Mara's," I announce with my hand on the front door. I turn around, watch her stand there in my bedroom doorway falling to pieces, watch Dad pretend nothing's happening, and I say, "I hate this place, I really hate this place!" Then I slam the door as hard as I can. My hot tears steam up my glasses as I walk.

I almost wuss out by the time I get to his street. The only light issuing from the entire house is the dim glow of the TV in the living room, flashing through the curtains. I walk up the front steps and slide my glasses into my coat pocket. My phone says 11:22. I stand there listening for any sign of movement from inside. I try to think of what I could say, about earlier, about last night. I feel dizzy, suddenly, as everything inside of me seems to rush to the surface of my skin all at once. I sit down on his front steps—I just need to collect my thoughts for a minute, that's all.

At 11:46 his cat prances up the walkway. She runs up to me as if she'd been waiting for my arrival. She presses herself against me, weaving her agile body between my legs, nudging her head into the palm of my hand. She jumps in my lap and just lies there, letting me pet her. Even if I am just a stupid mouse, she keeps me company. Her purring sends calming vibrations through my body, warming my hands up against the bone-chilling night. I look at my phone again: 12:26. He wrote *I hope I'll see you later*. I know that's what it said. I shift my position to try to get the note out of my pocket and the cat looks at me accusingly.

The door screeches open. I turn around.

She leaps out of my lap and is inside the house in one swift movement. I take a breath to prepare an explanation, but the door's already creaking shut—he doesn't even see me. He was only letting the cat in. I have to say something. Now.

"Josh, wait!" My voice sounds so small against the vast, empty night.

"Shit!" He jumps back, eyes wide. "Shit," he says again with an uncertain laugh. "You scared me."

"Sorry. I was just—hi."

"Uh, hi. . . . It's freezing. How long have you been out here?" He steps out into the cold, letting the screen door slam behind him. He's wearing sweatpants and a dingy-looking T-shirt, his feet bare. He rubs at his eyes like he had been sleeping. He crosses his arms as the wind picks up a small cyclone of leaves and drops them at my feet.

"Not long," I lie between my chattering teeth. What's long, anyway? An hour and four minutes is actually a short amount of time, relatively speaking.

He looks around at the stillness of his darkened street, at the nothing that is going on. He holds out his hand. I take it. His skin feels like fire, but I guess that's only because I'm so cold.

"Why didn't you come in or ring the bell or something?" he asks once we're inside.

I shrug.

"Well, are you okay?"

"Yeah, I'm fine." But it comes out too fast, too sharp—too obviously a lie.

"Wait, I don't understand. Why were you just sitting there? I was waiting for you—well, I mean, I stopped waiting a couple of hours ago."

"I didn't know if you still wanted me to come, so I just . . ." My eyes drift to the TV. Then I look around. He's turned the living room into shambles. The afghan that's usually on the back of the couch is pulled down and twisted, stuck in the crevices between the cushions. The couch's matching pillows are on the floor and have been replaced by two pillows from his bed, positioned at TV-watching angles. The coffee table is covered with stuff: a slightly ajar pizza box, multiple cans of soda, a plate with half a pizza crust left on it, three different remote controls.

"Eden?" he says slowly.

I focus my attention back on him.

"What's going on?" he asks, looking at me suspiciously. "Are you . . . high?"

"No." I don't get high. "Why would you say that?"

"Your eyes . . ." He holds my face in his hands, inspecting me. "They're all glassy and bloodshot, like—"

I move my face so that I don't have to look at him while I admit it. "No, I was just—" But I stop before I can say the word. Because maybe I would rather him think I was high than crying.

"Look," he begins, "I'm glad you came—you'll probably think this is really lame, okay—but if you're on something right now, I really don't want you here. I'm not trying to be mean. I'm just not into that stuff, okay?"

"Well, I'm not either! And I'm not on anything, I swear." He doesn't believe me, obviously. "God, what do you think, I'm just, like, this screwed-up, horrible person or something?"

"No." He sighs. "But are you high, Eden? Really, just be honest."

"I'm not high! I was just"—I clear my throat—"crying." I try to mumble it into only one syllable, as quietly as possible. "Earlier. Okay?"

"Oh." I guess he doesn't know what to say to that. His face wavers between skepticism and pity, both equally undesirable. "Um . . ."

"If you want me to leave—" I start.

"No, stay. Really. You can stay." He takes the backpack from my shoulder and sets it on the floor.

Looking down at my feet, I fidget with the zipper of my jacket, feeling shy and uncomfortable—vulnerable—now that he's seen yet another chink in my armor.

"So, what do you wanna do?" I let my arm swing forward so that my fingers touch his fingers. It's a rhetorical question. I know what he wants to do. Why else would he ask me to stay?

"I don't care," he says, taking my hand. "Come here." He pulls me toward him and just hugs me. He smells like soap and dryer sheets and deodorant.

I pull away too soon because, damn it, I just can't seem to get these things right. I feel dizzy when he lets go, like we'd been spinning in circles, but we were just standing still.

"Are you hungry? There's pizza." He gestures to the square, grease-stained cardboard pizza box sitting on the coffee table. "Or there's other stuff too, if you want something else."

I open my mouth. I'm about to say no, by default, but there's this pang inside of me. I am hungry. I know I'm not supposed to need anything. Not supposed to want. But I hadn't really eaten since that granola bar at lunch. I clear my throat. "Maybe. I mean, pizza kinda sounds good. I mean, only if you were going to have some. Were you?"

He smiles. "Sure."

And I'm thinking: *He's nice, really nice.* I think I smile too as he takes the pizza box into the kitchen. I hear some dishes clanging and then random beeps as he presses buttons on the microwave, and the familiar buzzing moan. He steps into the doorway between the kitchen and living room, leaning against the wall. Just looks at me from across the room. He's a little blurry without my glasses. I can't tell what he's thinking, but for once, not knowing doesn't seem so frightening. We don't speak. It feels okay. *BeepBeepBeep.* "Be right back," he whispers. I say okay, but I don't think he hears me.

He comes back into the room, balancing two mismatched plates in his hands while switching off the kitchen light with his elbow. Setting the plates down on the coffee table, he sits next to me and asks, "You wanna watch something?"

I nod. "Sure."

He flips through tons of channels, without even waiting to see what's on before switching. That's something Caelin does all the time. It annoys the shit of me, but not now, not with Josh. "Nothing's really on, sorry." He sighs. "How's this?"

I have no idea what this is, some sitcom with a laugh track. Stupid. Perfect. "Doesn't matter. This is fine." I do know that I feel more normal right now—sitting on his couch eating rubbery reheated pizza, him in his shabby pajamas, me with no makeup, hair a mess, watching something mindless on TV—than I've felt in a long time.

He finishes his slice in, like, forty-five seconds flat. I've never understood how boys can eat like that. Don't they feel like pigs? I guess not, because he just leans back into the pillows and alternates between watching me and the TV, grinning.

"What?" I finally ask him.

"Feeling better?"

I nod, "Mm-hmm."

"Good. Do you always eat this slowly, or is it just 'cause I'm here?" He smirks.

"It's called tasting, maybe you've heard of it?" I must be feeling better, good enough to be a smart-ass, anyway.

"I've never seen you eat before. You look cute." He laughs—it sounds so real it makes me want to laugh too.

I stick the last bite in my mouth, thinking this was maybe the best pizza I've ever had in my life. "When I'm shoving food into my face?" I say with my mouth full.

He nods his head yes. "You have, uh, like, sauce"—he touches the corner of his mouth—"right there."

"Eww, stop watching me eat!" I wipe my mouth with the back of my hand. "Did I get it?"

"Uh-uh, come here, I'll get it." I lean in, still wiping my face. "Closer," he says, "let me see." I'm practically on top of him by the time I realize he's messing with me. He grins as he moves in to kiss my mouth. "Got it."

I shove his arm gently and lean against him. And he puts his arm around my shoulder. On the TV a man is walking down a city street wearing some ridiculous bunny costume.

"What the hell are we watching?" he laughs.

"I have no idea."

He reaches for the remote and turns it off, sinks down into the couch and tugs the afghan out from under us, pulling it up around my shoulder so that I'm lying with my head on his chest. "So, why were you crying?" he finally asks.

"I don't know," I breathe.

"Was it because of me, 'cause of last night, I mean?"

"No. No, it wasn't anything to do with you." I feel him exhale beneath me. "I'm sorry about all that, by the way. I don't even know what happened." It amazes me how the apology just slips out, so easy.

"I'm sorry too."

We breathe against each other, and with every exhale I feel like I'm getting lighter, cleaner, like the residue from all those old, stagnant emotions is working its way out of me. I start drawing these invisible lines on his forearm, connecting the constellations of tiny, sparse freckles. "I got in this big fight with my mom," I volunteer.

"How come?"

I take a breath and start to tell him about the stupid fight. But then I keep on talking; I tell him about how things have been bad with my parents in general, especially since Caelin has been gone. How they think I'm at Mara's house. How sometimes I feel like Mara isn't really my friend at all. How I think I am beginning to truly hate my brother. Words, so many words.

I have an image of the Tin Man stuck in my head. Dorothy and Scarecrow finding him rusted solid in the woods, oiling his mouth and jaws, and then, magically, squeak, squeak, squeak, much like a mouse, he says "M-m-m-m-my goodness, I can talk again." It is like that. Cathartic. I feel like I might never shut up again.

He listens patiently as the words flow out effortlessly, offering up mm-hmms and yeahs at the appropriate times.

"Sometimes"—I'm not sure if I should say something this terrible out loud—"sometimes, I don't think I believe in God." Because what kind of God lets bad things happen to people who so desperately try to be good? "I know I used to, but now—I'm just not sure. That's really bad, isn't it?"

"No. Everybody has that thought," he answers casually.

"Really?"

"Yeah, really. I think that too. It's hard not to when you look at the way things are. How fucked up the world is, I mean."

"Mm, yeah," I agree. But the truth is that right now, in this moment, the world feels pretty amazing to me.

"We all think things we're not supposed to think sometimes," he continues. "Like how sometimes I don't even like basketball."

"I thought you *lived* for basketball?"

"Actually, sometimes I fucking hate basketball," he says with a laugh. "You know, if you think about it, it's just stupid—pointless, really. It's not like you're actually doing anything or helping anyone. It's basically just a big waste of everyone's time. I hate that just because you happen to be good at something, people automatically think that's what makes you happy, but it's not really like that, you know? It's not that simple."

"Yeah," I agree, kind of in awe. I knew he was smart, as in he got good grades, but I had no idea he actually thought this deeply about things, that he was maybe more complex than I imagined, more than just a nice guy with killer eyes.

"You know, I got this basketball scholarship, and I don't even really want to go to college. I want to take a year off. Travel or something. I don't even know what I want to go to school for, but my parents won't hear me. They want me to be something big. Like a doctor or a lawyer or a CEO, or something. Not that they would have any clue what's involved—neither of them even went to college." He laughs, and then says, "My parents." That's it.

"What about them?" I ask.

"They're just—" he starts, but stops. "You know, they're not really at my cousin's wedding. They just think that's where I think they are." He stifles another laugh so it's just a short burst of air. "My mom doesn't know how to clear her browser history, that's how I know where they really are. . . ."

"Well, where are they really?"

"They're at this retreat—I guess you could call it a counseling thing."

"Like for couples, you mean?" I ask, just to clarify.

"Like rehab," he says flatly. We both pause, neither of us knowing exactly how the air suddenly became so thick and heavy. I notice my hand has stopped touching his arm. His fingers stopped running along my back. He holds his breath. I can hear his heart through his shirt, feel its beat accelerating. "My dad," he says uncertainly, answering the question I was silently asking. "He's been in and out of rehab for—well, forever, really—my whole life, anyway."

I raise my head to look up at his face. He stares at the ceiling, his Adam's apple bobs as he swallows once, not looking at me.

"He just can't stay clean." He goes on like he's having a conversation with someone else that only he can hear. "I don't understand why. Things will be going really good for a while, sometimes for even a year or so, but then he just goes back to it. Nothing works, this won't work either."

"Rehab," I say, like a moron morbidly unprepared for the realness this conversation requires of me. "What for?" I ask.

"I'm not sure. He's gotten into drugs before—nothing illegal—like prescription stuff. I mean, not that it's actually prescribed to him or anything." He laughs bitterly. "But drinking is always the biggest, you know, problem."

"Oh," I breathe.

"I remember this one time when I was a little kid, my dad was supposedly on a business trip, and he had been gone for what seemed like a really long time." He pauses, like he's remembering it all over again right now. "But then I overheard my mom on the phone with my one aunt, saying something about how my dad was at a halfway house." He laughs again. "And I thought it was like, half a house, or something. So, I remember I drew this picture of my dad sitting in this house that was like, sawed in half, right down the middle," he tells me, his hand dividing the air in front of his face. "And when I showed my mom, I remember she started crying and I didn't know why. I guess that was when I first understood—in some really vague way, anyway—that something was wrong with him."

I wish—wish to God—I knew what to say right now. I open my mouth, but there's nothing in my brain, so I just touch his face, his hair, try to help him relax.

"I was cleaning the leaves out of the gutters the other day," he continues, "and I found five bottles in the gutters, like, just sitting there. Full. I don't get it, I really don't. I mean, when? Why? When did he even do that? Why the gutters? Who does that?"

"Oh God, I don't know," I whisper. Except I think I might—they were there, just in case—and it scares me that I might kind of understand.

"I knew it had to be bad this time, so I told my mom and the next thing I know they're going out of town for a wedding. I just wish they would tell me the truth, it's not like I'm a kid anymore. It's not like I don't already know what's going on." He repositions his body against me, and while I'm listening to him, I am also acutely aware of the fact that I have never felt so completely unthreatened in my life. "When I busted my knee sophomore year, I got a script for painkillers, and my mom made me hide them from him. My own dad."

I open my mouth. I'm about to say something useless, like *I'm sorry*, or *That really sucks*, but thankfully he just keeps talking.

"The thing is," he continues, "when he's sober, he's great. He really is. Like, we do stuff together and everything, you know, like, he takes me to games and camping and fishing and all that shit. I mean, he's basically a good dad, but then there's this thing that, like, controls him. My friends all say they wish he were their father. Of course, I would never let them see him when he's fucked up. So, they don't really know shit about it."

Somehow, when we had started talking, I was in his arms, and now it's the opposite.

"So then that's why you wanted me to leave earlier, when you thought I was high, because of your dad?"

"Oh, maybe," he says, as if he hadn't realized the connection. "It's not just you, though. I don't like being around my friends when they're doing that stuff either. I don't even like being around them when they're drinking. Because you never know what could happen. People do things and say things that are just—things can get out of control so quickly. It just makes me . . . I don't know, nervous, or something," he mumbles.

"I want you to know I don't do anything like that. I really don't. I smoke, that's all—cigarettes. I mean, I don't even drink."

"Sorry I thought that. I guess that's just the first thing I think of whenever anyone is acting weird. Well, not that you were acting weird. I mean, it's just that sometimes you seem, I don't know, distracted. Like you're not really there or something. And that's how he gets all the time—he gets this look on his face, you just know he's somewhere else. That's how it seems with you a lot of the time."

"Oh."

"Or like tonight," he continues. I really didn't think I needed any more examples of my weirdness, but he keeps talking. "I don't know—it just seemed familiar, that's all."

"Oh" suddenly seems like the only word I'm capable of speaking.

"Sorry, I'm probably making it worse. I'm not trying to. I'm just trying to explain. I'm not trying to make you feel bad. I'm sorry, I'll just stop talking."

"No. It's okay. I know." I know I act like a complete freak, I just didn't think it had gotten to three-ring-circus sideshow proportions. Enough to make the person I've been fooling around with think I'm on drugs.

"Okay. Sorry," he says one more time. He kisses my hand, which is resting on his shoulder, and takes a deep breath. He exhales slowly and says, "You know, I've never told anybody about that. Some of my friends I've known since first grade, but I could never tell them, and I've only known you, what, a couple of weeks?" He laughs a hollow nonlaugh.

“Why can’t you tell your friends?” I ask.

“Maybe they’re not really my friends. No, I don’t mean that,” he corrects himself right away, as if he’s committed sacrilege against the divine covenant of popular kids. “It’s just embarrassing is all.”

“It’s not embarrassing.”

He shrugs.

“I’m glad you told me,” I whisper. I open my mouth again, the words almost there, wanting so badly to come out. All that honesty saturating the atmosphere, filling in the gaps that exist between us. It does stuff to my brain, like a drug; it makes me want to tell the truth. I feel dangerously capable.

“I’m glad too,” he says quietly. “Don’t tell anyone, okay? Please,” he adds, a weakness to his voice I had never heard before.

He’s in luck, doesn’t know just how well I can keep a secret. “I would never,” I whisper back. “Promise.”

And so, at 3:45 in the morning, after hours of talking, he reaches up to turn the lamp off and kisses me good night, pulling the afghan tighter around us. As he lays his head back down on my chest he says, “I can hear your heart.”

It’s a simple, sweet thing to say. I smile a little. But then I feel my heart do something funny—it’s the thump, thump, thumping of the proverbial part of the organ. And around the time the moon and sun are coexisting in the sky, turning the room inside out with that eerie, yet calming, pale glow, I have a terrible thought: I like him. I really, really like him. Like, *love*-like him. Like, with my metaphorical heart. Like, if I had an x-ray, it would show an arrow lodged right into the center of that bloody, bleeding mass of muscle in my chest. And I know, somehow, that things have changed between us.

"ALL RIGHT!" MARA SAYS, as she walks into my bedroom that weekend. "Let's download. It's time you start spilling, Edy—I'm supposed to be your best friend, right?"

I close and lock the door behind her.

"What do you mean?" I ask as she plops down on my bed and takes her coat off.

"I mean, do I ever get to see you anymore? You're spending everywakingminute with Joshua Miller and you haven't given me any details whatsoever. So, it's time to spill your guts."

"I don't know." I shrug. "What is there to tell?"

"Tons! Okay, let's start with where are you going when you're together every day? Are you going to Joshua Miller's house?" she asks, raising her eyebrows.

I laugh. "Yes, I've even been in Joshua Miller's bedroom."

"No shit. Joshua Miller's bedroom," she repeats in awe.

"Okay, you need to stop calling him Joshua Miller, Mara. It's weird."

"But . . . he's Joshua Miller, Edy."

"I'm aware of that." I sit down in my desk chair and look at her, so excited for me, and I try really hard not to get excited for me too.

"So what do you call him? Sweetie? Sexy? Sugar? Greek God?"

"Yeah, Mara, I call him Greek God." I laugh, throwing a pillow at her face. "Josh usually does the trick, though."

"Josh . . . ," she repeats, rolling the word around in her mouth. "So, what's he really like?"

"I don't know. He's nice. He's just . . . he's really nice, actually."

"And hot, don't forget," she adds, like I could ever forget that. "So have you . . . you know? Had sex?" she whispers.

I nod my head yes.

"Oh my God! What was it like? What was he like?" she asks awkwardly, scooting to the edge of the bed.

"No, I'm not discussing this."

"Come on, I need to live vicariously through you," she pleads.

"Well, what's going on with you and Cameron?"

"Nothing." She sighs. "Not even close. Still just friends." And suddenly, the way she looks at me, I feel an entire ocean between us, and we're standing on opposite shores, staring at each other from the farthest ends of the world.

"So, come on, tell me about your hot boyfriend. Please?" she asks, rather than acknowledging this great distance.

"He's not my boyfriend," I correct her.

"He doesn't want to be your boyfriend?" she asks, scrunching her face up. "What, he just wants to sleep with you and—"

"No. It's me. I don't want to be his girlfriend."

"Are you insane?" she asks immediately.

"Maybe." I laugh.

"Seriously, though. Are you totally insane?"

"I just—I don't know. I don't like the idea, I guess. I don't wanna be tied down like that. Obligated. Stuck, you know?"

"That doesn't make any sense at all. But okay. As long as he's not trying to keep you guys a secret or anything scummy like that?"

"He's not. I promise. And it's not scummy to want a little privacy."

"Whatever you say, Eeds. I wouldn't know anything about it, I guess." She relents, a hint of something like resentment there beneath the surface. But she quickly pushes it back down wherever it came from and grins. "So is it good? Or fun? Or whatever it's supposed to be." She laughs, embarrassed. "Is he, you know, nice to you, when you're together, I mean?"

I nod yes.

She smiles. "He better be."

"TELL ME AGAIN," he says breathlessly, moving his fingers through my hair, "why you can't just be my girlfriend?"

"Why?" I groan. God, even if he is nice, he can annoy me.

"Because," he mumbles, with his mouth against my neck, "I don't like thinking about you with other guys, you know. . . ." His voice trails off, swallowed by his kisses.

"Then don't."

He stops and looks at me in that intense way he sometimes does that terrifies me. "It's not that easy to just not think about."

I don't answer. I know I'm supposed to tell him he has nothing to worry about, that I'm all his, that there aren't any other guys. But somehow, I can't. Instead, I say, "When would I even have time to spend with anyone else? We're together every night."

He grins that grin of his, and I think, for just a moment, he's going to let it go. But finally, after all these weeks, he begins the conversation I assume must have been on his mind ever since he realized my name was plastered all over the bathrooms.

"So, I'm just curious . . . ," he says, playing with a strand of my hair.

"About?"

"Who else did you, uh . . ." He trails off again.

"What?"

"Who else have you, you know, been with?" he finally finishes.

"Why?" I ask, and not in a nice way.

"I don't know," he mumbles.

"Does it matter?"

"I guess not."

"Good." Because I didn't want to have to think about it, let alone talk about it. I didn't want to even acknowledge the fact that there had been someone else.

"But . . . ," he begins again, "I still wanna know."

"Just pretend you're the first, okay?" That's what I'm doing, after all.

"That's not what I meant. It's not like it bothers me or anything. I was just—"

"It bothers me." Goddamn it, my stupid mouth—it needs to be wired shut. I roll away from him so that I'm on my own side of the bed. I feel my underwear down by my legs. I put them on under the sheets.

"What? Why? It's not like I haven't been with other girls."

"Yeah, I guess." It's definitely not the same thing, though. I clamp my teeth down on the insides of my cheeks—need to stop myself from saying anything else. I taste blood, I bite harder.

"No big deal or anything, I just wondered is all." He pauses a beat, two, three, four, then inhales and says, "So . . . was it more than one person?"

"Seriously, Josh! I really, really don't want to talk about this!"

"All right." Pause. "I'll tell you mine. . . ."

"No, don't. I don't care, okay? It doesn't matter to me. I don't want to know." Of course, I already knew his, because he was never exactly a low-profile type. Until me. "And I don't want to talk about this anymore. Really, I mean it."

"I just—sometimes I feel like I don't know anything about you. It's weird."

"You do too." But I know that's not the complete truth.

He just sighs.

"All right, ask me anything else, really, anything else and I'll tell you, okay?"

"God, it must've been pretty bad, huh?" I turn my head to look at him; there's no other way to tell him how incapable I am of discussing this. "What? I'm just saying the guy's a fucking asshole. Whoever he is."

"Why?" I smirk. "Because of all the nasty things written about me on the bathroom walls?"

"You know about that?" he asks quietly. "Eden, you know that I don't believe any of those things, right? I mean, I know the truth."

Truth. Truth! Truth? He doesn't know shit about the truth. I open my mouth, and I almost tell him that. "Never mind," I mumble instead.

"What now? I'm just trying to—" I pull away from him. "Oh, come on. I'm just trying to tell you I wouldn't do that. I think that's really shitty."

It was a shitty thing to do. He's right about that. I don't say anything though. We need to drop this immediately. I think he finally gets it too, because he's quiet for once. Quiet for a long time.

I stare up at the ceiling of his bedroom. His house is soundless like always—parents sleeping or somewhere else, I don't know which. I turn to look at him, lying there, still facing me.

"Tell me a secret," he whispers. I always get the sense he knows I have a secret. A deep, dark one. "You know, something that I don't know about you—a secret."

"Right." I grin, trying to erase what just happened. "Because you don't know anything about me . . ." I'm only halfheartedly mocking him.

"I know," he says, pulling me closer, covering my mouth with his, "that's why I want you to tell me something." I wonder what he would say if I told him. What he would do. If I told him my deep, dark, black-hole secret, the one that had the potential to swallow up the entire universe.

"Okay, my middle name is Marie." That's a lie. My middle name is Anne. "Now you?"

"That's not a secret. I meant something real." Kiss. "Matthew."

"What?"

"Matthew," he repeats. "Joshua Matthew Miller."

"Oh." Kiss. "That's nice." Kiss. "Tell me something else."

"No, it's your turn, Eden Marie McCrorey." He smiles that crooked smile of his and lays his head down on my chest, waiting for me to be honest, to share some tidbit of truth with him, a detail, anything. I should've told him then that Marie wasn't really my middle name. He seemed to like saying it, though, like he thought that small scrap of information made him know me a little better, made him like me just a little more.

"I used to play clarinet in band." True, although not really a secret, per se.

He lifts his head and grins at me. "You did not."

"Yes, I did, I swear," I tell him, putting my hand over my heart. "You can even check the yearbook. But wait—don't—because I looked like a real dork last year."

He laughs, still looking at me like he doesn't quite believe me. "For real?"

"I was even in this book club thing last year," I offer.

"You don't seem like a book club kind of girl to me," he says, eyeing me suspiciously.

"I don't?" I ask, pretending to be surprised. "I even started the book club with Miss Sullivan." I laugh.

A smile spreads across his face as he decides I'm telling the truth. "That's cute," he finally says, grinning wider. "That's really cute."

"No, it's not," I mumble.

"No, it's not. It's kind of hot actually." Then he kisses me seriously, deeply—the kind of kisses that lead somewhere. But he stops and looks at me, his eyes so soft. "You're really beautiful, Eden," he whispers.

I don't ordinarily like to hear things like that—nice things—but maybe it's the tone of his voice or the look on his face. I smile. Not on purpose, but it's just that my face won't let me not smile.

"You know, I already had sex with you," I try to joke, "so you don't have to say stuff like that."

"Stop, I mean it." And then he leans in and kisses my lips, so sweetly. Sometimes he uses his words like weapons to chip away at my icy exterior and sometimes he can break through to the slightly defrosted layer beneath. But then again, sometimes he just hits solid iceberg. For instance, he knows what he's doing when next he says, "And you should smile more too."

I look away, embarrassed. He has no way of knowing how sometimes it physically hurts to smile. How a smile can sometimes feel like the biggest lie I've ever told.

"No, I love your smile," he says, with his fingers on my lips, which only makes my smile widen.

Only it doesn't hurt this time.

"Eden Marie McCrorey . . . ," he begins, like he's giving some big lecture about me, "always so serious and gloomy . . ."—my eulogy maybe—"but then you have this great smile nobody ever gets to see. Wait, are you blushing?" he teases. "I can't believe it. I made Eden Marie McCrorey blush."

"No, I'm not!" I laugh, placing my hands over my cheeks.

He takes my hands in his, though, and gently moves them away from my face. "You know what I think?" he asks me.

"What do you think?" I echo.

"I think . . ." He pauses. "You're not so tough—you're not really so hard," he says seriously, his smile fading, "are you?"

My heart starts racing as he looks deeper into me. Because he's right. Tough girls don't blush. Tough girls don't turn to jelly when a cute boy tells them they're beautiful. And I'm terrified he'll see through the tough iceberg layer, and he'll discover not a soft, sweet girl, but an ugly fucking disaster underneath.

He brushes the hair out of my face and runs his index finger along the two-inch scar above my left eyebrow. "How'd you get this?" he asks. "I've been wondering, but every time I notice we're—eh-hem—busy." He smirks. "And then I always forget to ask."

I touch my head. I grin, remembering the sheer absurdity of the accident.

"What?" he asks. "It must be something embarrassing. . . ."

"It happened when I was twelve. I fell off my bike, had to get fifteen stitches."

"Fifteen? That's a lot. Just from falling off your bike?"

"Well, not exactly. Me and Mara, we were riding our bikes down that big hill, you know, the one at the end of my street?"

"Mm-hmm," he murmurs, listening to me like I'm saying the most interesting things he's ever heard in his life, paying such close attention to every word out of my mouth.

"And there're those train tracks at the bottom, right?" I continue.

"Oh no."

"Well, I guess at some point I kind of flipped over my handlebars and rolled the rest of the way down the hill, that's what Mara said, anyway. I don't really remember, think I blacked out. My face smashing into the tracks broke my fall, though."

"That's terrible!" he says, even though he's laughing really hard.

"No, it's stupid. You should laugh at me. I'm the reason the town had to put up fences at the end of all the streets in my neighborhood."

That makes him laugh even harder. Me too.

Then I start thinking about everything that came after.

That was the day I fell in love with Kevin—or what I thought was love, with the person I thought he was. And he knew it too. And he used it to get to me. This was the day I wish I could go back to—the day I need to undo to stop it all from happening. It was so hot, and the air so thick, it felt like my lungs couldn't even breathe it in. Mara and I were just two twelve-year-olds in our pathetic two-piece bathing suits, which revealed nothing because we basically had nothing, drawing with sidewalk chalk in my driveway, ice-cream-sandwich ice cream dripping down our arms and legs.

We were drawing suns with smiley faces and rainbows and trees and hideous, artless flowers. We played tic-tac-toe a few times, but it was boring because no one ever won. We made a hopscotch court, but the cement was on fire, too hot to hop on. I wrote in big bubbly pink letters, across the driveway:

MARA LUVS CAELIN

I only did it to embarrass her. So then Mara swung her two long braids over her shoulders and hunkered down with a fat lump of pastel blue. In huge block letters she wrote:

EDY LOVES KEVIN

Which caused me to scream at the top of my lungs and throw the stick of white at her, which missed, of course, and shattered into a million tiny slivers that were from then on useless, which was all right because white was always boring anyway. And then I said, "Mara, you should really marry Caelin. Then we'd be sisters and that would be so awesome!"

"Yeah, I guess." She frowned. "But I think Kevin's cuter."

"He is not. Besides, Kevin isn't my brother, so if you married him, we wouldn't be sisters."

"You're just saying that so you can marry Kevin."

"Well, I can't marry my own brother—that would be disgusting!"

"Oh yeah," she realized, as if those two were our only options in the entire world. Our world was small—way too small—even for twelve-year-olds.

"So, you marry my brother and I'll marry Kevin and then we'll be sisters and Kev and Cae will be brothers. It makes sense because everyone already thinks they're brothers anyway."

She considered this for a moment, then said, "Yeah, okay."

Now that we had our lives all figured out, I asked, "You wanna ride bikes?"

"Yeah, okay."

We tried not to let our feet touch the molten pavement as we ran inside the house to throw on our shorts and flip-flops. Mara's dad finally left for good that summer. There was a lot of fighting going on at home. So she spent most days at my house even though she was the one with the swimming pool. She agreed to almost anything as long as it kept her out of her house and away from her parents. So, when I said marry my brother, she said okay. When I said let's ride bikes, she said okay. And when I said let's ride our bikes as fast as we can down the big scary steep hill at the end of my street so that we could see if there was a train going by on the railroad tracks at the bottom, she said okay.

It was not one of my brightest ideas, I'll admit. The last thing I remember hearing before plummeting to my near-death was the sound of Mara screaming. The last thing I saw was the rotted gray wood of the railroad ties, flying toward my face at an enormous speed. My skull clunked against the steel rail with a dull thud. And then everything went dark.

When my eyes opened, I was staring up at an impossibly bright sky and my legs were tangled in my bike. My glasses were gone. And I felt water dripping down my face. I raised the arm that was still capable of moving. It was covered in dirt and hundreds of tiny cuts. I touched my head. Red water. Lots of red water. And then I heard my name being called from far, far away. I closed my eyes again.

"What the hell were you two doing?" It was Kevin's voice, loud, close.

"We wanted to see a train go by." Mara, innocent.

"Edy, can you hear me?" Kevin, his hands on my face.

"Uh . . ." was all I could moan. I opened my eyes long enough to see him take his T-shirt off and press it against my head. I felt his hands on one of my legs. Which one, I couldn't even tell.

"Edy, Edy, try to move your leg, okay? If you can move it, it's not broken. Try," he demanded.

"Is it? Is it moving?" I think I asked out loud. I didn't hear an answer.

And then I was weightless. He carried me up the hill and then he laid me down on the grass. He called 911, even.

I decided that night with Mara, I was definitely marrying him. The damage: a fractured left wrist, a sprained ankle, a thousand scrapes and bruises, a broken pinkie, fifteen stitches in my forehead, and one utterly demolished ten-speed bike. And, of course, a severe delusion about the kind of person Kevin truly was. *You were very lucky and very, very stupid*, I was told over and over and over that day.

⁂

"You're lucky there wasn't a train coming!" Josh's voice says, pulling me back into the present. My eyes refocus on his bedroom ceiling. He's still laughing. I had stopped.

"Am I?" I accidentally say out loud. If there had been a train coming, then I would have been killed or at least seriously and irreparably injured. And 542 days later I would have been lying in either a grave or a hospital somewhere, rotting away or hooked up to machines and not in my bed with Kevin in the next room and me thinking he was the greatest person in the entire world, incapable of hurting me in any way, because, after all, he had saved the day. Maybe if that day never happened, maybe I wouldn't have become so smitten, so pathetically infatuated. Maybe I wouldn't have flirted with him over a game of Monopoly earlier that night. And maybe I would've screamed when I found him in my bed at 2:48 in the morning, instead of doing nothing at all. And maybe it was essentially all my fault for acting like I liked him, for actually liking him.

"Of course you are," I hear a dim voice say through the fog in my mind. But now his face has changed to serious. I can't remember the last thing either of us said.

"I am what?" I ask.

"Lucky!" he says impatiently.

"Oh, right. Yeah, I know."

"Then why would you even say that? That's not funny."

"I know."

"It's really not. I hate when you say stuff like that."

"Okay, I know!" I snap at him.

He doesn't say anything, but I can tell he's mad. Mad because

I'm always getting upset with him for no reason, saying fucked-up things, or just being generally weird. He doesn't say anything else. He just rolls away and lies there next to me. Now he's the one staring at the ceiling and I'm the one on my side, facing him, wanting him to look at me. I put my head on his chest, try to pretend things are okay still, pretend I'm not a freak. Reluctantly, he puts his arm around me. But I can't take the silence, can't take the thought of him being mad.

So I whisper, "Tell me another secret."

But he's quiet.

After a while, a very painfully silent while, I think maybe he has fallen asleep, so I pretend to be sleeping too. But then I feel him press his face into my hair and breathe. Quietly, almost inaudibly, he whispers, "I love you." His big secret. I squeeze my eyes shut as tight as I can and pretend not to hear—pretend not to care.

After I'm sure he's really fallen asleep, I sneak out as quietly as possible.

"SO WHAT ARE WE gonna do for your birthday this year, Edy?" Mara asks me at my locker after school the next day.

"I don't know. Let's just go out to eat or something," I tell her as I pack up my things for homework.

"Oh my God, Edy. Look, look, look," Mara says quietly, barely moving her mouth, smacking me in the arm over and over.

"What?" I turn around. Josh is walking down the hall, headed straight for us. "Oh God," I mutter under my breath.

"Edy, shut up, and be nice!" Mara says low, just as he approaches earshot. She looks at him with this enormous smile on her face. "Hi!"

He gives her one of those winning smiles of his, and she giggles—*giggles*.

"Hi!" he returns her greeting with the same level of enthusiasm. Then he turns to me and it's just a dull, "Hey."

I don't know what to do. Two totally opposite worlds are in the process of colliding right at this moment, and I'm stuck in the middle.

"So, Joshua . . . Miller, right?" Mara says, as if she doesn't always refer to him by his full name.

"Yeah—well, Josh. And you are?"

"Mara," she responds.

"Oh, right, Mara. It's nice to finally meet you."

"You too."

They both look at me, like I'm supposed to somehow know how to shepherd this mess. When I don't say anything, Mara takes over: "So, Josh, we were just talking about what we're gonna do for Edy's birthday tomorrow."

"Your birthday's tomorrow?" he asks, his eyes searching mine.

Mara frowns at me. "Edy, you didn't tell him your birthday's tomorrow?"

"Yeah, *Edy* must've forgotten to mention it," Josh answers. "Just like *Edy* must've forgotten to say good-bye before she snuck out of my house last night," he says in this way that tells me he's not going to let it go, not going to just sit back and take it this time.

"Well, um," Mara begins, uncomfortably, "I guess I probably have somewhere to be, so . . ." Pause. "I'm gonna go there now. It was great to meet you, really," she tells Josh with a sweet, sincere smile.

"Yeah, definitely," he responds, like he genuinely means it.

As she walks away she looks back at me over her shoulder with her lips tight and her eyes wide, and she just points her finger at me, like *You'd better not fuck this up!*

"It was nice to finally meet *one* of your friends."

"So, what are you doing here?" I ask, ignoring his comment.

"You know, I'm really sick of your rules, okay? We need to talk. And we need to talk now."

"Fine. Can we go somewhere a little more private, at least?" I look around, taking note of all the people watching us.

He takes my hand. I pull away from him involuntarily. He looks at me like he's hurt, but just holds on tighter, leading us down the hall. We stop in the stairwell and he sits down on one of the steps. I stand more still than I ever have before. I'm scared. Really scared he's about to leave me. And more scared because I don't want him to.

"Will you sit?"

My heart and thoughts race, bleeding together in a cacophony of why, why, why? "Why?" I finally say out loud, my shaky voice betraying the look of cool, calm collectedness I'm attempting to secure on my face.

"I told you already. I want to talk. I'm serious."

I hold my breath as I sit down next to him. He turns to face me, but I interrupt before he can even begin. "Just tell me now—are you trying to end this?"

"No! Not at all. I just—I can't go on like this. I can't have this be all there is. We have something more. You have to see that, right?"

"I told you before, I don't—the whole boyfriend-girlfriend thing—I'm not comfortable with—"

"I'm saying that *I'm* not comfortable, Eden!" he interrupts, raising his voice, suddenly upset. Then quieter, "I'm not comfortable with us sleeping together every night and then acting like we don't even know each other at school. You won't come out with me and meet my friends. Clearly, you don't want to introduce me to your friends. We've never been anywhere together except my bedroom. I mean, why can't we at least go to your house sometimes?" He pauses, taking my hand. "Why do I always feel like we're sneaking around?"

"I don't know," I say quietly, feeling so exposed.

"Yes, you do, so just be honest with me."

"What do you mean?"

"I mean, is there a reason that we should be sneaking around?" he asks, his real question finally emerging.

"What reason?"

He looks at me like I'm totally dense.

"What, like another person?" I clarify.

"Yeah, like another person."

I stare at him and wish that I could somehow make him understand everything. Everything that's happened, everything I think and feel, about him, about me, about us together. How my heart—that stupid, flimsy organ—aches violently for him. But it's too much for words, so I just utter that one syllable, the one that matters most right now: "No."

He exhales as if he was holding his breath. Obviously, that was not at all the answer he was expecting. "Then if there's no one else, why does it have to be like this?"

"I don't know, because then everything gets complicated and screwed up and—"

"This is complicated, though," he says, raising his voice slightly. "This is screwed up." Then quieter, "It is."

I can't argue with that, so I just look down at my hands in my lap.

"Look, I don't want to fight or anything, I just—I just care about you. I really do." He kisses my lips and then, quietly, with his mouth next to my ear he whispers, "That's all I'm trying to say."

I should say it back. I care about you too! I care, damn it,

I fucking care—I want to scream it. "I—I—" *Care*, say it.

He lifts his head, a small glint of hope in his eyes.

"Look, you don't understand. It's not like this is easy for me, I can't just—I can't—" My voice squeaks, mouselike, as I try to make my brain and mouth work in concert. I feel the tears in my throat, filling my eyes. He looks confused, worried, and I think, almost relieved—relieved that I'm really not so tough, not so hard.

"Okay," he breathes, dumbfounded by this sudden, unprecedented display of emotion. "Baby, don't—" he says softly. "Look, I know. It's okay, come here." He pulls me into him, and I let my body fall against his side. And I don't even care who sees us right now. I just hold on to him as hard as I can. Everything that's been coming between us seems to dissolve, and for once I don't feel like a complete liar. For once I feel calm, safe. Terrifyingly safe.

"Hey, let me take you out for your birthday—out to dinner or something."

"Okay," I hear myself answer right away.

"Seriously?" he asks, pulling away from me, holding my shoulders at arm's length. "I'm gonna need to get that in writing." He reaches for his backpack like he's getting a pen and paper.

"Stop," I say with a laugh, smacking him in the arm. "I said yes."

"Okay, it's a date!"

His hands find their way around my body with a practiced fluency. "You know . . . all this talking," he mumbles as he kisses my neck. "You wanna come over?"

"Tomorrow, okay? After dinner, right?" I smile.

He moans like it's agony, but then smiles and whispers, "Okay."

✻

When I arrive at my locker the next morning, I'm greeted by Mara's handiwork. She has gone all out decorating my locker. It was tradition. She taped up balloons and crepe paper and bows and curly string and a sign that reads: HAPPY 15TH BIRTHDAY. I cringe.

I tear the sign down as fast as I can, but I have a feeling it's too late, that he's already seen it. I discreetly slip the piece of paper into the garbage on my way to homeroom. I hear footsteps jogging up behind me and I take a deep breath because I know they belong to him and I know he knows, somehow. He pulls me by the elbow into the boys' bathroom with this wild look in his eyes.

"Get out!" he yells at the kid who is peeing into one of the urinals at the wall. To the right of the boy's head I notice these black letters glaring at me, the fluorescent lights bouncing off the grimy powder-blue tiles: EDEN MCSLUTTY IS something illegible—it had been scribbled out by a marker that was not quite opaque enough. As soon as the kid had scrambled out of there, forgetting to even zip up his pants, Josh is in my face.

"How could you do this? After everything, how can you still be lying to me? You said you were sixteen. I'm eighteen, you knew that! I trusted you!"

"I didn't—" I was going to remind him that, technically, I never told him that, but I can see that he's not about to hear it. He just paces back and forth, ranting, fuming.

"I mean, fourteen? Fourteen? Fourteen!" he shouts, the volume elevating with each repetition.

"Calm down. It's not that big of a deal." I had never expected him to be this mad about it—age isn't something we had even really discussed. Besides, there are plenty of senior guys who date freshmen—that would be the same age difference, if not more. Nobody cares about these things.

"It's a big fucking deal! All those nights—in my bed—you were fourteen. Right?" His words are so sharp they sting. "Right?" he repeats.

"Yeah, so?"

"Do you realize that I could be accused of raping you? Statutory rape, Eden, ever hear of it?"

I laugh—wrong thing to do.

"This isn't funny—this is not funny! This is serious, this is my life here. I'm an adult, okay, legally an adult! How can you be laughing?" he shouts, horrified at me.

How can I be laughing? I can laugh because I know what the real crime is. I know that the kind of wrong he's talking about is nothing. That people get away with truly wrong things every day. I know that he doesn't have anything to worry about. That's how I can be laughing.

"Look, I'm sorry," I tell him, trying to stop my mouth from smiling, "but you're being ridiculous. You didn't"—I lower my voice, inhale, exhale, inhale again—"you didn't . . . rape me." There, I said it. The word I've been spending so much time and energy not saying, not even thinking. Of course he couldn't appreciate what it took for me to utter that grotesque four-letter word out loud. He just continues, his tirade only gaining momentum.

"Yeah, of course I know that, but it doesn't matter. Your parents could still press charges against me, Eden."

"They won't, though. They don't even know about—" *You*, I was going to say, but he interrupts me again.

"You don't get it," he continues. "I'm talking about Actual. Criminal. Charges. I could get arrested, go to jail even, I'd lose my basketball scholarship and everything. Everything could get completely fucked up."

He stops. I watch him take a few shallow breaths, watching me, waiting.

"Well?" he finally says, sweeping his arm in my direction.

"What do you mean, 'well'?" I ask, my voice as harsh as his.

"I mean, don't you care?" he yells. Then quieter, "Don't you care about anything? About me?" His stare pierces me, searching to see if I remember any of what happened yesterday in the stairwell. Of course I remember, but since I'm really good at pretending, I just look right back at him—right through him. My face is a stone. My body is a stone. My heart is a stone.

"No." That one syllable. The biggest lie. The worst lie.

"What?" he breathes.

"No," I tell him calmly. "I don't." My words like knives destroying everything we had created. "I. Don't. Care." I repeat with icy precision.

You would think I just punched him in the face the way he looks at me. But that only lasts for about one, two, three . . . and a half seconds, and then he quickly resumes his anger. "That's fine—great, actually! That's great. Because we can never see each other again, I hope you know that, Eden. We can't—"

"Puh-lease." I laugh bitterly. "Listen, you know I had fun, but this was pretty much over anyway, don't you think?" Some other person has taken over my brain and I'm screaming at her to shut up—stop talking now. But if it's ending anyway, and it is, I can't let him think he is in charge. I'm in charge, damn it.

His face sort of caves in a little around the edges. He looks so defeated I almost start apologizing, almost start begging him not to leave me, begging because I'm so fucking alone, and I do care about things, about him, especially. But then he straightens himself up and chokes out, "Yeah. Definitely over."

I leave him in the bathroom. I push through the door effortlessly, walking tall and calm, and he stands there shaking his head at me.

CAELIN AND KEVIN COME home on Christmas Eve. They barrel through the front door struggling with duffel bags and sacks of dirty laundry and backpacks full of schoolwork and textbooks. Mom and Dad falling all over them. "Edy, can you help the boys with their bags?" they both ask me more than once. But I just stand there in the living room, cross my arms, and watch.

It takes a few minutes before the commotion settles, before either of them sees me there. Caelin walks across the room toward me, his arms outstretched, but something stops him in his tracks, and for a split second his smile gives way to a look of confusion as his eyes take me in.

"Edy." He says it slowly, almost like a question. Not really addressing me, but as if he's trying to make sure it really is me.

"Ye-es?" I respond, but he just stares.

"No, it's just—" He forces himself to smile. "You look—" He turns his head to look at our parents, searching. Then back to me. "You just look so . . . so—"

“Beautiful.” Mom chimes in, smiling, even though I’m pretty sure she’s still as freaked out as I am about that slap, which neither of us has mentioned again.

He folds his arms around me stiffly, like he doesn’t want to get too close to my breasts. “You just look so grown up. I mean, how long have I been gone, right?” he says with a laugh, pulling away uncomfortably. He looks at me like he wants to say more, but he just walks off, carrying his bags into his bedroom.

And now Kevin stands before me, five feet away maybe, staring me down. Giving me the secret look he must’ve been perfecting over the past year. The look that is clearly supposed to deflate me—make me shrivel and wilt and retreat. And even though my legs feel flimsy and boneless, like they might give out at any moment, and my heart is racing and my skin feels like it’s on fire, I don’t flinch, I don’t run, don’t back away this time. I want to believe that somewhere beneath that knifelike stare he can see just how much I’ve changed, how different I am from that girl he once knew. I don’t move a muscle, not until he walks away first.

“Okay, Edy!” My mom claps her hands together twice. “We have to get to work here. Grandma and Grandpa will be here in the morning so there won’t be any time tomorrow. We have to get everything that can possibly be done ahead of time, done ahead of time.”

I follow her into the kitchen, dreading the next eight hours of my life. She’s in her manic, deceptively chipper, but just on the verge of a nervous breakdown mode—there’s something about Grandma and Grandpa coming over that always sets her on edge. I watch as she slips into the laundry room and neatly unfolds the stepladder into an A at the front of the junk closet. I know what’s next. She pulls her ancient radio/cassette/CD player out by its handle and sets it on the kitchen counter.

"Oh, Mom, do we have to?" I moan. I can't take it—cooking all day while listening to Christmas music.

"Yes, we do. It'll put us in the spirit!"

I get started chopping up insane amounts of celery, onions, and garlic. Next, the butternut squash. Just as I'm in the middle of struggling to cut it into little cubes like Mom wants, the rhythm of her chopping is interrupted. "Oh my God!" she shouts. I nearly cut the tip of my middle finger off.

"What?"

"Goddamn it!" she gasps, "Silent Night" playing softly in the background. "I knew I forgot something. The goddamn cream of tartar—I always forget it! The last thing I want to do right now is fight my way through the grocery store the day before Christmas!"

"Do we really need it?"

"Yes." She braces herself against the counter and breathes deeply, closing her eyes. "Yes, we do. Okay, new plan. I'm going to run to the store. You keep chopping. And when you're done with the squash, put it in the big bowl in the cabinet above the fridge. Then, will you do these dishes so they're not piling up while we're trying to work?"

She's already got her jacket on—over her apron—and is slinging her purse over her shoulder.

"Caelin!" she yells. "Caelin?"

"Yeah?" I hear him answer, his voice muffled from the other side of the house.

"Can you come in here please?" she calls back, using all her restraint to not flip out and start screaming. "I am not going to yell across this house!" she says under her breath, as she wraps her scarf around her neck in a tight noose. He appears in the kitchen. "What are you two doing right now?" she asks as she pulls on her gloves.

"Nothing. We're just playing a game. It's paused. What do you need?"

"Where's your father?"

"Snoring. On the couch," he answers.

"Fine. Look, I need you to go into the garage and find a box—it's labeled 'Christmas Decor'—it has the nice tablecloth and place mats and centerpiece that we used last year. I'm going to the store. Can anybody think of anything else that we need?"

Caelin and I both shake our heads. And she's gone.

"Wow," he says. "She's freakin' out early this year. Is it some kind of a record, or what?" He laughs.

"I know, right?" I try to act like things are the way they used to be, but I think we both know they're just not. "Can you please shut that off?" I ask him, pointing to the radio. He reaches over and flips the dial to off.

"So, what have you been up to?" he asks, leaning against the refrigerator. "Other than growing up too fast. I haven't heard from you much at all this year." He smiles at me, crossing his arms while he waits for me to respond. But I know him. And I know it's a fake smile, an uncomfortable smile.

"Well, I haven't heard from you much either." It comes out sounding nastier than I meant.

"Yeah, I guess so." He frowns.

I start filling the sink, squeezing in the dish soap like it's an exact science that requires my undivided concentration.

"Sorry," he continues, after I don't say anything. He has to raise his voice over the sound of the water running. "I've been unbelievably swamped. This semester's kicking my ass."

I just nod. I don't know what I'm supposed to say. It's okay? It's not. And it's not okay that he brought Kevin here—again.

"Okay, well, I guess I'd better go look for that stuff, then."

"Yeah."

After I hear the door to the garage close, I shut the faucet off and dip my hands in the hot water. It feels peaceful, somehow, quiet. The music off, the TV on low in the next room, the muffled clanging of the dishes underwater. Then, faintly, I hear footsteps creep up behind me. It's Kevin—it's like my body knows before my brain does, my senses heightened, my skin suddenly hot and itchy. Like I'm allergic to him. The proximity of his body to mine causing an actual physical repulsion, like a warning sign, flashing neon lights: DANGER DANGER DANGER. Get away from him, my body tells me. But it's hard to get away from someone like him.

Before I can even turn my head to look, I feel his thick hands wind around my waist, feel his body pressing up against my back. And then his voice, his breath in my ear, whispers, "Lookin' good, Edy." Then he moves his hands down over the front of my jeans, then up over the front of my shirt, then all over all of me, his mouth open against my neck.

"Stop," I breathe. "Stop it!" I pull my hot soapy hands out of the water, but I can't stop him. He has me pinned against the sink. And his hands can do whatever they want. I consider pulling the paring knife I used to chop the garlic out of the water and plunging it into his heart. But he finally lets go, backing away while he looks me up and down. Smiling, he says, "Is this for my benefit?"

I should've killed him, I should've done a million things to him, but instead my shaking voice just asks, "Is what?" But he doesn't answer, just keeps smirking and looking, up and down, my heart pounding so hard I can hear it in my ears. Clearly, I had gotten too bold. Forgotten the extent of him. He was letting me know. Then he walks away silently, just as he came in, leaving me properly terrified.

At 1:17 in the morning, officially Christmas day, I wake up to the sound of metal rattling. My heart racing because he's there to do it again, I'm convinced. It's him clanging at the doorknob.

"Edy?" he whispers.

"Who's there?" I choke out.

"Cae. Come on, Edy, let me in," he whisper-shouts.

I walk up to the door and press my ear against the wood. "Are you alone?" I finally ask.

"Am I alone? Yeah."

I unlock and open the door just enough to see that it is really my brother, and that he really is alone. "What?"

"I have to talk to you," he whispers. "You gonna let me in?"

I move aside, closing the door behind him.

"What, are you sleeping on the floor?" he asks, stepping over my sleeping bag.

"It's my back," I lie.

As he sits down on the edge of the bed, it howls. I feel my

insides tighten. "Edy, sit," he tells me, patting the empty space next to him. I pull up my desk chair instead.

"What?" I sigh, crossing my arms while I stare at him.

"Edy, me and Kevin, we went out with some of the guys tonight." He pauses like I'm supposed to say something. "Some of the guys we used to play ball with." Pauses again, waiting for some reaction on my part. "Some of them are *seniors* now?"

I can see where the conversation is heading, but I'm going to make him say it—say every word. "Yeah, and . . . ?"

"Okay. And some of them were saying things. About you, I mean. Lies, of course. But I just wanted to make sure nobody's been, I don't know, like, harassing you or something?" he says uncertainly.

"Why, what did they say?"

He opens his mouth but starts laughing. "I can't believe I'm even telling you this. I mean, it's crazy, it's so stupid. They said—they were saying that there're all these rumors about you being some kind of"—he stops himself, and then mumbles—"slut, or whatever. But look, don't worry, I stuck up for you. You know, I told them you aren't like that." He shakes his head back and forth, still smiling at the absurdity of it. "Christ, I mean, you don't even know Joshua Miller, do you?"

"Yeah, I know him," I answer.

"What?" he says, his voice unsteady.

"I know him pretty well, actually." I grin.

The color drains from his face, and then returns abruptly. He laughs again. "Oh God, you're kidding! You're kidding. Jesus, you scared the shit out of me for a second there." He continues laughing nervously as he studies my face.

I don't laugh, don't crack a smile. Blank.

"Wait. You are fucking with me, right?"

I just stare straight at him—no emotion, no regret.

His smile fades then. "Please tell me you're joking, Eeds. Please," he begs, hoping this is another one of those times when he just doesn't get it.

I shake my head, shrug. No big deal.

And silence.

A lot of silence.

I don't mind. In fact, I'm really beginning to like the silence. It's become my ally. Things happen in silence. If you don't let it get to you, it can make you stronger; it can be your shield, impenetrable.

"I can't—Edy, what are you even . . . thinking?" he accuses, tapping his index finger against his temple. "I'm gone for a year and all of a sudden you're—I can't believe—you're just a kid, for Christ's sake!"

"A kid?" I snort. "Um, hardly."

"No. Eden, you can't do this."

"Oh, really? Who are you to tell me what I can't do?" I challenge.

"I'm your brother, okay—that's who! I mean, do you have any idea what they're saying about you?" he whispers, pointing his thumb at my bedroom door as if all the guys who were calling me a whore were packed into our living room like sardines, just on the other side of my bedroom wall.

"I don't care," I lie.

"No," he declares, as if his *no* changes things. "This isn't you, Edy," he says, waving his hand over me. "No, no." He repeats as if his *no* is the definitive end to all things about me that don't fit with his idea of who I'm supposed to be.

"Maybe it is," I tell him. He looks like he doesn't understand. "Me," I clarify. "How would you know? You've been gone."

Sidestepping that question, he just goes on to make more demands. "Look. You're absolutely not seeing him again—Miller. He's too old for you, I mean it, Edy. You're fourteen; he's eighteen. That's four years apart. Think about it, that would almost be like you and Kev—"

"Just stop, all right!" I can't possibly let him finish that sentence. "First of all, I'm fifteen now. And second, I'm not seeing him again anyway, but that's only because *I* don't want to." Lie. "But I'll see whoever I want and I'll do whatever I want with them and I don't need to ask your damn permission!"

"You know they're just using you, right?" he blurts out. "I mean, you can't be that blind to think that they actually—"

"No one is using me! You have no idea what you're talking about. No one's using me, Cae. No one."

"Edy, come on, of course they are. I'm only telling you this because I care, okay? They prey on girls like you. Edy, you have to—"

"Girls like me? Please, tell me, genius, what am I like?"

"Naive and innocent—stupid—that's what they look for, okay. They'll just chew you up and spit you out. You have no idea. They just throw you away when they're done with you. I should know, Edy, I've seen them do it a million times. Those guys, they don't care. Do you really think they give a shit about you? 'Cause they don't!"

"It wasn't like that. Josh wasn't like—" But I stop myself. "What makes you think I even want them to give a shit about me? What makes you think I'm not using them, huh?" Not that there had been anyone other than Josh yet, but that's completely beside my point right now.

He screws up his face like I'm trying to explain nuclear physics to him or something. "Using them for what?"

I turn his patented you're-the-stupidest-person-on-the-face-of-the-earth tone back on him: "Um, isn't it kind of obvious, Caelin?"

That shuts him up. He shakes his head slightly, as if he could erase the images from his mind, like an Etch A Sketch. "Look," he finally says, "I don't know what the hell is going on with you, but I do know that you're going to get yourself into trouble if you keep this up."

"Get out of my room now, please," I tell him, totally calm.

"Promise me, Edy, you're at least being safe. You have made them use—"

"Caelin, please, I'm not a complete moron."

"I'm just worried about you, Edy," he says in this oh-so-very-concerned tone.

His sincerity ignites a tiny fire in my rib cage. "Oh, now you're worried?" It spreads to my vital organs, engulfing my heart and lungs in thick black smoke. "Wow, well, isn't this just a great time to start worrying about me," I hear myself growl. "Thanks a lot, but that really doesn't do me any good now!"

"What the hell is that supposed to mean?"

But I've said too much. "Just worry about yourself." It takes everything I have within me to not add "asshole" to the end of every sentence I say to him. "Mind your own business." Asshole. "I can take care of myself, okay?" Asshole. "Leave. Go. Now!"

He throws his hands up and stands to leave. He turns around

at my door, looking so far away, and says firmly, definitively, "You know, I don't even recognize you anymore."

And then he's gone.

I shut the door behind him, lock, unlock, lock, and pull.

"HEY," A GUY'S VOICE whispers in my ear, "I hear you're real dirty."

I swing around to face him. I remember he was with Josh that day in the hall, Jock Guy, in this exact spot, in fact, when Josh gave me the note at my locker. But it wasn't just a him, it was a them—two guys. The other one I recognize too—a senior, not a jock, but still in with Josh's clique. He is more like page-sixteen Abercrombie catalog model; his are weight-room fitness-equipment muscles, not sports muscles.

It's the first day back from winter break. There isn't another person in the hall. It's late, after school. I stayed to help Miss Sullivan catalog a shipment of new books. "What did you just say?" I manage, thinking for sure I must've heard him wrong.

"I said you really like fucking, don't you?" Jock Guy answers, trying to touch my cheek. I back away, slam my locker shut, loop my arms through the straps of my backpack and start walking. DANGER DANGER DANGER: my skin getting hot and itchy again.

The other one—Pretty Boy—says, "Don't run away. We just have a question for you."

"Yeah, what?" I ask sharply, trying to seem brave, calm, and tough while moving myself down the hall, away from them, toward the front doors of the school, as fast as I can.

Pretty Boy answers, "Yeah. We wanted to know if you wanna be in our movie?"

Then Jock Guy chimes in, "It's just a little film we're doing and we hear you have a lot of experience in that, uh . . . genre. We figure you could have the leading role."

The human brain is a truly amazing organ because, despite all the nauseous thoughts electrifying my neurons at that moment, somewhere in the dark folds and recesses I was genuinely impressed that he used the word "genre" correctly.

"You'll be happy to know you have excellent references," Pretty Boy adds quickly before spitting his laughter all over me.

I walk faster, as the fear sinks in, as fast as I can without running, my feet getting heavier with every step. They follow behind, cackling and wheezing.

"Wait, is this you doing hard to get? Because word is that you're actually pretty easy." Jock Guy laughs, catching right up with me. Pretty Boy gets on the other side. "Come on," Jock Guy continues, "don't you wanna be a star? Get paid for what you do? You'd make a killing."

Where the hell is a janitor when you need one, damn it?

"No, we're just kidding, there's no movie. But you know," Pretty Boy says, putting his arm around my shoulder, his fingers coiling around a strand of my hair, his mouth close to my ear, "if you let me fuck you, I'll be real gentle, I promise."

And then they crack up.

All I can hear is Caelin's voice in my head: *They'll just chew you up and spit you out.* Girls like me. Girls like me, he said. And then Pretty Boy licks his lips like he might just devour me. Why am I not screaming? Why am I not screaming-running-fighting for my life? They wouldn't do anything, not in school, not in a public place. There could be people around, not any that I can see or hear, but there has to be someone somewhere, right? Right? My heart is about to explode—about to implode. I feel that bullet buried deep, dig in, piercing through some fresh warm meat inside of me. How could this possibly be happening?

"Stop, okay? Don't touch me!" I finally shout, trying to pry his fingers out of my hair. My voice echoes through the hall, mingling with the sound of their laughter.

"'Don't touch me,'" Pretty Boy mimics. "That's not what you said to Josh."

I break into a jog but only make a few strides before he's caught up with me again. "Get away from me!" I finally yell.

"Or what, you'll get your big bad brother to come and beat me up too?" Pretty Boy says. "I don't think so." He grabs my backpack and it stops me dead in my tracks.

"Dude. Come on," Jock Guy subtly reprimands.

All the feeling just drains out of my body, like slowly being novocained from head to toe, so much that I feel like I'm about to pass out. He spins me around, holding on to my arms so tightly, pulling me in so close, I'm afraid he might kiss me. I try to break out of his clutch, but I can't move an inch.

"Relax, she loves it," he tells him. "Don't you?"

"Come on, bro," he calls out, stepping closer. "We gotta go, come on! Let's get outta here, all right?"

Pretty Boy's evil grin fades and he allows some distance, and then hesitantly, he finally lets go. I stumble away from him, backing myself right up against the lockers, and I see something like remorse flicker in his eye, like a neurological twitch. I guess even a psychotic asshole can see I'm terrified.

"Come on, McSlutty"—he claps me on the shoulder—"we're just fucking with you," he says casually, glancing over at Jock Guy.

"Yeah, just fucking around," Jock Guy echoes, reassuring Pretty Boy, or himself maybe, but not me.

"Take a joke," Pretty Boy adds, instantly resuming his phony bravado, running a hand through his perfect hair.

"Leave me alone," I try to say as firmly as possible despite the fact that I'm shaking uncontrollably and my voice is scarcely above a whisper.

"You can't have your brother fight all your battles for you," Jock Guy says, smiling as he hitches my chin up with his knuckle. I want to spit in his face.

They shuffle down the hall, snickering and high-fiving their job well done.

I practically run all the way home. I slip on the ice at least a dozen times because I'm not being careful at all. My brain is like scrambled eggs. Josh wouldn't have told them to do that, I know he wouldn't have.

Caelin was still home on vacation from school, and I was going to get answers out of him if I had to hold a knife to his throat. He obviously did something to make things worse. I throw the front door open and he flinches, slouched on the couch, watching some ridiculous reality TV show.

"What the hell, Edy?" he whines.

"What did you do?" I demand, rushing toward him, not bothering to take my boots off, dragging dirty wet slush in on the carpet.

"Edy, take your fucking shoes off—you're ruining the rug!"

"What did you do?" I repeat, snatching the remote out of his hand. I almost throw it right at his face, but I stop myself at the last second and throw it on the floor instead. It cracks open and the batteries go flying out in opposite directions.

He's on his feet, just needing to show me how much bigger and stronger he is than me. As if I could ever forget. As if the entire world wasn't organized just to make sure I never forget, even for a second, that any boy, anywhere, even my brother, could take me. "What the hell is with you?" he finally shouts, looking down at me.

"What did you do?" I say, losing my voice to the tears.

"What are you talking about?"

"You don't even know what you did! You made everything worse! I told you to stay out of it and now everything's worse! Do you even realize what you've done? Do you even care? God, I hate you!" The tears stream down my face, my words fading to nothing as my voice strains to make him comprehend how much he's hurt me: "I hate you I hate you hate you so much I hate you hate you I fucking hate you . . . hate . . . you . . . hate . . . I . . . hate . . ." I see his mouth moving, but I can barely hear the words he's screaming back at me. I want to fight now. It's deafening, blinding. I want to fight so hard. To the death.

"Edy, stop it! Stop!" he keeps saying over and over. I realize that his hands are now around my wrists. And it's because I had been pounding my fists against his chest. "Would you just calmthefuckdown, sit, and tell me what the hell happened." He pulls me down onto the couch but doesn't let go of my arms. I look at his hands gripping on to me; his knuckles all red and swollen, the skin broken and raw. So he got in a fight with him, with Josh—that's what they meant.

"So, what, you beat him up?"

"Edy, you don't understand what happened—"

"No, you don't understand. You don't understand what happened!" I sob.

"Edy, I had to," he continues, ignoring every word out of my mouth, as usual.

"No, you didn't! Why couldn't you let me deal with it? It was over. Everything was fine and now—" But how could I admit what had just happened? Because if they had wanted to, they could've done anything. And I was not tough. I was weak. So fucking weak, like I always knew I was, like everyone always knew I was. It's too humiliating. "When did you even see him?" I ask instead.

"New Year's Eve. We were at this party, drinking, whatever, and then a bunch of the guys start talking shit—things that he told them, Eden—things I never wanted to hear about my little sister, by the way! And so then he shows up later and he's drinking and saying all this stupid, fucked-up shit. . . . We got into it, okay?"

"Got into it—let go of me—what is that supposed to mean? Let go of me!"

"No, I'm scared!" he roars back. "I'm scared of you! You're out of your mind. I'm not letting go."

"Let. Me. Go." I jerk my arms with each word.

"Don't. Don't. Hit me. Again. I'm so fucking serious, Edy,"

he says, his voice low, as he tightens his grip. We stare each other down, brimming with some kind of deep-seated rivalry that's about to drown us both, then he finally releases my wrists.

"What did they say he said, Caelin?" I take my coat off, wipe my eyes on the sleeve of my shirt.

He leans back, crossing his arms, sulking like a child. "I can't even repeat it."

"If it's that bad, then it didn't come from him. He's not like that—you don't know him! He doesn't even drink. He doesn't like being around drunk people. Was he even really there, or did you have to go find him?"

"Edy." He looks up at me and grins. "Come on, all he had to do was say one thing to these assholes. It came from him, no matter what he said to start it. And he was there. And completely fucking trashed, okay? God, you're so naive," he says with a laugh.

"You're the one who's naive! Did you actually think they would just let something like this go?" That piques his attention—the sudden realization that he's not all powerful, that he's not in control of everything anymore.

"Did somebody say something—did he actually have the balls to talk to you again?"

"No, not him—I didn't even see him at school today."

"Who, then?" he demands. "Who?"

"Why, do you want to make it ten million times worse? Maybe get me killed or something? You'd like that, wouldn't you? Then you wouldn't have to be so embarrassed of me."

"Edy, come on, don't say that." He tries to reach for me. "You know that's not—Edy . . . ," he calls.

But I'm already gone.

I slam my bedroom door as hard as I can.

I turn the lock, ninety degrees, and slink down to the floor.

And suddenly everything in my body goes quiet. Everything in my mind—quiet. Like I've exhausted every emotion, every reaction, every thought, and I have nothing left to offer, not to Caelin, not even to myself.

I hear him shouting on the other side of my door, pounding. "Edy. Edy? Eden!" Pounding, pounding, pounding. "Open this fucking door!" He rattles the doorknob, trying to get in. "Edy? Are you okay? Edy, damn it."

I say nothing. I do nothing. I feel nothing.

"Edy, please," he says quietly, almost sadly. "Please, Edy." I can hear him breathing on the other side of the door, breathing oddly, like, unevenly. But no, it's not just him breathing, I realize slowly. He's crying. And I kneel there on the other side of the door that might as well be the other side of the galaxy, feeling so empty, so dead inside. He tries the knob one more time and then I hear nothing. Until the front door closes, then the rumble of his car starts in the driveway.

Later, after I am a no-show at family-dinner theater, where we play the parts of a loving, functional family (sans little sister—no understudy), after Mom and Dad (reading for the roles of doting mother and father) go to bed, Caelin (wholesome, caring big brother) lures me out of my room with my favorite food in the entire world. Caelin McCrorey's famous pizza sandwich, which is exactly what it sounds like: a sandwich filled with pizza toppings—sauce, tons of cheese, pepperoni and mushrooms, and black and green olives—grilled in the sandwich maker to buttery golden perfection. Sinfully delicious and a time-tested, never-failed peace offering. I can't resist.

We stay up late like we did when we were kids, with the TV on low, mocking infomercials and horrible nineties music videos, genuinely entertained by ridiculously corny children's cartoons. And when I fall asleep on the couch, he covers me with the old, scratchy, dusty-smelling but incredibly warm blanket from the hall closet. It is a temporary truce, anyway.

I finally see Josh at school the next day. He looks pretty roughed up—purplish green under his right eye, left cheekbone scraped, a yellowish bruise fading from his jaw. He watches me intently as I walk toward him, like I'm speaking and he's trying really hard to listen to what I'm saying. I'm going to tell him that I didn't have anything to do with what my brother did to him. I want him to tell me he had nothing to do with what his friends did to me. I want to say sorry. I want to make up. I want, even, to tell him how much I've missed him and how much I want to be with him again, but really with him this time. I'm going to tell him all these things. I am.

But suddenly Jock Guy appears next to him, sneering at me. He cups his hand over his mouth and coughs "slut," nudging Josh in the ribs with his elbow. Grinning wide, he looks to Josh, then to me, then back to Josh. I stop walking. I wait for his reaction, like Jock Guy waits for it. Please don't laugh, please don't laugh, I silently beg.

I barely hear his voice carry through the jungle of noise, but I see him glaring at Jock Guy, see his mouth taking the shape of words: "Don't fucking do that, man—that's so stupid!" Jock Guy looks embarrassed, mad—mad at me. Mad as hell at me. He exits, stage left, a rabid dog with its tail between its legs.

Enter stage right, beautiful brunette in a miniskirt and tight sweater, inexplicably tan for the dead of winter; interlacing her French-tipped fingers with Josh's, standing on her tiptoes to kiss his cheek, her smile dripping with honey. I guess she's my replacement—an upgrade, clearly. She nuzzles her face into his arm like some kind of adoring pedigree kitten, but when her eyes meet mine, that sweet smile is all feral and fanged. It scares me more than slut coughs, almost as much as secret after-school ambushes.

Obviously, I have stumbled onto the wrong side of the invisible but ever-present velvet rope. Even Josh isn't immune to these cruel taxonomies. He opens his mouth like he's going to say something, call out to me, like he's been waiting to say something, just as I have. But then, remembering the order of things, he stops himself, looks down at the girl latched to his side. Things would have to stay unsaid. And so I put on my game face, my new face, my tough face, and just walk away.

PART THREE

Junior Year

"YOU REMEMBER THE PLAN, right?" Mara asks me as we pull into the gas station in her brand-new old car. Her dad gave her his beat-up brown Buick for her sixteenth birthday. It was the one he'd had since we were kids. But basically it was a guilt gift for being such a crappy father, for having a girlfriend, for canceling his weekends with Mara all the time.

"You really think this will work?" I check my lipstick in the rearview mirror just once more.

"I think so. I mean, if that sophomore can pull it off, we sure as hell can," she reminds me. We'd overheard this girl bragging on the first day of school about how she'd been scoring beer from some guy who works weeknights at this particular gas station—all you have to do is flirt a little, she'd said. "Just act natural," Mara whispers as we push through the door.

A bell dings over our heads. The air-conditioning blasts down on us and the fluorescent lights blare overhead. I meet eyes with the guy behind the counter. He grins, looking us both up and down, simultaneously, then down and up, from our heels, up our legs still tan from our summer spent in Mara's pool, to our skirts, to our too-tight shirts.

"Hey," Mara says in his direction, a little too casually. "Just a minute," she says to me, "I have to grab a couple of things." She walks toward the back of the store to the freezer section and casts a look at me over her shoulder.

I walk up to the counter, as planned. "Can I get twenty on pump four?" I ask him, sliding the bill across the counter. Mara said we need to make sure he knows we're driving, that way we'll seem older. "Can I also have a pack of menthol lights in the box, please?" I add, remembering to smile.

He looks at me closely, a knowing smirk, but reaches up over his head and pulls out a pack of cigarettes from a shelf I can't see. "Anything else?" he asks, tossing the box onto the counter in the space between us.

I look behind me as Mara makes her way up the aisle with a six-pack in each hand.

"It's all together," Mara tells him as she sets the beer on the counter. "Oh, and these too," she adds, picking up a packet of little foam tree air fresheners from the impulse-buy row of random merchandise littering the counter. She is still thinking the car is the key to all of this, and not our breasts and lips and bare legs. Still, he doesn't ask any questions. He just reserves the right to gawk at us without needing to hide it.

I can feel Mara holding her breath as we pay. I can feel her holding her breath as she slips the trees and the pack of cigarettes into her purse. Holding her breath as she hurriedly ushers us out of the store. We don't dare speak or even look at each other until we're back inside the car. "Oh. My. God. Edy." Mara says to me, barely moving her lips as she drives past the storefront windows and waves to the guy behind the counter, still watching us.

"Holy shit, I cannot believe we just pulled that off!" she says with a laugh as soon as she pulls out onto the road. "You were amazing!" she yells, wide eyed.

"So were you!"

"I was good, wasn't I?" Lavishly, she stretches her arm out the window. "This is going to be the best year, Edy!" she shouts, looking over at me with an enormous smile. She turns the radio up so loud, I can't even hear myself laughing.

"So where are we going again?" I yell.

"What?" she yells back.

"Where are we going?" I repeat, my voice straining.

"A surprise!" And then she turns down all the familiar roads we've been turning down our entire lives, past the churches and the fast-food chains and the car wash. And at the town-limit sign, just when I expect her to turn left, she keeps going straight. Every time we meet an intersection, I expect her to make a U-turn and go back. But she doesn't.

I lower the volume on the radio. "Okay, really, where are we going?" I ask her again.

"It's a surpri-i-ise," she sings.

"I'm positive there is nothing in this town that will be a surprise! It's literally a copy of ours, except it takes about eleven minutes to drive from one end to the other instead of ten." I laugh. "It's just as dull and boring as—"

"Not so fast, my little cynic," Mara interrupts, shaking her finger at me with a grin, as she turns the wheel again and again, steering us down short, dark streets. "Okay." She finally turns the radio off. "Look familiar?" she asks as she slows the car over the gravel parking lot.

"I can't believe it—I completely forgot about this place, Mara," I tell her, opening my car door before she's even come to a complete stop.

I once believed this was the most magical place on the planet. I walk closer. It's smaller now, it seems, than when we were kids, but still wonderful. The giant wooden playground is what we always called it, but it's so much more than that. It's a wooden castle the size of a Hollywood mansion, with towers and bridges and turrets and secret passageways. Elaborate swings in the shape of life-size horses with black rubber saddles.

"I knew you would love this." Mara trudges up behind me with the beer. "Okay, how many rules are we breaking right now?" she asks as we approach the park-rules sign. "It's past dusk so the park is officially closed—number one. No smoking—number two. We're bringing in alcohol, number five, while simultaneously breaking rule number seven—no glass containers. That's not too bad, actually." Mara laughs.

We take the wooden drawbridge across the sand moat, climbing to the upper level. We sit down on one of the bridges that connect the two highest towers of the castle. We rest our backs against the wooden slats that form the sides of the bridge, and I look up as our eyes adjust to the star-filled sky.

"Remember how we would beg our parents to bring us here when we were little?" Mara asks, opening a beer for each of us.

"Yeah, and they would always, always say it was too far away! I had no idea how close this place was. It took, what, like fifteen minutes to get here? I always imagined it was hours and hours away!"

"Another lie." Mara snorts, taking a swig of beer. "Just like Santa, the tooth fairy." Swig. "Marriage," she adds, staring into space. "Anyway." She segues. "Yeah. I had no clue this place still existed—my dad brought me here to practice driving in the parking lot."

"My parents still won't even talk about letting me get my learner's permit. So at least you have your license and a car—they get points for that, right?" I try.

"Whatever." She shrugs, lighting a cigarette.

I want to remind her of the fact that her parents were never happy. That they made each other miserable—and her, too. That it's been more than three years. And she needs to accept it. But I know these things are off limits, so I light a cigarette too, and look out over our little kingdom.

"You know, when we were kids I would climb up there"—I point with my bottle—"to the highest tower. Pretend I was some kind of princess. Trapped, waiting," I tell her, exhaling a cloud of smoke.

She turns and smiles. "Waiting for what?"

"I don't know. Life to begin? For something to happen!" I shout, hearing my voice echo.

"What are you talking about? We're still waiting for that!" she shouts back, into the night sky.

"Okay, well, maybe we're still waiting, but now we're doing it with a car!" I laugh, raising my beer in the air.

"And alcohol!" Mara shouts, as we clink our bottles together.

She falls forward with laughter, her beer sloshing out everywhere. And I laugh along with her, for no reason, louder than I think I've ever laughed in my life. Until it feels like my lungs might burst. Until it feels like freedom.

"Hey! Who's up there?" someone yells from down below. Footsteps crunch through the cedar chips that line the ground, getting closer.

"Shhh-shhh-shhh," Mara whispers, with her finger across her lips. "Cops?" she asks, turning toward me, her eyes wide with fear.

I press my face against the wooden slats and look down at two shadowy figures, one using his phone as a flashlight. Cops wouldn't do that. "Not cops—two guys," I whisper to Mara.

Mara slides up next to me and looks down at them. "Watch," she whispers. She places two fingertips in the corners of her mouth and lets out the loudest, most eardrum-piercing whistle. I remember the summer when her dad first taught her how to do that, she couldn't stop—for months, it was her response to any and every situation. Though I'm sure her dad didn't intend for her to get drunk and trespass and whistle like that at strange guys.

The one with the phone aims the light in our direction. "Who is that?" he shouts.

Mara stands up and leans over the railing, waving her beer in the air, "Up here!" she calls.

"Mara!" I shout, trying to pull her back down. She grabs my arm instead, and pulls me up to my feet.

"Hey, ladies!" the other one yells. "Want some company?"

"Come on up!" Mara yells back.

"What are you doing?" I laugh.

"Something is finally happening!" she says under her breath. "Let's just have fun, okay?"

I bring the bottle to my mouth and finish off half the beer in one gulp. "Okay," I answer, wiping my mouth with the back of my hand. We watch as they climb up the tower to meet us, whispering and laughing, just like we are. Something switches inside of me, in my head and my heart and my stomach—a lightness, a weightlessness takes over me—and I feel the corners of my mouth turn up. "Okay," I repeat.

Mara repositions her hand on her hip and adjusts her stance a few times, brushing her hair back with the other. As they approach I get a better look. They appear to be our age. Their faces seem soft—unthreatening.

"Hey," the first one says, pushing his too-long hair behind his ears. "I'm Alex. This is Troy," he tells us, pointing to the other. Troy raises his hand and says, "Hi."

"I'm Mara. And this is E—"

"Eden," I interrupt. No Edy with these guys.

"Awesome," Troy says, nodding his head with a ridiculous smile. They're both dressed like they just don't care. A sort of disheveled, grunge look. I kind of like it. Takes the pressure off, somehow.

Alex looks at us closely and asks, "You two don't go to Central, do you?"

"No," Mara offers. "How could you tell?"

"Because Central is full of total douche bags," the other guy, Troy, answers.

"Except for us, of course," Alex adds.

"So, what are you guys doing here?" I ask them, which happens to be the best conversation I'm capable of making.

"This is our spot," Troy answers. "What are you doing here?"

"Celebrating," Mara says. "My birthday."

"All right! Well, happy birthday," Alex offers. "It just so happens we have the perfect birthday present." He nudges Troy, who reaches into his back pocket and pulls out a small, flat, rectangular silver box. Mara raises her eyebrows at me. We lean in as he opens it, revealing a neat row of tightly rolled joints. "So, can we, uh, join in the party?" he laughs, gesturing to our stash of beer.

Mara smiles and sits down. Alex sits next to her. Then Troy and I sit opposite them. He smiles at me in this peaceful, silly way, and I think he must already be a little stoned. Mara passes around bottles for each of us. And Troy lights up. This sweet, pungent smoke spreads over me like a wave. He exhales and passes it to me. I hold it between my fingers for a moment, considering it.

"What, you don't smoke?" Troy asks, as if that would be the most absurd thing in the history of the world. Alex sets his phone in the middle of our circle and starts some music.

"I don't know," I mumble with a shrug. I look at Mara. *Are we really doing this?* I try to ask her without words.

"What she means is . . . birthday girl goes first. Right?" she says as she takes the joint from me.

I don't care if I'm not being cool; I don't want her to do it.

"Mara—" I start, but I'm too late. She closes her eyes as she inhales, then exhales a stream of smoke. She opens her eyes and looks at me with a smile and a nod. She passes it to Alex, who's staring at me.

He watches me as he inhales and then passes it to Troy.

"She's scared," Alex says, still holding on to the smoke in his lungs, grinning.

They all turn their heads toward me.

"I am not scared," I lie.

"I feel fine," Mara tells me. Then she turns to Alex, "I feel really, really fine." And they start laughing hysterically.

"It'll help you relax, that's all," Troy says softly, passing it over to me again. "Try it. Just go slow."

I place the paper between my lips and inhale.

"Okay," Troy instructs me, "now hold it. Just a second. Okay. Let go."

And I exhale. I pass it to Mara, who's still laughing. It goes around the circle, from one person to the next, in slow motion.

"How do you feel?" Troy asks.

"I don't know," I say, my words jumbled up together. Even I can hear the panic in my voice. "Dizzy, light-headed—"

"Please don't freak out!" Alex says like he's annoyed.

"You're not freaking out," Troy assures me. "Here, try again."

I have no idea why I do, but I do. Then Mara takes it from me.

"My heart is racing," I tell Troy, holding my hand over my chest.

"That's normal," he tells me, and he takes my hand and puts it over his heart instead. "See?"

"But your heart's not racing," I tell him.

"Neither is yours," he says, giggling.

"What?" I ask. "That doesn't even make sense," I tell him, feeling my mouth spread out into a smile.

"It doesn't?" he laughs. "I thought it did."

Suddenly this all feels like the funniest thing that's ever happened, so I start laughing too, until I can barely breathe.

I feel like one second I look and I see Mara and Alex laughing and the next I look and they're not there anymore. "Where did they go?" I ask Troy.

"Over there," he says slowly, pointing down. He's pushing her on the giant horse swing. They're laughing slowly.

"Mara?" I yell.

"Hi-ii-iii," she yells back, waving her arm over her head.

"This is so weird," I whisper.

"Yeah," he agrees with a smile, and he lies down, stretching out the length of the bridge.

The next thing I know, I'm opening my eyes, Mara shaking my shoulder. Alex standing behind her, their voices blending together, saying, "Wake up! Get up! Get up!"

"Dude, get up—Troy!" he shouts.

"Edy, it's three in the morning—we need to get out of here!"

"Oh, man," Troy mumbles, moving his arm from behind my neck.

I sit up slowly from this total stranger's arms. "What happened?"

"We all fell asleep," Mara answers. "Now we have to hurry the hell up and get home before we're on house arrest until we're twenty-one!" Mara shouts, pulling on my arm.

We hurry to gather all our things and race down the stairs and across the bridges, holding our shoes in our hands.

"OhmyGodohmyGodohmyGod," Mara mutters under her breath the entire way to the car.

"Bye!" the guys call after us.

"We are so fucked!" Mara yells once we get in the car.

"Okay, calm down. There's a perfectly good lie that can explain everything. Let's just think. You said you were staying at my house. I said I was staying at your house. Change of plans. We stayed at Megan's house instead."

"Who's Megan?" she cries as we peel out of the parking lot.

"It doesn't matter," I tell her, my mind thinking quickly. "We stayed up late and we were all having a good time until she started being mean and we got in an argument and left. That's why we're coming home in the middle of the night. See? Not fucked, okay?"

"You think that will work?" she asks frantically.

"Yes. Just stick to the story and act like it's the truth. Remember how good you were with the gas station guy?" I remind her.

"Uh-huh," she murmurs, looking like she might actually cry.

"Same thing. Except easier, because my parents will believe anything. Trust me," I assure her.

We make it to my house in only eleven minutes. Mara and I tiptoe through my front door and pause, listening for any signs that we might be caught. I silently lock the door behind us and we move to my bedroom as fast as we can. I press my hand gently against my bedroom door so it just clicks into place. I turn around to face Mara, who's standing in the middle of my bedroom with her hands palms up, her mouth hanging open.

"Did we just seriously pull this off?" she asks slowly, her mouth closing with a grin, grabbing both of my hands in hers.

"I think we did!" I whisper back.

"Holy shit!" Mara squeals, jumping up and down.

"Shh-shh," I mouth, silently laughing.

We change out of our weed-stenched clothes and into pajamas. I roll out my sleeping bag on the floor as Mara climbs into my bed. I lie down and take a deep breath.

"We are totally badass, you realize that, right?" Mara whispers.

I feel myself grin. "Good night."

"SO, EXPLAIN TO ME how you wound up here last night?" Dad says, standing over Mara at our kitchen table. It has only been a few hours since we crept in; Mara meets my eyes cautiously as she scoops up a spoonful of cereal and puts it in her mouth. This was about our fifth bowl of cereal each.

"I told Mom already," I lie. "Megan started with us, and we decided to leave. Now that Mara has a car." I smile at him.

"I never liked Megan, anyway," Mara adds. And we can't help it, we burst out laughing.

"Scary thought, you girls behind the wheel," he says, blowing on his coffee. He walks into the living room, shaking his head.

"See?" I tell her.

"Hurry up, Edy. There's something I wanna go do," Mara whispers.

Twenty minutes later we're sitting in Mara's car in the parking lot of a seedy strip mall I've never even seen before. There's a liquor store, a watch-repair shop, a hydroponics place, and a dollar store.

"Okay, you got me, Mara. What the hell are we doing here?"

"Look," she says, pointing to a detached building at the very back of the plaza. The sign says: SKIN DEEP: ALTERNATIVE BODY ART.

"Again, I ask, what are we doing here?"

"You kno-ow . . . ," she sings, unbuckling her seat belt.

"Are you still high?" I shout.

"It's my birthday!" she yells back.

"No, your birthday was Thursday. Remember, you got your car and we went out to eat. And then your birthday was Friday—I'll give you that one, okay? And we bought alcohol illegally. And then we got baked with two complete strangers from our rival school. But now it's Saturday. It's not your birthday anymore, Mara. And I am absolutely not letting you do anything you can't undo, if you're thinking what I'm thinking you're thinking!"

"Okay, Mom," she says with a laugh, getting out of the car.

I open my car door. "Wait!" I call after her. She turns around and grins, walking backward a few steps. I run to catch up with her. "Okay, just hold on. This seems like a super shady place, Mara."

"It's not shady! Cameron works here. It's fine," she says, shooing me with her hand as she walks ahead of me.

"Him again?" I moan. "Mara, please."

"Not him again. Him . . . still. Look, he's my friend, Edy. He's not a bad guy. I don't know why you hate him so much."

"He hates me too!" I try to defend myself.

"He does not!" she snaps, reaching for the door. "Edy, please just be nice to him. I want you with me for this, okay?"

"Okay, okay. Just tell me it's not going to be a tattoo."

She smiles. "Nose ring."

I smile back. "Fine. Let's go in." I even hold the door for Mara, just to show her how cool I am with this.

"Hey, you!" Cameron calls out from the back of the room, walking toward us with a smile. Toward Mara with a smile, anyway.

"I told you. As soon as I turned sixteen. I'm here."

"Wait, don't you actually have to be eighteen?" I ask.

"Sixteen with parent's consent," Cameron corrects.

"But you don't have parent's consent," I say to Mara.

Cameron rolls his eyes and looks at Mara like I must be the most tedious square on the planet.

"Well, we didn't have parent's consent last night, either," Mara says, laughing.

Cameron grins at her. "Do I even want to know?"

"You would definitely not approve, Cam," Mara tells him. "We were bad girls."

"Then don't tell me," he says, pretending to cover his ears. "I don't believe you could do anything bad." He looks at Mara so sweetly, like maybe he really is into her, finally. Then he looks to me: "Edy, on the other hand . . ."

I roll my eyes at him.

"Kidding, Edy." But I know he's not. "Okay, come on back," he says, leading the way down a hall to a little room. "Have a seat." He gestures to what looks like a dentist's chair. It's all very clinical and sterile. Smells like rubbing alcohol or iodine, or something. It leaves a bitter, chemical taste in my mouth.

"You're sure you want to do this, right?" I ask her as she climbs into the chair. "It is your face, you know?"

“Is it gonna hurt? Tell me the truth?” she asks Cameron, instead of answering me.

He dabs at her left nostril with a cotton swab and smiles as he looks down into her face. “I’m not gonna lie. It really will hurt. But only for, like, two seconds, and then it’s over, I promise.”

“Okay,” she whispers. Then she looks to me, taking my hand.

“Cameron, do you really, really know what you’re doing? Not being rude, I promise. Just—you can really do this, right?” I ask him.

“Yes, Edy. I do this every day. Really. It’s okay.”

“Cameron’s going to be a tattoo artist,” Mara says.

Yeah, sure he is, I want to say. “Fine, just be careful.”

“I will,” he says softly, gripping on to her nostril with this creepy-looking pair of silver tongs. “Your eyes are going to water, but it’s okay. That’s totally normal,” he tells her, placing a tissue in her hand. “Okay, Mara, turn your head toward me and close your eyes.”

I watch him bring the biggest needle I’ve ever seen in my entire life up to her tiny little nostril. I squeeze her hand harder than she squeezes mine.

“Okay, take a deep breath,” Cameron says. I do. “And exhale.” I close my eyes, and feel Mara’s whole body go tense. But she doesn’t make a sound. “That was it, now I’m just putting the ring in. Take another breath. Okay. And exhale. That’s it! That’s it, you did it!” He laughs.

I open my eyes. Mara has a little sparkly stud in her nose. Tears are streaming from her eyes, but she has the biggest smile on her face as she looks up at Cameron.

“That was it?” she asks him.

"Yeah, look. Here," he says, handing her a mirror.

"Oh my God!" she shouts, sitting up straight.

Then she looks to me, then back to the mirror, then back to me. "Do you like it?"

"I love it!" I tell her, and I mean it.

"This is the best day of my life!" she says, throwing her arms around Cameron's neck. He smiles as he leans in and hugs her back. Then she lets go and hugs me, too. Cameron and I smile at each other, truthfully, for the first time ever.

THE NEXT WEEK AT school we walk down the hall, Mara alongside me with her nose ring and freshly dyed cranberry hair. It seems like she's grown ten inches taller. Something radiates from inside of her. I don't know what, or how. But I wish some of whatever she's got would rub off on me.

After school on Thursday I wait for Mara at her locker so we can ride home together. But she's late. I pace up and down the hall, checking my phone. I'm not paying attention when suddenly I feel someone ram into my shoulder like a linebacker, spinning me around. I look up quickly. My mouth opens to apologize, but I stop short. Because it's Amanda glaring back at me.

"Watch it," she snarls, her eyes cutting through me.

I open my mouth again, searching for the words to put her in her place, but she's gone before I can think of anything. "Fuck you," I mouth at her back.

I go sit down on the floor by Mara's locker and watch as everyone filters out. Watch as the guys—jocks and geeks alike—watch me, wondering what the truth is, if I really am all the things they've heard. And the girls, they watch me too, like I'm contagious, not really caring about the truth.

I text Mara: where r u?

She writes back right away: on my way . . . 5 mins.

But just as I'm about to text her back I get another text. It's from a number I don't recognize: Eden, still wanna party tomorrow?

Who is this?

Really???

I stand up and pace the hall, looking into the classrooms, making sure no one's lurking around watching me, fucking with me.

Yes, really. Who is this?

Troy

How did you get my number?

You gave it to me! LOL

???

You told me to let you know about the party at my house tomorrow night. You don't remember??

I don't remember giving that guy my number. I don't remember anything about a party. I barely even remember that guy.

"Edy, sorry!" Mara calls from down the hall. "I was talking to Cameron after class."

"That's okay, come here. Look at this," I tell her, holding my phone out. "It's that guy, Troy, from the playground. Apparently I gave him my number. And apparently there's some kind of party tomorrow. I don't know, I don't remember any of this. Ringing any bells?"

Mara takes the phone from me and writes: Hmmm . . .

don't remember, LOL. But tell me about this party . . . ?

Cool. I'll text you the address. Make sure you bring your friend :)

OK

"There," she says, handing me my phone back with a grin. "I kissed that guy, Alex, you know."

"You tramp!" I gasp. "I have no idea what I did with the other one, I guess."

"You didn't do anything," she says with a laugh, smacking me in the arm. "I honestly think you two just passed out on each other," she says quietly, even though there's no one else in the hall. She would never say it, but I know it still weirds her out that I've had sex. Or maybe it's just knowing that people think I'm a total slut, that people talk about me like I'm a total slut. Especially when she's standing there next to me, not one.

"So, what's the deal with Cameron, exactly?" I ask her as we walk out to her car.

She throws her arms up in the air. "No fucking idea, Edy. I swear to God! He's driving me crazy. Sometimes I think he likes me just as a friend. Other times I feel like he's about to kiss me! I don't know, I don't know, I just don't know!" she yells.

"Yeah, it kind of seemed like he liked you—the way he was talking to you and looking at you at the piercing place. And how he's had to come and find you every single day just to ask how your nose is doing. But then he doesn't ask you out or anything?"

"Exactly!" she shouts, swinging her car door open. "Well, I'm done waiting for him. He's had almost two years to figure it out—two years!" she tells me, looking across the hood of the car at me, this fire in her eyes.

"Okay," I tell her carefully. "That's good, Mara. You don't have to wait for anyone."

"Exactly!" she says again, except this time with conviction as she slams her door shut.

"Are you okay to be driving?" I ask her, confused by this sudden anger.

"Oh, I'm more than okay—I'm great!" She laughs, shifting the car into drive.

I'm not sure if I should be laughing or concerned, so I just quietly say, "Okay."

"Maybe I want to go out with this Alex person. See what he thinks of that!" She looks at me when I don't respond. "Right?"

"Right. I guess. But—" I begin.

"But what?" she interrupts.

"But it just seems like those guys are, I don't know, probably fun to hang out with or whatever, but I mean, they're big-time stoners. Obviously not boyfriend material. For you." She looks at me like I'm crushing all her dreams. "Probably. I mean, I don't know them. Maybe not."

"But we'll go to the party, right?"

"Sure."

"Good."

She smiles and turns on the radio.

WE MAKE FIFTY WRONG turns getting to this house in the middle of nowhere. As we walk up the driveway the noise spills out. It's a huge house—at least three stories—with light shining from every window.

"So this is a real party, huh?" Mara asks, holding on to my arm as we walk up the front steps in our skirts and skimpy shirts.

"We'll find out."

We push through the open door and the smell of alcohol envelops us. We stand in what was formerly a living room but now looks to be a foundation for a landfill. The wood floors are covered in litter—potato chips, popcorn, pizza, glass bottles, plastic cups. Music, bodies, yelling, pushing. It's like the animals escaped from the zoo.

Mara and I look at each other, neither of us really knowing what we're supposed to do next. We had only been to the kind of parties at skating rinks and Chuck E. Cheese's.

"Text Troy, Edy. Let them know we're here," Mara tells me.

I take my phone out, but some guy shoves another guy into me, nearly knocking me over, and I drop my phone. "Watch it!" Mara yells after the guy, but I can barely even hear her over the blaring music.

"You all right?" Someone shouts from behind me, putting his hands on my shoulders. I turn around quickly, and this guy grabs each of my hands, holds my arms out to my sides, and looks me over. "You look good to me," this guy with a smooth voice and a dangerous smile says as he picks my phone up off the floor and hands it to me.

I turn to Mara, who's ogling this mystery guy. Obviously attractive, obviously older than us. He smiles as I turn back to him. A smile that seems to mean a lot. Mara comes closer and yells, "We're looking for Alex and Troy?"

This guy looks back and forth between Mara and me, confused. "Why would you be looking for them?" he says with a laugh, steering us farther into the house with one hand on my back and the other on Mara's shoulder.

"They invited us," Mara explains as we're herded through the living room and into a kitchen that's been turned into one huge bar, with a keg and an endless supply of bottled beer.

"They invited you?" he asks, coming to a halt, looking at us alternately, repeating himself with exactly the same intonation as the first time. "Wait. They invited you?"

"Yes," Mara tells him innocently. And he just starts laughing.

"All right," he says, shaking his head. "Gotta give 'em props for that!"

"Hey," he calls to another guy standing in the kitchen filling a plastic cup from the keg. "Hey, man, why don't you get some drinks for these two lovely ladies—friends of Troy and his tool bag, Alex!" And they both start laughing.

Mara looks at me like she doesn't get it. Clearly our Alex and Troy are not of the top tier here. Keg Guy hands both Mara and me a plastic cup full of beer, still laughing.

"They're not our friends," I correct, setting my cup down on the counter. "We don't even know them," I protest, but they're not listening.

I look at Keg Guy—he's older too. I look all around us. Everyone's older. This is not a high school party. Clearly, this is a college party.

"The only reason they're even here is because Troy's my little twerp brother. You'll find them out by the pool—they'll be the heads attached to the bong," he says with a laugh, pointing in the direction of the back door, dismissing us like we're just these silly little girls. "Go on, go get baked so you have something to talk about in home ec on Monday!"

Mara starts walking away, unfazed. I follow her through the sliding screen door, and sure enough, there they are in a cloud of smoke with a small crowd encircling them. Everyone laughing and talking slowly. They look up and Alex yells, "Hey, you made it! Awesome. Come join us." He slides over on the bench they're sitting on, making room for us. Now they suddenly don't seem so cool. I want to just turn around and leave.

"I forgot my drink," I tell Mara, but she's already left my side to go sit down with them, smiling and girly, already over our humiliation in the kitchen. I turn back to get my beer, the only thing that's going to make this bearable. That guy's still leaning against the counter next to his friend, his eyes following my every move as I walk back into the room. "Excuse me," I say, sharply. "My drink. You're standing in front of it." I have to step in close, reaching around him. But he snatches the cup and holds it up high over my head.

"First, tell me which one you're for? I gotta know," he says, waving the cup in the air.

I look up at the smirk on his face. The way he looks at me like I'm some kid he can tease. Which is the total opposite of the way he was looking at me in the doorway five minutes earlier, like he liked what he saw, before he knew I was connected to Troy. I cross my arms. "I'm not *for* anyone. And I'm not jumping for that, so you can just stop embarrassing yourself," I tell him, looking around like I'm embarrassed for him. I sound tougher than I've ever sounded in my life. In fact, I feel tougher than I've ever felt in my life—invincible.

"We got a live one!" Keg Guy whistles.

"I didn't know," he says, his face changing from amused to intrigued. "Sorry." He finally hands me the cup. His eyes narrowing on me, he asks, "You go to school with my brother?"

"No. We just met. He told us about this party. Thought we'd check it out. Not impressed," I add, looking around like I'm completely uninterested in anything that's going on here.

"How old are you—the truth?" He grins.

"Jailbait!" Keg Guy coughs under his breath, smacking him on the shoulder before he runs off, leaving us alone in the kitchen.

"The truth," he repeats.

The truth. I take a big sip from the cup. His words echo in my head. Truth. What is that, anyway? No such thing.

"What's your problem?" I ask, sure to sound positively bored out of my skull. "I'm eighteen." Except that is a total lie. Not the truth at all. "Calm down."

"All right, all right," he says. "Just bustin' your chops." And then he smiles his smile from the doorway. "So, not impressed, huh?" he asks.

"Not particularly." I shrug.

"Don't you wanna join your friend out there?" he gestures beyond the sliding door to the patio, where Mara sits between Alex and Troy, her head thrown back in laughter.

"That's not really my thing," I tell him.

"Oh, really? Well, what is your thing?" he asks, looping his arm around my waist, pulling me closer to him.

I feel my heart race, and the corners of my mouth turn upward, somehow, as I look at him. "I don't know," I answer. And that is the truth.

"Well, how 'bout a tour of the house?" he asks. "What kind of host would I be?"

"Okay," I agree. I look at Mara once more before I follow him out of the kitchen. She's having a great time. She's fine. He leads me up the staircase to the second floor.

"Maybe we can find something a little more exciting for you?" he says, looking over his shoulder at me.

"Maybe," I reply, not sure who is doing my talking right now. He grabs my hand when we reach the landing, and takes me down to the end of the hall, past people in rooms smoking and drinking, laughing and kissing. Then we go up another flight of stairs. My legs feel like they're jelly by the time we reach the top. There's a short hall with only two doors on either side, both closed. There's no one on this floor.

"It's quiet up here," I say, feeling my confidence slowly beginning to drain as I realize just how far away I am from everyone, just how far this has already gone.

"Exactly. This is only for special guests," he says, taking a key ring out of his pocket as he approaches the door.

"Special guests, huh?" I repeat, standing close behind him.

He turns around and puts his hands on my waist, and suddenly I'm up against the door, and he's kissing me fast and moving his hands all over me. I feel this rush of energy flow from my toes up to the top of my head and out through my fingers, the confidence flooding back through me. And now I kiss him the same way he kisses me. Move my hands over him the way he does to me. Careless, hard, dangerous. He fumbles to get the door unlocked. We tumble inside the darkened room. I barely have a chance to even look around to see where we are, because it's all happening so fast. There's a bed, a dresser, a mirror. That's all I can make out before he slams the door behind us and locks it, turning back to me before I'm even able to take a breath.

We're in the bed. The weight of his whole body on top of me. Cold metal belt buckle pressing against my stomach. Hands pushing my skirt up. Underwear peeling down my legs. Belt buckle comes undone, scraping against my skin. The sound of a zipper. Heavy breathing.

It's over before I even fully believe it's happening. Before I've even fully decided I'm going to do it. And I lie here staring up at the ceiling fan, this guy panting next to me. I don't even know his name. He doesn't know mine. We stay like this for what feels like a long time, but I can't be sure how much time actually passes.

He finally lets out a sigh, and sits up slowly. Smoothing out his shirt and buttoning his pants, he looks over at me like he's forgotten I'm here. "Thanks," he says quietly. "This was fun."

"Yeah," I whisper, slipping my underwear back on.

We don't speak as we make our way back downstairs to rejoin the party. And I realize I feel a little strange, like, out of my body in a way I've never been before. In a way that feels so much better than drinking too much, or even that night at the playground when we got high. Better than any feeling I've ever had. Empty and full, all at the same time.

I somehow find my way to Mara, still sitting outside, laughing just like she was when I left. It's like I was never gone, like time just stood still. They call me over, my name echoing through the thick air. I shake my head and walk to the edge of the crystal blue pool instead. Sitting down slowly, I take my shoes off and dip my feet into the cool water. I swirl my legs in figure eights over and over again as I look up at the stars, the warm breeze floating through me. I don't know who I am right now. But I know who I'm not. And I like that.

IT BECOMES DIFFICULT TO avoid someone while simultaneously using them. That's Troy. I know he's had a crush on me these past three months. And I've been trying not to lead him on. Not too much, anyway. Still, he tells us about every party that's happening in a thirty-mile radius. And I don't tell him about how I had sex with his older brother back in September.

Not that I enjoy the parties all that much. But I enjoy losing myself. And there's always someone there. Ready, waiting. Waiting for something to happen. Just like me. I've gotten good at picking them out right away. Finding that someone. Not a bad person. Someone who just wants what I want. To disconnect. For a little while, anyway. From themselves, mostly. I think. I wouldn't really know, though, because it's not like we ever talk about these things. It's not like I really care, anyway.

That's what I'm thinking about, lying on this lumpy futon next to some guy. The bedroom window is open, and the winter air flows in easily, cooling my whole body. I can almost see my breath.

"You're that girl," he tells me, propping himself on his elbow as he lights up a joint. "I didn't even realize it when we first started talking."

I turn to face him, and see that he's looking down at me with a grin.

"What girl?" I ask.

"Let's just say people know who you are at our school," he tells me as he exhales a cloud of smoke. "People talk about you," he says, his words slowing down. "A lot." He offers me a hit, but I shake my head. I haven't smoked pot since the playground with Troy. It turns out getting high really isn't my thing. This is my thing.

The smoke begins to fill the room, making me feel dizzy. I close my eyes, and try to sink down into this moment a little deeper—into my body, my mind—so deep I can come out the other side and forget how I even got here. I can hear the muted shouting and music on the other side of the door. But it can't touch me in here, somehow.

"You know," the guy says, reaching over to brush my hair back away from my face, his voice pulling me away from this feeling. I open my eyes and try to focus on him. "I can't tell if you're really pretty," he continues so sincerely, a soft smile on his face, "or really ugly."

It's like when you're falling in a dream and you wake up, shocked back into reality by your body hitting the bed with a crash. That's what his stupid, clumsy words do to me.

And in that instant an image forms in my mind, quick and fleeting.

Josh. I see his smile. Feel his sweetness. His arms around me. For just a moment—just a flash. It disappears almost immediately.

As soon as my consciousness kicks in, he's gone. But he was there just long enough and just clear enough to jolt me, to shock my system with a surge of fresh heartache. It leaves me with this sick underwater sensation, something dangerously close to drowning. Josh would never, ever say anything like that to me, not even after the way I treated him.

I sit up fast. I find my shirt and my pants. I get dressed. This guy lies there, watching me, smiling at me.

"Where you going?" he asks, taking too long to realize what I'm doing.

"Where do you think?"

"I don't know," he says slowly.

"Look, I realize you're stoned, but you don't say fucked-up things like that to a girl you just had sex with!"

"What did I say? I said you're really pretty, didn't I?"

"No, actually that's not what you said!" Leaving in a hurry was easier in the warmer months. Now I have layers to keep track of—I pull on my boot laces with force as I tie them in a double knot.

"Oh." He laughs.

I look at him before I leave. He's just lying there shirtless, grinning, and oblivious. "You know, I can't tell if you're really mean or really stupid!"

He cracks up at that. "You're so funny," he's saying as I'm closing the door on him, stepping out into the noise again.

Fuck off.

There are too many damn people crammed into this house. As I squeeze through the bodies, people look at me and I wonder if they all know me as *that girl* too. I find Mara in the basement.

She's sitting between Troy and Alex on a dusty old couch. Mara's talking. Alex isn't listening. She acts like she likes him when we're at these parties—lets him put his arm around her shoulder, and she'll touch his leg with her foot, kiss him good-bye before we leave—but I think she's just using him too. The only time she even mentions his name is when she's around Cameron. Still, after all these months of partying, they've only kissed.

"Hey," I call to Mara, barely able to find an empty place to stand. "I'm going outside," I shout, pointing toward the door.

"Wait," she says, peeling Alex's arm off her shoulder, "wait, I'm coming with you."

We push our way against the wall of bodies, weaving through the cases of beer stacked up on the floor of the kitchen like a maze. As I open the front door and step out into the cold, a welcome silence rushes over us, and I feel like I can breathe again.

"What's wrong?" Mara asks.

"Nothing."

She eyes me closely. "No, there's something."

"It's nothing. I was just hanging out with this idiot—he said something kind of mean to me. It's okay, though. I mean, whatever. I'm fine. I don't care." I shrug, taking in a deep breath of icy air, allowing it to fill me before I release it.

"What did he say?"

"It doesn't matter," I tell her, looking up at the sky.

"Let's go," she says.

"Really? You don't want to stay? What about Alex?"

"It doesn't matter," she says with a laugh. "I don't think he'll even notice, honestly."

We drive to this twenty-four-hour Denny's that's right in between our town and Troy and Alex's. It's only ten thirty. I order a big breakfast and Mara gets an enormous banana split.

"Tell me what that guy said to you?" Mara asks me again as she picks the cherry off the top of a swirl of whipped cream. "I really wanna know."

"Fine. It's kind of funny, actually. He said he couldn't tell whether I was really pretty or really ugly," I finally admit.

"You've gotta be fucking kidding me, right?" Her face is caught between a smile and a frown.

"No. Those were his exact words, Mara."

"That's heinous!"

"Yeah." I laugh. "But what's worse is the way he said it—so sweetly—like it was a compliment or something! Not exactly the kind of thing you want a guy telling you right after you sleep with him."

"No, I guess it's not," Mara agrees, her laughter fading. "Do you—do you do that a lot, Edy?" she asks me awkwardly, looking down at her banana split, like she's counting the scoops of ice cream over and over: vanilla, strawberry, chocolate, vanilla, strawberry, chocolate, vanilla, strawberry. "I mean, with guys you don't know?" she finishes.

"Sometimes." I shrug. "I mean, it depends, I guess."

"Do you think—I don't know, do you think that's such a good idea? I mean, that's kind of dangerous, isn't it?"

I bite into a warm buttered toast triangle. I don't know how to have this conversation with Mara. I don't know how to explain it. "Is it any more dangerous than getting wasted with a bunch of strangers?"

Her mouth drops open slightly. She's obviously insulted that I would even attempt to compare the two.

"I'm not saying there's anything wrong with that—you know I've done that too—I'm just saying it's kind of the same thing, don't you think?"

"No, I don't think it's the same thing at all," she says, sinking her spoon down into the softening mound of strawberry ice cream. "Isn't sex," she whispers, "supposed to be special? You know, with someone special?"

"Says who? A lot of things are supposed to be special that really aren't."

"I guess, Edy," she says, not convinced.

"Besides," I continue, "it's not like there are all that many special people just hanging around anyway."

"Still, I feel like I should tell you I'm concerned or something, tell you to stop doing that."

"I know what I'm doing." I reach across the table and steal a spoonful of her chocolate ice cream. "No cause for concern, I promise. It's honestly not a big deal. Really."

She shakes her head and shrugs, returning her attention to her banana split. "Do you think Alex and Troy are ever not high?" she asks, trying to change the subject.

"Not that I've ever seen," I say with a laugh.

"They're nice though, at least," she points out.

I nod. I take another spoonful of ice cream. "I did something kind of not nice to Troy, Mara."

"Oh no, did you have—you know—with him?" she asks. "When?"

"No, not with him. I kind of slept with his older brother," I confess. "At that party way back, at his house—it was really his brother's party. I've been feeling guiltier and guiltier about it every time we see him."

"Why did you do that?" she asks.

"Well, I didn't plan on it, or anything. It didn't mean anything. I never even spoke to him again after that. What—why are you looking at me like that?" I ask her, her face more horrified with every word I say.

"Sorry. I'm not judging. I'm just surprised—I just didn't know that had happened. That's all."

"Well, it did happen. But it didn't mean anything. I don't even know why I'm telling you, actually."

"No, I want you to tell me. I don't want you keeping all these secrets from me."

"I don't keep secrets from you," I lie.

"Okay." She pushes the banana split across the table. "You have to help me finish this—it's melting."

"IT'S BEGINNING TO LOOK a lot like hmm-hmm," Mom half sings as she stands on top of one of the dining room chairs holding a string of tinselly green garland. "Edy, hand me that thumbtack," she calls over to me as I fidget in my seat, gnawing on my fingernails, counting down the minutes until Caelin gets here. I take my phone out of my pocket. Nothing. No calls, no texts, no distractions.

I'm desperate.

I text Troy: can we meet up in a while? need a little help *relaxing*

"Edy!" my mom calls again. "Bring me one of those."

"Oh, right. Sorry. Here," I say, holding out a palm full of metal tacks.

"Thanks." She smiles, catching my eye. "You know, it's nice to have you around for a change. We never see you since Mara started driving. You girls always have something to do, somewhere to be." She sighs.

My phone vibrates in my pocket. Troy: no prob. for u . . . anytime

"That reminds me," I tell her, thinking fast. "I know Caelin's coming home tonight, but I have to go do some last-minute shopping at the mall. Mara's picking me up," I lie.

"Edy!" she says, pursing her lips, hand on hip. "You have to plan better than this."

"I know, I just forgot a couple of things." I text back: thx. 6:00 @ playground?

"Well, you'll be hard pressed to find anything decent two days before Christmas." She *tsk-tsk-tsks* her tongue at me, shaking her head. "Why don't I just take you now before Caelin gets here?"

Troy: can't wait :)

"Mom, you hate the mall. Besides, Mara needs to go too. And you're in the middle of"—I look around at the mountains of decorations and fuzzy snow—"you know, all this," I finish.

"Fine." She relents. "But let's take it easy for the next couple of weeks, huh? Your brother doesn't get to make it back here as often as we'd like—as often as he'd like—we need to all make an effort to spend some quality time, okay?"

"Why are you telling *me* this? He's the one who's going to be spending all his time with Kevin."

"Well, Kevin won't be joining us this year, so you don't have to worry about that."

I shove my phone deep into my pocket. "What do you mean? Did hell freeze over?"

"Edy, stop." She rolls her eyes. "I don't know. Caelin just said Kevin would be staying there, at the Armstrongs'. That's all I know," she says, throwing her hands up.

"That's good," I tell her.

"Well, it's not good. But, I suppose, it's normal. I mean, they are technically his family," she says.

"That's what I've been saying forever."

"Well," she begins. But that's it. Just "well."

I consider texting Troy back and telling him to forget it. But then I feel this tightness creeping up inside my chest at the thought of seeing Caelin, even without his other half.

I text Troy again: how's 5:30?

Mara gave me her extra car key in case of emergencies while she and her mom are at her grandmother's house for the week. Her mom would flip out if she knew. My parents would flip out if they knew. Mostly because I only just got my learner's permit and I'm not supposed to be driving any car. But this is the most legal thing I'm planning on doing tonight, so I really don't care.

Troy's already there when I pull in the parking lot. "Hey," I yell to him as I'm getting out of Mara's car. "Have you been waiting long?"

"Naw," he says quietly, batting at the air. "No big."

I walk up to him. He looks different to me, standing here with the sun going down, still daylight barely. I've never seen him in the sunlight. But even the way he stands, the way he looks at me, everything feels different, somehow.

"What's wrong?" I ask, standing in front of him. I never realized we were the same height. Although, I don't actually think we've ever stood face-to-face like this before. He's always sitting down, on a couch, a floor, somewhere, slouched, smoking.

"What? Nothing's wrong," he tells me, shrugging as he tucks his hair behind his ears. A terrible thought crashes into my mind:

He found out, someone told him about me and his brother.

"Why do you seem like that, then?" I ask.

"Like what?" he asks, looking around, confused.

"Like—not normal. Are you mad at me for anything?" I pry.

"No, of course not," he says, grinning slowly. "Been smoking already? You're paranoid, girl," he says with a laugh. And even that sounds different.

"No, you just seem like something's . . . different?" I tell him.

"Well, I'm straight—that's probably why I don't seem normal!" He laughs again. "This is not my natural state! I was waiting for you."

"Oh." I hadn't even thought of that. I hadn't even considered he could exist while not under the influence. "Oh." I laugh. "Okay. That makes sense."

"You do need help relaxing, don't you?" He smiles. Then he reaches forward and places one hand on each of my shoulders, kneading the muscles up to my neck, gazing at my face with a concentration I've never seen in him before. He steps in. I back away. I can't let him kiss me. Not right now. I look down. Then back up. He looks down too, embarrassed.

"Let's get in the car," he says, rubbing his hands together. "It's freezing out here."

"Thanks for meeting me," I tell him as I turn the heat on.

"Course." He shrugs, placing one of his expertly rolled joints between his lips. He lights it, then inhales. "What's got you all tense there?" he asks, looking at me sideways, still holding the smoke in his lungs as he passes the joint to me.

I inhale shallowly, still a little bit afraid of what might happen. And exhale. "Family."

"Hear that." He sighs. He turns the radio on, adjusting the volume perfectly.

We pass the joint back and forth several times, not speaking. He reclines the passenger seat so he's almost lying down. He stares out through the windshield at the sun setting behind the wooden castle. I follow his gaze and watch as the colors bleed and mingle like something out of a dream. This is not the black-and-white world I once thought I was in. This world is alive and vibrating. And I'm alive in it—and that feels amazing.

He nudges my arm. I look down. He's passing me the joint. And I hear his words, their pace slow, as I inhale and pass it back to him. "Do you always look like that?" he's asking.

"Like what?" my voice echoes on some kind of delay. He takes one last deep drag, letting it nearly burn down to his fingers before he throws it out the window.

"Pretty like that," he says, looking up at me, his eyes wanting to close.

I feel my mouth smile at him. Then I lean over slowly, everything moving slowly, and kiss him. His hands gently touch my face, in a way that makes me think too much of Josh. It seems like we kiss and kiss, forever. He does it softly, slow like honey, nothing like that brother of his. He whispers, "I hope I can remember this," and then we both start laughing and laughing.

The next thing I know, a soft dim light wants my eyes to open. The next thing I know, I feel movement all around me. And someone takes my shoes off. Someone pulls my arms out of my coat. Footsteps surround me. I open my eyes. I'm looking up at my bedroom ceiling;

my desk lamp casts a warm golden glow over everything.

My eyes close again. Then I see a flash of me parking Mara's car in her driveway. Me trudging through the snow in the dark. Me putting my key in the door. The TV in the living room flashing.

They open again. Caelin stands over me.

"Caelin?" I hear myself mumble.

"You're fine," he tells me. "You reek of weed, Edy," he whispers, his hands firmly planted on his hips.

"Why am I in my bed?" I ask him, pushing the blankets off. "I don't wanna be in my bed."

"Shhh," he says, jerking the covers back up. "I don't even want to know how you got home or where you were or who you were with or what the fuck you were doing!" he whisper-shouts over me.

"Stop," I tell him, covering my ears. At least, I think I say the word.

"You walked in the door and passed out, Edy! Mom and Dad don't know. They're in bed already."

"Go away," I moan.

"Sleep it off."

Then dark.

"HEY, MARA," CAMERON SAYS, walking up to our table in the library. He glances at me as he sits down. I have my headphones in, so he doesn't bother speaking to me. I nod at him, though, and turn the volume down all the way so I can listen in on their muffled whispers. I absently thumb the pages of an enormous SAT study guide that Miss Sullivan brought over when she saw that I was reading a magazine instead of studying. Ever since we got back from winter break, it's been SAT fever around here. Suddenly everyone's deadly serious and slamming energy drinks and overthinking the importance of their entire lives.

"Hey!" she responds, smiling with her entire body.

"What are you doing? Studying?" he asks.

"Trying to, anyway." She sighs, her head falling into her hands. "This is evil!" She lets the pages of the book fan over, losing her spot.

"Well, why don't we study together?" he asks. "What are you doing tomorrow night? Steve's coming over, we're just gonna be studying. You should come over too. It'll be like a study group. Moral support, you know?" He laughs. "She can even come if she wants," he adds, gesturing to me. I turn another page.

"Oh, thanks for offering. But I have plans tomorrow night. We both do. Or probably, anyway. I'm going to a party with this guy Alex I'm seeing, so . . ." She makes a point of referring to him as "this guy Alex I'm seeing" whenever she talks about him to Cameron. And he cringes more noticeably with every mention of his name. She knows exactly what she's doing, just like I know what I'm doing. Most of the time, anyway.

I glance up. Cameron's just gazing into Mara's eyes, not saying anything.

"What?" she asks innocently.

"Let me know when you get sick of that." He lays his hand on her shoulder for just a moment as he stands. And then he walks away. Mara turns around in her seat and watches him leave.

I take my headphones off just as she turns back to face me, her eyes wide. "Oh my God," she whispers, reaching across the table to grab both my arms. "What just happened? Did you get all that?"

"Yeah, I did."

"What am I supposed to do? Should I follow him? Is he mad at me?" she asks, talking fast. "Should I go after him?"

"No, you're not supposed to follow him. And he's not mad. He's jealous." I smile. "Congratulations."

"What do you mean?" she asks, her face blank.

"Come on, wasn't this the whole point of Alex?" I close the book—this conversation is definitely going to take up the rest of the period, if not the rest of our lives. "To make Cameron jealous?"

"No. No, not really. I mean, not entirely, anyway." But as the thought sinks in deeper, a slow smile forms across her face. "This is good, isn't it?" she asks.

"Well, considering you've been in love with him for the past three years, and now he's finally here—yeah, I would say this is good." I laugh.

"He's finally here," she repeats in awe.

I never would've thought I'd be spending a Friday night at Cameron's house—in Cameron's family room—with Cameron's mother and father and shih tzu roaming in and out, bringing us snacks and drinks. I never would've thought Cameron, with his piercings and hidden tattoos that Mara swears are there, his punk-goth style, and his infamous blue hair, was the product of a *Brady Bunch* household.

We sit cross-legged on top of these giant pillows his mother insisted upon, Cameron and I opposite each other across a big round, shiny wooden coffee table. Mara excuses herself to go to the bathroom, probably to reapply her lip gloss for the hundredth time. I look around—everything decorated in the most traditional way imaginable. A painting of a boat sailing peacefully under a bridge hangs above the couch, delicate neutral colors adorn every surface, a vase of soft yellow tulips sits perfectly centered on top of a tiny table that could serve no other purpose than to hold a vase full of soft yellow tulips.

"What's her name?" I ask Cameron as his little dog nuzzles her face into my hand.

"Jenny."

"Why Jenny?" I raise my eyebrows at him, amused he would choose such a sensible name, and for such a sensible dog—but mostly just amused at his super-sensible life.

"I don't know," he mumbles. "I guess because when I was eight—that's when we got her—I had a crush on a girl named Jenny. It was the best name I could think of." He shrugs.

"And now you have a crush on a girl named Mara?"

"Yeah, I guess I do," he says quietly. "Look, pretend I'm someone else for second, okay?" he whispers, leaning over the coffee table toward me, keeping one eye on the door. "You're her best friend. What do you think my odds are? I mean, this Alex guy—he sounds like a total loser."

"I don't know what your odds are," I lie. "Mara's a pretty special person—you know that, right?"

The doorbell rings. His mother yells, "I'll get it," from the next room.

"Yeah, of course I know that," he whispers.

"Good. Well, then, I'd say you have a shot. I mean, she's here, isn't she?"

"Okay. Thanks, Edy," he tells me, very seriously.

Just then a guy appears in the doorway.

"Steve's here," Cameron's mother calls.

Cameron instantly breaks eye contact with me as he hops up from the floor. "Hey, man!" He does that guy-handshake thing where he holds his hand out, but just cups his fingers enough to slightly grasp Steve's hand, moving in to hug him briefly with his other arm. "Come in, sit down, get comfortable." Then to me, "Edy, you know Steve."

"Eden," I correct. "Hi."

"Hey," Steve says slowly, staring at me. "Wow, I—I didn't know you'd be here," he says, looking from me to Cameron.

"Yeah, I texted you," Cameron tells him. "Mara's here too. She just went to the bathroom."

Steve sits down on the floor between me and Cameron—the only free spot left. "I guess I didn't see your text," he says under his breath.

I look at Cameron. Then back to Steve. Something's going on. Steve is clearly not happy I'm here. I look at him closely. He almost doesn't even look familiar anymore. He's changed so much, I almost question if he really is Stephen Reinheiser, aka Fat Kid. I look at him again. No, not fat, not gawky, not awkward. Not Stephen. Maybe some alternate universe Stephen. Steve Stephen. He doesn't look anything like that kid who always took my side in book club arguments. Not the same shy, dorky, four-eyed kid who once sat at my kitchen table with me, trashing Columbus. He could almost be sort of cute now. He's gotten taller. Not thin, but a good solid, medium build. He's actually fit. Reasonably confident. But he kind of has that look about him—like a sad, waiting-for-something-to-happen kind of look. If I didn't know any better, he could almost be someone I would hook up with at a party.

Cameron sucks in a deep breath of air and holds on to it, swinging his arms in front of him, nervously catching his right fist in his left hand over and over. I pick up a Triscuit from the cheese-and-cracker plate his mother brought us. No one says a word. It's just the sound of Jenny panting faintly in my lap and the cracker crunching between my teeth. Thankfully, Mara comes back right then, her lips perfectly pink and shiny.

"What did I miss?" she asks, smiling happily at all of us, touching Cameron's back as she walks behind him to take her spot on the floor between us, opposite Steve.

"Well, Steve's here," Cameron says, finally exhaling.

"I see that! Hey, Steve," she tells him.

"And you're here too," he says with a playful, friendly smile, like he's relieved to see her. Suddenly I feel like a total outsider.

"Cameron," his mother says, standing in the doorway clipping on an earring. "Your father and I are heading out—we have those tickets for tonight, remember?"

"Yeah, okay, Mom," he answers.

"Call if you need anything. We'll be home early," she says, and I swear she looks at me when she says it, like maybe she knows, like everyone across at least two school districts knows, I'm *that girl*.

"Bye," he tells her, Steve chiming in.

"Have fun," Mara calls to them.

I hear the front door close and lock. I exhale too loudly. They all look at me. "Any chance there's anything to drink around here?"

Cameron pushes a can of ginger ale toward me.

I look at Mara—*You've gotta be kidding me, right?*

"Edy, come on," she giggles, "we really do have to study here."

"In that case, I'm gonna need a cigarette, at least," I tell them, standing up.

"You have to go outside," Cameron tells me quickly.

"I was going to, don't worry." I roll my eyes at him as I put my coat on.

The backyard is so impeccably landscaped and orderly, I'm afraid to move my feet because I'll make too many shoe prints in their flawless white snow. I light my cigarette and try to make it last as long as possible. I never did ask Mara what she said to Alex about us not showing up tonight. I don't mind too much anyway. I don't really want to see Troy again. Especially not after our altered-state sweet and slow make-out session in Mara's car. Especially because I still can't really put all the pieces back together to figure out how that night ended. I close my eyes and try once again, but it doesn't happen. What I see instead is Caelin, the next day, standing over me in my bedroom, grilling me. His angry voice still echoing through me: ". . . fucked up, Eden . . . not okay . . . not cool . . . are you listening . . . you could get seriously hurt . . . in serious trouble . . . why are you laughing . . . this is not funny . . . are you listening to me—"

"Eden?"

I turn my head. My cigarette has burned all the way down, the ashes still holding its shape. Steve is standing there. "What?" I answer.

"Um, hey. I brought you your phone; it keeps going off, so . . ." He stops midsentence, extending his arm all the way to hand me my phone, keeping us an arm's length apart.

"Thanks." I take the phone from him. Then he stands there and puts his hands in his pockets. I light another cigarette. A series of texts from Troy are still visible on the screen in reverse order:

are you mad at me?

I want to see you. . . .

hey, pretty girl, it's been a while. are you coming tonight?

I look over at Steve, looking down at his sneakers. He obviously saw the texts. I put my phone in my pocket without responding. "Want one?" I ask him, holding the pack of cigarettes toward him.

"No," he says, holding up his hand, "but thanks, I guess." He tries to smile. I can't quite tell what he's all about these days. He wears some kind of comic-book-superhero-type T-shirt over a long-sleeved thermal. His hair is just slightly unkempt, but his eyes are bright and clear and focused, not at all like Troy's, or any of the guys I've been around recently.

"Do you not like me or something?" I finally ask.

"No. I thought it was the other way around?" He looks me straight in the eye; he's bolder than I remember.

"Why would I not like you?" I ask, instead of answering him.

"I have no idea," he says, crossing his arms. "Why do you not like me?"

"I never said that," I tell him. "I don't not like you."

He nods his head and looks up at the sky. He opens his mouth to say something, but Cameron opens the screen door, interrupting us, yelling impatiently, "Okay, really, it's time to start studying this shit! Seriously." Then he pops his head back inside and slams the door.

"All right." Steve laughs. "I guess it's time to start studying this shit," he echoes, gently mocking Cameron, like maybe I'm not such an outsider after all. I stub my cigarette out and follow him inside.

PART FOUR

Senior Year

I'VE BEEN WITH FIFTEEN different guys—sometimes it seems like too many, other times it seems like not nearly enough. But each one takes me just a little farther away. I'm so far gone now, sometimes I feel like maybe it's almost enough. Because, honestly, there isn't the slightest trace left of that frizzy-haired, freckle-faced, clarinet-playing, scared-silent little girl. And her big secret is really not such a huge deal anymore. It was all so long ago now, it practically never even happened.

After all, I'm only one month away from turning seventeen, twenty-two days to be exact, which means I'm almost eighteen, which means I'm practically an adult. Which means I'm allowed to be cutting my last class of the day. Which means it's perfectly fine to be doing what I'm doing with this guy in the back of someone's crappy old Dodge Caravan that smells like dog-chewed sneakers. And so what if I bombed the SATs last spring. It's all fine—great, actually.

I slide the side door open and hop down onto the damp pavement.

I look at him once, trying to remember his name before slamming the door shut. It doesn't matter anyway. I make my way across the student parking lot, boots clicking in time with my heart, pounding from that empowering rush of making out with some guy I don't know or care about, already unable to conjure up his face in my brain. It feels like I'm flying. I check the time on my phone and pick up my pace. I know Mara's waiting for me.

She smiles when she sees me coming.

"Hey!" I call out as I take my spot next to her, leaning up against the driver's side of her car. And like every other day she hands me an already lit cigarette, complete with her lipstick print on the filter. We wait for the stream of cars to empty before entering the fray.

"Where you been, girlie?" She exhales a stream of smoke and laughs, because she already knows where I've been.

I shrug. "I don't know. Nowhere, really."

"Hmm," she mumbles through the cigarette hanging out of her mouth as she picks a few pieces of lint off her sweater. "Nowhere with someone special, perhaps?" she asks, her voice all light and hopeful, thinking maybe I had finally found someone like she had.

"Not anyone special, that's for sure." I don't know why I say that; I regret it instantly. This isn't parking-lot conversation.

"Well, you know . . . ," she starts, but looks away, not finishing. She flips her hair over her shoulder and looks out across the parking lot; she'd let the cranberry grow out and now she has these streaks of pink running through her dark hair underneath. She had somehow managed to seamlessly and fully segue out of her dork role into this new cool, unconventional, artsy girl.

And me, well, before it was like you had the girl and then you had the rumors about the girl, but now there's only the girl, because the rumors aren't just rumors anymore, they're the reality—they are the girl.

"Edy, you know Cameron's friend—" she tries again, but I interrupt before she can even finish.

"No, Mara."

She flicks her cigarette against the side mirror over and over, not looking at me.

"Sorry, I just—I'm really not interested. Thanks anyway, though."

"Okay. Yeah, I know. It's fine. Whatever." She slides her sunglasses from the top of her head to her eyes, letting her bangs fall down into her face. "What do you wanna do tonight?"

"I thought you'd be busy with Cameron—date night and all?"

"No. He's hanging out with Steve tonight." She pauses. "You know, Edy, Steve really is a good guy, and he —"

"Yeah, I know," I interrupt again. "Really, I'm not looking for that. Not with anyone. And most of all not with Stephen Reinheiser, okay?"

"All right, all right. Girls' night in, then?" She smiles, raising her eyebrows. "We haven't done that in so long, it'll be great. We can order takeout and have a movie marathon?" She laughs, staring out at the emptying parking lot. "Sounds fun, right?" she asks, nodding her head enthusiastically as she slides into the driver's side, closing the car door on our conversation.

Like always, we split another cigarette and keep the music just loud enough to drown out our thoughts, to silence the things we should be saying to each other.

When we get to my house, she turns to face me. “How ’bout you come over after dinner? Maybe you could . . . I don’t know, procure us some refreshments?” she hints with a smile.

“Got it covered,” I assure her. The gas station guy has become more partial to me than Mara ever since her nose ring and pink streaks; his tastes are a little more conventional, I suppose.

My house is quiet. The sound of Mara’s car pulling out of the driveway fades to silence. And leaves everything feeling too still, too vacant. Empty, haunted—this house. Not by ghosts, but by us, by our own history, by the things that have happened here.

I choose the cracked ceramic mug from the cupboard—the one with flowers on it that no one uses anymore—and fill it halfway with the gin Vanessa keeps at the back of the spice cabinet, as if the mint leaves, and cayenne, and cream of tartar can hide the thick glass bottle, or its contents, or the reason she needs it to be there in the first place. I take my cracked mug into the living room, turn the TV up loud, close my eyes, and just float.

When my eyes open again, the shadows in the room have shifted. The mug is nearly tipped over, my hand slack around its cylinder body. I sit up to see the clock: 5:48. Vanessa and Conner will be getting home any minute. I take the last gulp of gin and swish it around my mouth. I carefully rinse out the mug and put it in the dishwasher. Then I dump my books out of my backpack onto my bedroom floor and throw in a change of clothes, my toothbrush, hair stuff, and makeup. I find the notepad on the kitchen table, with Vanessa’s note from last weekend scribbled in blue pen:

Went to the store. Leftovers in fridge.

Love, Mom

I rip out the page and begin a new one. Our preferred method of communication these days.

Sleeping at Mara's. Call you in the morning.

-E

THE NIGHT IS A total blur. We didn't order takeout. We didn't watch movies. We just sat on Mara's bedroom floor and drank. And drank. And drank until there was nothing left.

"Morning," Mara mumbles as I sit up too fast.

"Oh God, my head. Not so loud," I grumble. I can't remember whether I fell asleep or passed out.

She gets up from the floor, wobbly, and stands in front of the mirror licking her hand and wiping the mascara stains from under her eyes. I follow her out of her room and down the stairs to the kitchen like a shadow.

"Are you hungry?" she asks me, opening and closing the cupboard doors, trying to find something edible.

"A little, I guess."

She carries an assortment of cereal boxes to the table. I get the bowls and spoons and skim milk from her fridge.

"So, I have an idea—a plan—if you'll just please think about it for at least ten seconds before you say no," she tells me as we sit at the little breakfast nook her father built when we were kids.

I pour my Cap'n Crunch with Crunch Berries. The clinking sounds of the small pinkish-red spheres and the pillow-puff-shaped corn-oat amalgams falling against the ceramic bowl echo through the empty kitchen.

"Edy?" Mara says.

"Oh, what?" I pretend I didn't hear; I'm much too busy pouring my skim milk.

"I said I want you to listen to this idea I have."

The spoon dives in; I put it in my mouth. I chew. Chew, chew, chew. I swallow. "Yeah, okay, I'm listening."

"Good. I want you to come out with us tonight."

I stop chewing. I stop blinking. I stop breathing. "Uff?" I mumble through my mouthful of cereal. Swallow hard, try again. "Us?"

"Yeah, with me and Cameron. We're going to the mall." She smiles as if that's not the most absurd thing she's ever said.

It takes me a few seconds to recover. "With Cameron? To the mall? You're kidding, right?"

"I know it's lame, Edy, but we're going to the movies and we would only have to walk through a small, tiny little baby section of the mall to get there, okay?"

"Mara, why? We've tried this before. Cameron and I do not like each other. Please accept that."

"Well, it's not just that," she begins slowly. "Steve's coming too."

I wonder how Cap'n Crunch would taste with a little splash of vodka, or maybe half the bottle.

"So, will you come, Eeds, pleeease, pwetty, pwetty pwease?" She clasps her hands together and gives me her best doe-eyed pouty face.

"But this is like a date, right? You're trying to set me up on a date. At the movies. That's just pathetic. What is this, middle school?"

"Seriously, I think it'll be great!" She smiles at me like she actually believes what she's saying.

"Okay, Mara. Look, we no longer party like we used to, or hang out with guys who are trouble. In fact, I barely even get to see you anymore. I've done a lot to accommodate you and little Cameron-two-shoes, including putting up with Steve constantly hanging around. So please, please, please, I beg you—not the mall."

Her smile fades, her face crinkling with frustration. "He's cool and nice and sweet, okay? And cute, so stop being all judge-y."

"Oh my God." I sigh.

"He is," she whines. "And he's perfect for you."

"I don't know why we're still talking about this—I told you already—not interested."

"Why?" she asks, pretending to be surprised.

"Because, Mara, I'm not going to fucking double-date with you and fucking Cameron, okay?" Too harsh, my tone, I know. I can't help it though.

"Well, excuse me—God, Edy, you can be so mean sometimes! You know, I already promised Steve you would come. And besides, you owe me."

"How do I owe you?"

"Please, I've covered for you more times than I can even count—probably more times than you even know!"

I stand up with my cereal bowl in hand; I walk over to the sink and dump the excess milk down the drain. "I can't. I'm sorry."

"Thanks a lot, Edy. Way to be there for me. I never ask you for anything!" She crosses her arms and jerks herself back in her chair, pouting like she's a twelve-year-old.

I stand there, trying to calculate how serious she is, how mad she would be if I bail. "Oh God," I moan. "Look, I'll go with you, but please just make it very clear this is not a date."

She rolls her eyes. "Fine."

"I have to go."

"Wait, don't go," she says, standing up like she might actually try to stop me.

"No, I told Vanessa I'd help her do something." But that's a lie. I scrape my soggy cereal into the garbage can under the sink. "Just call me later and let me know what time I should meet you."

"Are you mad at me?"

"I'm sorry." I relent, realizing how nasty I'm being. "I'm not mad. I'm just hungover, you know, I need a cigarette, my head hurts."

I don't bother getting dressed, or brushing my hair or even my teeth. I just grab my backpack and jacket and I'm out the door as quickly as possible. Mara's house is the one place in the world I've never been in a hurry to leave. But things change all the time. As I take steps farther away from her, the sidewalk seems a little unstable under my feet. I cut through two backyards and have to outrun a rabid terrier just to avoid walking past Kevin's house—Amanda's house.

I stand outside the food court, sure to be early—a peace offering for Mara—proof that I'm not above going to the mall if it truly means that much to her. I sit on the edge of a big concrete planter near the drop-off area and light a cigarette. I notice my hand shaking as I bring it to my lips. I feel on edge. Nervous. I'm dreading this entire night. It's just too wholesome and purposeless. I switch my cigarette to my other hand, but this one shakes so frantically, it slips right through my fingers. I have to jump to my feet so it doesn't fall into my lap and burn me.

Just as I'm brushing the ashes from my coat sleeve, Mara's voice startles me: "You all right, there?"

"Oh!" I gasp. "Hey. Yeah, I just dropped my—whatever, never mind—hi."

"Hey." Cameron raises the hand that's conjoined with Mara's, black nail polish peeling from his fingernails. "Glad you could come with," he lies. The streetlight glints off a metal ball inside his mouth as he talks, off the rings curled around his bottom lip and left eyebrow. "Steve's parking."

As we stand there waiting, Mara grimaces through a smile, as if to tell me to play nice. Then I see Steve power walking through the parking lot in his sweater-vest—his wallet chain all shiny, dangling from his back pocket, his Converse sneakers too clean. Like he's dressed for a date. He hasn't even arrived and already he's trying too hard. "Hi, Eden!" He waves as he approaches us, smiling so hugely.

"Hey." I try not to sigh too loudly.

During the movie Mara and Cameron hold hands. She leans her head on his shoulder. He kisses her forehead, then gives me an awkward smile when he catches me staring. I turn to look at Steve next to me. He smiles shyly and focuses intently on the movie screen. There are few things in this world that will make you feel like more of a loser than this.

The movie's in French, with subtitles. I guess Mara forgot to mention that part. After the first five minutes I've stopped reading them altogether. At some point I shut my eyes instead. And right in that space between being asleep and being awake, I hear my own voice, whining: "No, I wanna be the dog—I'm always the dog, Kevin."

And it's like I'm back there, but not as myself. I'm there as someone else, like a bystander sitting at the table with them, watching her slide into the seat opposite him. It's like I'm watching it in a movie—looking for signs of what's going to happen in only a few hours. He reaches his arm across the kitchen table and places the little metal dog in front of her with a smile. "Thank you," the girl sings. She can feel her face turning pink, blushing for him.

"I guess I'll be the hat." He's resigned.

"Be the shoe—the shoe's better." Their options were pretty limited. The dog was obviously everyone's first choice. They had lost the car several summers earlier in an ill-fated outdoor game of Monopoly that got rained out, so they were left with only the wheelbarrow, thimble, hat, and shoe. In the girl's mind, the shoe was at least a little more relevant than the others—it could walk. Theoretically, anyway. Hat, thimble, and wheelbarrow just seemed too arbitrary to her.

"Okay. If you think the shoe's better, I'll be the shoe." He smiled across the table at the girl. They placed their pieces on the GO square at the same time, and she couldn't tell if she had made their fingers brush against each other or if he did. "You want me to be the banker, right?" he asked her. She nodded. And her stomach suddenly felt sick, but in a strange, good way. He had remembered that she hated being the banker. And she was flattered. Her face was burning pink like a total idiot's.

He made it around the board twice while she was stuck in the cheap properties: Baltic Avenue, then Chance, which had her back up three spaces to Income Tax. Monopoly had never been her game, anyway.

"Where's my brother?" the girl asked him casually. It was unlike him to be detached from Caelin. It was unlike him to be treating her like a human being, to voluntarily be spending time with her like this.

"On the phone." He rolled an eleven and bought St. Charles Place, giving him a monopoly on the pink properties; he put two houses on Virginia.

"With who?" she asked, desperate to keep him talking to her. She rolled a one and a two and wound up back on Chance: another fifteen dollars for Poor Tax. "Shhhoot!" she said in her good-little-girl voice. She couldn't possibly have said shit.

Then he smiled at the girl in a way nobody had ever smiled at her before. For the first time, she felt like she should be embarrassed to be wearing that childish little flannel nightgown covered with tiny sleeping basset hounds in front of him. "His girlfriend—who else?" he answered, taking the money from her hand.

"Do you think she's pretty?" she asked as she watched him roll two fours and scoop up New York Avenue for the orange monopoly.

"I don't know, yeah, I guess. Why?"

She shrugged. She had only seen pictures of her brother's college girlfriend, but she could tell the girl was really pretty. She didn't know why she suddenly cared if Kevin thought the girl was pretty or not. Maybe because she knew deep down that she herself wasn't. Because she was just all angles and flatness. Because she didn't look like a girl someone like Kevin might think is pretty, and she was afraid she never would.

She rolled a six and a four. Community Chest: Go to jail. "Oh, come on! I have to go to jail now?" she said, flipping the card over for him to see.

"Oh, shoot!" he mocked in a girly voice.

"Hey!" She grinned, but only once she realized he was making fun of her. And then she kicked his foot under the table.

"Oww, okay, okay." He put houses on Illinois Avenue and Marvin Gardens while the girl waited to roll doubles to get out of jail.

When it was her turn, she shook the dice in both hands and then unleashed them. A six landed off the board at the edge of the table and the other fell on the floor under Kevin's chair.

"Oooh, what is it? What is it?" she asked, trying to see.

"It's a six," he announced from under the table. He placed the die in the center of the board, six side up. "You're free." He grinned.

"Was it really a six?" she asked him. After all, the girl was not a cheater.

"I swear to God," he proclaimed, holding his hand up in an oath.

She looked across the table at him suspiciously, finally deciding. "I don't believe you."

"Ouch. How do you not trust me by now? That hurts, Edy. Really." He spoke in a strange way, almost seriously, but not really because he was smiling. The girl didn't quite understand. All she knew is that it made her feel nervous and excited at the same time. Like there was maybe something else happening, but she wasn't sure what.

"All right, I believe you—I trust you," I hear the girl tell him.

I want to slap the girl. I want to stand up and sweep my arm across the table, knocking over the little dog and the little shoe, the plastic houses and the paper money. Because as the girl smiles demurely, I look in his eyes and I see now what the girl couldn't then: that this is the moment. He had been thinking about it for some time and was pretty sure, I could tell, but this was the moment he knew not only that he would do it, but that she would let him get away with it.

"Good." He grinned again. "It's your turn."

She moved her dog ahead, not thinking about anything except the way he kept looking at her, like she was a girl and not just some annoying kid. She pretended to have something in her eye so that she would have an excuse to take her glasses off. "So," she started, trying to sound as nonchalant as possible, "do you have a girlfriend?" And I remember how her heart raced as she waited, taking mental inventory of every pretty girl she'd ever seen him with.

"Yes," he answered, as if that was the most ridiculous question anyone had ever uttered in the history of the world.

"Oh. Oh, you—you do?" She tried so hard to sound casual, but even she knew she just sounded pathetic and sad. She rolled again and tried desperately to add the two numbers together.

"That's eight. You only moved seven," he told her matter-of-factly. She moved her dog one more spot. "Are you disappointed?" he asked, reading her thoughts somehow.

She looked up at him. He was slightly blurry without her glasses. "Disappointed? No. Why—why would I be?"

"Do you have a boyfriend?" he asked.

Her breath caught in her throat. She thought, for sure, he's making fun of her. "A boyfriend? Yeah, right," she mumbled, reaching to pick up her glasses. But suddenly the girl felt his hand on top of hers, just for a moment.

"You look good without your glasses, you know that?"

She literally could not breathe. "I . . . do? Really?" She tucked her messy, grown-out bangs behind her ears. She passed GO, she collected her two hundred dollars. Her heart skipped some vital beats.

"Yeah, I've always thought that." He leaned in across the table ever so slightly, looking at her intensely. "You still have that scar," he said, touching his own forehead in the place where her scar was, the place where my scar is still.

She mirrored him, too bewildered by what was going on to make sentences. She started to get scared she might actually faint.

"You remember that day?" he whispered, smiling through the words like it was something to him, like that day meant something to him the way it meant something to her. "In the emergency room," he reminded her. "Your bike accident?"

"Uh-huh," she breathed. It was as if he knew that she thought about that day all the time. How she thought it was probably the most romantic thing that would ever happen to her in her entire life.

"So, do you want a boyfriend?" He narrowed his eyes at the girl. "You finally like boys now, don't you?"

"I—yeah, I do, but I—" She was confused, though. Because what was he really asking her? It sounded, in a way, like he was asking if she wanted him to be her boyfriend, but no. No, of course not, she told herself silently. She looked down at her flat chest and thought, definitely no, that couldn't be it. Besides, he had a girlfriend—he'd just told her that. Plus, he was too old, too mature for her, the girl thought. But, still, she couldn't make sense of that smile.

The girl's brother emerged from his bedroom, standing at the head of the table, looking at their game. "Kev, you don't have to babysit her. She can amuse herself, man." He grinned. The girl didn't even know that she was supposed to be offended. She was supposed to get mad at her brother when he said stuff like that about her. But she didn't. Her brother disappeared into the kitchen and returned seconds later with a bag of chips under his arm and two beers in each hand. "Let's go," her brother whispered to Kevin, making sure his father wouldn't see them stealing his beer.

But the girl wanted to keep playing whatever game this was. She wanted to finish. Because this, she thought, could be the biggest night of her life.

"Edy." Caelin grabbed the girl's attention. He pointed a finger at her and then placed it against his lips, the universal sign of silence. "Got it?"

She nodded, thinking they were just so cool, feeling so special to be in on their delinquency.

Kevin pushed his chair out and stood up. "Good game, Eeds."

Then the boys left the room with their bootleg beer and chips. The girl tried to breathe normally, and then she slid her glasses back on her face where they belonged. She cleared away the colored money and the plastic houses, the dog and the shoe. She folded the board up inside of the falling-apart box and set it back on the game shelf in the hall closet where it belonged. But something still felt out of place.

She tiptoed into the living room, kissed her mother and her father good night, and sent herself to bed promptly at eleven. She knew because as she shut her bedroom door, she heard the news say: "It's eleven o'clock, do you know where your children are?" She tucked herself in tight and pushed all her stuffed animals away, up against the wall—stuffed animals were for kids, and, God, how the girl was so sick of being a kid, that stupid, stupid girl.

As the girl closed her eyes, she was thinking of him. Thinking that maybe he was thinking of her, too. But he wasn't thinking of her in that way. He was holding her in the palm of his hand, wrapping her around his fingers, one at a time, twisting and molding and bending her brain. I try to whisper in the girl's ear: "Edy, get up. Just lock your door. That's all you need to do. Lock your door, Edy, please!" I shout, but the girl doesn't hear me. It's too late.

I open my eyes. I'm breathing heavy. My forehead is beaded with sweat. My hands are wrapped tight around the edges of the cup holders. I look around quickly. Mara touches my arm and whispers, "What are you doing? Are you okay?"

I'm okay. I'm safe. It was a dream. Only a dream. And now I'm awake.

I nod my head and breathe the words, "Yeah. I'm okay."

FOR THE SECOND MARKING period, Mara and I are placed in the same study hall. Which is the only way I am going to be able to spend any time with her at all. Of course, Cameron and Steve come with the package, a bonus feature I could do without.

Me, Mara, Cameron, and Steve all sit at one table. And as luck would have it, Amanda sits at the table next to ours, giving me evil looks anytime I so much as glance in her direction. On the first day I waved and tried to smile at her, tried to silently tell her that I really don't care if her lies turned me into the school slut. No big deal. I'm fine with it. In fact, I owe her one. She's given me someone to be, after all, someone interesting and reckless, someone who doesn't have to care so damn much. About anything. But her coal eyes just stare right through me, unchanging.

She even trains her tablemates to shoot eye daggers at me as well. One of them, I know; that snarky girl who added "totally slutty disgusting" to my epithet on the bathroom wall. I try to be cool, ignore it, let it roll off me. Plenty of girls at school hate me, think

I'm trashy, worry about their boyfriends. I'm not blind, I'm not deaf, either. I see the way they watch me like I'm dangerous, hear the way they talk about me, their smirks behind cupped hands and their whispers. I'm used to it. The other girls, they don't matter. But Amanda's different. Because what right does she have? I should be the one hating her. If I cared enough, that is. Which I don't.

Mara places her fingers against her lips and kisses them, and then lays her hand flat in front of her mouth, palm side up, and blows. The kiss is sent across the room. Cameron stops sharpening his pencil, catches her kiss in his fist, and then smacks his hand against his mouth.

"So, you really haven't—you know—yet?" I whisper to Mara.

"Not yet, but soon. I think," she says sedately, gazing dreamily at Cameron, who continues sharpening Mara's drawing pencils like nothing in the world could make him happier.

She's been so busy with Cameron and dreaming about their future, she hasn't even asked about my birthday. Every year we're supposed to go out to eat, just the two of us. It's tradition. This year's pick, I've decided, is going to be the Cheesecake Factory, but she doesn't know that yet because I haven't had a chance to tell her, mainly because she hasn't asked.

"Mara, you do remember that tomorrow—"

"Shhh." Mr. Mosner, our study hall teacher, places a finger against his mouth. "Ladies, please . . . this is called study hall for a reason—it's for studying, not talking."

"What were you saying?" Mara whispers to me.

"Nothing."

✳

That night I wait for my annual midnight happy birthday phone call from Mara. I wait and wait and wait. Maybe she just fell asleep. Or maybe we're getting too old for midnight birthday calls.

The next morning when I get to my locker there are no birthday decorations. That's fine, maybe we're also getting too old for birthday locker decorations. But then when I see her in math and lunch and study hall and four times in between classes, she never says anything that gives me any indication she knows it's my birthday. And when she drops me off at home after school, she doesn't ask where we're going for dinner, she doesn't say when she'll be back to pick me up.

"Edy? I thought you'd be out with Mara," Vanessa says, walking in the house to find me lying on the couch. She sets down her purse and keys and the mail that was tucked under her arm, and then looks at me, almost too concerned. "We haven't seen too much of Mara around here lately. You two haven't had some kind of falling-out, have you?" she asks in that pseudocasual, too-high tone, which lets me know she's trying really hard to do the whole worried-parent bit.

"No, she just has this boyfriend she's been spending every-wakingminute with."

"So you're still going out for dinner then? 'Cause I could make something—I don't mind."

"No, yeah, it's fine. I mean, we're still going out."

"Well, good. Where are you going?" she asks as she thumbs through the envelopes, tossing them into junk and bill piles.

"Cheesecake Factory," I lie. "I have coupons," which is technically true, even if I won't technically be using them.

"Good." Junk. Bill. Junk. Junk. Bill. "Looks like you got a card from Grandma and Grandpa, oh, and one from your aunt Courtney in Phoenix," she says, handing me a red envelope and then a purple one. She always does that—Aunt Courtney in Phoenix, Uncle Henry in Michigan, Cousin Kim in Pittsburgh—as if I have more than one Aunt Courtney, Uncle Henry, and Cousin Kim.

I open the purple one first. From my grandparents. The front of the card has one teddy bear giving a balloon to another teddy bear; on the inside: "I hope your birthday is beary special." The card was probably meant for a five-year-old, but it also contains a check for seventeen dollars, and on the memo line, in my grandmother's shaky cursive, it says: "Happy 17th Birthday, Eden." Last year it was a sixteen-dollar check, next year it will be eighteen. Aunt Courtney sent a twenty, which I graciously stuff in my pocket.

Heaving my body off the couch, I go into my room, change my clothes, and make a big show of getting ready for my great birthday celebration. I have no clue where I am actually supposed to go for the next two to three hours.

"Have fun," Conner calls to me from the kitchen as I'm leaving.

"Edy, wait, just in case we're in bed when you get home, happy birthday again." Vanessa proceeds to give me an awkward hug in the doorway. "We love you," she adds at the last moment.

They're trying—I give them credit for that.

I just can't anymore. It's too hard.

IT TURNS OUT THE public library is the perfect hideout, even better than the school library. You can feel like a completely desperate, pathetic loser in solitude, without judgment.

I have my phone out. Right there in front of me, waiting for her call. I can even hear the ring in my head, anticipating the moment when she realizes how silly she's been to forget her best friend's birthday.

I idly flip through the pages of one of my school notebooks. Every page starts the same way, with the date and nothing else. I guess I attempted to take notes at the beginning of the year, but now it's just the occasional "Does this pen work??" scribbled in the margin. With each turn of the page I notice my hands trembling more and more. I shake them out. I stretch my fingers in front of me, as far as they can go. Then I close them tightly in a fist. I do it over and over. I rub my palms against my thighs, trying to get the circulation going, or whatever the problem is. But it only gets worse. It starts to make me nervous, which only makes them shake harder. I slam the notebook shut and lay my hands flat against the cover. They will not stop.

I'm breathing heavy as I pick up my phone and the rest of my things and head up to the reference desk to sign out a computer. Even if it's a completely lame excuse, it would make me feel so much better right now. I check my inbox: No Mara, but there is a message from Caelin. The subject line reads, "happy birthday." I double-click:

Dear Edy,

Happy Birthday

—Cae

Well, concise. But at least he remembered.

RE: happy birthday

Dear Cae,

Thanks. Are you coming home for Thanksgiving next week?

—Edy

He responds right away:

Yep—I'll be there! Maybe we can spend some time just you and me next weekend, what do you think?

I don't respond. I gather my things. I need to leave. Need to go somewhere. Anywhere. Go home, if necessary.

I walk. And walk. The cold November air licks my skin with its icy tongue. I walk and walk, without knowing where I'm going. Until I realize I'm there, standing on the sidewalk, in front of a house I used to know so well. I stand on the curb. I reach out and touch the red flag on the mailbox with my index finger, gently letting my hand flow over the raised sticker letters along the side of the black metal box: *M-I-L-L-E-R*.

I quickly pull my hand back. How strange must I look if anyone's watching? The TV in the living room is casting a dim bluish glow against the walls. A light in his parents' room is burning as well. His bedroom is, of course, dark. Because he's not there. He's away at college.

Suddenly, in the shadows, I see his cat—her fast, smooth body darts out from behind the front steps. She walks toward me stealthily, down the driveway in a straight line, light on her feet like a ghost. I freeze. Because I have the strongest urge to pick her up in my arms and take her home with me.

I actually consider it.

"Get a grip, Edy!" I whisper out loud.

I put my hands in my coat pockets and force my feet to keep moving down the sidewalk. I turn around. She's following me.

"Get away!" I yell. "Go home!" I shoo at her, but she just keeps walking toward me.

I practically run, my heart pounding fast.

"YOU'LL NEVER GUESS WHAT I did last night!" Mara says as I get in the passenger side and buckle up. Face-to-face with her, right now, I'm angrier than I thought I would be. Angrier than I thought I was. She's practically erupting with giddiness, so I know the thing she did last night must involve Cameron. She backs out of my driveway, then shifts into drive. "Well . . . we did it." She glances over at me, so excited.

"That's great." She had sex with her boyfriend, and I almost stole a cat. "Really great," I repeat.

"What, I thought you'd be happy for me? Excited?"

"Congratulations." I slowly clap my hands together twice.

Her smile inverts itself as she slows to the stop sign. "What's your problem?"

"My problem is you left me all alone last night!"

"What are you talking about?"

"Think, Mara. What was yesterday?"

"I don't know, Thursday?"

"You know what, just forget it, it doesn't even matter."

“Fine,” she says shortly. She floors the gas as we pull out onto the main road.

We don’t say anything the rest of the way to school. The air in the car is stuffy, filled with all kinds of sour unspoken words and the things we’ve been stifling for too long. The pressure is enough to crack the windshield. When we finally park in the student lot, I throw my seat belt off and just as I’m about to open the door, the valve that will keep us from exploding in here—

“Wait, Edy,” Mara says. I stop. “I wasn’t going to tell you this, but . . . well, I am now.” She takes a deep breath and exhales. “You’re really hard to be around lately. It’s really, really hard to be around you. It seems like ever since I started going out with Cameron, you’ve been such a—” She pauses, searching for a diplomatic word.

“What, such a bitch?” I laugh as I say it—very bitchy indeed.

“Yes,” she slowly agrees.

“Well, ever since you’ve been going out with Cameron, you’ve been a shitty friend. And it’s been really hard to be around you too, because you’re so completely self-centered and oblivious to anything and anyone else outside of yourself! And no one is forcing you to be around me, Mara, so if you have better things to do, then please, don’t let me get in your way—” I only stop because I have to catch my breath.

“Wow. Are you really that jealous?” she accuses.

“Jealous? That’s a laugh!”

“You just can’t stand to see me happy, can you?” she asks, as if I’m supposed to answer a question that’s that hurtful. “Well, I’m not going to stay miserable just because you are, and if you were really my friend, you wouldn’t want me to—you would be happy for me!”

"I'm not miserable. And I don't want you to be miserable either—God, I can't believe you would even say that to me!"

"Yes, you are, and you always need to drag everybody else right down with you. I'm not going to do it anymore—I'm out, all right? Go ahead and be unhappy if you want, but leave me out of it from now on, okay? I'm in love with Cameron and I'm finally happy and you act like that's a bad thing, like you think I'm an idiot or something!"

"Yeah, well, maybe you are. Maybe it's pathetic to let some guy totally control your life!" I shout, my blood racing into every cell in my body.

"And maybe you're the pathetic one! I'd rather have someone in my life who really cares about me than—" But she stops herself before she says what she really wants to say, what she's been wanting to say to me for a long time.

"Hey, finish now, Mara—you're almost there!"

"Face it," she says, her words hard, "all you have to do to get over a guy is take a shower—that's pathetic!"

I'm out of there before my brain even processes, slamming the door so hard, I feel something rip in my shoulder.

We don't talk or even look at each other for the rest of the day. And then Saturday goes by with nothing. She calls on Sunday. I let it go straight to voice mail but listen to it immediately:

"Hi. It's me. Look, I'm really sorry I forgot your birthday. Maybe I have been a shitty friend. I'm sorry about what I said to you. I mean, I'm sorry about the way I said it. I was serious though, Edy. And I think we should probably talk about it. So, just call me back when you get this. Okay, bye."

I WALK TO SCHOOL on Monday, getting there way too early. I use the time to clean out my locker. I hear footsteps walking lightly—I know it's Mara without even needing to look. I pretend I don't see her, even though we're the only two people in the entire hall.

"Hi," she says, standing next to me. "I stopped by your house. Your mom said you left early."

I don't respond. Just continue rummaging through the papers that have gotten crammed into the bottom of my locker.

"What, you're not talking to me now?" she asks, her voice sharp.

I finally turn to face her.

"Thought I'd hear from you over the weekend," she continues. "Didn't you get my message?"

"Yeah, I did," I finally answer.

"Okay, so you were just never going to call me back?"

"Well, that wasn't quite the apology I was looking forward to, Mara."

"You don't think you owe me an apology too?"

We stand there opposite each other, our arms crossed, both waiting for the other to say it first.

"Okay. I really am sorry about what I said," I admit. "I don't think you're pathetic for being with Cameron. And I do want you to be happy, I promise. You just—you really hurt my feelings."

"Edy, I know. I have felt so guilty about what I said to you, really, I didn't mean it the way it came out. I'm just worried about you, that's all. And I am the biggest effing idiot in the entire universe for forgetting your birthday. I still can't believe I did that!"

"No, it's okay, really. I overreacted."

"No. It was really, really shitty of me. It's unforgivable."

"It's not unforgivable," I tell her. "We're allowed one fight in seven years, right? How about I forgive you if you forgive me?"

"Deal." She smiles.

"So . . ." I knew she'd been dying to tell me. "How was it?"

She takes a deep breath and sighs, falling against the lockers, gazing up at the ceiling dreamily. "Amazing. It was so great, Edy, really. I never thought I would feel this way about anyone. Wait, I can't talk about this here, Let's get outta here before anyone sees us—we'll go get breakfast, sign in late. My treat, okay?"

I slam my locker closed. "Hey, you had me at 'Let's get outta here,'" I say with a laugh. We run for the nearest exit.

CAELIN COMES HOME FOR Thanksgiving as planned. He tries to act like things are fine between us, but we both know better. After dinner on Friday he comes to my room, knocking on my door. He pokes his head inside, and says, "So, Edy—tomorrow? You and me. We still on?"

"I guess." I shrug.

"Great." He smiles, then stands there awkwardly. "Well, I'm heading out, so . . ." He raises his hand to wave, starts to walk away.

"I'm heading out too," I call after him, like it's some kind of competition.

He reappears in my doorway. "You are?"

"Yeah, so?"

"Nothing," he says, but he gives me this grave look. "Just, you know, please be careful, okay, Edy?"

I roll my eyes and go back to picking out clothes from my closet.

✻

There's a buzz, a vibration in the air, as Mara and I, and Cameron and Steve, drive to this party at the dorm of a friend of a friend of a roommate of a friend who knows Steve's cousin. Which is almost like being invited. And that's good enough, because everyone has been trapped in small, confined spaces with their families for more than two days and is about to spontaneously combust. Or maybe that's just me. We hold a one-two-three-not-it contest in the car to see who will be our designated driver. Cameron was the slowest; thus he must remain sober.

"I don't care, I just want to be with Mara," he announces. "I don't have to get wasted to have a good time."

Steve opens the damn car door for me. I ignore him.

"That's nice, Cameron. I, however, do have to be wasted to have a good time, so can we just get in there already?" I start walking ahead, toward the music. Steve laughs. It wasn't a joke, I almost tell him. In fact, I couldn't fucking be more serious. Not only do I need to be wasted to have a good time, I need to be wasted to even be conscious right now, knowing I still have the whole weekend ahead of me before Caelin leaves, and Kevin along with him. I feel like I need to go shoot heroin or something. If only I knew where to get some, I just might.

Mara catches up with me. "All right. So, are you interested or not?"

"In him?" I nod my head back at Steve. "No, of course not."

"Come on, Edy, why not?" she asks, looping her arm in mine so our elbows are locked.

"Because he's so . . ." I glance behind us, and he waves an arm in the air at me. "He's so—"

"What, so nice? He's too nice for you, too smart, too adorably cute and sweet?"

I kick a loose chunk of pavement down the pathway in front of us. "Just don't expect me to sleep with him, all right?"

"I don't!" she shouts, rushing ahead a few steps to kick the rock before I can, jerking my arm, making me stumble forward.

"Yeah, well, he does!" I take a big step and give it one last good kick, launching it into a row of hedges lining the sidewalk and putting an end to our little diversion.

"He does not—" She stops, then whispering, pulling herself closer to me, says, "Expect you to sleep with him."

"He expects something, I can tell." I look back at him and Cameron again; they're laughing, shoving each other's arms as they catch up with us.

"You're hopeless, you really are," she says with a laugh. "He's a nice, decent guy who's interested in you. Can't you just let it happen?"

Four and a half red plastic cups later, I'm standing in a crowded, alcohol-drenched, bass-filled hallway with Steve asking me inane questions about myself.

"So, have you decided where you're going to school next year?" he shouts above all the other noise.

I'm not going to school next year, but it's not worth saying. So I just take another sip and let Steve keep talking.

"Have you thought about going here?" he asks me. "I know it's a state school and all, but it's close to home—so that's good, right?"

"Uh-huh." I take another big gulp; it burns on the way down. Caelin could've gone here, stayed home. But he was too good for state school. He could've had a free ride—full scholarship and everything. I'll never have anything like that, never know what that must feel like, but it wasn't enough for him. He had to leave. Leave me here to rot. Leave me to take on Vanessa and Conner all by myself. Asshole.

"I'm stuck between . . . ," Steve begins. But I have no idea what he's saying because two guys are running shirtless through the hall screaming at the top of their lungs, and he doesn't even seem to notice. "So . . . basically . . ." I catch bits and pieces. "They have this amazing liberal arts program, but it's just so expensive, so I don't know. It's not like my grades are that wonderful that I could get scholarships."

I nod along, pretend I'm listening.

"So, do you like photography?" he shouts.

"Huh?"

"I said do you like photography?" he repeats even louder. I had actually heard him the first time, I just couldn't figure out where that came from. Maybe it was part of what I missed before. I remember he did photography for the yearbook freshman year.

"Uh, yeah. Sure."

"You should come by my house this weekend. I'll show you my darkroom."

I laugh. That's a new one. He gets at least a couple of points for creativity.

"What's funny?" he asks, his mouth in a confused smile.

"Nothing, it's just—your darkroom—what is that supposed to mean?"

"My darkroom. I turned my bedroom closet into a darkroom. You know, to develop pictures."

"Oh, a darkroom." Literally.

"Right."

"Right."

"So?" he asks.

"So . . . ," I repeat, "what?"

"So, do you want to?"

"Want to what?"

"Come over."

"Oh."

"No?"

"No, I said *oh*," I tell him, louder.

"Oh. So, yes then?"

"Um . . ."

"What?"

"Fine."

"What time?" he asks. "I don't know, whenever you want, I guess. I work mornings, so . . . I don't know, maybe, like, in the afternoon?"

And this is why people don't have conversations at parties like these. I finish off what's left in my cup. Goddamn talking. "Hey, Steve?" I smile sweetly, manipulating his wholesome little heart. "Would you mind getting me another drink?" I'm going to need it.

"Yeah! Yeah, of course. Yeah, I'll be right back." And he happily disappears with my red plastic cup into the sea of faces.

"Hey, looks like you need a drink there?" says a guy who just sauntered up and is leaning against the wall next to me, holding a brown beer bottle in each hand.

He's not particularly attractive. But then again, he's not

particularly anything. And that's kind of exactly what I'm looking for. "Maybe," I answer.

"You don't live in this building, do you?" he asks as he hands me the bottle.

"No." I take it. It's opened, though. I hope I'm sober enough to keep remembering not to drink from it. Although he wouldn't have to drug me to get me to leave with him; I'm ready to go right now.

"Didn't think so, I'd remember seeing you." He smirks as his eyes travel down. I'm definitely sober enough to see what this is all about. "Where do you live?" he shouts, reluctantly meeting my eyes.

"Off campus." Which is not a lie.

"Listen, I can barely hear you. . . . You wanna go down the hall . . . there's a room. . . ."

I take a huge sip of the beer he just placed in my hand.

Next thing I know, I'm following him down the hall, him dragging me along with a limp, dead-fish grip on my hand. He leads me into one of those suites like you see on TV with a common room and then separate bedrooms off to the sides. There are all kinds of people everywhere, laughing, shouting, making out on couches and chairs and coffee tables. We go into a room that has a RESERVED FOR RACHAEL—ALL OTHERS WILL BE TOWED sign on the door. There's a lava lamp casting creepy purple and blue underwater shadows over everything. Rachael could be back anytime. He takes the bottle from my hand and sets both of our beers down on Rachael's computer desk.

Stepping closer, he runs a couple of fingers down my arm, "So, uh, what's your major?"

"We don't have to talk," I tell him, kicking my shoes off.

"Right on," he says through beer breath.

We waste no time with pretense. He rips a button as he clumsily gets my shirt off. At this rate, Steve won't even know I was gone. In just four steps, we're tumbling into Rachael's tiny bed. He unbuckles, unbuttons, and unzips his pants. "God, you're fuckin' hot," he murmurs into my mouth while trying to simultaneously kiss me, get my pants off, and get his hands inside my bra. I reach into my back pocket for my just-in-case-Steve-turned-out-to-be-not-just-a-dull-polite-guy condom. He takes his shirt off. His body feels soft and flabby against mine. That's fine. I don't care about that. I care only about this moment—about forgetting, about leaving myself behind.

Just as he's sliding my pants down over my butt, the door opens. I look at the doorway. Two bodies: Rachael, I presume, and the guy whose hand is attached to her hand.

"Dude, what the fuck?" the guy who's on top of me shouts at the two dark figures.

"This is *my* room, asshole!" A very tiny Rachael marches in and flips the light switch on; I cover my eyes with one hand, my body with the other.

"What the fuck?" I hear a strangely familiar voice say very slowly.

I spread my fingers and peek through. No. No, no, no.

"Eden, get up!" he shouts. "Hey! Get up right now, you fucking asshole, that's my sister!" he yells at the guy.

"Get out of my bed—this is disgusting!" Rachael screams at us, with her skinny jeans and faux-punk haircut, near tears. She could pass for cool, or at least interesting, out on the street. Too bad in here, her tweenie magazine centerfold posters of steamy, shirtless celebs give her away. She's more of a poser than I am, even. I start laughing. I want to ask her if her nose ring is magnetic, but I can't seem to remember how to use my voice at the moment. The guy hovers over me, looking down at me like I'm nuts.

"I'll kick your fucking ass"—Caelin charges the bed—"if you don't get the fuck off my sister right now!"

"Dude, chill the fuck out," the anonymous guy on top of me says as he tries frantically to zip his pants back up so he can get off me.

"Everybody needs to get the hell out of here now!" a high-pitch-voiced Rachael shouts, hands on hips, looking not at all threatening, just comical.

Finally the guy is standing and I struggle to button and zip my jeans. "Caelin, whaddaareyou . . .doing—" *Here*, I was going to say. It surprises me how much I'm slurring, how slow I'm talking, how dizzy I suddenly feel, as I brace myself against the desk.

"What the hell are *you* doing?" he screams in my face. I can barely stand without falling over—I'm definitely drunker than I thought I was.

"And you," he says, pushing the guy up against Rachael's wall, knocking over a stack of books on the floor. "She's sixteen years old, you pervert! What the hell do you think you're doing?"

"Stop it!" Rachael yells. "You're destroying my room."

"Dude, chill—I didn't know that, okay? I don't want any trouble, really." He holds his hands up in the don't-shoot-I'm-innocent way. He seems genuinely scared of my brother.

"I'm not six—" *Teen*, I try, but Caelin's eyes flash over to me and he has this look of disgust and hate in them that makes me freeze. Just freeze. Because my brother just caught me almost having sex with some guy in a room that he was supposed to be having sex in, with the girl whose room this actually is, and now I'm standing here in my lacy black bra and it's obviously hard for him, my own brother, not to look at my breasts.

"Jesus-fucking-Christ, Edy! Would you put some fucking clothes on?" He looks down and backs away from the guy.

"I'm outta here," the guy says, scooping up his shirt as he stumbles out into the noise.

"Were you actually going to have sex with that guy, Eden? Do you even know him?"

I finish buttoning my shirt and pick the unopened condom up off the bed, shoving it back into my pocket. "So what, do you even know her?" I ask, gesturing to Rachael, who's inspecting her things to make sure we didn't steal or ruin anything.

"You know what, I really just want you both to get the hell out of here now—right now," Rachael says, thrusting the two beer bottles into my brother's hands.

"I'm so sorry about this," Caelin says, pulling her aside.

Rachael crosses her arms and rolls her eyes. "Just go," she orders.

"Yeah," he whispers, "sorry."

We file out of Rachael's room and into the common area without a word, without eye contact. "I cannot motherfuckingbelieve this," he says under his breath as he sets the beer bottles down on top of a stack of papers on the table next to the door. Once we get out in the hall, he yells, "What the hell are you even doing here,

Edy?" Partially because of the music, but mostly because he's mad, really mad, madder than I've seen him in a long time.

"Apparently, the same thing you're doing here, Caelin."

"Don't do that. Don't. Fucking. Do. That. Don't be a smart-ass."

"I'm *fucking* not!" I yell in his face, not sure yet if he's making me want to be mean or funny. I feel my mouth grin. "Or are you just mad because I fucked up your fucking plans. That I fucked up your plans to get fucked, I mean." Still, that's not what I meant to say. "You know what I mean. You wanted to fuck that girl." I laugh because the word "fuck" sounds like the funniest word ever.

"You're drunk, Edy. You're really drunk and that guy was trying to take advantage of you! You're lucky I came in when I did," he says, dead serious, as if getting taken advantage of would be the worst thing that could happen, as if that wasn't something that happens to girls on a daily basis.

"Take advantage of *me*?" I laugh, hysterically. "Me?" It's funny. "Are you drunk, Caelin?" I mean to shove his shoulder, but I just fall into him. "It's more like the other way around, if you wanna know. Don't you get it? I'm not your sweet, stupid, innocent little sister. I'm not—"

"All right, all right, just stop." He puts his hand up as if he can just shut me up with nothing more than a small gesture. He looks around like he's embarrassed.

"No. What do you think? Do you think that I don't drink and smoke and fuck—"

"Jesus Christ, Eden!"

"Oh, sorry—have sex, or make love—what do you call it?"

"Stop."

"Do you think I haven't had sex with hundreds of guys, Caelin?"

"Shut up!"

"Okay, maybe not hundreds. More like a hundred, give or take a few, of course." So, the exact number would have been sixteen had we not been interrupted, but I'll bet if I included all the ones I've messed around with and not actually had sex-sex with, it probably comes close. And one hundred just sounds so much more appalling than a measly fifteen. Sometimes just messing around is enough. Not lately, though. Lately, nothing seems like enough.

"Shut up, Edy, I mean it!" he says under his breath, through his teeth.

"Edy," I hear behind me. I turn around quickly, lose my balance. Caelin grabs my arm. I shrug it off. "We've been looking for you." It's Mara, with Cameron and Steve trailing behind. "What's wrong?" she asks, looking back and forth between me and Caelin.

"What's wrong, Mara?" Caelin shouts. "Neither of you should be here!" Then he stares down Cameron and Steve. "And who the hell are you?"

I decide to make the introductions: "Caelin, this is Cameron, Mara's boyfriend, and he's so wonderful and dreamy and he doesn't need to get wasted to have a good time, you'd like him, he's the designated driver. And this"—I throw my arm around Steve's shoulder—"this is Steve. But you don't have to worry about Steve. Don't let his appearance fool you—he may look like an ordinary guy, but he's just a shy little dork underneath, right Steve?"

I turn my head to look at him, but my feet follow and my body sways into his. I grip on to his shoulder tighter, trying to balance, and he pulls me up straight. "See?" I laugh. "What I'm saying is Steve is a nice guy, Caelin—such a nice, decent guy—but—" I shout, pausing to catch my breath. "But he did invite me to his darkroom and he's my date. My date, Caelin. Yes, I came here with a date!" I feel Steve slither out from under my arm, but I don't take my eyes off Caelin's face—I want to memorize everything about his reaction.

"Edy, please, please, please just shut the fuck up!" he screams. I record it, try so hard to brand it all into my brain—his cheeks turning pink, the vein in his temple pulsing, his voice unsteady, his hands shaking—the way he's losing control.

"Hey, hey, now—" Mara starts to defend me.

"No, it's okay!" I scream, louder than I meant to. "Caelin is just having some trouble dealing with the fact that his sister's a big whore. Right, Cae? That is what it is, right? Or is there something else that's bothering you?"

He looks at me, for just a moment, really at me, and he looks so angry, angry enough to hit me, maybe. I almost wish he would, because that would feel better than being eternally ignored by him, better than being made to feel like I'm just some inconsequential speck of dust dirtying up his otherwise immaculate life. But then the moment passes as quickly as it came—he doesn't see me anymore.

"Look, she is way too drunk," he says, turning to the three of them. "Can you guys get her home, or not?" he asks, pretending I don't exist, a game he plays even better than basketball.

"Yeah, man. Sure. We will, I promise," Cameron says, nodding his head all serious and responsible-like. I feel like screaming *GO FUCK YOURSELF* to everyone within earshot, Caelin,

Cameron, Steve, Mara even, the people standing around staring at us, Rachael, that would-be-sixteen guy, Kevin, if he's around, which I'm sure he is.

Caelin walks away. Doesn't look at me, doesn't say another word. Just walks away from me. Everybody gives me these sideways looks of uncomfortable pity, like I had just lost some really important game. Whatever it was that we were playing, they all seemed to think I was the loser. I wasn't. He lost! He was the loser. They were all losers. Not me.

"Are you okay?" Mara asks me, touching my shoulder.

"Yeah, of course." I snort. I'm tough. I can take it. So what?

"Honey, you're crying," she says, looking worried.

"I am not!" That's ridiculous. But I rub at my eyes with the back of my sleeves and it leaves two dirty, black streaks from my mascara.

"She never cries," she tells Cameron and Steve.

"I can hear you, and I'm not crying! Maybe my eyes are watering from some reason, but not because I'm crying," I shout.

Nobody really says much the whole way home.

Caelin doesn't speak to me at all the next day. Needless to say, we don't have our special brother-sister outing like he wanted. And he's gone by the time I wake up Sunday morning.

And then nobody really says much to me in school on Monday. Or Tuesday. Or Wednesday. I don't care if Cameron doesn't talk to me. I honestly don't care if Steve doesn't talk to me. And Mara, it can't rightfully be said that she's ignoring me, she just doesn't seem particularly happy that I exist.

"All right, so why is everyone being weird?" I finally ask Mara in the hall by her locker on Thursday.

"What do you mean?" she mumbles, not even glancing up at me.

"Ever since the party no one's been talking to me."

"I'm talking to you right now."

"Yeah, barely."

"Well, can you really blame them? You were so mean, Edy."

"Not to you, I wasn't."

"No, but you made fun of Cameron." She pauses, waiting for me to react. "And Steve, you know he actually liked you and you were horrible to him."

"I was not. Not *horrible*." If he was stupid enough to actually like me, then that's his problem.

"Edy, you obviously ditched him to go hook up with some other guy. But I guess he's just a little dork, right? So who cares, anyway?" she says, rolling her eyes.

"Well, when you say it like that, it sounds mean, but that's not what I meant—that's not how it happened. Not really."

She just crosses her arms and shakes her head.

"I was drunk, Mara. I didn't mean anything by it, you know that."

"Yeah, exactly." She inhales sharply. "And I really think you have a problem, Edy."

"What, a drinking problem? I don't drink that much—you drink more than I do."

She slams her locker shut, all exasperated, like it's such a big project to talk to me. "No, that's not what I mean. Not a drinking problem, but you have some kind of problem. You didn't mean anything by it, right?"

"Yeah, that's what I said," I snap, getting impatient.

"But you never mean anything."

"So?" I wish, wish to God, that she would say what she means, instead of having me jump through her psychological hoops.

"So, nothing ever means anything to you. You're just out there lately, Edy, way out there. It worries me."

"Out where, what are you talking about?"

"Like—I don't know—I just feel like you're about to go over the edge or something." Her fingers walk an imaginary line through the air, and then she lets her hand plummet downward, like she's enacting her hand falling off a cliff.

"You're completely overreacting."

She shakes her head firmly back and forth. "No, you're out of control this time. Really. You know, you're acting crazy—crazy for you, even."

"Where is this coming from? I drink a little too much and then I'm not perfectly polite to your little boyfriend and now all of a sudden I'm crazy?"

"Edy, just stop. You know what I'm talking about. It's everything."

I feel my face contorting into a smirk—that really condescending way Caelin does it that makes me want to punch him in the mouth just to shatter that stupid crooked line of his lips. "Thanks for the concern," I snarl, "but I can take care of myself just fine."

"Edy . . ." The corners of her mouth turn down in that way that means she's trying not to cry but is going to start any second. "I don't like you like this."

"Like what?" I ask, not nicely. It pushes her over the brink.

"You're not thinking right and you're—you'regoingtogethurt." She has to say it really fast so she can get it all out before the tears. "Please. Listen. Okay?" Then she takes a breath and just like that, her eyes are full to the brim, just on the cusp of spilling over. Then one drop rolls down, then a whole army of them, like rain on glass. She cries. And then, because I'm such great friend, I just walk away.

IT'S AFTER MIDNIGHT. The snow is falling hard outside, the wind howling. Can't sleep. Can't get comfortable. Goddamn lumpy sleeping bag. I turn my head and my eyes focus on my ninth-grade yearbook, sandwiched between the floor and the leg of my desk, leveling it out. I pull on it from the flimsy spine—it releases easily. And the desk rocks forward without its support.

I absently flip through until I reach the clubs and organizations section.

Lunch-Break Book Club.

Miss Sullivan posing behind the circulation desk, her glasses pushed down to the tip of her nose, her index finger in front of her lips, making the shhh face. The six of us stood around her, three on either side, each of us making our most angelic faces and holding out six shiny red apples for her—very nerdy, so very, very nerdy. It was my idea. Steve had set up the tripod with his camera exactly where I had marked with masking tape on the floor. And I was a stickler about the apples, too. Cortland, Empire, Gala,

McIntosh, and Red Delicious were permitted, but no Ginger Gold or Golden Delicious, and absolutely no Granny Smiths would be allowed in any yearbook picture I was orchestrating. I even sent out an e-mail to that effect so no one would show up with the wrong apple and fuck up my picture. I guess that was the beginning of the end of Lunch-Break. But if there were a contest for best group photo that year, Lunch-Break Book Club would've won by light-years. I compare the grainy gray hues of our apples; they match perfectly. A yellow or green one would've thrown the whole thing off, I'm sure of it.

I examine it more closely—everyone's goofy faces—Steve's chubby cheeks, Mara's sincerity, Miss Sullivan playing along, and then there's me. It's me in a ponytail and my old glasses. And I have this smile on my face, but it's all wrong because there's this look in my eyes—this dull, dead darkness. Like something is missing. I can't say what. But that missing something is something important, something crucial, something taken. Something gone now. Maybe for good.

I flip to the sports section. Boys varsity basketball. He'd been sitting there in the back of my mind like someone incessantly tapping on my shoulder. Ever since the night I found myself outside his house. I shoved him back into his corner where he belongs. But now I have to look. I can't ignore him anymore. Not when I'm this close. I trace my finger over the faces. And there he is. In his Number 12 jersey. Josh. My heart thumps hard and fast the way it used to. I force my eyes to close. I force my fingers to turn the page. So I can't look at his face again, so I won't see his name listed there, so I can go back to forgetting all about him for the rest of my life.

Instead, I flip to the ninth-grade section to visit the ghost of that girl I used to be. And there she is, right between Maureen Malinowski and Sean Michaels. Glasses and all. A stupid innocent smile plastered on her stupid innocent face. That picture was taken on the very first day—the first day of high school—the day I thought her life was about to begin. How could she have known her stupid, pathetic, flat-chested days were numbered?

I envy her, that awkward, not-quite-ugly-not-quite-pretty girl. Wish I could start over. Be her again. I look deeply into her eyes as if she holds some special secret, a way to get back to her. But her eyes are just pixels. She only comes in two dimensions. She doesn't know shit. I start out grinning, grinning because of the irony, and then I snicker a few times, shaking my head back and forth. Then I'm laughing, laughing because of the absurdity, and then I have to use both hands to cover my mouth because I'm laughing so hard. And then I have to use both my hands to cover my eyes, because they're crying, crying because of the atrocity of it all, of regret and time and lies and not being able to do anything about any of it.

Only now I can't remember, damn it, where the lies ended and I began. It's all blurred. Everything suddenly seems to have become so messy, so gray, so undefined and terrifying. All I know is that things went terribly awry, this wasn't the plan. The plan was to get better, to feel better, by any means. But I don't feel better, I feel empty, empty and broken, still.

And alone. More alone than ever before.

I feel these forbidden thoughts creep in sometimes without warning. Slow thoughts that always start quietly, like whispers you're not even sure you're hearing. And then they get louder and louder until they become every sound in the entire world. Thoughts that can't be undone.

Would anyone care?

Would anyone even fucking notice?

What if one day I just wasn't here anymore?

What if one day it all just stopped?

What if? What if? What if?

"EDY?" VANESSA SAYS, pushing my bedroom door open. "I asked you ten times, very nicely, to go out and shovel." It started snowing Wednesday night. And then on Thursday school is canceled, work is canceled—life is canceled, trapping me in the house with Vanessa and Conner all weekend. There's a driving ban for the entire county, and everyone's cars are buried under two and a half feet of snow that is only getting deeper and deeper with every hour that passes.

I really just want to ignore her, because she has in fact interrupted me about twenty times already, not ten, to bother me about shoveling. What the hell are snow days for, anyway? What would be so wrong with just sitting at my desk pretending to do homework while I drown in the sheer rightness of a day off?

I take my headphones out of my ears and look up at her like I didn't hear. "Huh?"

"What are you working on?" she asks, trying to smile at me.

"Homework. English," I lie.

"Well, do you think you could take a break? Your father shouldn't be out there this long."

"Then why doesn't he just come in?" I counter.

"Edy, I'm asking you," she tells me firmly.

"Yeah, but it doesn't even make sense to be shoveling during the snowstorm. Doesn't it make more sense to just shovel after it stops? None of our neighbors are out there shoveling right now. Why do we always have to do this?"

"No, why do *you* always have to do this?" She points her finger at me. Then I watch as she takes a deep breath, like she does when she's trying to calm herself. Watch as she takes one deliberate step backward. I wonder if she's afraid she might slap me. "What I'm saying is," she begins again, more restrained, "why can't you just do what I've asked? You know, why do you have to challenge everything I say, Eden? I don't understand."

"I'm not challen—"

"There you go again," she accuses, waving her hand at me. She starts getting that look in her eye. The one that gives its victim the sense that everything wrong with the world—war, famine, global warming—is her fault. "This is exactly what I'm talking about."

"I'm not challenging anything. God. I'm just pointing out the obvious. Why should we have to shovel all day long, instead of just once?"

She throws her arms up and walks away, muttering to herself, "I can't take it anymore. I can't. I just can't."

"Fine," I call after her, tossing my book down against the desk. "I'll go out there even though it's the stupidest thing I've ever heard of!"

By the time I shovel to the bottom of the driveway, the cold has infiltrated my core, but it's invigorating somehow. I look out, squinting my eyes so that my vision blurs beyond the identical houses and cars and streets and trees, until I am the center of this frozen nowhere suburb-scape.

I refocus my eyes and turn around to look at the house. At the rate the snow is falling, it looks like I never even started shoveling. The cars are still blocked in, and my extremities now feel like they are about to fall off. And somehow, this satisfies Vanessa. "Thank you," she says when I come inside with icicles dripping from my eyelashes.

"It doesn't even look like I did anything."

"That's really not the point, is it?" She smiles, licks her index finger, and turns the page of her magazine.

"Isn't it?" I ask, hanging my coat up on the hook by the door.

"Isn't what?" she says absently.

"The point," I reply, "of shoveling?"

"Oh. Well . . ." She places her finger on a word and looks up from the magazine, stares into space for a moment, squinting her eyes like she's thinking of something to say to me. I stand there, in actual suspense, waiting. But then her eyes refocus on the dingy wallpaper, and she swats her hands in front of her face, like she's shooing some annoying insect. She goes back to her magazine, never finishing.

I send myself to my room, lock myself in, crack the window, and light a cigarette. I've never smoked in my house before. I was always afraid they would smell it and they would be disappointed in me yet again. Nobody was noticing anything, though. She couldn't even be bothered to finish a sentence.

After dinner Vanessa knocks on my door, asks if I want to help decorate the tree. I don't answer. I close my eyes and cover my ears and will her to just please walk away. She doesn't ask a second time.

As I sit on my bedroom floor smoking cigarettes—listening to the sound of the TV under my door, and the rustling of Christmas ornaments being unwrapped and unpacked—I have this intense longing to call Mara. To make up with her, and just say whatever words I need to say to put things back in place. But I know the only way to do that is to apologize to Steve first. I shake my head as I reluctantly dial his number.

It only rings once before he picks up.

"Steve, hey. It's Eden."

"I know" is all he says.

I pause, consider hanging up.

"Look, I'm sorry about the party," I finally tell him.

Silence.

"Sorry if I was jerk," I try. "I was messed up. Sorry."

Finally he sighs into the phone. "It's okay. You know, I get it."

"Thanks, Steve. Well, I'll talk to you—"

"So, what's goin' on?" he interrupts before I can say good-bye. "I mean, what've you been up to—all this crazy snow?" he asks awkwardly.

He wants to keep me on the phone.

"Not much," I answer, suddenly realizing I kind of want to be kept on the phone.

"Yeah, me neither."

Silence.

"Well, what are you doing now?" I ask him.

I RING THE DOORBELL at Steve's house. I don't know yet what it is I really want from him. I only know that I couldn't stand to be in my house another minute.

"Hey!" He answers the door with that warm, shy smile that never fails to make me feel bad for not being nicer to him. I look at him and wish, for just a second, that I could be the kind of girl who could like him, really like him. Sometimes I wonder how hard it would be to pretend. "Come in, come in," he tells me.

I take my coat and my boots off in the entryway of his house. Everything's neat and clean and quiet. The house is laid out the exact same way as Josh's house was, just in reverse. But, then again, most of the houses in our neighborhood are exactly the same. There are only about three or four different versions.

"Can you believe we actually got a snow day?" he says. "It looks like they're probably going to close tomorrow too, my father said. He just called from work. He said the roads aren't cleared yet at all, so . . ." He drifts off. "Anyway, I'm so glad you called. We can go up to my room. I'll show you my photo stuff. I mean, if you're really interested."

"Yeah, definitely," I lie.

I follow him up the stairs to his room the way I used to follow Josh up the stairs to his room. Then down the familiar hallway, a familiar floor under my feet.

"So this is it," he says, holding his arms out as we stand in the middle of his bedroom. Except all I can see is Josh's bedroom when I look around.

And instantly Josh is there, again, in my mind, taking up all the space, consuming all the thoughts, making my heart go wild. I can hardly breathe. I find myself, for once, not wishing that I were the one who was different, that I were someone else, but that *Steve* were someone else. That Steve was Josh. That Josh was here instead of Steve, but feeling the way Steve feels about me.

But that's not what's real. That's not what's happening. In fact, nothing is happening.

And I realize, abruptly, that is the problem. I need something to happen. Need to make something happen. Anything. Now.

I close his door behind us and turn around to face him. "What—" Steve asks, looking at me, alarmed, confused, as I walk toward him. "What are you doing?"

"Come here," I say, reaching out for him.

"What?" he says slowly.

"It's okay, just come here." Cautiously, his hands reach out to meet mine, but he still looks uncertain. And then something passes over his face—he just got it. He moves in to kiss me, but stops, like he needs permission. "It's okay, I promise," I whisper. So I close my eyes, focus everything in my mind and my body on pretending that the boy I'm kissing is Josh, and that I am some better version of myself—the girl I used to be, the one that Josh once felt the need to say "I love you" to.

I kiss him, pull him toward me. He kisses back. I pour myself into it, but I don't feel any different. I need more to happen. More, damn it. I back him up to his bed and he pulls me on top of him. But this isn't enough. I start to move my hands down his chest and stomach, but he grabs my hands as my fingers touch his belt. He stops kissing me altogether. "Wait, wait, wait. Edy," he whispers, holding my hands in his. "What are we doing?" he asks, with his eyes darting back and forth between mine, searching melodramatically.

"It's okay, I promise. I really, really want this to happen." But that's such a lie. I feel like I'm close to pleading.

"Well, me too," he whispers, "but let's go slow. We have time, right?" He smiles.

I nod, but I barely even understand him. Time? Time for what? This is urgent. There's no time at all. We need to do this right now. He doesn't get it—he doesn't get anything!

He kisses me and touches my hair and my face like he means it; in fact, he doesn't touch me anywhere else at all. It feels like this goes on forever. And with every second that passes, the less I can pretend, the more real this becomes, the less like Josh I can make him. I get a sick, churning sensation in my stomach. Because I'm using him, using him bad.

Between kisses he whispers all kinds of things to me, in my ear, like, romantic, sweet things. "I've never known anybody like you, Edy. You just don't care what people think—that's so amazing, that's so cool."

But the more he talks, the more I'm just thinking of ways I can get out of this. *How can I get out, how can I get out?* I repeat in my mind, over and over.

"You're so pretty and interesting . . . and smart—"

"Steve, please." I have to stop him there. "I am not." Smart girls don't get themselves into mess after mess after mess.

"Ye—" he starts again, but I stop him.

"I'm not any of those things, okay?" I tell him, more firmly.

"Yes, you are." Pulling me closer, he doesn't seem nervous anymore, not scared. "I've liked you since we were in ninth grade, with the Columbus project, and then the library thing, remember?"

"Lunch-Break," I mumble absently, maneuvering myself so that my back is facing him. At least this way I don't have to look him in the eye while I calculate my exit strategy. He reaches his arms around me from behind, his hands crisscrossing over my stomach. My skin wants to crawl off my body.

"You know, I wouldn't even do the reading for my classes, but I would read all those stupid books cover to cover just so I would have something to talk to you about. And I'd feel like such an idiot because I never understood any of it, but you always did."

"Wow," I whisper, looking at the window, not through it, but at the glass, at the mini snowdrifts caught in the corners of the window, the condensation trickling down. It all makes me feel like I could cry. Because, in my heart, I know, I'm not who he thinks I am. Not even close. And he's not who I want him to be, either.

"I'm so glad this is finally happening," he whispers. "I really want to get to know you now, Edy. For real. I want to know everything. Like . . . what are your interests, what do you like to do, what kind of music do you listen to?"

I shrug.

He says, "Favorite movie?"

I can't do this.

"Okay, how's this: What are you thinking about when you get quiet all the time?"

I have to concentrate all my energy on not allowing myself to cry.

"Edy?" He pulls his arms around me tighter and tighter.

"What?" I finally answer.

He moves my hair and kisses the back of my neck. "Just—I don't know, tell me anything."

"I can't." I hear my voice and it sounds so wrong, like that's not what I'm supposed to sound like. I feel my body curl into itself a little more, pulling away from him.

"What is it?" he asks. "What's wrong?"

That's it!

I break out of his arms and turn around. I sit up straight, ready to have a face-off. "Steve, will you please just shut up? God!"

He sits up too, looking so confused it makes me want to slap him.

"I mean, what is wrong with you? Can't we just have fun? You have to ruin it, really?"

It's almost like he flinches, almost like I really have slapped him. Like I hurt him. With just my words. Sadly, sickly, that makes me feel a little better, a little stronger.

"You wanted me to talk, right? Happy now?"

"I—" he starts. But I don't hear the next word out of his mouth because I'm on my feet. I swing his bedroom door open and I run down the stairs. I slip on my boots and my coat. I don't lace or button anything. I just need to get out.

Outside in the cold, I look up and wish on the entire universe of stars that I was anywhere—I close them tight—anywhere but here. But when I open them, I'm staring at the same sky, standing in the same town I've been stuck in forever, the same middle of nowhere, feeling the same as I did before. Only worse.

I light a cigarette but only get in a few deep drags before I hear the door screech open, followed by his footsteps shuffling through the snow. Then his voice, crushing the delicate silence of the frozen air.

"Look, Edy, I don't know what just happened in there."

I keep my back to him. He places his hands on my shoulders.

"I really have to go," I tell him, in as even a voice as I can muster. Hooking my shoulders inward, I try to shrug his hands off.

He lets go and steps around in front of me, wearing an expression I've never seen on him before. His standard slouching posture straightens as he puts his hands on his hips. He looks bigger than usual, imposing.

"I honest-to-God don't know what I did," he says, the words cutting the air. "I'm trying to do the right thing, and you're acting like you hate me or something!" His eyes get wider as he speaks, colder.

I say nothing. He stands there, waiting for me to deny it, getting angrier every second. I fill my lungs with smoke to stall my response. But then he throws his hands up abruptly, letting them fall heavy as they smack down against his thighs. It's like my entire body shudders. My cigarette slips out of my hand and falls to the ground.

"I'm just saying that—" He pauses and looks me once over, assessing my face, my body. I try to recover, try to act like I'm okay. "What do you think," he says slowly, "I would hit you or something?"

I shake my head no, but my mind isn't sure anymore. Of anything. Or anyone.

"Oh my God, what kind of person do you think I am, Edy?" he says, voice raised. But I don't know what kind of person he is—hell, I don't even know what kind of person I am.

I feel myself backing away.

"I wouldn't," he says after I don't answer. "I can't believe I have to tell you that. I would never do anything like that."

"Fine. Yeah, I know."

"Wait, I'm just trying to explain . . . ," he continues, stepping closer, but I can't even begin to listen. I nod my head in agreement to whatever it is he might be saying. "So does that make sense?" he finally finishes.

He reaches out to touch my face, my hair maybe, I don't know—I can't help but flinch away from him. "Jesus, Edy, you're not—you're not scared of me, are you?"

"Yes." I hear the word exit my mouth and my heart freezes. Because it's the truth. His mouth drops open. "I mean no." I try to fix it, try, I try but it's too late. I'm shaking, my fingers fucking tremble. Christ. "I meant no. I'm not scared, I'm just"—I'm trying but I can't breathe, like I have bricks on my chest—"just so . . . ," and suddenly, "so . . . fucking . . . ," and I'm crying, "tired." There's no way to hide it. "I'm just tired, okay?" I blather. "So. Fucking. Tired.

And I don't feel like having some big fucking conversation, that's all!" I cry out, near screaming, near hysterical.

He says nothing. I cover my eyes. I'm crying with my whole body and all I want to do is disappear. I feel his hand hesitate, hovering over my back, then rubbing awkward circles, and then his fingers in my hair. If he's saying anything, I don't hear. All can I hear is my blood rushing and my heart drumming in my ears. A pulsing in my throat, like there's a big jumbled ball of words stuck in there dying to get out. He puts both arms around me. But I feel suffocated. Don't want to be held. Don't want to be touched. Not by anyone ever again in my entire life.

I crunch my teeth together to keep myself from screaming. Screaming in general, screaming at him to get his hands off me, screaming for help, screaming because I can't make sense out of anything that is happening, has happened, will happen. Screaming because I still feel like I'm back there, always back there, in my heart I'm still that girl. I clench my fists tight and tell myself: *No more tears, stupid fucking baby.* On three, go. One, two, *push.* Push my body. Push him. Push, just push. Three. I break out of his arms like an explosion. He stumbles backward. But I'm free.

I'm walking away.

He grabs the sleeve of my coat. "Edy, come on."

I snatch my arm away from him the second I feel his hand on me. "Don't touch me!" I only realize I've screamed it as my words echo back at me, reverberating against the trees and the dark and the cold. He looks around, panicked, thinking maybe the neighbors are going to hear.

"Don't be mad," he says, reaching for me again.

“I’m not mad, just don’t—don’t touch me, okay?” My words shake as they hit the air, my mouth never having demanded such things before.

He holds his palms out in front of his chest. “Fine, fine, I’m not.”

We stand there, staring at each other.

“So what happens now?” he asks.

“You go in. I leave.” I try to be stoic about it, try to pretend I didn’t just have a total meltdown in front of him.

“I mean what happens with us?” Us. God. I can’t answer that question, and I think he knows it too because he changes his face, his tone, and asks instead, “Look, are you okay?”

“I really have to go, Steve,” I say impatiently, careful not to look him in the eye.

“Okay. So we’re okay—we’ll talk tomorrow?”

“Sure.”

“Okay. I’ll call you tomorrow.” He tries to smile.

I try to smile back.

“Wait—I want you to know, Edy, I would never hurt you.” He leans in slowly and brushes his lips against my cheek softly.

“Okay,” I whisper, terrified—more terrified than I’ve been in a long time, of anything or anyone.

“Okay,” he says. “Well, good night.”

“Good night,” I repeat, moving away from him.

"EDEN?" MOM KNOCKS ON my door, tries to turn the knob. I open my eyes; pray it's all been a dream. I fumble for my phone. One forty-three p.m. I've been asleep for fifteen hours. Ten missed calls.

"Yeah?" I moan, trying to scroll down the list: Mara, Mara, Mara, Steve, Cameron, Steve, Cameron, Steve, Steve, Steve. Shit. Shit. Shit.

"Eden!" she calls again.

"I said yeah!" I shout. Don't make me get up, Vanessa. Please.

"I'm not going to holler through the door!" she hollers through the door.

I drag myself up, dust myself off, whatever, shove the sleeping bag under the bed and throw my pillow on top. Unlock my door.

"You have a visitor," Vanessa whispers, tight-lipped, "some freaky-looking guy."

"What?"

"Cameron something or other, do you know this boy?" She tilts her head so I can see him standing in the center of our living room, opening and closing his mouth. He's playing with his tongue ring, another stupid, annoying thing about him that I hate.

"Shit," I breathe.

"Eden," she scolds. I stare at the straight line of her mouth. "Well," she says, resigned, "your father's out and I was just leaving to go to the store, but do you want me to stay? I just—I don't like the look of him," she murmurs, casting a glare over her shoulder. "Is he—will you be—he's not dangerous, right? He's your friend?" The thought of her being worried about leaving me alone in the house with a dangerous boy is just so laughable, I could throw up.

"It's fine," I mumble, my tongue and lips dry as paper. Or maybe it wouldn't be fine, but I don't need witnesses for whatever is about to go down. "Would you just tell him I'll be out in a second?"

I slip past her, locking myself in the bathroom. My heart starts beating erratically. I will not cry. "You will *not* cry," I whisper to myself. I wash my face and brush my teeth, try to tug a brush through my hair, which is in knots. I hear muttered good-byes and the front door closing. I pull my hair tight into a ponytail. No. Looks like I care what I look like, looks like I'm trying; I take it out and carefully pull it into a sloppy bun.

"You can't pick up a phone?" he blurts out while I'm still shuffling into the living room.

"I can—I mean, I'm capable, if that's what you're asking."

"Oh, okay. You just won't?" he says, all jittery from trying to restrain himself.

I cross my arms, shrug, absently pulling at a loose thread on my sleeve, a subtle signal that I can barely even be bothered to have this conversation.

"You're unbelievable. He doesn't deserve this. I mean, you do know that, don't you?"

I roll my eyes.

"You know, I told him a girl like you would just destroy him. Because girls like you—"

"Girls like me?" I laugh. Where have I heard this speech before?

"I don't know what the hell he ever saw in you, I really don't."

"Come on, it's pretty obvious what he saw. What he wanted. He had his chance, right? And he kinda blew it, sorry to say."

"Bullshit!" He spits the word before I've even finished my sentence. "Don't pretend you actually believe that. Unless you really are that heartless. Are you? I mean, are you really?" There's this vein in his forehead that throbs every time he raises his voice.

Stone-faced, I mumble, "Guess so."

"Yeah?" he asks, vein bulging, fists clenched at his sides. "'Cause you're so tough, is that right? You're just so tough?"

I grin, let out a sigh. What a dick. He's not getting to me, he's not. He takes a step toward me. I resist the instinct that tells me to back up, to run. But I do some quick physics in my head—mass, volume, density—I could maybe take him. Sure, he's taller, but scrawny. We'd have to weigh about the same. Yeah, if push came to shove, I could take him.

"So, that's why you were crying? Because you're, what, *tough*?" he asks, with this cool smirk. Or maybe he could take me.

I inhale a breath of something that doesn't feel like air, and then can't seem to remember how to exhale. My eyes can't hold their stare; they look down, the stupid cowards.

"Yeah, he told me about that," he continues. "He told me everything. He said that he was trying to be nice and you were being a bitch—" He pauses, letting the word cut through the air. "Well, I'm paraphrasing here 'cause you know Steve wouldn't actually call you a bitch, even if you are one, even if that's what he was thinking. Yeah, he said you started crying, crying like a little—"

Oh, I'm back. "Just shut the fuck up, Cameron! You don't know—you just don't even know, so stay out of it!" I can hardly take in enough breath to keep myself speaking. "You wanna talk about pretending to be tough? Take a look in the mirror! You think you intimidate people, the way you look? You think you're tough?"

"No. I never said I was. I hope I don't intimidate people, but that's the difference between you and me, isn't it? You want to take people down, you want to hurt people, but you know what?" He sneers, inching toward me.

I swear to God I'll hit him right in the face if he comes any closer. "What?" The word comes out strangled—not tough, not fierce—not the way I meant it to.

"Nobody's afraid of you," he says quietly, reserved, restrained, and suddenly in complete control of his emotions.

I swallow hard. I'm losing my shit here. Because I know he's right. I know it's true.

"You're so weak and scared, it's pathetic." He smiles, cocks his head to one side. "What?" He pauses, cruelty dripping off the silence. "You don't think people can see that?"

"Get out." My voice shakes.

"You think you're such a mystery? You're completely transparent—I see right through you."

"Leave!" I demand.

"You're toxic. You know, you just spread around your bullshit everywhere you go. It's so pathetic, I almost feel sorry for you—almost."

I had no idea Cameron could be so mean. Somewhere, a small part of me almost admires him—almost.

"You—you don't even know me. How can you—"

"Oh, yeah I do," he interrupts. "I know all about you."

I shake my head. No. I can't speak.

"I'll go now"—he backs away—"so you can cry. Alone."

"Fuck you."

"Yeah." He raises his arm and waves. "Sure."

"Fuck you!" I scream at his back. "Fuck you!" I pick up the ceramic coaster sitting on the end table, the closest thing to my hand, and chuck it at the door as it closes.

Back in my room, I pull my sleeping bag out from under the bed, toss and turn a few times. Then I'm up on my feet again. Rolling the sleeping bag into a ball, I throw open my closet door and shove it in. It flops out. I kick it, kick and kick and kick at it. I throw myself on the floor and push it back in, over and over, but it just keeps stumbling out again. Next, the avalanche of papers, boxes, a toppling-in-slow-motion stack of old clothes that no longer fit, a fleet of stuffed animals, a fucking stupid, useless clarinet. I lie down on the pile and try as hard as I can to stop crying.

I stay in my room all day. All night. I skip dinner.

Steve texts me at eleven: please don't do this.

He calls and leaves another voice mail at 11:44. And again at midnight.

I turn my phone off.

I GET THERE FIRST, before the bell. I've been dreading it all day. Study hall. Then the three of them walk in together like a gang, against me. Next, it's Amanda.

Mara marches up to our table. "You're not sitting here—no way."

"It's okay," Steve says, setting his stuff down.

"No, it's not, Steve—I've had it with her shit!" Mara yells at him. Then to me: "Move."

"Fine." I stand and scan the room.

Amanda nudges the empty chair next to her toward me with her foot. I think she even tries to smile, but it looks more like a facial tic.

"If everyone will take their seats, come on, Edith, take your seat please." Mr. Mosner smiles at me impatiently. I don't even have the will to correct him. *Edith*—I could just die.

I sit next to Amanda, pretending that it's a free world and I can sit wherever I damn well please. I glance sideways at her. Then I look at her friends: there's Snarky Girl, of course, and the boy who always looks completely baked, and the girl who looks like a bleached-out, negative version of Amanda—blond to her black, pasty to her tan, blue eyes to her brown. They all look at me like I'm some kind of alien.

I can't take my eyes off the clock. Only twenty-four more minutes until this period is over and I can get away from Steve and all the hurt feelings he's throwing my way. Away from Cameron and his words that still ricochet around in my head. And from Mara and this bitterness that lodges itself between us ever deeper.

"Can we talk?"

I turn. It's Steve.

"What, right now?" I ask.

"Yeah," he mumbles, glancing uncomfortably at Amanda and her friends, who are all staring. He starts walking away, toward the door. He glances at Mr. Mosner's back, then motions with his hand for me to follow. I don't know why I do.

"So, you're just not talking to me now, huh?" he asks once we're in the hall.

God, he really hates me. I can feel it in every cell in my body, every nucleus, every fucking ribosome.

"I'm not not talking to you, I just—"

"What?" he interrupts. "You just what?"

"I just don't have anything to say." I shrug.

"You don't have anything to say? How is that possible? How can you possibly not have anything to say?" he almost shouts.

"Okay, well, obviously you have something you'd like to say, so why don't you just go ahead?"

"Fine. It meant something to me—it means something to me. There. I'm not afraid to admit it." And then he just stares at me, waiting, wishing for me to spit his words right back at him.

"Okay, Steve. I'll be honest. It didn't mean anything to me." Truth? Lie? I can't even tell anymore. I know I'm being cold and heartless, but I can't stop myself. He touched. He got hurt. He comes back for more. He gets it. Not my problem.

"I don't even believe that. I was there, okay. I know that it did."

"Look, it's not your fault, it's just the—"

"What is this?" he interrupts, all jumpy and irritated, shoving his fingers back through his hair, almost like he wants to rip his hair out.

"What is what?"

"This! This act," he says, waving his hand at me. He clenches his jaw and his nostrils flare as he starts to breathe heavier. "What's with this act? What are you doing?"

"I don't know what you're talking about!"

"Maybe this works with other guys, but it's different with us, so just stop, okay?" He takes a step closer. I take a step back.

"Why? Because you think you're different? Don't lie to yourself. You're no different. You. Are. Exactly. The same. God, this whole damn thing is so fucking predictable, it makes me want to die!" My words carry through the empty hall, encircling us, holding us motionless in their orbit.

I look at him, turning shades of white, shades of hurt, and I feel my face start to smile.

"You know, I can take weird," he says quietly, the muscles in his face flexing and twitching. Then quieter, "I can take fucked up." And his eyes, they fill with water. Oh God, his voice shakes. "But you're just a . . . slut."

If words are weapons, if they could wound physically, then he just shot a hundred-pound cannonball through the center of my body. The kind of artillery built to take out a battleship, and certainly equipped to sink a stupid, mean little girl.

In shock and disbelief, I utter the word, "What?"

Steve's not supposed to say stuff like that to me.

He steps closer. I'm expecting him to scream, which makes it so much worse when he only whimpers quietly, "You're a fucking bitch. And a slut. And I can't believe I ever thought you were anything else." The words come out through his teeth, and he's unable to stop the tears, like it hurt him to have to say it, even more than it was meant to hurt me.

"I—" I touch his arm. I don't know what to do. He snatches his whole body away from me, though. "Steve, don't—" *Be mad, don't be hurt by me, don't leave angry and destroyed. Don't you know I'm not worth it?* I want to grab him and hold on to him and tell him I'm sorry. I want to do that even more than I want to run. Because Cameron was right, he doesn't deserve this. "Steve, Steve . . . please don't—"

"Fuck. Off," he chokes out, wiping his eyes on his sleeves. He turns around and starts walking off down the hall, past the classroom, getting smaller in the dim light, around the corner, and gone.

I walk in the opposite direction. I slink down the stairwell at the other end of the hall. Into the dirty, forsaken basement bathroom where there are no windows but it's still okay to smoke because no self-respecting teacher would be caught dead in here. I lock myself in. It smells like sewer. Perfect for a mouse, a little rat, like me. In the stall, I sink into the floor, press my back against the cold tiles, and light a cigarette. My breathing echoes. I flick the ashes into the stained toilet next to my face. I close my eyes and I wait. And wait.

I think about Josh again. Not anything in particular. Just little things, like the way he would smile at me, or the sound of his voice, the way I could sometimes make him laugh, the way he could sometimes make me feel so good, so free, so myself. How I thought things were so complicated with him. But they were so easy compared to this, compared to everything else.

I imagine him coming here. Finding me all the way down here in the basement bathroom dungeon like some knight, like some Tin Man in rusting armor, holding a bouquet of dandelions, ready to slay my darkest, most deranged dragons. He'd bust through the door and say something perfect like, "Baby, what's wrong? Don't cry. Let's get the hell outta here. You and me. I'll take you anywhere. We can run away. We can start over, we can be—"

But something interrupts the fantasy, and suddenly I feel my body again, gravity pulling me down, anchoring me to the cold cement floor. Something pinches my thigh, bringing me back to reality, pinching harder. And harder, burning, damn—no, not pinching. I open my eyes to see that my cigarette has burned all the way down to the filter, causing the cherry to fall off and burn through my pants like acid, right down to my skin.

"Shit!" I whisper-shout, smacking my leg to try to extinguish the stupidity.

Then the bell rings, screaming through the walls and the ceiling, vibrating through the whole building—through me. I wait until the distant noise of shouting and feet running and lockers clanging has passed.

I walk back into the classroom to find Amanda picking my backpack up off the floor. She's being so gentle with it, it's unsettling. Everyone else has gone except for her and Snarky. I linger in the doorway, listening.

"So, you're what, friends with her now? That's seriously fucked," Snarky says under her breath.

"Not friends. Just—I don't know, I guess I'm trying not to hate her." The way Amanda says "her," I know somehow that they're talking about me because I get this pounding in my chest. I freeze, stuck between fight and flight. "I'm trying to be Zen, okay?" she continues. "Isn't that what you're always preaching?"

"Even after she . . . ?" Snarky asks her quietly. "There's a limit to being all Zen and shit."

Amanda shrugs. "I don't wanna talk about it."

"After I what?" I ask, stepping forward, the decision made for me. I'll fight.

Amanda turns to look at me, startled. "Oh! Nothing," she answers quickly.

"No, what? What the hell did I ever do to you? I really want to know. I would love to know," I hear myself say, with a little laugh in my throat, feeling close to the edge of something, like I could say anything right now, do anything, and not give a damn about the repercussions.

"Just forget it," Amanda tells me, shaking her head.

But Snarky pipes up: "You and Kevin."

"Wh—what?" The word sticks in my throat. Me and Kevin don't belong in the same sentence, in the same thought, in the same fucking galaxy.

"Shut up!" Amanda snaps at her friend. "I was going to pick up your things for you," she says to me.

"What are you talking about?" I demand from Snarky.

"I'm talking about you and her brother—"

"Fucking shut up!" Amanda interrupts. "I said I don't care!"

"Doing it," Snarky finishes, looking me up and down like I really am a totally slutty disgusting whore.

I can barely hang on to a thought long enough to get the words out of my mouth. "I—I—what? I never—why would you say that?"

"Please," Snarky says with a laugh, "it's like, just, a known thing."

I refocus on Amanda, trying to speak instead of vomit. "You tell people this? Why would you make something like that up?"

"I'm not making it up—he told me!" She starts to get that hateful look in her eye again. "So you don't have to act like—"

"I never. Never. I never, you fucking liar! I hate him. I would never! I hate him more than anyone in the entire world. He disgusts me. In fact, you disgust me! You disgust me because you make me think of him!" I'm pointing and thrashing my arms around wildly, and they start to back away from me, I realize, because I'm getting closer.

"He said that you and him—" Amanda starts to speak, but I can't let her have one more word.

"I wish he were dead, okay? I hope. He fucking. Dies. Nothing would make me happier than for something really horrible to happen to him. Do you get that?" I'm inches from her face now. Can't stop moving toward her. "I mean, do you fucking get that?" I feel something savage and electrical flow through me, like my hands could strangle her, like they're controlled by some part of my brain that's immune to logic, the same part of my brain that's allowing me to say these things, these fucked-up things that are just going to give me away. I could just . . . my hands. Reach out. God. For anything. To hurt.

Next thing I know she's on the floor.

And her friend is screaming, "You fucking psycho, what the fuck?"

And I'm screaming, "I'll kill you if you ever say that again." Amanda looks up at me, tears rolling down her cheeks. It makes her look just like her seven-year-old Mandy self, but still I can't force myself to stop. "Don't you ever fucking say that again—do you understand? Not to me, not to anyone. Or I swear to God. I swear to God, I'll fucking kill you."

I cry the entire way home from school. I just walk down the streets sobbing. Not caring who sees me, or what I must look like, or what anyone thinks. I get home and lock myself in my bedroom.

I just lie awake, staring at the ceiling.

I made Mara cry. I made Steve cry. I made Amanda cry.

Anyone who has ever felt anything for me now hates me—after hours of dwelling on this, I've actually made myself physically ill.

I don't go to school the next day. Can't face anyone. I'm sick, sick, sick, I tell Vanessa. She feels my forehead and tells me I'm burning up. I just sleep and sleep. And no one bothers me at all. All day and all night, it's just me in my sleeping bag drifting in and out of consciousness.

"CALM DOWN, HONEY, it's going to be all right, I promise," I hear Vanessa say in a dream. In it, I'm crying and she's trying to take care of me, and I'm trying so hard to let her. I open my eyes. A dim light glows through the curtain. My alarm clock says 5:10 a.m.

"Everything's going to get straightened out, son, you'll see," Conner says, in a voice so tender, I question if I really am awake at all.

"No, Dad—you weren't there. I just don't think so." It's Caelin, and it's him who's crying, not me. And I am awake, I'm sure.

"Maybe you should call the Armstrongs, Conner," Vanessa says, her voice muffled behind my locked bedroom door. The Armstrongs—Kevin—I heard that. I sit up fast, listen harder.

"No! Don't call them. Not yet . . . not until we know if—" Caelin pauses and then I hear him sniffling again. But Caelin shouldn't be here. His winter break isn't for another week. No, something's not right.

I unlock my door, small steps to the living room. No one hears me come in. My brother is sitting in the middle of the couch, head in hands, Vanessa in her bathrobe and slippers sitting next to him, arm draped across his back; Conner on his feet, hovering, a hand resting tentatively on his shoulder. They're silent. Caelin's body bobs up and down.

"What's going on?" I ask.

They all turn their eyes to me. But they don't say anything. Caelin drops his head back down into his lap. Vanessa's chin quivers.

"It's Kevin, honey," Conner finally tells me.

"What—what did he do?"

"Do?" Caelin spits at me. "He didn't do anything!"

"Shhshhshh," Vanessa coos at him.

"Okay, well, what happened?" I try instead.

"It's all going to be all right, so everybody just calm down," Conner yells. "Edy, Kevin is . . . in a little bit of trouble, but it's going to get straightened out soon enough."

"What kind of trouble?" I scratch my arm, the anxiety bubbling up under my skin.

"This girl in our dorm is saying he raped her!" Caelin shouts. And then, at my lack of reaction, he adds, "He didn't, obviously, but I don't know what's going to happen. The police came and—"

I can't hear anything else because someone is yelling inside my head, taking a mallet to my brain. Screaming, *God, no, no, no, no.* I feel like I might fall over, like I might just stop breathing altogether. That old familiar bullet inches its way in deeper. I think it's headed for my heart this time. No, my stomach. I run for the bathroom. Make it just in time to lift the lid and throw up.

I sit down on the cold tile floor. My head is pounding, like there's literally a war going on inside my brain, complete with bombs and cannons and big guns and casualties. He did it. Of course he did it. There's no question about that. But, did I do it too? I listened to him, I kept my mouth shut, and then he went and did it again, to someone else. Except this girl, whoever she is, she was brave, smart. Not like me. I am just the same sniveling coward I was then. I'm a mouse. I am a fucking mouse.

On the other side of the door I hear some more sniffling and low, wordless whining. Gurgling sounds from the coffeepot. I emerge, hopefully not looking like someone just kicked my ass.

"You okay, Minnie?" Conner asks, squeezing my shoulder a little too vigorously. Minnie, I haven't heard that one in a while. How obscenely appropriate.

"Not really," I admit.

"Don't worry about school today." He smiles. "We're all taking a mental-health day. Sound good?"

I nod, try to smile back.

We sit around the house for hours, everyone looking devastated. Caelin's a mess. Conner tries to act like everything's okay. Vanessa vacillates between manic fidgeting and sitting too still. I feel like beating my head against the wall.

I can't imagine eating, but I help Vanessa make lunch anyway. She says it will help everyone feel better. I seriously doubt that. As we sit around the kitchen table, mostly just picking at our grilled cheese sandwiches and stirring our bowls of lumpy tomato soup, the story comes out disjointed and biased.

Caelin tells us, "It's his girlfriend. It just—it doesn't even make sense—I mean, why would he need to rape someone he was already sleeping with?"

It made sense to me, of course. He needed to make her feel worthless, needed to control her, needed to hurt her, needed to leave her powerless.

"She broke up with Kevin for some reason or other—I really don't know—but it wasn't a huge deal or anything. And Kevin asked her to come over the one night, because *she* was upset about the breakup, just to talk, and she says that's when he 'raped' her." He air quotes, and I want to lunge across the table and break his fingers off. "Kevin admitted to having sex with her—'consensual' sex." He air quotes again.

I don't bother telling him that if he's trying to make her the liar, then he doesn't want to emphasize the word "consensual."

"She didn't even report it for a couple of days," he adds, as if this is some important piece of information, as if it means anything. "If it really happened, then why didn't she report it right away?"

Compared to how long I've waited, two days seems nearly instantaneous, two damn days is nothing.

"And besides," he continues, "I was there. I mean, I was right there in the next room. I would have known if something was happening. If she was seriously in trouble, she could've screamed, or called for me—I mean, we were friends too. And I didn't hear anything!"

Oh, my heart. Stops. If he only knew the things he was capable of not hearing from the next room.

"Nothing at all," he repeats. "And that's exactly what I told the campus police when they questioned me last week. But then out of nowhere, they came last night—the real police, this time—and took him. That's why I'm here—I didn't know what else to do. I just can't believe they can get away with this. They can't just arrest someone for no reason, right? I cannot figure out why she would lie like this. She seemed so . . . normal."

"Maybe she's not lying," I finally blurt out, unable to hold it in any longer.

"How can you even say that? Of course she's lying!" Caelin looks like he's about to climb over the table at me.

"Well, they don't just arrest someone for no reason, and you just said yourself you didn't think she would lie," I remind him.

"No, I said I don't know why she *would* lie, not that I didn't think she was. And I don't know, Eden, maybe she just decided to invent some fucked-up story because she felt bad—breaking up with a guy and then sleeping with him anyway—for being a slut."

"Caelin, we don't talk like that at the table," Vanessa scolds gently.

But he ignores her. Instead he looks at me and mumbles under his breath, "You can understand that, can't you?"

My mouth opens. Out of shock or to speak, I don't know which. I can't even think in words—can't breathe, can't feel—but somehow my voice finds them anyway, and they explode off my tongue, those perfect words: "Fuck. You."

"Fuck you too!" Caelin matches me, in flawless reflex.

Conner slams his fist down on the table, rattling the spoons in their bowls. Rattling my heart. "All right, all right! What the hell is going on with you two? Both of you shut your goddamn mouths right now!" He points his finger in both our faces, alternately.

Caelin pushes his chair away from the table and storms into the kitchen.

I follow suit and stomp off to my room, slamming my door hard behind me.

I sit down on the floor, leaning my back against the side of my bed. I let my head fall against the edge of the mattress. I close my eyes. I can't keep it out any longer. Can't hold it back. I feel something break like a levee inside my head.

WHAT HAPPENED: I WOKE up to him climbing on top of me, jabbing his knees into my arms. I thought it was a joke—unfunny to be sure, but still, a joke. I opened my mouth. I tried to speak, but only got out "wwwh," the beginning of what. What, what, what is happening, what are you doing?

But he put his hand over my mouth right away, so my mom and dad wouldn't hear. They wouldn't hear, because my alarm clock was blinking 2:48 at me from the nightstand next to my bed. We both knew they were fast asleep on the other side of the house.

No joke.

Because now his mouth is on your mouth and his hand around your throat and he's whispering, "Shutupshutupshutup." You do. You shut up. You are stupid, stupid.

It's 2:49: He had my days-of-the-week underwear on the floor. And somehow you still don't understand what's happening. Then he yanked my nightgown up—my favorite nightgown with the stupid sleeping basset hounds on it—and I feel the seam rip where the thread was already coming loose. He pulls it up around my neck, exposing my whole body, my whole naked, awkward body. And he shoves a fistful of it into my mouth, choking me. I was gagging, but he just kept pushing it into my mouth, pushing, pushing, pushing, until it wouldn't go in any farther. I didn't understand why, not until I tried to scream. I was screaming, I knew I was, but no sound—just muffled underwater noise.

I managed to get my arms free, but they didn't know what to do first. They flailed aimlessly, striking outward without direction. Stupid limbs. A quick smacksmack against a wall of boy body and I was down again. So much for that adrenaline rush of superhuman strength I'd always heard about—the kind that could allow grandmothers to lift cars off children yet wouldn't allow me to just get out of his hands. Fucking useless urgency.

"Stop it," he warned me as he held my arms down against the bed, his knees digging into my thighs, grinding his kneecaps in hard until all of his body was smothering all of my body, my bones turning to dust. I remember you thought that hurt. But that was nothing.

His body was shaking—his arms from holding me down so hard, his legs from trying to pry himself between my thighs, trying to position himself to do the thing that even then, in that moment, I still didn't believe he was capable of doing. "Goddamn it," he growled in my ear—her ear, her ear. "Hold still or I—fucking do it, or I—I swear to God," he breathed.

I didn't care about the ends of those sentences because this can't be happening, this can't be happening, this can't be happening. This is not real. This is something else. This is not me. This is someone else. I tried to keep her legs squeezed together. I really tried—they were shaking from the strain of it—but by 2:51 he got them apart.

The bed frame creaks like a rusty swing swaying back and forth. Moans like a haunted house. And something like glass shatters. Shatters inside of you, and the tiny slivers of this horrible thing splinter off and travel through your veins, beelining it straight to your heart. Next stop: brain. I tried to think of anything, anything except it hurts it hurts it hurts so bad.

Quickly though, the pain became secondary to the fact that I thought I might actually die. I couldn't breathe. No sound could get out of my mouth and no air could get in. And the weight of his body was crushing me to the point I thought my ribs would snap right in half and puncture a lung.

He used one hand—just one—to hold both my arms over my head, grinding my wrist bones together. He kept the other hand around my throat, constricting every time I made any sound at all. The sounds were involuntarily: gurgling and sputtering—dying noises—noises the body just makes when it's dying. Did he know he was killing me? I wanted to tell him I was about to die.

At some point I guess I just stopped struggling. The thing, it was happening. It didn't matter anymore. Just play dead. He kept his face buried in the pillow and every time he moved, so sharp, his hollow, muted grunts and groans reverberating through the cotton and polyester stuffing, winding a meandering path that led directly to my ears, melting with the noises of my insides breaking, the voices in my head screaming, screaming, screaming.

By 2:53 it was over. He let go of my arms. It was over, it was over, I told myself. When he ripped the nightgown out of my mouth, I started coughing and gasping. I had almost suffocated to death, but he couldn't even let me have that—a simple bodily reaction. He clamped his hand over my mouth. He was out of breath, his mouth almost touching mine, his words wet: "Shut up. Shut up. Listen to me. Listen." He held my face still, so that I had to look directly into his eyes. His eyes were the eyes he always had, but they burned me now, burned right into me. "Shhshhshh," he whispered as he peeled away strands of tear-soaked hair from my face, tucking them behind my ears—like, gently—over and over again, his hands on me like it's the most normal thing, like this was just supposed to be.

"Look at me," he whispered. "No one will ever believe you. You know that. No one. Not ever."

He pushed himself off me then, a burst of icy air rushing in between us as he sat up. He was leaving and it would finally be over. I didn't care about what had just happened, or what would happen next, I only cared that it would be done, that he would be gone. I would be quiet, I would be still, if that's what it took. I shut my eyes and waited. And waited. Except he wasn't leaving, he was kneeling between my legs, looking down at me, at my body.

I had felt plenty ugly before, in general. But never ugly like this. Never as insignificant and repulsive and hated as he made me feel then, with his eyes on me. I tried to cover myself with my hands, but he tore them away and laid my arms flat against my sides, he put his hands on me instead. It wasn't over, not yet. This was still part of it. I grab handfuls of sheets in my hands to make my body stay put, like he wanted.

He wasn't even holding me down. Not physically. But he was holding me in some other way, a way that was somehow stronger than muscle and arms and legs. I couldn't even feel my body anymore, not even the hurt, but I could feel his eyes on me, showing me all of the places I was ugly, all the things he hated most about me, all the ways I didn't matter.

"You're gonna keep your mouth shut," he whispered into my mouth. I wasn't sure if it was a question or an order. Either way, there's only one right answer, I know. "I asked. A fucking. Question." Drops of spit fly onto my face with each word.

I stare . . . am I allowed to speak? Wasn't I supposed to be shutting up?

He grabs hold of my chin and a handful of hair and jerks my face up and down. "Yes?" he hisses, nodding slowly. I nod my head ferociously. "Say it."

My voice doesn't work right though; I can only get out the "s" sound.

"Say it," he demands.

"'Es. Yes, yes," I hear myself whimper.

"No one—do you understand? You tell no one," he says with his mouth close to my face. "Or I swear to God. I swear to God, I'll fucking kill you."

I hear my voice, no louder than my breath: "Please, please, please." And I don't even know what I'm begging for—him to just get it over with and kill me or for him to spare me.

He smears his lips against my mouth one last time, looks at me like I'm his, and smiles his smile. He gets up. Then he's back in his boxers. He whispers, "Go back to sleep," before shutting the door of my bedroom behind him.

I put both hands over my mouth, squeezed my eyes shut as tight as I could, and tried to fix my brain to disbelieve everything it thought and felt and knew to be true.

I OPEN MY EYES. I'm breathing heavy. Then barely breathing at all. My heart races. Then stops altogether. I'm in my room. Not then, but now. And I'm okay. *I'm okay. I'm okay,* I repeat silently.

I stand up.

I pick up my phone.

I pace my room.

I need someone. I actually fucking need someone. Need someone now. But I have no one to call—no one. I have left myself with absolutely no one in the world who would ever care about what is happening to me right now.

But then I have a thought. A very stupid, masochistic thought, but now it's there in my head and it's one of those thoughts that once it's there, there's nothing that can be done to make it go away. My fingers press the numbers even though my brain forbids it, just like it was two years ago, just like no time has passed at all. The sequence of numbers ingrained in my bones and muscle, I dial.

I practice his name: "Josh. Josh," I whisper.

I hate myself. It's ringing.

"Hello?"

I open my mouth. But what words could ever, ever undo these things, what words could ever tell enough of the truth?

I hang up.

What is wrong with me?

I redial.

"Uh, hello?"

I hang up.

Just one more time . . .

"Hel-lo-o?"

I hang up again. Damn it.

I take a breath.

Like some kind of junkie with no self-control, I just cannot stop myself. I dial.

"Who is this?" he demands.

Oh God. His voice. Just the sound of his voice makes my heart pound.

"Hello?" he inhales. "Hello?" he exhales.

I open my mouth. But then Vanessa's voice calls, "Edy? Edy, will you come out here please?"

I hang up fast.

In the living room, I'm met by two incredibly intimidating looking people: a man—a cop in uniform—and a woman who's wearing a power suit and introduces them both.

"Hello, this is Officer Mitchell and I'm Detective Dodgson. We're here to ask some questions regarding Kevin Armstrong. We understand that your family, Mr. and Mrs. McCrorey, is very close with Mr. Armstrong and his family, is that correct?"

Conner fumbles with the remote control as he tries to switch off the TV. And Vanessa does something I've never seen her do before—she reaches for Conner's hand.

Caelin is suddenly on his feet, looking entirely too confrontational considering the fact that both these people have visible guns on them. "I already told the police everything I know, which is nothing, because nothing happened!" Caelin practically shouts.

"We are aware of the statement you gave the campus police last week, but we're here today regarding a separate matter, a related but separate matter," the woman, Detective Dodgson, says. I feel my hand clutch at my chest. Because I know, right away, I know there's someone else, another girl, someone besides the ex-girlfriend. Okay, I take a deep breath and hold it; I plant my feet into the floor, and brace myself for something terrible.

"What is this all about?" Conner says shakily, putting his arm around Vanessa's shoulder.

"Look, he didn't do anything to her, I know it!" Caelin insists.

Officer Mitchell, towering over six-foot-tall Caelin, takes a step toward him; he doesn't even need to speak to intimidate. Detective Dodgson proceeds, "We'd like to ask each of you, separately, about Kevin and Amanda Armstrong."

The bottom of my stomach opens up and my heart drops through.

Amanda.

Of course—of course, it would be her. I try to fade. Try to hold still and just blend into the wall. Try to summon enough psychic power to disintegrate, to dematerialize right here before their eyes.

"What?" Caelin whispers, even though it's pretty clear he meant to scream it.

"Mandy?" Vanessa says, more to herself than the detective.

"Why would you want to ask us about her?" Conner asks, all of us getting afraid of the answer.

"But why? Why—what?" Vanessa can't seem to formulate a sentence.

"We're investigating a report of assault, ma'am," Officer Mitchell says.

Detective Dodgson looks at me in a way that makes me feel naked. But she couldn't know, because nobody knows.

"What . . . do you . . . mean, assault?" Vanessa stutters, unable to comprehend what we're being told.

Caelin sits back down on the couch and just stares at an imaginary point on the carpet—doesn't speak, doesn't blink.

"We'll want to speak with each of you," Officer Mitchell says. "Mr. McCrorey, will you join me in the other room?" He starts walking into the dining room, Conner follows, looking disoriented, clutching the remote control for dear life.

The woman looks at me dead on. "Eden, right?"

Breathless, I try my best to respond: "Yeah."

"Can we speak privately? Caelin, Mrs. McCrorey, Officer Mitchell will be in to speak with you two shortly."

I start toward my room, her footsteps trailing behind me.

"May I sit?" she asks, gesturing to my bed.

I nod. My heart is racing. My hands are shaking. My skin is crawling. She sits down, and the bed creaks like it's spilling its secrets out all over the place.

"I'd like to ask you a few questions, if that's all right."

"Okay, but I really don't know anything." Too jumpy, Edy. Calm down.

"Really?" she asks. "Because you didn't seem at all surprised when Officer Mitchell told your family about the allegations against Mr. Armstrong." That's not a question, though. I don't know how I'm supposed to answer, so I just stare. "I'd be interested in knowing why that is."

"Why what is?" Play dumb, that's it.

"Eden, if you have any information or knowledge regarding the Armstrongs, now would be the time to tell us."

"I don't, though. I swear. I had no idea he was doing that to her."

"Doing what, Eden?" she asks, pretending to be puzzled.

"I don't know. Whatever he was doing, whatever he did, I don't know." Oh God, she sees right through me.

"All right. Then back to my initial question?"

"Why I wasn't surprised, you mean?"

"So, you *weren't* surprised?"

"No, I—I was. I was surprised—am, I mean, I *am* surprised," I stammer.

"No," she says slowly, "your mother and father and brother were surprised—shocked—but not you. Can you tell me what was going through your mind?"

"Nothing, I don't know, I wasn't thinking anything."

"You had to have been thinking something?" And she looks at me with these eyes—these no-nonsense, no-bullshit, no-tolerance-for-lies-of-any-kind eyes. She looks so far inside of me, as if she can see everything. Everything I am, everything I'm not. I count the seconds of her staring into my soul: One. Two. Three. Four. Fi—

"Let me ask another question, then. Do you think that these allegations against Mr. Armstrong are plausible—just in your own opinion?"

"I don't know. How should I know? I mean, I wouldn't know."

"I have to say, you seem awfully agitated, Eden. Are you hiding something because you think you're protecting Mr. Armstrong?"

"Protecting? No. And I'm not hiding anything, really."

"Eden, I'll be frank with you," she says, folding her hands neatly one over the other in her lap. "I personally spoke with Amanda, and she specifically mentioned your name. Told me I should be talking with you." She gently points her finger at me through her clasped hands. "Do you know why?"

I shake my head too hard back and forth, back and forth.

"Well, she seemed to believe that you may have some kind of information about Mr. Armstrong. Kevin," she adds, as if she knows the spark of rage that just the sound of his name sets off inside of me.

I watch her watching my hands shake. I cross my arms and tuck my hands under my arms.

"Amanda told me about an incident that happened at school earlier this week. She said you became highly . . . emotional when discussing—"

"No! I said no. I don't know why she mentioned me. I don't know anything." I mean to shout it, to be firm and strong, but it just comes out in a piercing whimper.

She holds me in her poker-face stare. I cannot read her at all. She stands up, walks across my room. I think she's leaving, but she closes the door so it's only open a crack. "Eden," she says softly. "I'm going to ask you something and I need you to be very honest in your response." She lowers her voice and stands there like a mountain I will never be able to move. "Eden, has Kevin ever abused or assaulted you in any way, sexual or otherwise?"

I always promised myself that if only someone would ask, if someone would only ask the right question, I would tell the truth. And now it's here. It could be over in one syllable. I open my mouth. I want to say it. Yes. Yes. I try to make a sound. Yes. Say it! But my mouth is so dry, I can't.

I take a breath and I choke. I choke on the word. I'm actually choking. I stand up out of my chair as if that will help anything. I start pacing the room, losing my air quickly. I'm coughing so hard she has to race out of my bedroom to get me a glass of water. I'm still coughing when she gets back. I sip the water, but I choke even more, spewing it all over the carpet. My throat feels raw.

"Can you breathe, Eden?" she asks loudly.

I nod my head yes even though I really can't. I can't breathe. It's like there's something stuck in my throat. I cough and cough, but it doesn't do anything. I clutch at my neck. There's something there, I can feel it. Can taste it. Something lodged in my throat, something familiar, something dry like cotton, something like . . . like the end of that stupid damn nightgown that went directly into the garbage the next morning.

By then Vanessa and Conner have stormed in.

"Oh my God!" Vanessa screams.

"Do something!" Conner yells at no one in particular.

The room shrinks. I shrink. And now I'm back there. I see

myself over their shoulders, lying in my bed and he's on top of her again. I'm watching him shove the nightgown into her mouth and nobody does a fucking thing. She tries to hit him once, twice, but he has her arms down again and . . . and he . . .

Vanessa: "Edy, drink the water!"

Detective: "All right, everyone calm down, let's just give her a little space now. She's fine. You're fine, honey, you're fine."

But I'm not fine. She's not fine.

He's doing it, hurting her, again and again and again and nobody even turns to look! I try to point, want to scream: Behind you, look, damn it, notice something for once . . . it's right there, what you need to know, right there, happening . . . still. . . .

"EDEN EDY EDY EDEN EDY EDY," they scream at me all at once. I try to scream back. But nothing. Their voices fade into the background. White noise. Only one sound pierces through the veil of static: *No one will ever believe you no one will ever believe you no one will ever believe you.*

Be over. Be over. I thought it was over. It was supposed to be over.

Underwater voices and blurry words surface: "Better . . . Okay . . . Edy . . . Eden . . . She's all right, look."

My eyes open. I'm staring at the ceiling. I'm on the floor. There's Vanessa on one side, the detective on the other. I feel like Dorothy, waking up from the strangest dream, except to an even stranger reality. Caelin and Conner are behind them, leaning over me.

"What happened?" I ask, my voice scratchy.

"You fainted!" Vanessa screeches, tears threatening to overflow the shores of her eyes.

"Oh God," I moan, trying to sit up.

"Take it easy, now. Slowly." Detective Dodgson puts a hand on my back.

"Sorry. That's never happened before. God, I feel so stupid." I try to laugh at myself. It sounds fake as hell, though.

"Well," the detective says, standing up, "I do still have some more questions for you, Eden, but for now why don't you just get some rest. If you do happen to think of anything, please don't hesitate to call. I'll leave my card right here for you." She pulls a business card out of some invisible compartment of her jacket and sets it down on the corner of my desk, tapping it twice with her index finger.

I SIT AT MY desk and stare at the card for a long time. After Vanessa force-fed me about a gallon of orange juice and endless saltines, I was allowed back in my room unsupervised. I trace my finger over the embossed letters that spell out: Detective Dorian Dodgson. I take my phone out.

I scroll down and find the number in my outgoing calls.

"Hello? Hello?"

I hang up. I call back.

"Hello . . . are you there?"

I hang up. I redial.

"Hello?" he answers, edgy.

Hang up. Redial.

"Eden, is this you?"

My heart sinks deep.

"Eden, if this is you . . . just . . . hello?"

I hang up. Fuck. Then my phone starts vibrating in my hand. It's him. It keeps ringing. I silence it. Shit, but then it'll go to voice mail. I have to pick up. I do. I don't say anything. I listen. He breathes.

"Eden?

"Eden!

"Will you just say something?

"I hear you breathing. . . .

"Okay, listen." His voice is sharp, just like that day in the bathroom when he dumped me.

I listen. I listen closely.

"I don't know what you want, why you're calling me like this. Talk now. Or don't expect me to pick up again."

He pauses, soundless. Then hangs up.

My hands shake as my fingers punch in the numbers. I hold my breath. It rings. Once, twice, three times. I should hang up. I should. This is crazy.

"What?" he snaps.

I can't speak.

"Eden, come on. . . ."

No.

"Do you need some kind of help?"

Yes, yes.

"Is there something going on, is something wrong?"

God, yes.

"I can't—you're going to have to say something here!"

I wish I could.

"Eden . . . Eden, come on. Look, are you stalking me or something?"

Stalking him?

"There're laws, you know," he adds. "This has to stop. I mean it."

"No," I finally whimper.

"What?"

"No. I'm not stalking you."

"Then what are you doing? Because this—this is really fucking creepy, okay?"

"I'm sorry."

Silence.

More silence.

"Are you okay?" he finally asks.

"No." True.

"Wha—"

"I cared!" I blurt out.

"What?"

"I cared about you. I always cared about you."

"Okay," he mumbles, like a verbal shrug. Can't tell what it means.

"Okay?"

"Well, I don't know what to say, Eden. I mean, I haven't spoken to you in years. This is just—this is really weird."

"Did you know?"

"Did I know what?" he asks.

"That I cared?"

He hesitates, probably trying to decide if he should just hang up on me. He sighs and I can tell he's also rolling his eyes; I can see him so clearly in my mind. "Sometimes, I guess."

"I lied to you. A lot. God, I don't even know if you remember. Do you? Do you even remember me?"

"Yeah, of course I remember you, Eden. I remember everything."

"I wish you didn't."

"You don't sound good, Eden. Should I call someone for you?"

"Do you remember what I told you my middle name was?"

"Eden, why have you been calling me?" he demands, ignoring my question.

"Marie, right, remember?"

"Yeah, Marie, I remember."

"That was a lie too."

"What?"

"It's Anne."

"Are you drunk?"

"Why, do I sound drunk?"

"Yeah, you do, actually."

"Well, I'm not, but hey, that's probably a good idea. I'm just—I don't know, I'm just so—fucked up!" I laugh. It's funny. This. This conversation, it's ridiculous. "So completely fucked up." I laugh again. "I'm sorry. You can really hang up if you want."

"No, I don't want to hang up. I'm really worried, though. You don't sound right."

"I'm *not* right. I'm really not. I'm not right. I'm wrong—everything I have ever done in my entire life has been wrong."

"Eden, I don't understand what you want, what is this about?"

"I used to love the way you said my name, you know, before you hated me."

"I never hated you." He sighs.

"Yes, you did. I made you hate me. It's okay, though, everyone hates me. I would hate me too. I mean, I do. I do hate me. I'm a horrible, horrible person."

"Eden, please, just—look, what do you need from me? How can I help?"

"You can't!" I shriek. And then I cover my mouth because I can't let him hear that I'm crying. "Look, I'll let you go. I'm sorry," I gasp. "I shouldn't have called. I just—" I sniffle, struggling for enough air to finish this. "I just miss you so much sometimes, and I wanted you to know that I cared. I really did. And there wasn't anyone else. Ever. I hope you'll believe me."

"Wait, Eden, don't hang—" I do, though, I hang up.

I turn the phone off because I don't want to know if he calls, and even more so, I don't want to know if he doesn't call. I just want to sleep. I just want to fall asleep for a very long time, for forever, maybe.

But I do wake up, 5:45 a.m., like every other morning. And like every other morning, I shower. I brush my teeth. I do my makeup, my hair, get dressed, the usual. I pack my bag, pretend to be getting ready for school. All the while I try to convince myself that last night didn't happen. Hell, that all of yesterday didn't happen. I didn't cry and snivel on the phone to Josh. I didn't pass out while being questioned by Detective Dorian Dodgson. In fact, I don't even know a Dorian Dodgson. I don't know an Amanda, either. Kevin Armstrong? Never heard of him. And rape . . . all I know about rape is that it's a terrible thing, something that happens to other people. Not me.

I tiptoe through the living room, past Caelin asleep on the couch. "I'm leaving," I whisper, too quiet for anyone to actually hear. And then I do. I leave. It's only six thirty. I try to think of somewhere to go—school is out of the question and the library won't open for another two hours. The streets are empty and silent. A fresh layer of snow absorbs all the sound in the world.

I turn my phone on. Fifteen missed calls, nine new voice mails.

11:10 p.m.: "Eden, it's Josh. Please just call me back, okay?"

11:27 p.m.: "Eden, I—I don't know what's going on, but please call, just to let me know you're all right."

12:01 a.m.: "Eden . . ."

12:22 a.m.: "Damn it, I'm really worried. . . ."

12:34 a.m.: ". . . (breathing)."

12:45 a.m.: "Eden, I just want you to know that I don't hate you. I never hated you. Fuck, will you just call? Please."

1:37 a.m.: "I'm starting to get really scared that you might be doing something stupid and I don't want—just please don't, all right. Just call me and we can talk. Please."

1:56 a.m.: "Look, I don't know what happened, but it will be okay. It really will. Just please call me, I'm going crazy here."

2:31 a.m.: "Eden . . . if you won't call me . . . fuck it, I'm coming there."

End of messages.

Coming there? Here? No, no, no, no. I dial. It doesn't even ring on my end before he answers.

"Hello, Eden?"

"Yeah, it's me."

"Jesus Christ, I called you like twenty times!"

"I know, I'm sorry, I just now listened to your messages. Just please don't come. It's not worth it. I'm really not that—it's not an emergency or anything. I'm really sorry if I worried you."

"Worried me? Yeah, you fucking worried me. I've been thinking you were *dead* for the past seven hours!"

That word—"dead"—it just cuts. Like a blade. Through everything. "I didn't—" But I can barely speak. "I didn't mean to—that's not what I wanted. I didn't want you to be worried, I was just—oh God, I don't know."

"You what? Why were you calling me?"

I have to stop walking while I try to think of the answer. Well, maybe not *the* answer, but an answer. "I was just . . . lonely. I'm just lonely, that's all. I'm sorry. I know it was stupid to call. I don't even know why I did it. I shouldn't have involved you."

Silence.

"I feel like such an idiot," I tell him.

I hear him cluck his tongue, then sigh sympathetically. "No, come on, stop. Don't say that."

"No, I do. I'm really embarrassed."

"I see you."

"What?"

But he hangs up. I start to call him back, but a car horn shatters the icy quiet that blankets the entire neighborhood. I turn to look. An old beat-up Ford slows down as it pulls up behind me. I stop walking. It stops moving too. I bend down and look inside through the steamy passenger window. It's really him. He reaches over and unlocks the door.

We stare at each other from across the table at the IHOP off the highway. I feel like I'm looking at a ghost. He looks the same, but different—grown up, more like himself, like the way he's supposed to look, somehow. He sips his coffee; he takes it black, very grown up indeed.

Next to the syrup corral, there's a cup of broken crayons. I can't stop staring at them.

"So . . . ?" he says, and I literally have to push the crayons out of my field of vision so I can focus on him.

"I just can't believe I'm sitting here with you," I finally say, after staring for far too long.

"I know. I can't believe it either." Except the way he says it is so much different from the way I said it.

"You had to have been driving all night?"

Pointedly, he says, "No, just half the night, the other half I was calling you."

"I *am* sorry. I didn't mean to make it sound so dire. I was just upset, I guess."

He doesn't say anything. His face is a cross between pissed, annoyed, and confused.

And because I can't stand that look, my mouth keeps saying the stupidest things. Things like: "Um, you look really good," and, "So, I guess this is finally our date, huh?"

He doesn't respond though, he just sits there, looking like he's in pain.

Blessedly, our waitress comes to my rescue with two heaping plates of pancakes. "Just let me know if I can get you anything else," she tells us. "Enjoy, guys."

We both reach for the butter-pecan syrup at the same time. Our hands touch.

"Eden, I should tell you something up front, right now, okay?"

"Okay?" This sounds important; I balance my fork on the edge of my plate, make sure I look like I'm paying attention.

"I'm seeing someone. I have a girlfriend, and it's serious, so . . ."

"Oh." I pick my fork back up, stab at the pancake, try to wipe the devastated look from my face, and sound as blasé as possible. "Right, yeah, right, of course." I carefully cut off a triangle of pancake and stuff it in my mouth. It's hard to swallow.

"So I just want you to know that I didn't come here to—what I mean is that I'm only here as a friend."

"Sure, yeah, I get it." Be cool. Eat. Be normal. And for the love of God, don't say anything else. "Does she know you're here right now?" I mumble into my mug. It echoes.

He nods, taking a sip of his coffee.

"What did you tell her, you had to go talk some crazy, lying, stalker girl down off the ledge?" I smile. My face cracks.

"No." He grins uncomfortably, just slightly. "Not like that anyway. I told her that you were an ex-girlfriend, and I know, I know that's not how you thought of it, but that's what I told her, just for the sake of simplicity. And I told her I thought you might be in trouble and I wanted to see you and make sure you were all right."

"Wow," I whisper. I don't know which is harder to believe: the fact that he actually told her the truth, or that after he told her the truth, she let him come anyway. If he were mine, really mine, I wouldn't let him anywhere near someone like me. "And she was okay with that?" I ask in disbelief.

"Yeah." He shrugs and finally starts eating. Then he looks up at me for just a moment and says, "So *are* you?"

"Am I what?"

"In trouble?"

Just as I'm trying to figure out how to even begin answering that question, the waitress is back, asking "How is everything, guys? Need a topper there?"

"This is really good, huh?" I say after she leaves, pointing at the pancakes with my fork. "Or am I just that hungry?"

"Eden, are you gonna tell me?" he asks impatiently.

"Tell you what?"

"I don't know." He waves his hand in my direction. "You tell me. Whatever it is you called to say—you don't call that many times unless you have something to say."

I nod. I do have something to say, many things to say. Too many. "I think I mostly just wanted to tell you how sorry I am," I admit. "I know it doesn't change what happened. I know it doesn't change anything, but I wanted you to know anyway."

He takes a bite of pancake. Takes his time chewing. And swallowing. And just when it looks like he's going to say something, he takes another bite. Finally he looks at me, like he's choosing between saying something mean and saying something nice.

"Eden," he begins, taking a breath. "Look, I knew things weren't exactly how they seemed. I guess I sort of understood that you had issues, or whatever. No, that's a lie," he corrects right away. "I didn't understand, actually. Not at all. Not back then, anyway, but I do now." He flashes me a sad smile before going back to his food. "I thought about you a lot, you know, worried about you a lot," he says with his mouth full, not looking at me.

"Why?" I whisper, afraid that if I speak too loudly, I'll wake myself up from this dream.

"Because you were always so—you just never really seemed okay."

"I guess I wasn't okay." I tie my straw wrapper in knots, over and over. "But now?" I laugh. "Now I'm so far past not okay, I don't even know how I got here. You must think I'm out of my mind. I might be."

"You keep saying that, why? Did something actually happen?" he asks. I watch him watching me squirm, and I know there's no way to get out of this now, not without actually telling him. The truth. He deserves the truth, after all.

I had been waiting for three years for somebody, anybody, to say those magic words. And I've already let the opportunity pass me by once—when it really mattered—I can't do it again. My whole body goes tingly. I panic that I might pass out again.

And I hear my voice, smaller than usual, "Yes. Something really bad happened."

He's waiting, watching, and looking more and more concerned with every second that passes. "What?" he finally asks. He sets his fork down and leans in toward me.

I look down at my plate, at the puddle of syrup, crumbs of wet pancake. My hands are shaking; I put them in my lap. I open my mouth. "I was . . ."

"Yeah?" he prompts.

I try again. But nothing comes.

"Eden, what?"

I look around. My eyes set on those crayons again. Then back on him, waiting for me to say a word I just cannot say.

"What?" he repeats.

I reach across the table and pull the cup of crayons toward me. I pull out a broken red. I peel the paper back and rip off a corner of my place mat. My hand wants to break as I press the waxy crayon against the paper. *R*, I start to write it neatly, but an ugly word need not look pretty. My *A* becomes a shaky triangle. *P* is jagged. And the *E* and *D* come fast and furious. I look at the word "RAPED" for just a moment before I fold it in half and slide it away from me, across the table, past my plate and his coffee cup. Careful not to let it touch the few stray drops of syrup that have dripped down the side of the bottle, I move it toward him, along with every last shred of trust and faith and hope I have. He pulls the tiny piece of paper out from under my fingers and all I can do is sit there, staring at my lap, my trembling hands digging into the edge of the seat.

He has the word. It's out there. He has it—my secret. The truth. I can't ever take it back now. Can't lie it away. I close my eyes, wait for him to say it, to say the word, to say something. But he doesn't. I force my eyes open and I look at him, looking at me. I can't read his face.

"You—you were—did you—did you tell somebody, did you go to a doctor, I mean—are you okay?" His eyes dart all around me, in a clinical manner, scanning for injuries that aren't visible.

"No, I never told anybody, and I didn't go to a doctor, either. And no, I don't think I'm okay"—my voice falters—"I really don't." But no, I can't cry, not here.

"Eden, I'll take you. Come on. We can go right now." He picks up his keys and pushes out his chair like he's about to get up.

"No, no." I reach across the table and grab his arm. "It's—it's not like it just happened," I whisper. "It was a long time ago."

"What?" He pulls his chair back in. "When?"

"Three years ago—almost exactly."

"Eden, what do you mean?" He's doing the math in his head, I can tell. "That was before we ever—how did I not know this, Eden? Why didn't you ever tell me?"

I just shake my head. There always seemed to be so many good reasons—excellent reasons, in fact—but sitting here across from him, I can't think of a single one.

I look around. The Earth is still intact. I'm still alive. The floor didn't open up and swallow me whole. I haven't spontaneously combusted. I don't know what I thought would happen if I told, if I let that that one word exist, but I didn't expect nothing to happen. Everything is just as it was. No giant meteors collided with the planet and completely wiped out the entire human race. Dishes still clang in the kitchen, the radio still softly hums the oldies station it's set to, the people around us continue their conversations. My heart, it's still beating, and my lungs, I test them, in and out, yes, still breathing. And Josh, he's still sitting here in front of me.

"Eden, who—" he starts.

"Everything still okay?" our waitress asks, suddenly appearing at our table.

"Fine, fine, um, can we just have the check, please?" he asks her.

"Sure. Do you need some boxes?" she asks, looking back and forth between us.

"No, thanks. I'm finished," Josh says, pushing his nearly untouched plate away from him. The waitress looks confused by his disgusted expression, and then turns to me, her eyes begging us not to give her a hard time about the food.

"No, I'm done too, thanks." I try to smile at her—we're not those kinds of customers, I tell her silently. She looks relieved.

"All right, well, thank you." She fishes around in her apron pocket for a few seconds before she finally sets the slip of paper down on the table. "You two have a great day."

"Do you wanna leave?" he asks me.

I nod. "Um, yeah, I just—I don't have any money with me, I'm sorry."

"Please"—he bats at the air between us—"it's fine." His hands are trembling as he pulls two twenties from his wallet and lays them out on the table. I don't even know if he's aware of what he's doing. The waitress is getting an eighteen dollar tip. He's shaken. As we make our way through the tables, his hand hovers over my shoulder, never quite connecting, like he's afraid to touch me.

He walks around to the passenger side door to let me in first. He unlocks it but then stands there, staring at nothing.

"Are you okay?" I ask him.

"Eden, I'm so sorry. I should've—"

"There's nothing you could have done, I swear." But that might be a lie too. He stands there, close to me, and he looks like he doesn't know what to do. I certainly don't know what the protocol is either, but I step forward and put my arms around him. He hugs me back. We stay like that for a long time, not saying anything, and I feel like we could stay like this forever and it would still never be long enough.

"Let's get inside," he says, finally letting go. He opens the door for me, closes it too. I watch him jog around the front of the car, and I think about how nice it must be to be his girlfriend. His real girlfriend. They're probably perfect together. She's probably smart and funny and pretty in this wholesome, natural way. And he probably loves her and gives her thoughtful gifts on her birthdays, and he's probably met her parents and they probably love him because, well, how could they not, and they'll probably get married when they graduate and I'm sure they don't play games or lie to each other. She's probably the complete antithesis of me.

He turns the car on and cranks the heat. It takes a long time to warm up.

"Eden, have you really never told anyone?" he asks.

I nod.

"Who did it? I mean, do you know who it was?"

"Yeah, I know who it was."

"Who?"

I feel the tears working their way up from the pit of my stomach. "I can't tell you that," I say automatically.

"Why?"

I pull at a strand of yarn that's coming loose from my scarf.

"Why, Eden?" he repeats.

"Because I just can't."

"Do I know him, is that why?"

My brain fights against my body. I tell it to remain still, to not give anything away, but damn it, it won't listen. I nod. And the tears, they roll down, falling faster than I can wipe them away. I can't do this.

"You can," he says, as if he can hear the thoughts in my head, "really, you can tell me."

"You won't believe me," I sob.

"Yes, I will," he says softly. "I promise."

"I know that I've lied about things before, but I wouldn't lie about this, and I know that everyone thinks I'm a slut and I probably am, but this happened before all of that. I mean, I had never even been kissed—you were my first real kiss, you probably didn't know that. I never even held hands with a boy; I had never even so much as given out my phone number! I was just a kid—I—I—" I have to stop, I can barely breathe I'm crying so hard. I look at him, but everything's blurry through my tears.

"I know. I know. Here." He hands me a McDonald's napkin that was hiding somewhere in the car.

"This isn't who I was supposed to be. I used to be so nice. I used to be a nice, sweet, good person. And now I just—I just—I hate. I hate him. I hate him so much, Josh. I really do."

"Eden"—he turns me toward him, smoothing my hair back from my face—"look at me. Breathe, okay?" he says with his hands on my shoulders.

"I hate him so much that sometimes, that"—gasp, gasp, gasp. "Sometimes I can't feel anything else at all. Just hate"—gasp—"hate, that's all, that's everything. My whole life is just hate. And I can't—I can't get it out of me. No matter what I do, it's always there, I just—I can't—"

"Who is it? Just say the name, please, Eden. Just tell me." He's gripping my arms so tight, he's actually hurting me, and all of this pressure builds inside my chest, inside my head. "What's his n—?"

"Kevin Armstrong!" I scream it. Finally. "It was Kevin! It was Kevin."

His hands ease up. "Armstrong?" He lets go of me. His brain

is working something out, I can't tell what. "Armstrong," he says again. I don't know if the disdain in his voice is because he thinks I'm lying or because he believes me. I open my mouth to ask, but he brings his fists down against the steering wheel. Hard. He mutters something indecipherable, and then, ". . . Fucking son of a bitch . . . that fucking . . ." He shakes his head back and forth, and he wraps both his hands around the steering wheel so tight, I think he might rip the thing right off.

"You believe me, don't you?" I ask, desperately needing someone on my side.

He jerks his head up, and says, "I'm going to fucking kill him, Eden, I swear to God I'm gonna kill him."

"You believe me, right?" I ask again.

"Eden, of course I believe you, I—I just . . ." He inhales, and exhales slowly, trying to calm himself. "I just—you could've told me—you should've told me. Back when we were together. Why? Why didn't you ever say anything? I would've believed you then, too."

God, I almost wish he didn't just tell me that. I wish he'd said that he wouldn't have believed me, because then I could feel justified in not telling him. I just look down at my hands, shake my head.

"There were so many things that never made sense. About you, about what happened between us. God, it seems so obvious, I should've known. Eden, I was with that guy like every day. I mean, we were on the same team. Kevin Armstrong, I—"

He reaches out and takes my hand. I lean my head against the headrest and close my eyes. Breathe. Just breathe. "I'm so exhausted," I whisper.

"Do you want me to take you home?"

"I can't be there right now," I tell him, my voice so quiet.

"School?"

I open my eyes. "You're kidding, right?"

He smiles an equally exhausted smile at me. "I think we both probably need a little rest. We could go to my house. My parents are already at work. Just to sleep, I promise," he adds. "Then we'll figure out what to do, okay?"

"I SEE THEY PAINTED your room," I say, standing in the middle of my own personalized twilight zone. I sit down on the edge of his bed and unlace my boots.

"Oh yeah, I forgot they did that. So, you can have the bed. I'll just go crash on the couch or something," he says, fidgeting in the doorway.

"Oh." I shouldn't be disappointed. I shouldn't be surprised. "Yeah, sure." But I am.

"Is that not—I mean—well, is that okay?"

"I don't know, I was kind of thinking you might stay with me, but if you're not comfortable—I mean, I could take the couch, too, if you want."

"No, I'll stay," he says, entering his room cautiously.

Awkwardly, we lie down next to each other, neither of us wanting to point out the obvious clumsiness of the situation. Side by side we stare at the ceiling. The lightning bolt crack is still there, exactly as I remembered it. I turn my head to look at him and my body moves on its own, its muscles having long ago memorized this routine. He tenses when I place my hand on his chest.

"Sorry, can I?" I ask, realizing that while in my mind we are still intact, in reality I no longer have permission to do this, to touch him. At all.

"Yeah," he whispers. I watch his throat move as he swallows hard. He's nervous. He's probably worried I'm going to try something. I'm a little worried about that too.

I lay my head in its old spot.

And I fall asleep easy, so easy somehow.

I'm facing the other way when I wake up. Josh—Joshua Miller—is spooning me. I press my face into the pillow and breathe it in—it smells so clean, like him, like his sheets and clothes and skin always smelled. With his body molded to mine like this, I get the feeling that his arms are the only thing holding these broken pieces of me together. And I don't ever want him to let go.

I feel him press his face into my hair and kiss.

I close my eyes. Want to freeze this moment, want to stay just like this, and never have to do or think or feel or be anything else at all. His hands seem to move purposefully. I shouldn't turn my head, shouldn't twist my body around to face him, but I do. And his mouth finds my mouth. The warmth of his body is something I could never remember properly—that is something that has to be felt, in the present.

"I miss you," he whispers, his lips moving against mine.

"I miss you, too," I echo.

"Eden, it could work this time," he says softly, inching his face away so we can look at each other, brushing my hair behind my ear. "I know it could. We could make it work."

I start to nod. Start to smile. But "this time"—"this time," he said. I don't want it to be this time, though; I just want it to be then. I just want to go back. I want to start over and not become who I became. "This time"—those two words like a one-two punch in the gut.

"Your girlfriend," I remind him. And myself.

"I know, I know," he whispers, closing his eyes like it hurts to even think about having to hurt her. "But I love you, I still love you," he whispers, coming in to kiss me again.

I feel my hands push against him. "I can't. You can't either. You'd hate yourself for it and I don't want to be the reason you hate yourself. I don't want to hurt anyone. I can't just keep hurting people."

"I know, but—" He holds on tighter. I feel like I might fall apart if he lets go, if I make him let go. "All I ever wanted was for you to let me know you—and now you are. . . ."

His hands, his arms, can hold the pieces in place temporarily, maybe even for a long time, but he can never truly put them back together. That's not his job. He's not the hero and he's not the enemy and he's not a god. He's just a boy. And I'm just a girl, a girl who needs to pick up her own pieces and put them back together herself.

I sit up. Out of his arms, I'm still here. I didn't crumble to dust. I let my back rest against the headboard. I stare at my hands—these steady, capable things—capable *of* things. I try to figure out why everything suddenly feels different. Lighter. Why I feel like, for once in my life, I might really have some control over what happens next. That things will happen next, instead of this perpetual nightmarish loop my life seems to be cycling.

He sits up too and moves next to me, waiting for me to say something. Waiting for me to explain what the hell is going on. I look at him and it's like the first time I'm really seeing him.

He looks puzzled. "What is it?"

"I always thought that somehow you'd be the one to save me, you know, all along, all those years ago, even. I think that's why I called. Maybe I wanted this to happen. I wanted you to come and, you know, rescue me or whatever."

"So let me," he says, like it's easy, like it's possible.

"You can't, though. Nobody can."

"That's not true, Eden." He reaches for my hand, and strangely, that, too, feels like the first time he's ever touched me. It feels new, tingly, electric almost. It's like the first time anyone has ever touched me. Which, in a way, is true—I've never really been this person before.

"No, I just mean, I can't keep thinking of myself as someone who needs rescuing."

He opens his mouth, but pauses, "Okay, I get that. I do, but just let me—I don't know, let me help you."

"You are."

"I can do more, though. I'll be with you—really with you—if you'd just let me. We have something, Eden. We do. You can't deny that."

"Remember that day when you came over to talk to me?" I ask him.

He looks at me blankly.

"Remember, I was sitting in the grass by the tennis courts and you had just gotten out of practice and you were waiting for your mom to come pick you up?"

"I . . ." He stares hard at his ceiling, trying to recall this moment that was so fresh in my mind. "I guess," he finishes uncertainly.

"You were telling me about dandelions?"

He thinks for a second. "Right, yeah."

"Before you left, you gave me the in-between one, that's what you called it. Remember?"

"Oh God, yeah," he says with a laugh. "That was pretty stupid, huh?"

"No, it wasn't. I kept it. I still have it."

And now he looks at me like maybe it's the first time he's really seeing me, too.

"I thought it was really sweet," I continue. "But of course I couldn't bring myself to tell you that. I loved it—" My mouth shuts out of habit, not used to sweet words exiting, but I make it open again, for the important part. "I mean . . . I loved you."

He nods, only once. "Past tense," he states matter-of-factly, not looking at me.

We sit in silence like strangers.

"Eden, this isn't gonna happen, is it? Us, I mean."

"I wanted it to—I really did, but . . ." I shake my head gently. "I think you're right, though. We do have something. I'm just not sure what."

There's a brief moment of silence for what we've lost. And in that moment, it ends. Finally. The past of us officially comes to an end.

"Eden, I think I'll always have feelings for you, you know that, right? I don't know that they'll ever go away, but—" He stops. "But I'll be your friend. I mean, I want to be your friend. Do you think that would be okay?"

"Yeah. That would be okay," I say with a laugh. "That would be very, very okay. That would be perfect. I think I want that more than anything in the entire world."

"Okay. Friends." He grins and knocks his shoulder into mine.

"Friends." I smile. I have a friend.

He smiles back, but only briefly. "Eden, I know you don't want to hear this, but as your friend, as someone who cares about you, I really think you need to tell someone about this. I mean someone besides me, someone who can do something. Like the police."

And suddenly the reality of it all comes crashing down like a storm inside of me—it feels like someone's taking my internal organs and twisting them into demented balloon animals.

I guess it shows on my face, because he says, "I know it'll be hard, but it's important."

He gives my hand a squeeze and says the one thing I really need to hear: "They'll believe you, don't worry."

There're probably a million things I should say to him. I'm sure there are some things he wants to say to me, too. But we just sit, side by side on his bed, in silence. We sit like this for a long time, just being together, not really needing to give voice to all those unsaid words, just knowing and accepting the truth of what we really mean to each other. There's not enough language, anyway, for these things.

He kisses my cheek on his front porch. Even his cat comes

outside to see me off. He offers to drive me to the police station, then he offers to drive me home, then he offers to walk me home, but I need to walk myself. And I have one other person to talk to before I can go to the police.

I take one step off the porch and turn around. He stands there with his hands in his pockets. "Josh, are you okay? I mean, how is everything?" This should've been my first question, not my last.

He smiles. "Yeah. I'm good, basically."

"Good. I'm glad. School's good?"

He nods. "School's good, yeah."

"And how's your dad? You know, with his problem?"

He forces a smile, looks off somewhere above my head, trying to find the words. "He's—you know, it's just"— he meets my eyes, and I understand—"it is what it is, right?"

I nod, stand there for a second, take a breath as I try to memorize him, and then finally I turn away.

"Hey," he calls after me as I'm halfway down his driveway. I stop and turn. "You're gonna call me, aren't you?"

"Yes." I've never answered any question so honestly in my life.

"And you're gonna speak this time, right?" He grins.

I smile. "Yes."

He nods, takes his hand out of his pocket, and waves good-bye.

"WHY AREN'T YOU AT school?" Caelin mumbles at me, still lying on the couch where I left him hours earlier. Not asleep, just staring off into space. He can't force his eyes away from the nothing to even look at me.

"Cae, I need to talk to you."

"Edy, please. I can't right now, okay?"

I actually feel bad for him. I feel bad for the things he found out about his best friend, for the things I'm about to tell him. Feel bad that things are going to get so much worse. "Can I get you anything?" I ask.

He shakes his head and closes his eyes.

I go into the kitchen and pour him a glass of the good cold water from the fridge. "Here." I sit down on the floor next to the couch with the glass.

He sits up slowly and takes a sip of the water. "Thanks."

"It's important," I find the courage to say, feeling for the first time like maybe this actually is important, like it matters. Like *I* matter.

It takes him a few extra seconds to hear me. He sets the glass down on the coffee table. "All right," he says finally, rubbing his eyes, looking totally disinterested.

"Caelin, I have to tell you something and it's important that you listen and that you don't interrupt me."

"Okay, okay, I'm listening."

I take a breath. I can do this. "All right, this is hard, really hard. I'm not even sure where to start."

"At the beginning . . . ?" he offers sarcastically, not knowing he's being helpful in spite of himself.

"Okay. I'll start at the beginning. There was this night," I start. I stop. I start again, "I was a freshman—and I never told anyone about it, but this night—okay, there was this night that—everyone was asleep and—Kevin came into my room—"

"For the love of God, Edy, can you just pick one sentence and finish—"

"Please." I hold my hand up; it silences him for once. "He came into my room in the middle of the night and . . ." I can't look at him when I say it. I close my eyes and cover them with my hands because it's the only way I'll be able to get it out. "And he got in my bed." I take a breath. "He raped me. He did, okay, Caelin. And I never told anyone because he said he would kill me if I did. And I believed him. So I know that what they're saying is true because he did it to me, too. And I'm sorry, because I know you don't want to hear this, but if you don't believe me, Cae"—I gasp to catch my breath—"then you're not my brother anymore." I breathe. And wait. And breathe. And wait.

Silence.

I slowly uncover my eyes. I expect him to be looking at me. But he's not; his hands are covering his ears, his eyes shut tight. He's slumped forward, toward me, his body folded in on itself. He doesn't move; I don't even hear him breathe. I don't know what to say next so I say nothing. I leave him be. Let him process. Hope that he believes me, that he picks my side. I wait.

"I . . . ," he begins, but stops. I look up at him. "I—I just don't understand what you're saying, Edy," he mumbles into his hands. Then he pulls himself up and looks at me. "I don't un-der-stand how this happened." He says each word, each syllable, separately—precisely, carefully. He studies my face, searching, but I don't understand either.

Then he's on his feet fast. And he's pacing, like he's thinking too many things all at once. "No," I hear him mutter as he walks out of sight around the corner and into his bedroom. I almost call after him, but just as I open my mouth I hear what sounds like a dump truck driving into the side of the house, and Caelin screaming "FUCK" over and over, in this guttural, animal way.

My feet can't resist taking me to his door. I look at what he's done, what he's doing. Everything that was sitting on top of his dresser—all the relics of his high school glory: basketball trophies, medals, certificates, photos, and these model cars that he and Kevin spent eternities working on together—is now just a broken, mangled pile of memory vomit on the floor. And he's kicking his closet door over and over, with his bare feet.

He always keeps such a tight lid on everything. I mean, I've seen him mad, of course, I've seen him nasty at times, but never like this. He spins around, now at his dresser again and his hands grip the edges so tight. I put my hand over my mouth to keep from yelling at him to stop, because I know what he's about to do—he's about to throw the dresser on the floor. This dresser has to weigh more than both of us combined; it's old, antique-old, it belonged to our great-grandparents. It's probably worth something too. I have a vision of it breaking through the floor and crashing into the basement. But I just stand there, bracing myself, and I watch as it teeters forward, the floorboards creaking under its shifting weight.

And then it all stops. The dresser rests again on four feet, and he's stopped yelling. He just stands there, breathing heavy, square in front of me, and he looks at me like he sees me, like maybe he finally gets it. He pinches the bridge of his nose as his eyes fill with water, and then he shoves his knuckles into each eyeball, trying to thwart the tears. "I don't understand," he says again, except this time it's not measured but messy and trembling. Because he does understand.

I watch as his body melts down to the floor and I start to understand something too. That this isn't all about me. This thing, it touches everyone.

MY HANDS ARE SHAKING as I hold her business card. As the phone rings, I just read her name over and over and over.

Caelin drives me downtown, to the precinct. I bite my nails until they bleed. Caelin keeps taking these enormous breaths that he doesn't seem to be exhaling. But neither of us speaks until we're walking up the massive, terrifying steps of the building.

"Caelin, you don't have to come in with me," I tell him, wanting to spare him. I don't think I could bear for him to hear the details.

"No, I'm not leaving you here by yourself, Edy."

We have to empty our pockets and walk through a metal detector; police officers in bulletproof vests wave those wands over our arms and legs. And then we follow the signs that lead us on a winding path to the fourth floor. I slowly push through the double doors and search the large room full of desks and computers and chairs and phones ringing and people rushing around with clipboards and serious looks on their faces, scanning for Detective Dorian Dodgson.

"Eden, I'm so glad you could make it down here so quickly," she says, appearing next to us. "Caelin. Good to see you again. Shall we find a quieter place to talk?"

"Detective?" I start.

"Dorian, please," she corrects.

"Okay, Dorian. Caelin doesn't need to stay, does he?"

"Not at all."

"Edy, I'll stay," Caelin insists.

"Sometimes," Dorian tells him, picking up on my fear, "with this kind of discussion, the fewer people present, the better. You understand," she says.

He nods, and I think he's partly relieved, too. "I understand," he says to her. "Call me when you're done, Edy, and I'll come pick you up. I'm gonna go to that bar right up the street, the one with the white-and-green awning, so I'm not far."

He holds out a hand to shake with Dorian's, and nods, very gentlemanly.

"Thank you for bringing her in, Caelin," she tells him. "You take care now."

She leads me to a room that has a window and a plant and a couch and a coffee table, not at all like those interrogation rooms you see on TV.

"It may be difficult to remember some things," she cautions as she sets a Diet Coke down on the table in front of me, "but just try, as best you can, to describe exactly what happened."

I wish it was difficult to remember.

"He came into my room. It was 2:48—I looked at the clock—by 2:53 it was over," I tell her, but that's not the complete truth.

Five minutes. Three hundred seconds, that's all it is. It can seem like a short amount of time or a long amount of time, depending on what's happening. You press the snooze button and wake up five minutes later—that's no time at all. But if you're giving a speech at the front of the classroom with all those eyes on you, or you're getting a cavity filled, then five minutes can feel like a long time. Or say you're being humiliated and tortured by someone you trusted, someone you grew up with, someone you loved, even . . . five minutes is forever. Five minutes is the rest of your entire fucking stupid life.

But there's no way to really explain his mouth almost touching mine. No way to describe how completely alone I felt, like there was no one in the entire world who would be able to help me or stop him. Ever. No way to say how much I truly believed him when he said he would kill me. I take a breath and look Dorian in the eye, and try to find words to explain what words could never explain.

I tell her, as best I can, every gruesome detail.

She says things like, "Mm-hmm, mm-hmm, mm-hmm . . . in what way was he restraining your arms? Can you show me? And he penetrated you?" God, that word, "penetrate," how could she say it? "How much force—would you say excessive? Was this before or after? Could you yell for help at that point? Can you describe, again, exactly how he inserted the nightgown into your mouth? Did you lose consciousness at any point? Did you, at any point, fear for your life? And he told you that he would kill you if you told anyone what happened?"

It takes hours. I have to say everything a million times by the end, and then she hands me my own clipboard and pad of paper and a pen, and I have to write it all down while she sits there watching.

My hand cramps up after the first couple of pages. I stop and shake it out, extending my fingers.

"I guess it's pretty awful that I never told anyone?" I ask her.

"How do you mean?"

"Well, what if I would've told, and then he wouldn't have—I mean, maybe I could've stopped all of this from happening?"

"When someone threatens your life, those aren't empty words," she states matter-of-factly.

"But what if—"

"No. No more what-ifs," she tells me firmly. "You did the right thing by coming in, Eden."

"How can you be sure what's right?" I ask her, thinking about how everything has to change now.

She smiles soberly and says, "It's my job to know the difference between right and wrong. This is right."

I try to smile back.

"We're going to get this little bastard," she says. "I'm sure of it. And he won't be able to hurt anyone else, okay?"

"Do you know about what happened to him?" I clear my throat. "When he was a kid—with his uncle, I mean?"

"Yes," she answers. Her face doesn't change, though. She just continues looking at me, unflinching. "That was a terrible thing—yes. But it's not a free pass. Not an excuse."

My heart floods, so full of every emotion I've ever known, all at once. Because she's right. It's no excuse. Not a free pass. Not for him. And not for me. I nod my head.

"I won't lie, Eden," she tells me. "It'll get harder before it gets easier, but everything will be okay, I promise."

"Everything will be okay" always sounds like a generic, useless thing that people just say when there's nothing else to be said for a situation, but those words coming out of her mouth—it sounds like the most profound thing anyone has ever said in the history of humankind.

Outside, it's dusk. Nearly night already. I can just make out the white-and-green awning. I start to descend the stairs, but I sit down on one of the steps instead. I breathe the cold air in deeply and it fills my lungs in a new way.

I take my phone out and dial a number I had memorized years ago. It rings.

"Hello?" Mrs. Armstrong answers, sounding just exhausted.

"Hi, Mrs. Armstrong. It's Edy. Is Amanda there?"

"Honey, I'm not sure she feels like talking right now. Wait—hold on a second." And I hear her hand cover the receiver, her words muffled. Something's happening. Static and movement. It seems like a long time passes.

Then finally: "Hi," Amanda says quietly. "Sorry, I had to go in my room." And suddenly she sounds like herself again, the girl I used to know.

"Hi," I respond, but I don't know what else to say to her.

"I had to tell," she says, not wasting any time with chitchat. "I just had to."

"Amanda, I'm sorry."

"I'm sorry too—about everything—I'm sorry for things you don't even know I should be sorry for, Edy," she admits.

"How did you know?" I ask her.

"I could just tell. The other day at school. I could just feel it—I don't know."

"Did he really tell you we actually slept together, like you said?"

She pauses, and says, "You know, I always looked up to you so much when we were younger. I don't know if you ever knew that. He knew that, anyway. And he tried to make me believe that it was okay. Normal. That you—if you did it, wanted to, I mean—then, you know, what could be wrong with that?" Her voice breaks up, as she tries not to cry. "The sickest part is that I actually believed him—about you—I believed every word. Until the other day."

"I never knew any of that, Amanda, I swear."

"I hated you. So much. As much as I should've hated him—I hated you instead. I don't know why. It's all fucked up, isn't it?" She laughs, even as she cries.

"Yeah. It's all fucked up," I agree. "But I think it's going to get better now."

"It has to," she says.

"It will."

As I walk the two blocks up the street, the air feels different, my steps against the ground feel different, the world—everything—feels different.

I push through the heavy wooden door at the bar and I'm strangled by smells of beer and smoke. I spot Caelin right away, down at the end of the bar, looking pathetic and crumpled, his hand curled loosely around a shot glass.

"Hey, hey, hey, you—girl!" the bartender yells at me. "ID."

"No, I'm just here for my brother—over there," I yell to him, pointing at Caelin.

The bartender walks down the length of the bar and raps his knuckles twice on the shiny wooden counter in front of Caelin. He raises his head slowly. "Time to go, buddy," he tells him, nodding his head in my direction.

Caelin turns toward me, wobbling a little as he stands, moving slowly as he reaches for his wallet. "Edy, I said I would pick you up," he says while ushering me out the door.

"It wasn't that far. I felt like walking anyway."

"I don't like you in there," he mumbles.

We walk in silence to the parking garage.

"I should probably drive, huh?" I ask, watching him sway back and forth.

"Here," he says, tossing his car keys to me.

After I adjust the seat and mirror, I decide to light a cigarette—no more secrets. He looks at me like he's about to chide me, his kid sister, but then he looks forward and says, "Can I bum one?"

I feel myself grin as I hand him mine and light up another.

He tries to smile at me. We drive home, finishing our cigarettes in silence.

I park the car in the street. "Edy, wait," he says as I start to get out.

"Yeah?"

Uncomfortable, he does one of his half-shrug-head-shake gestures and opens his mouth, taking a few extra seconds for the words to come. "I don't know. I'm sorry. I'm so sorry, Edy." He looks me in the eye. "I'm your brother. And I love you. That's all. I don't know what else to say."

I think that's really all I ever wanted to hear from him. "You'll stay with me when I tell Mom and Dad?"

He nods. "Yeah."

He holds my hand as we walk up the driveway. It feels like it's a million miles away, like it's taken a million years to finally get here. But it gives me a chance to think. And I think: Maybe I'll explain this to some people. Maybe Mara. Maybe I'll apologize to some people. Maybe Steve. Maybe I'll try a real relationship someday, one without all the lies and games. Maybe I'll go to college, even, and maybe I'll figure out that I'm actually good at something. Maybe he'll get what he deserves. Maybe not. Maybe I'll never find it in my heart to forgive him. And maybe there's nothing wrong with that, either. All these maybes swimming around my head make me think that "maybe" could just be another word for hope.

Though this book is a work of fiction, I recognize the millions of real-life teens who have, in some way, shared Eden's experience. Unfortunately, theirs are not new stories, but they are ones that need desperately to be told. Over and over and over.

If you need to speak with someone, there are people who will listen. There are people who will help. For free, confidential, secure support, visit the Rape, Abuse & Incest National Network at rainn.org or call the RAINN hotline: 1-800-656-HOPE.

ACKNOWLEDGMENTS

I must acknowledge the tenacity, passion, and extraordinary work of Jessica Regel, who helped to shape this book in ways that far exceeded anything I could've ever imagined or expected from an agent—thank you, Jess, for believing in this book and fighting so hard to make sure it saw the light of day!

Sincerest thanks are also due to my editor, Rūta Rimas, for being such an incredible partner on this journey, for taking a leap of faith on a new author, and most of all, for your sensitive, thoughtful, and discerning work on this book—thank you for being one of those rare people who just *gets* it.

And an extended shout-out to all the wonderful, dedicated, and talented people at Margaret K. McElderry Books, Simon & Schuster, and Foundry Literary + Media, who have helped to turn what was once a dream into reality.

I am infinitely indebted to my family, to my inspiring and supportive friends, and to Holly, my best friend and the brave soul who graciously served as this book's first reader way back when.

Lastly, I am grateful for life's many mentors and guides, for the good and the bad, for the never-ending ebb and flow.

After you finish reading

THE WAY I USED TO BE,

use the following questions to facilitate a discussion.

DISCUSSION QUESTIONS

1. The morning after Eden is raped, she is hesitant to tell her mother. What did Kevin tell Eden to discourage her from telling anyone? What about her mother's tone makes Eden change her mind? Discuss what might have happened if Eden's mother had been a more supportive listener.

2. Eden and the guy she calls "Number 12" crash into each other in the hallway, and Eden has a strong reaction. Describe Eden's thought process after their encounter. What word(s) does she use to capture how she is feeling? The reader is given no reason to believe that Number 12 bumped into her on purpose, so discuss why Eden reacts this way.

3. Near the end of her freshman year, Eden decides to start standing up for herself, beginning with her parents, because "it was with them that it began." What began with her parents? Do you think it is possible for her to stand up for herself *and* win her parents' approval?

4. During the beginning of her sophomore year, Eden discovers that "All you have to do is act like you're normal and okay, and people start treating you that way." Predict what will happen if she continues to act like she is okay without dealing with her underlying emotional issues.

5. Mara asks Edy if she is afraid that Joshua Miller will want to have sex with her. What does Edy actually fear, and how does she decide to address her fear moving forward? Do you think that her method of coping might be common among rape victims?

6. Eden describes how Josh and Kevin talk differently. How is Josh's voice different from Kevin's, and how does Eden interpret this difference? What exactly does Eden mean when she says that "everything about him is different"?

7. Eden admits that something about Josh makes her "want, so badly, to be vulnerable." Why does she resist becoming vulnerable with Josh? Rather than open up to him, what does she do instead? How is Eden's struggle with balancing control and vulnerability evident in future relationships?

8. Josh says that his father is "basically a good dad, but then there's this thing that, like, controls him." How does he define a "good" dad? What is the thing to which he refers? Do you agree that Josh's dad is still basically good, despite this particular flaw?

9. Eden tells Josh the story of when she fell off her bike when she was twelve. Reread the conversations she remembers having with Mara that day, and look for details that exemplify Eden and Mara's childhood innocence. Then, describe how Eden is forced to grow up after being raped by Kevin.

10. Interpret the following quotation: "I don't know who I am right now. But I know who I'm not. And I like that." Who is Eden "not" anymore? What did her dad used to call her when she was younger, and why does Eden resent that nickname now?

11. Eden describes in detail what happened the night Kevin raped her. Why does she tell the story in third person? What effect does this point of view have on the reader? How might Eden's story and response to being raped seem different if the author told the story from another character's point of view?

12. Eden explains how she picks out guys at parties. Discuss how Eden thinks of her own sexual behavior and compare that with the reputation she has at school. Why does Eden choose to have multiple partners, and how is her behavior viewed by her peers?

13. How do the characters in the story view Eden? How do Amanda and Steve describe her? Do their descriptions differ? Why?

14. At the beginning of Part 4, Eden begins referring to her parents by their first names instead of *Mom* and *Dad*. What brings about this change? Discuss the significance of this change, keeping

in mind how her relationship with her parents has changed throughout high school. Will she revert to *Mom* and *Dad* when she gets older?

15. Amanda and Eden's relationship is tense, but they have a very open and honest conversation during Eden's senior year. What does Amanda reveal to Eden? What did Kevin say happened between him and Eden? Discuss how Amanda and Eden's relationship evolves throughout the story.

16. After Eden tells her story to the police, what does Detective Dorian Dodgson say to comfort her? How does Eden react to this statement? Do you think Eden's trust in the police is common for young women in her situation?

17. Describe Eden's relationship with her brother, Caelin, and how it changes as the story unfolds. Does Eden feel safe discussing her feelings with her brother? Why or why not? How does Caelin respond to Eden's rape? Does he feel guilty?

Guide written by Pam B. Cole, Professor of English Education & Literacy, Kennesaw State University, Kennesaw, GA.